MARY DAHEIM

LOCO MOTIVE

A BED-AND-BREAKFAST MYSTERY

AVON

An Imprint of HarperCollins*Publishers*

This book is a work of fiction. The characters, incidents, and dialogue are drawn from the author's imagination and are not to be construed as real. Any resemblance to actual events or persons, living or dead, is entirely coincidental.

AVON BOOKS
An Imprint of HarperCollins*Publishers*
10 East 53rd Street
New York, New York 10022-5299

First Avon Books mass market printing: May 2011
First William Morrow hardcover printing: September 2010

Avon Trademark Reg. U.S. Pat. Off. and in Other Countries, Marca Registrada, Hecho en U.S.A.
HarperCollins® is a registered trademark of HarperCollins Publishers.

Printed in the U.S.A.

10 9 8 7 6 5 4 3 2 1

To David, with thanks for the more than forty-four years of love and laughter, and for making me not just a better writer, but—I hope—a better person
RIP

Chapter One

Judith McMonigle Flynn hurried out of Hillside Manor, stared up at the second-story window, and screamed, "Don't jump! You'll kill yourself!"

The small man with the slicked-back hair crouched on the ledge and waved a sinewy hand. "Move it, lady! Here I go!"

"No!" Judith cried. "No, no!"

The man ignored her. He leaped out the window, somersaulted in midair, and landed upright in a rhododendron bush. "See?" he shouted, brushing glossy leaves off his chamois shirt. "Your better half just lost fifty bucks. Doesn't he know who I am?"

"Unfortunately," she murmured, "he does, but he didn't think you'd be stupid enough to try that stunt at my B&B."

"Where is Whazisname?" Wee Willie Weevil said, gazing around the quiet cul-de-sac. "He knew I'd jump at"—he peered at his watch's hodgepodge of numbers and symbols that Judith figured could launch a NASA spacecraft—"thirteen hours."

"Mr. Flynn told you he had a lunch meeting," Judith said.

"He should've canceled. I do what I do when I say I'm going to do it." He belched. "I'm off to run up and down that steep street you folks call the . . . what?"

"The Counterbalance," Judith replied wearily. "It's the steepest part of Heraldsgate Avenue. Years ago, a kind of cable car went . . ."

Weevil had taken some deep breaths and counted to three before taking off like a shot toward the cross street that led to the avenue. Shaking her head, Judith walked over to the porch steps.

"Yoo-hoo!" a voice called. "Judith! What on earth was that?"

Turning around, Judith saw her neighbor Arlene Rankers emerge from behind the gigantic laurel hedge between the two properties. "Wee Willie Weevil, jumping out of room two," Judith replied. "Why did I let Justin Weevil talk me into letting his uncle stay at my B&B?"

Arlene joined Judith at the porch steps. "Because Justin is a very nice young man and a friend of your son's? Because you're kindhearted and had a vacancy the week before Halloween? Because you're insane?"

"All of the above," Judith agreed. "Weevil checks out Friday. I'm booked for the weekend because Halloween falls on Sunday this year."

Arlene's pretty face was sympathetic. "Then you've one more full day to put up with Willie." She gestured at Judith's porch decorations. "Your gourds look better than mine. That jack-o'-lantern reminds me of Marie Klumpf from church. So many missing teeth. The Dooleys' witch was stolen last night," she went on, gazing at the big white house looming behind the cul-de-sac. "It's a shame their front porch faces the other street. I feel safer where we are. Too many cars cruise around here lately, but so far they haven't come near us since Carl's been Block Watch captain. He's always alert. Unless he's taking a nap."

Judith was used to Arlene's contradictions. "Carl's very reliable," she agreed. "Too bad he couldn't ban Willie. No decent hotel will let him in, which is why he's here. I wish I'd known that before I agreed to let him stay at the B&B. Mike thought it'd be fun. As a kid, he idolized Willie's daredevil antics, including his movies and cartoon shows."

Arlene clapped a hand to her cheek. "I'd forgotten about

his early exploits," she said. "He'd come to town on publicity tours and visit his relatives. Our kids were big fans, too. But every time Willie was in town, his shenanigans upset the local hotel employees and their guests. The newspapers and TV were full of his wild stunts." Arlene paused, appearing to revel in the memories. "He never used the elevator when he stayed at the Cascadia. He'd climb up the hotel's exterior and swing into his penthouse suite on a rope. At the Naples, he rode his motorcycle up and down the hall at all hours. Oh—I forgot the Wetmore, where he walked a tightrope between the hotel's two towers."

"How did I miss all that?" Judith asked, her head swimming.

Arlene frowned. "This was almost thirty years ago when you were living out south on Thurlow Street. Did you take a newspaper back then? Or watch TV?"

The memories of Judith's disastrous first marriage were stashed in a dark corner of her mind where she seldom ventured. "Those last years before Dan died were like living in exile. He wouldn't let my relatives visit and pitched a five-star fit if I spent time with them. Not that I had time to spare while working two jobs and Dan not working at all. The newspaper canceled us and the TV was repossessed. Even though he was in charge of paying—or not paying—bills, he got furious, especially about the TV. He couldn't watch *Crusader Rabbit* with Mike. For six weeks Dan tried doing finger puppets to amuse Mike but gave up when his hands went numb. Dan had poor circulation due to his diabetes and weighing four-hundred-plus pounds."

Arlene looked puzzled. "That doesn't sound right. Are you sure?"

"Sure of what?" Judith responded, feeling chilly as the wind picked up off of the nearby bay. "You know my pathetic life story."

"Yes, certainly," Arlene agreed. "But wasn't *Crusader Rabbit* on TV much earlier when we were kids?"

Judith smiled ruefully. "You're right. Whatever it was, Dan and Mike couldn't watch it." Maybe, she thought, it was one of Willie's action cartoons.

Arlene nodded. "Rags the Tiger, Crusader Rabbit's faithful sidekick. Rags was a good sport, the boon companion who didn't mind playing second fiddle. And speaking of companions," she went on before Judith could start up the steps, "is Willie married to that redheaded floozy who's with him?"

Judith sighed. "Who knows? Maybe she's a circus acrobat."

"That sounds like Willie's type," Arlene said. "Flash and dash, danger and . . . contortions?" She shrugged. "I'd rather not think about that, though Willie was popular with his marital arts movies."

"*Martial* arts," Judith corrected.

"Oh." Arlene frowned. "Yes, I know. Carl and I just had a big fight. I misspoke." She glanced toward her house, where only the second story could be seen above the hedge. "It's turning cold and windy. I should go make up with Carl—if he's regained consciousness."

"Okay." Judith didn't ask for details. She was never sure when Arlene was exaggerating. Her neighbors had been married for over forty years, a devoted couple who enlivened their wedded state with an occasional rumpus. Passing through the entry hall where Sweetums was hissing at her, she went into the dining room, where she heard the phone ring. A woman answered the call in the kitchen. Pushing aside the swinging half doors, Judith saw Pepper, the wife, companion, or God-only-knew-what to Willie. "Who?" Pepper shouted, dancing around the orange and white blur of feline fury as Sweetums streaked to the back door. After a pause, Pepper barked, "Never heard of her," and hung up.

"What was that?" Judith demanded.

"Who cares?" Pepper snapped. "It wasn't Wayne. He should've called by now."

Judith didn't know who Wayne was and didn't care. "The guest phone's in the upstairs hall," she said pointedly. "Don't you have a cell?"

"It needs charging." Pepper's freckled face was hostile. "I'm a guest. Why can't I use any damned phone that's handy?"

"My phones are for professional and personal use. You're welcome to use the guest phone upstairs on the end table by the settee. It's right outside your room. There's a charge for long—"

The phone rang again. Pepper reached for the receiver.

"No!" Judith shouted. "Don't!"

The younger woman snatched up the receiver. "Wayne?" she barked into the phone. "Hey—knock it off with the calls, you moron!"

Fuming, Judith glared at Pepper. "Give me that. Now."

"Oh, for . . . here." Pepper shoved the phone at Judith. "It's that same idiot. You deal with it."

A volley of obscenities bombarded Judith's ear. Recognizing her cousin's voice, she waited until Renie ran out of steam—and cusswords.

"It's me, coz," Judith said as Pepper stalked off down the hall that led to the back stairs. "Sorry about guests who don't follow house rules. What's up?"

"I'm down," Renie replied, suddenly sounding glum. "Bill and I had a huge fight about his Boston trip. I can't fly there with him unless I'm really drunk. He swears that if I guzzle a pint of Wild Turkey before I get on the plane and sit in the lap of another Olympic gold medalist, he'll kill me."

"You only did that once," Judith said.

"He was so good-looking," Renie asserted. "He'd won the decathlon, for God's sake!" She paused. "Maybe I never told you about the Argentine tenor or the American League MVP. If God intended humans to fly, He'd have tucked a fifth of Wild Turkey in with the fetus."

"You're not making sense," Judith pointed out, trying to obliterate other embarrassing incidents Renie had caused when the cousins had flown together. "Are you sure you haven't gotten a head start on the booze?"

Renie grimaced. "I hate the stuff. The odor's too strong."

"You've taken several plane trips. Can't you do it sober by now?"

"No."

"Then you'd better stay home."

There was a pause before Renie spoke again. "Bill already bought the tickets. We leave Tuesday. The psychology conference starts Thursday." She paused again to clear her throat. "But I have an idea."

Judith was afraid to ask. "What?" she inquired.

"Well . . . I called Amtrak to ask if the Empire Builder had sleeping car availability Sunday. They did, so I reserved a sleeper for two."

"Bill doesn't mind going by train?"

"Uh . . . he does, actually." Renie paused again. "Bill sleeps poorly on trains. I don't know why—I sleep like a baby in a cradle. But he's giving a speech the first day and has to be well rested. That's why he booked a Tuesday flight; he insists sleepless nights on the train would ruin him for the entire conference."

Judith was wary. "So you take the train and he flies."

"And pay for four round-trips to and from Boston?" Renie started speaking very fast. "It's foolish to waste all that money. You and Joe could join us. Our husbands can fly while you and I—"

"Whoa!" Judith cried. "You're asking me to drop everything on short notice and go to Boston? Why would Joe want to tag along with Bill to attend a nutso conference? This is your goofiest idea yet!"

"It's a not-so-nutso conference," Renie said. "The focus is helping patients get normal. Or pretend they're normal. Or . . . something." Her voice had grown uncertain, but she rallied. "Boston's wonderful. You've never been there, and neither has Bill or Joe. There's so much history and the rest of New England is—"

"Stop. Please." Judith held her head. "I'm sorry you're in a bind. There's no way Joe and I can put our lives on hold and take off for . . . what? At least ten days if I were to travel with you on the train?"

"Twelve," Renie said, uncharacteristically meek.

"I pass. Find another pigeon." Judith looked up as Joe came through the back door. "My husband's back from lunch with his new client. I have to go." She broke the connection.

Joe took off his dark green suit jacket. "Was that Willie I saw running the Counterbalance?"

"Yes." Judith reached for the Excedrin bottle on the windowsill. "He jumped out the second-floor window. You owe him fifty bucks."

"Take it off his bill," Joe said.

"I will." Judith poured a glass of water. "How was your meeting?"

Joe frowned. "If you've got a headache, I'd better not tell you."

Judith's dark eyes widened. "It didn't go well?"

Joe sat down at the kitchen table. "Too well. Brewster Cartwright's a golf buddy of a Wirehoser timber biggie. The Wirehoser guy was impressed by my background work in choosing their new CFO, so Brewster asked me to do ditto for SANECO Insurance."

"That's great," Judith said after swallowing the Excedrin. "Wirehoser paid you big bucks. I assume Cartwright will, too."

"Oh, yes." Joe passed a hand over his ruddy forehead. "I'd be an idiot to turn him down. But there's a problem."

"What?" Judith asked, sitting down across the table.

He sighed. "In two weeks, the candidate at Bullfinch Life & Casualty is off for a month in China. Brewster wants him checked out ASAP so everything is settled by year's end." Joe's gaze avoided Judith. "I have to leave Tuesday."

"Leave for where?"

Joe finally looked at his wife. "Boston."

There's a crow on the telephone wire outside," Judith said, standing on her cousin's doormat. "Can you shoot it and roast it for my dinner?"

Puzzled, Renie ushered her cousin into the entry hall. "Why?"

"I'm eating crow." Judith flopped into a brocade armchair by the hearth, but avoided looking at Renie. "We're having a Boston Tea Party after all."

Renie gaped at her cousin. "You're kidding!" She shook her head. "No, no, of course you aren't. Are you that desperate to get away from your mother?"

"I had nothing to do with it." Judith heaved a big sigh. "I'll make this quick. I have to go to Falstaff's Grocery before my new guests check in. Joe came back from his lunch meeting and told me that . . ."

Renie was grinning by the time Judith finished her explanation. "Coz, that's great! This could be fun."

Judith's expression was wary. "It could? With us? When was the last time we went anywhere and had fun?"

"Might you be referring to your penchant for finding dead bodies?" Renie inquired archly. "If so, I suggest you avoid any potential murder victims. I realize that with your history, you'll probably come across a couple of corpses somewhere between the Pacific and the Atlantic, but I'd enjoy a trip with you that didn't involve fleeing from a crazed killer."

"You think I wouldn't?" Judith snapped.

Curled up on the green sofa, Renie seemed skeptical. "I don't know. Only you can answer that. Boston has some intriguing cemeteries. Maybe you could read the tombstones and figure out if the people buried there died from natural causes or foul play. You might solve some centuries-old murders. Would that satisfy your morbid curiosity?"

"Knock it off," Judith snapped. "You made your point and I'm in a bind."

"The Rankerses can handle the B&B. They're old hands at it, and they like keeping busy since Carl retired. They also get along with Aunt Gert."

"I don't feel right asking them to take over for such a long period of time," Judith said. "I'd prefer getting a professional B&B sitter."

"You know best."

"You're smug." Judith stood up. "I like it better when you're ornery."

"I'm versatile," Renie said, walking Judith to the door. "There's enough time for Bill to transfer my plane ticket to Joe. The train leaves Sunday at four forty-five. I've requested a lower level bedroom so you won't have to climb so many steps. Bill can drive us to the station. We'll pick you up at a quarter to four. Dress warmly," she called to Judith, who had kept going to her car. "Bye."

Judith drove up Heraldsgate Avenue in a daze. Too much had happened too fast. She'd have to talk to Joe, to the Rankerses—and to her mother. Gertrude Grover took offense at her daughter going anywhere more than ten minutes away. Fixated on such daunting tasks, Judith almost drove past Falstaff's Grocery. It was after three when she finally got home.

"You look frazzled," Joe said, gesturing at the four shopping bags his wife was placing on the counter. "Got any more?"

"Three," Judith said tersely.

Joe headed outside. Judith was hanging up her car coat in the hallway when she heard someone coming down the back stairs. Since guests used the entry hall stairs, she assumed it was her cleaning woman, Phyliss Rackley.

Judith was wrong. She didn't recognize the fair-haired young man with his uncertain smile. "Mrs. Flynn?" he said, stopping by the pantry.

"Yes? Did you check in early?"

The young man shook his head. "I'm not a guest. I'm visiting Mr. Weevil." He held out a slim hand. "Wayne Fielding. You're the owner?"

Judith nodded and allowed her hand to be shaken. "How can I help you?"

"You can't." Wayne smiled disarmingly. Up close he didn't look as young as Judith had first thought. There were small wrinkles around his hazel eyes and his mouth, and on his forehead. She guessed he was closer to forty than thirty. "I'm going outside," Wayne explained. "Is the back door off-limits like the phones?"

"You spoke to Pepper," Judith said without her usual tact.

"Oh, sure," Wayne said breezily. "She's quite a character."

At that moment Joe entered with the rest of the groceries. He nodded to Wayne and kept going into the kitchen.

Judith, who was still rattled, tried to focus on Wayne's question. "You mean . . ." She nodded at the door. "Go ahead. Family and friends generally use our back door. Is there something you need outside?"

Wayne pointed to a camera case hanging from his left shoulder. "I'm taking some pictures. I'm Mr. Weevil's publicist."

Judith forced a smile. "You're photographing my B&B? Or Mr. Weevil?"

Wayne chuckled. "I never know exactly what with Mr. Weevil."

"What don't you know?" Joe asked, coming up behind Judith.

She gave a little start. Joe's casual, mellow tone had served him well during his career as a police detective. She took his arm and smiled. "This is Wayne Fielding, Mr. Weevil's publicist. He's taking photos."

Joe didn't offer his hand. "I'll go with you," he said to Wayne. "You better be quick. It's going to rain."

Wayne's grin widened. "Doesn't it always around here?"

"Constantly," Joe said. "Show me where you're shooting your photos."

The men went out the back door. Judith's curiosity was piqued. She was about to step onto the porch when Phyliss emerged from the basement with a hamper of laundry.

"Ungodly," Phyliss muttered. "Is Weevil really a movie star?"

"He used to be," Judith said. "He's famous for several things."

"Piety isn't one of them," Phyliss retorted. "Taking the name of the Lord in vain, cavorting with that red-haired harlot, and pretending he's the Angel Gabriel by jumping out the window. What kind of heathen does those things?"

"Mr. Weevil is famous for his daredevil escapades," Judith said wearily.

Phyliss set the hamper on the floor and wagged a finger. "You see? Daring as the devil. If that's not irreligious, what is?"

"Don't ask me," Judith continued as she moved onto the porch. "Oh, drat! Here comes Mother."

Gertrude Grover had driven her motorized wheelchair down the ramp of the converted toolshed where she'd chosen to live rather than share a roof with Joe Flynn. The old lady never called her small apartment home, but described it as anything from a packing crate to a pay-as-you're-going coffin.

"I'm cross as two sticks," Gertrude shouted, zipping by the small patio, the birdbath, and the statue of Saint Francis. "Why didn't you tell me it was Christmas? I haven't addressed a single card!"

"Christmas?" Judith met her mother on the sidewalk by the porch. "What are you talking about? It's not Halloween yet."

"Mad as a hatter," Phyliss remarked from her righteous position on the porch. "That's what happens when you play with a necklace that's got a cross with our Lord on the end of it. More sacrilege."

Judith shot the cleaning woman a warning glance. "It's October, Mother," she said to Gertrude. "Why do you think it's Christmas?"

"Why else would somebody . . ."

Gertrude's words were drowned out by raised voices that came from around the corner of the house. One belonged to Joe, whose usually mellow tone had turned harsh. Ignoring Gertrude and Phyliss, who had begun yet another stare-off of mutual contempt, Judith hurried to the driveway.

Joe and Wayne were craning their necks to look up at the roof. "Get down, you crazy moron!" Joe yelled. "If you jump, I'll call the cops!"

Dressed in red sweats, Wee Willie Weevil was standing by one of the roof's two chimneys. The wind was blowing hard enough that the fabric flapped against his sinewy physique. Somehow his dark hair stayed in place. "Beat it, buster," he shouted back. "I'm exercising."

Wayne was fiddling with his camera. "Move to your right," he called loudly. "The light's not so good from this angle."

Joe grabbed Wayne's arm. "Put that thing away or I'll break it. This is a B&B, not an amusement park. Do you want to run us out of business with Weevil's loony risk-taking stunts?"

Wayne was unruffled. "He knows what he's doing."

Joe noticed Judith a few feet away. "Did he sign a special waiver?" he asked, jerking his thumb toward the roof.

"You mean Willie?" Judith glanced up at the daredevil, who was coming around to the north side of the chimney. "I don't think so. He registered like any guest, agreeing to the standard B&B rules."

"So he's screwed if he kills himself. I should never have said I bet he couldn't jump out the second-story window. I thought he was joking."

Wayne had moved out of sight. Judith heard her mother ask if he was one of Santa's elves. Phyliss accused him of consorting with the devil. "I know Satan when I see him," she declared. "Red suit and all."

"That's Santa Claus, dummy," Gertrude said to Phyliss. "What happened to his elves and the reindeer?"

"Pagan practices," Phyliss snapped. "Worship of unnatural creatures and animals. Satan, Santa—just switch the letters around. And it's not Christmas, though why you heathens care about it, I don't . . . ahh!" She jumped as Sweetums brushed up against her leg. "Beelzebub's familiar! Help!"

Judith tried to block out the familiar rant. She followed

Joe to the rear of the house where Wee Willie seemed poised to make his jump.

"Much better," Wayne called, trying to brush his wind-swept hair off of his forehead. "Any time. I'm starting to shoot."

His subject didn't hesitate. Wee Willie took a deep breath, squared his shoulders, and made a running leap to the roof's edge. Joe shouted; Judith screamed. Willie went airborne just as a gust of wind blew him off course. He missed the lily-of-the-valley bush he'd apparently aimed for and crashed into a thorny pyracantha. His howls of pain and agonized writh-ing horrified Judith. Wayne was frozen in place. Joe yanked out his cell to call 911 before approaching the stricken man. Phyliss lifted her hands skyward, appealing to heaven. Ger-trude moved her wheelchair closer to the carnage. "Serves him right," she muttered. "He'd better not have ruined that bush. Grandpa Grover planted it during the Depression. It cheered him up—until he had his nervous breakdown."

Judith barely heard her mother. The wind whipped her shoulder-length hair into her eyes, cut through her merino sweater, and made her teeth chatter. Wayne was trying to extricate Willie from the shrubbery. Joe grabbed Wayne by the scruff of the neck and pulled him away. "You'll do more harm than good," he warned. "Wait for the medics."

Sweetums was creeping under the lily-of-the-valley bush, apparently to enjoy a close-up view of human suffering.

"My leg!" Willie cried. "I think it's broke!"

"Help's on the way." Joe sounded as if he was talking through gritted teeth. "The EMTs know how to get here." His ironic sidelong glance at Judith added fuel to her ag-gravation.

"But those thorns are gouging him," Wayne said. "See—he's all scratched up and bloody."

"Ugh," Phyliss said. "He looks like he's already in hell. I'm going to put the laundry away. It's cold out here."

"For once," Gertrude muttered, "I agree with that crazy

religious battle-ax." The old lady revved up her wheelchair and zoomed off to the toolshed. She didn't bother to turn back when a garbage can lid blew down the driveway, clattering loudly before bumping into a tire on Judith's Nissan. Leaves from the cherry tree sailed to earth along with twigs, dead camellia blooms, and small branches from the tall cedar behind the Dooleys' fence. As a leitmotif for the winds of October, Willie continued moaning and groaning.

Judith couldn't endure watching the excruciating drama. Without another word, she followed Phyliss inside and slammed the door.

"Didn't I tell you that man in the red suit was Satan?" the cleaning woman demanded as she picked up the hamper. "He got what he deserved. A fallen angel, that's the devil." She turned on the fat heels of her corrective shoes and started up the back stairs.

Judith headed for the Excedrin on the kitchen windowsill. Soon the cozy cul-de-sac would resound with a cacophony of sirens and a glare of flashing lights. The scenario was all too familiar. A couple of months earlier, another guest had been injured by falling into the pyracantha. The bush seemed cursed. Or she was. Maybe a break from the B&B was overdue. She swallowed two tablets as the doorbell sounded. The old school clock showed it was just past four, time for guests to check in. She hurried to greet the new arrivals.

The two young women who stood on the porch didn't fit Judith's information about the expected guests. They certainly weren't the older couple from Tennessee who were celebrating their fiftieth wedding anniversary or the two middle-aged couples from Alaska or the father-son combo from Montreal.

"I'm afraid I'm booked tonight," Judith apologized, "but I can find you alternate lodgings at another B&B."

The newcomers giggled. "We're here about the rental in the cul-de-sac," the blond girl said, exposing deep dimples. "Is it you or your daughter who's showing it?"

Judith frowned. "Oh? Oh! You mean Mrs. Rankers. Her daughter is in real estate." She pointed at the hedge. "Try next door."

The blonde pulled up the hood of her green raincoat. "We'll do that."

The taller, dark-haired young woman used one hand to clutch her billowing red jacket closed and held the storm door with the other hand to keep it from blowing shut. "Thanks," she said. "Where's the owner?"

"She moved." Judith couldn't bear to revisit the disaster that had forced Joe's ex-wife to leave town the previous August.

"Thanks again," the taller girl said as they started down the steps.

Judith grabbed the storm door to keep it from banging. "Good luck," she called, using her free arm to prop up the sheaf of cornstalks that had blown over. Luckily, the jack-o'-lanterns, the autumn leaf wreath, and the colorful gourds remained in place. She turned to go inside when she heard sirens whining nearby. Luckily, the young women had disappeared behind the laurel hedge. A moment later the medic van turned into the cul-de-sac. Judith hurriedly shut the door.

She wasn't in the mood to face the medics and the fire-fighters and the ambulance drivers and whichever other emergency personnel might arrive at Hillside Manor. She went into the front parlor and peeked through the tall, narrow window overlooking the driveway. Joe was motioning for the medics to come ahead. Maybe, Judith hoped, the rest of the usual crisis crew wouldn't show up. Joe could handle the situation. He knew the ins and outs of city departments, how to deal with disaster, cope with all sorts of . . .

Her shoulders sagged. *I really am worn out. Maybe I haven't recovered from dealing with Vivian and the dead body in her backyard. Maybe sitting in a private compartment and watching the world go by would do me good.* She closed her eyes and tried to relax. To her relief, there were no more sirens. Guests wouldn't have to trip over firefighters and ambulance attendants.

"There you are!" Pepper shrieked, coming into the parlor from the living room. "We'll sue! WeeWee's a mess! His leg and arm are broken! We won't pay you a dime. We're checking out and we never want to see you except in court!" She flounced out of the parlor.

"Good riddance," Judith muttered, collapsing onto the window seat. She didn't care if Willie canceled his payment, left the B&B's best room vacant, took the Flynns to court, or bad-mouthed Hillside Manor in the media. Weevil and Company were out of her life. Judith felt as if Fate were smiling on her.

She didn't bother to consider that Fate was often fickle.

Chapter Two

It was after six o'clock when Judith was able to sit down with Joe and discuss travel plans. The new guests had finally arrived, triumphing over a seven-car pileup on the north-south freeway, a late flight out of Anchorage, and a long line at U.S. Customs and Immigration on the Canadian border. Judith had gotten all eight of them registered, settled into their rooms, and served the appetizers for the social hour. She'd waved good-bye to Phyliss, tried to explain Wee Willie's antics to Gertrude, and informed Ingrid Heffelman at the state B&B association that Hillside Manor had an unexpected vacancy. Predictably, the conversation with Ingrid had been rancorous despite omitting the guest's name, who, as Judith had put it, "took a tumble in the garden." Her innkeeper's reputation was already sullied by too much murder and mayhem for Ingrid's taste. It had been an ongoing struggle to keep the association from revoking the B&B's license.

"Hey," Joe said, sitting at the kitchen table with his frazzled wife, "stop fussing about media coverage. Two good things have come out of the Weevil disaster. He's gone, and from what Wayne told me, there won't be any media coverage. Willie's too embarrassed to let the world see he's not infallible."

"Oh, he's fallible," Judith muttered. "He fell right into the pyracantha bush. He's lucky he didn't kill himself. Or somebody else."

Joe made a face. "If I'd had time to shove your mother under Willie . . ."

The flippant remark didn't amuse Judith. After forty years, she was used to the antagonism between Joe and Gertrude. Judith's mother had loathed Dan McMonigle, too. Despite frequent criticism of her daughter, no man was good enough for Gertrude's only child. Judith took a sip of diet soda and changed the subject. "Are you going to use Renie's plane ticket?"

Joe nodded. "It's a done deal. I stopped by their house when I went to get gas for my MG. Bill was pleased."

"You two seem to have a good time together," Judith said.

"We do." The gold flecks in Joe's green eyes danced. "But what really pleases Bill is not spending five hours on a plane with his drunken wife. My ticket money will be reimbursed by whichever company picks up the tab."

"Thank heavens Renie doesn't need to get looped on a train," Judith murmured. "I'm starting to get excited. I haven't taken a cross-country train trip since she and I went to New York to sail to England."

"Over forty years ago," Joe said softly, cradling his can of beer. "Strange—it doesn't seem that long. Back then, the twenty-first century was so far away. We were just getting used to being grown-ups. Which," he went on, looking more serious, "we didn't always manage very well."

Judith touched Joe's hand. "We finally got it right, didn't we?"

"Oh," Joe said with a deep intake of breath, "we did, but only after twenty-odd years at hard labor with our first spouses. Fate plays tricks on us. It's as if you and I were destined to be together, but Fate got the puppet strings tangled. Vivian should've married Dan. They would've drunk themselves to death or killed each other. You and I could've raised Mike together instead of having Dan fill my place. It took a long time for Fate to untangle those strings."

"Didn't it, though?" Judith said softly. After a long, wistful pause, she changed the subject. "Do you think the Rankerses should take over the B&B?"

Joe shrugged. "You know Carl. He'd saw off an arm or a leg if you asked him. I'll be here until Tuesday and get back Sunday," he went on, getting up to toss the empty beer can in the bin under the sink. "As long as the Rankerses can deal with your mother and Phyliss, I can help with everything else."

Judith nodded. "We aren't fully booked next week. That's good for Carl and Arlene, but not for us."

Joe had gone over to the stove and lifted the lid off the Dutch oven. "Your dumplings are done. Shall we eat?"

Judith cocked an ear to listen for sounds from the guests who'd congregated in the living room. "I think most of them have taken off for the evening. You dish up our dinner while I deliver Mother's."

Joe eyed Judith warily. "Have you told her yet about the trip?"

"No." She made a face. "I'll do it now. Mother loves beef stew and dumplings. Maybe she'll be in a good mood."

"If she is," Joe said, taking silverware out of a drawer next to the fridge, "check the time of day. We'll have to include all the details when we contact the media to report an unprecedented event like that."

"Not funny," Judith muttered.

To her surprise, Gertrude was indeed in a good mood. "Well, toots," the old lady said as her daughter put the dinner tray on the card table, "what time will Mike and Kristin and the grandkids be here?"

Judith stared blankly at her mother. "You mean . . . what?"

"He called me this morning," Gertrude replied, studying the beef, carrots, potatoes, and dumplings on her plate, "or was it this afternoon? Anyway, he told me they'd be here for supper."

Judith frowned. Was her mother delusional? It would hardly be surprising, given the old lady's advanced age. "Tonight?"

"You bet." Gertrude looked puzzled. "You didn't know?"

"Um . . . no. That's odd."

Gertrude was slathering gravy over the food on her plate. "Now that I think about it, Mike said something about your phone being out of order. He called you twice . . . or more than that?" She paused to take a bite of beef and shrugged. "I told him something around here was always out of order. Like Lunkhead, for instance."

Judith ignored her mother's disparaging reference to Joe. "Our phone isn't out of—oh!" The light dawned. "One of the guests kept answering the phone and hanging up on people. She was expecting a call. She didn't follow the house rules about which phone she should use. If Mike and the gang are coming to dinner, I'd better make extra stew." Judith started for the door, but turned around to face Gertrude. "Did Mike say why they were coming?"

Gertrude was chewing more beef. "It had to do with that goofy guy dressed like Santa Claus," she said after pausing to swallow. "Mac and Joe-Joe wanted to see him." She shook her head. "But I didn't know he played Santa until the crazy fool fell off the roof. Where's those reindeer when you really need them?" She paused, fork in hand. "Wait. It wasn't Santa—it was Superman."

"No," Judith said. "He never played Superman."

Gertrude glared at her daughter. "'Course he did. He told me so himself." She stabbed a fluffy dumpling.

"But . . ." Judith surrendered. "I'd better scoot. Maybe I can catch Mike and Kristin before they leave their place up at the summit."

Back in the kitchen, Judith dialed the ranger station's number and got Mike's recorded message: "This is Michael McMonigle. I'm unavailable at present, but in an emergency, dial—" Judith clicked off and tried her son's cell phone. Her daughter-in-law picked up on the second ring.

"Where are you?" Judith asked.

"In your driveway," Kristin said. "The boys are at the back door."

Sure enough, Mac and Joe-Joe raced into the kitchen. "Hey, Grams," Mac shouted, "where's Spider-Man?"

"Spider-Man?" Judith cautiously bent down to hug the boys. "You mean Wee Willie Weevil?"

Joe-Joe nodded, his dark curls dancing. "Is he like Spider-Man?"

"Ah . . ." Judith turned as Joe entered the kitchen.

"Hey!" he cried. "Look who's here. What's the occasion?"

"Wee Willie, for one thing," Mike answered as he and Kristin came through the hallway. "I'm kind of excited about meeting him, too."

Judith and Joe exchanged bleak looks.

"I didn't know . . ." Judith began.

"You should've called . . ." Joe said at the same time.

Mike held up his hands. "Whoa! Is something wrong?"

Joe put a hand on his son's shoulder. "Wee Willie checked out."

Mike's eyes darted in his mother's direction. "You mean . . . he's . . ."

"No, of course not," Judith said with a nervous little laugh. "Willie slipped and fell. He went to the ER, but he won't be back here before they head out of town." Seeing the disappointment on not only the little boys' faces, but Mike's, Judith suffered guilt pangs. "I'm sorry, guys. Maybe he'll visit here again." *Not if I can help it,* she thought. *I'd rather play host to a bunch of man-eating tigers.*

"Hey," Kristin said, her Viking-like form leaning over the little boys. "We'll get some of Willie's movies from the video store after dinner."

Mac glared up at Kristin; Joe-Joe pouted. "You promised!" they chorused.

Mike knelt by his sons. "If you help, maybe we'll find some of my Wee Willie posters and comics around here. I think I saved a couple of his *Robbing Hood* videos, too." He looked at Judith. "Do you know where they are, Ma?"

"Wherever you left them," Judith replied. "You promised to go through all that stuff years ago when you were transferred to the summit."

Mike looked sheepish. "We don't have much extra room up there. Maybe I can take some back with us."

"That'd be nice," she said. "I might be able to find room for the CDs and DVDs we've bought in the last ten years."

"Sorry," Mike mumbled. He stood up and spoke to the boys. "We'll start with the basement while Mom goes to the video store. You'll like the *Robbing Hood* shows. Willie wears a hood so nobody knows who he is and he steals from bad guys to give to poor people. At the end of each show, somebody asks, 'Who was that hood?' Lots of fun action and adventure."

"Actually," Judith said, "the stew's not quite done, so you should say hi to Gee-Gee. She's excited about your visit."

"Good idea," Joe said. "How late do you plan to be here tonight?"

Kristin, who had eyed the two place settings on the kitchen table, frowned at Joe. "Through the weekend. Didn't Gee-Gee tell you? Mike's taking a couple of days off. He still has vacation time because summer's so busy." She turned to her husband. "Hey, Big Daddy, you and the kids can bring in the sleeping bags and the rest of the stuff. I made dill pickles a couple of months ago, but I keep forgetting to bring them. I put up peaches, too, and pears and . . . Wait up, guys!" she called after Mike and the boys. "Don't forget my homemade jams and jellies. They're under the quilt I just finished."

As always, Kristin never ceased to amaze Judith, who considered her the most efficient, energetic, organized person on Planet Earth—with the possible exception of Aunt Ellen, who lived in Beatrice, Nebraska. At less than half Aunt Ellen's age, Kristin was catching up fast. Just listening to her daughter-in-law's feats was exhausting. Kristin made Judith feel lazy, old—and short.

"I think," Judith said, "I'll have a cocktail. Can I fix you something, Kris?"

"No, thanks. I made two kinds of cider—one hard, the other kiddy-safe." She opened a tan canvas bag on the counter. "Want some?"

Judith hesitated. "Oh . . . sure. Why not?"

Kristin turned to Joe. "How about you, Daddylawman?"

Joe managed not to wince at the nickname Kristin had bestowed on him. "No thanks. I'll help the boys unload the Rover."

Kristin had beaten Judith to the cupboard where the glasses were kept. "It looks as if you thought we wouldn't get here in time for dinner," she said, gesturing at the kitchen table. "Did Gee-Gee warn you we might be late if traffic on the pass was heavy?"

Judith hedged. "You never know with cross-state highways."

"Right," Kristin agreed, pouring the thick amber liquid into two glasses. "I checked all the sites on the computer and timed it so we could avoid any serious tie-ups." She handed a glass of cider to Judith. "Cheers!" The women clicked glasses. Kristin beamed at her mother-in-law. "This is going to be a great weekend. The kids can't wait to go trick-or-treating in the city."

"Ah . . ." Judith tried not to look surprised.

"Go ahead, taste it," Kristin urged. "It turned out fairly well. Oh, this should be such fun. It's the first time since the boys have been old enough that Halloween has fallen on a Sunday. Being a leap year, Saturday got skipped. Mac and Joe-Joe can't wait to be in the Heraldsgate Hill Halloween parade Sunday."

If Judith hadn't already been jolted by the first sip of hard cider, Kristin's words would have left her just as bug-eyed. Worse yet, the little boys ran down the hall, each carrying gym bags and making whooping noises. Joe-Joe dropped his bag with its frog motif at Judith's feet and grabbed her by the legs. "Wanna see my costume?" he asked.

"No!" Mac shouted, clutching his tiger-themed bag. "Grams can't see it until we get ready to go to the parade."

Judith's heart sank even lower. For the past decade, Heraldsgate Hill denizens of all ages dressed in every imaginable costume—or, as in the case of the ersatz Lady Godiva the previous year, no costume at all except for a long, dark wig. From infants to golden agers, the fantastic and the mundane promenaded the length of the commercial district on top of the hill. Inspiration often came from current pop culture: superheroes, presidents, characters from the latest hit movie or book. The revelers represented every category of animal, vegetable, and mineral. One year there were several babes-in-arms wearing pea-pod bodysuits, while their older siblings dressed as bananas, pumpkins, and a fruit salad that kept losing his—or her—grapes.

Traditional outfits weren't forgotten: angels, devils, witches, and ghosts, mingled with monsters, princesses, and skeletons. The imagination and handiwork of the hill's residents always amazed Judith. She and Joe never wore costumes, but they joined Renie and Bill at one of Moonbeam's curbside tables. The foursome drank mochas and hot chocolate while watching the steady flow of celebrants seeking treats—or store coupons—from local merchants. For the past few years, Judith had longed for the day her grandchildren would take part. Renie always hoped that she and Bill would become grandparents, but so far the three married Jones offspring hadn't granted her wish.

The event began at three and lasted until dark settled over the hill. *Damn,* Judith thought with pangs of guilt, remorse and disappointment, *I have a train to catch. I've always known life isn't fair. But do my grandchildren have to find out when they're only five and seven?*

Mac's inquisitive dark eyes gazed up at Judith. "What's wrong, Grams? You look sad."

"Nothing." She forced a smile. "I'm guessing what your costumes will be."

"Want a hint?" Joe-Joe asked, finally letting go of Judith's legs.

Mac grabbed his younger brother's arm. "No! It's a surprise! We promised Dad!" he said as his father and grandfather hauled cartons, luggage, and bedding through the hall. "Joe-Joe wants to tell Grams what we'll be for Halloween."

"He won't," Mike said. "Help Gramps with the stuff that goes upstairs, okay, guys?"

Joe's rubicund face was rosier than ever and he seemed short of breath. "What . . . about the . . . jellies?" he asked.

Judith hurried into the hall. "Set them down here. I'll put the canned goods in the pantry."

"Let me," Kristin volunteered. "Grams is cooking dinner."

Dinner. The old schoolhouse clock showed it was seven-thirty. She'd forgotten about dinner. The McMonigle clan's arrival hadn't merely overwhelmed her; it had killed her appetite. "How about pizza?"

"I'll do it," Kristin said. "Have you got fifteen-inch round stones?"

"Ah . . . no. I don't often make pizza," Judith admitted. *As in never.*

Kristin looked thoughtful. "I can use cookie sheets. Let's see . . . I'll need pepperoni, Italian sausage, ham, hot dogs, mushrooms, onions, grated mozzarella cheese, and tomato sauce. Or canned chopped tomatoes, if you have them. Oh! The dough, of course."

While Kristin listed her needs, Judith downed more hard cider. "This packs a wallop," she said. "What liquor is in it? I can't tell."

Kristin smiled slyly. "It's my own recipe."

Feeling as if fog had invaded her brain, Judith wasn't sure what her daughter-in-law meant. "You mix a couple of kinds together or . . ."

Kristin winked at Judith. "Not exactly."

"Then how . . ." Judith paused. "Moonshine?"

"Living in a forest has its advantages," Kristin said, opening the fridge. "I'm a country farm girl." She searched the shelves, apparently for pizza makings. "I shouldn't talk about it. I wouldn't want Mike to get fired."

"No." Judith took another sip. "No, not fired. How about

sued?" she asked, reeling just enough that she had to lean against the sink.

Kristin laughed. "As in going blind or crazy? I know what I'm doing." She closed the fridge. "I found wieners and ham, but no sausage or pepperoni. Do you keep pizza makings in the pantry or the freezer?"

"Pantry? Freezer?" *What's a pantry? What's a freezer?* Judith wondered. After a long pause, she compelled her brain to function. She'd drunk only half a glass of cider. Kristin had finished her drink and seemed in complete control of her faculties. *She has a hollow leg,* Judith suddenly remembered. *A large and long hollow leg.* Noticing that her daughter-in-law looked apprehensive, Judith set her glass down on the kitchen table. "I don't have all the ingredients you need," she blurted. "You're kind to offer, but let's call the pizza parlor at the top of the hill." She gestured at the bulletin board by the half doors. "The number's there along with a menu and some coupons. Go ahead, call and get something the boys like. I'm so sorry about the mix-up, but Mother can be forgetful. We really didn't know you were coming."

Kristin grimaced. "I wondered. Gosh, I'm afraid we've upset you. I should've double-checked. Maybe we should go home."

Judith's step was unsteady as she moved toward Kristin and hugged her. "No! We're delighted to see you." She let go of Kristin before the younger woman crushed her rib cage. "Get pizza. I'm going to the living room and pass out."

Kristin's anxious expression returned. "Are you sick?"

"No," Judith said, teetering toward the half doors. "I'm drunk."

When Judith woke up an hour and a half later, she realized that the hard cider wasn't the only cause of her cave-in. Ever since the Flynns had returned from their trip to Scotland in March, she hadn't taken a day off.

Innkeeping was no nine-to-five, five-day-a-week job. Judith had to keep close to the premises. She'd considered cutting back by closing the B&B on Mondays, but that meant raising rates. Still, the B&B was usually free of guests from morning checkout to afternoon check-in. Except for breakfast and the social hour, it was rare for Judith to provide anything more demanding than a Band-Aid or information about sightseeing tips.

Still, she reflected, sitting up on one of the matching sofas by the fireplace, the August debacle with Joe's ex-wife had been a huge physical and emotional drain. Maybe she hadn't yet recovered. Getting to her feet, she realized that the house was remarkably quiet, considering that two young boys and their parents were in temporary residence. The grandfather clock in the living room informed her it was nine-twenty. The kids were probably tucked into their sleeping bags in the family quarters on the third floor.

Judith went to the kitchen. The dishwasher's green light was on, indicating it had finished its load. The counters were spik-and-span, as was the sink, the floor, and every other surface. The garbage and the recycling bins were empty except for fresh liners. Checking the fridge, she saw three slices of pizza covered in plastic wrap. Judith realized she was hungry. As she took out the pizza, she heard voices from the back stairs.

"Ma!" Mike called, coming down the hall with Justin Weevil. "You okay?"

Judith smiled as the two young men entered the kitchen. "Yes." She hugged Justin. "Your uncle Willie . . . let's face it. He shouldn't have jumped off the roof when it's so windy." She looked at Mike. "Have you heard what happened?"

Mike grinned. "Oh, yeah. Incredible. Or not, given Willie and his wild ways. Justy brought over one of his uncle's old butt-kicking movies. Mac and Joe-Joe loved it, but they think Willie must still look like that, all buff and wrinkle-free. They want to see him in the hospital."

In spite of all the trouble Willie had caused, Judith felt sorry for him. "He really broke an arm and a leg?"

"He'll be fine," Justin said. "He's broken just about everything over the course of his career. Even when he got older, he refused stunt doubles until one of the movie insurers balked and Uncle Willie had to let his stand-in do the stunts for the last live-action film he made. He still gets money from those old movies and cartoons. I hoped he'd mellow when he hit sixty, but it hasn't happened." Justin's handsome face grew serious. "I shouldn't have mentioned your B&B to him. I'm sorry. I'll talk to Pepper and make sure you get paid for their stay."

"You don't have to," Judith said. "It's a relief to have them gone. Did you stop by the hospital this evening?"

Justin laughed. "Are you kidding? I keep my distance from that crazy old coot. So does Mom. She solved that problem by leaving town. She hasn't spoken to her brother-in-law since she dumped my dad almost thirty years ago and moved here from Montana."

Judith was puzzled. "I thought Willie came to see his family."

Mike frowned at his mother. "Don't get Justy started on that one."

"Oh." Judith was embarrassed. "I'm sorry, but . . ."

Justin smiled ruefully. "No apology required. Mike's heard me bitch about my uncle ever since we met. When I was a little kid growing up in Montana, Uncle Willie dissed the rest of his family, including my dad, unless he needed us for some self-serving reason. Back then, Willie was already well known for his daredevil stunts. My mom and dad and my sister and I hardly ever saw him unless he had to dump off his spoiled brats while he went off on one of his outrageous exploits. My cousin Ricky was my age, the oldest of the three kids, and he made my life hell. He was totally out of control. Mom tried to discipline the little beast, but it was hopeless."

Mike laughed. "I've told Ma about the time Ricky got his

head stuck in a bucket. You got back at him that time with your hammer."

"Right," Justin said, his tone ironic. "Too bad it was a plastic hammer."

"No wonder you moved here," Judith remarked.

"Not soon enough," Justin said. "It got worse later on when Willie got his first movie deal. He needed publicity showing he wasn't just a badass rebel, and conned all of us into photo ops. Willie the family man with wife and kiddies, Willie at a family picnic, Willie grinning all over the place when Granny Weevil baked him a cherry pie. After we did our posing for him, he'd ignore us until the next time we were needed. He was a user, a taker." Justin paused. "You've heard all this before. Mike must've talked about it."

Judith glanced at her son. "I recall the bucket story, but not much else."

Mike looked embarrassed. "When I first met Justy, you weren't home a lot. Even on weekends, you were always tired from coping with . . . Dad."

The reference to Dan McMonigle evoked bittersweet memories. Dan had raised Mike as his own son. He'd done a decent job as a surrogate father, but he'd been a rotten husband. "I was an absent mother, what with holding down two jobs," Judith acknowledged. "I also had to do what I could for Grams."

Mike shrugged. "You didn't have much choice." He turned to Justin. "Speaking of fathers, didn't your dad always side with Willie?"

"Oh, yes." Justin sounded resentful. "My father was a few years younger than Willie. He looked up to him and envied his courage and determination. But the rest of the family, especially my mom, didn't feel that way."

"But," Judith put in, "didn't he come to see you and your mother this time?"

Justin's expression was sour. "That was what Pepper said when she called to say they were headed this way. There was another reason, though. A local computer company had expressed interest in developing an action game using Willie. I don't know if he got together with them."

Judith shook her head. "If he did, it wasn't face-to-face. Except for jumping out of windows and off roofs, he stayed close to the B&B. The only visitor was the publicist who took photos when your uncle got blown off course."

Justin shrugged. "Family isn't a Weevil priority. Pepper had mentioned getting together at Mom's condo at the bottom of the hill. That's why I thought the B&B would be a perfect place for them to stay—especially since Willie's been banned from every local hotel that doesn't have cockroaches for doormen."

"And?" Judith prodded.

"And . . . nothing." Justin shook his head. "Not a word from Pepper—or Willie—after I gave them your contact information two weeks ago. They never called to confirm the get-together, so Mom decided to leave town. I would've, too, if I hadn't had to work." He glanced at his watch with its plain black face and silver hands. "Speaking of work, it's going on ten. I've got an early HR meeting tomorrow." He bent down to kiss Judith's cheek. "I won't let Uncle Willie and Pepper cheat you out of the money for their stay here."

"Don't be silly," Judith said. "You're like family."

Justin stopped on the porch, his face serious. "You've all been family since the first time Mike asked me to come for dinner. Before Mom moved here, I was lost, a hick from the sticks." He took a notebook out of his inside jacket pocket. "I'll make out an IOU." Justin scribbled a few words and handed the page to Judith. "We'll both sign."

Judith laughed at what he'd written: *We're in this together. The payoff is one cooked goose.* "You don't need to do that," she insisted.

Justin looked earnest. "Years ago I said I'd roast a goose for Christmas or Thanksgiving dinner. Now I'll make good on that promise, but I'll cook it at Mom's condo. Goose is greasy. I don't want the fire alarm going off at my apartment or scaring your guests. Besides, I can't think of another way to make up for saddling you with my crazy family. I should never have suggested your B&B."

Judith glanced at Mike, who was looking bemused. "Well?"

"Why not?" Mike said. "Hey, Justy, tell your mom Kristin can help. Her granny's an expert on roast goose."

Visions of the know-it-all Kristin and Justin's indomitable mother, Germaine, facing off with basting brushes over a roasting pan made Judith blanch. "Please," she begged, "forget about your uncle's stay. It's over."

"Oh, no," Justin countered. "Sign here. I wouldn't feel right about this whole mess if you didn't."

Judith scribbled her initials. "Okay, but it's not necessary."

"It is to me," Justin said, starting down the steps. "One way or another, I'll make darned sure you get what's coming to you."

Watching Mike and Justin walk toward the driveway, Judith realized that Justin's last words had a double meaning—and one of them wasn't good.

Chapter Three

As Judith slipped Justin's IOU into the strongbox where she kept cash and credit card receipts, the golden-wedding-anniversary couple returned. Judith hurried to meet them before they headed upstairs. The seafood restaurant on the bay had been excellent; their room was very comfortable; they had no idea what to expect of the city, never before having gone farther from Memphis than Little Rock, where their son and his family lived. After more than fifteen years of innkeeping, Judith could ask questions, hear answers, make appropriate responses, and establish rapport while her brain was otherwise engaged. None of her guests seemed to realize she wasn't really listening. According to Renie, Judith was so adept at exuding warmth—and telling lies when the need arose—that she could probably fool Saint Peter when she arrived at heaven's Pearly Gates.

As soon as the Tennessee couple headed upstairs, Judith went back to the kitchen, where Mike was pouring himself a glass of milk.

"Are the boys asleep?" she asked.

"They should be," Mike replied, closing the fridge door. "They went on a sugar high after Gee-Gee let them plunder her box of chocolates. She never let me do that. Then she told them Santa Claus got drunk, fell off the roof, and killed himself. It took Kris and me ten minutes to make them stop crying."

Judith shook her head in bewilderment. "I honestly never know when Mother is genuinely gaga or just putting me on."

Mike shrugged. "She's earned the right to be muddled. The boys like her. Maybe they sense she's got a good heart."

Judith shot her son a hard look. "A strong heart, anyway."

"Ma . . ." The single word conveyed reproach.

"I know," Judith responded. "I get frustrated. I'm glad the boys have a great-grandmother. You got shortchanged with grandparents. Only Mother was there for you—and for me. My father died too young." Feeling her eyes grow moist, she turned away, wishing as she often did that Donald Grover wasn't such a distant, yet dear, memory. "I'm so glad you're here," she said, and turned around to hug her son. "Your boys are such darlings. I hope they're having fun."

Mike laughed. "They are," he said as Judith moved out of his embrace. "But they're worn out. After they watched the movie with Willie in action, they wished he was still here. It's hard for them to understand that thirty years later, Willie doesn't look like the guy on the screen."

"He may dye his hair and he's got wrinkles, but he seemed very fit. I don't remember his movies. I suppose his fans would recognize him."

Mike took a big drink of milk. He nodded—and shrugged. "Justin told them that Willie couldn't be exactly like the movie version and Kristin reminded them that the most fun would be Halloween. That made up for missing Willie."

"Good." Judith tried to sound pleased rather than guilty about being unable to share the entire holiday with the children. "They'll have a grand time."

Mike drained the glass. "It'll be huge. Is it so popular that you have to reserve a place on the avenue to watch the parade?"

"No," Judith replied. "But get there early if you want a seat outside."

Mike looked puzzled. "We'll walk with the kids. You

can't stand around too long on your bum hip. Should we leave first to get a table for you?"

"Ah . . . I meant if you want to drive and not walk up the Counterbalance."

"It's only three blocks," Mike said. "Living at the summit, we walk uphill a lot. The boys are so excited they'll practically fly there."

"Oh. Of course." Judith couldn't look Mike in the eye. "Walking isn't easy for people with hip problems." She had to reveal her travel plans, but hesitated, playing for time to figure out how to attend at least part of the parade. Maybe Renie or Joe would have some advice. "Where's your father?" she asked.

Mike laughed. "He dozed off about twenty minutes into *Extrema Escrima,* leaving Willie at the mercy of a Mongol horde."

"I didn't know Willie made historical films. Was Genghis Khan after him?"

"No." Mike took a couple of snickerdoodles out of the sheep-shaped cookie jar on the kitchen table. "These Mongols were part of a motorcycle club from Southern California."

"I hope the bikers won," Judith murmured. "It's after ten, so I'm going to lock up. The guests who are still out on the town will have to use their keys. Wake your father so he can go to bed."

"Will do." Mike glanced at the dishwasher. "I almost forgot—Kris told me to unload that thing when the green light came on."

"I'll do it," Judith said.

Mike shook his head. "I told Kris I would."

Judith scrutinized her son as he opened the dishwasher. "Hold it," she said. "I don't like asking, but is all this drill sergeant stuff from Kristin part of the deal you agreed to after she wanted to separate?"

Mike's face flushed slightly. "In a way. That is, Kris felt useless after she resigned from her ranger's job." He grabbed a handful of silverware and put it on the counter. "You know we'd tried from the get-go to be posted to the same place, even if it meant moving across the country. That didn't happen." Mike took out the rest of the silverware. "Even after we had the boys, she still felt she'd lost her identity and become just another wife and mother." The stew pot and the lid were next. "It wasn't fulfilling."

Judith was staring incredulously at her son. "Wife and mother don't qualify as possibly the most important jobs on earth?"

"Oh, sure," Mike replied, stacking a half-dozen plates in the cupboard next to the stove. "But that was all about the boys and me. She wanted something that was . . . how did she put it? Exclusively hers." Glassware was next. "Kris realized she needed to get back to her roots. All the women in her family through four generations were raised on farms, including Kristin on her parents' wheat ranch." He paused, juggling several bowls before putting them in the cupboard. "They did organic before the rest of the world caught on. Crafts, too. Almost everything was homemade, including clothes and bedding and rugs."

"Odd," Judith remarked. "I can't picture Kris's mother building a tractor."

Mike made a face at Judith. "I said 'almost.'" He was holding a salad bowl. "Kris does pottery, too. Where does this go?"

"One cupboard over, second shelf." Judith considered taking more Excedrin. Her headache had come back.

"Getting in touch with the earth and letting it nurture her was what Kris wanted, which is why she became a forest ranger in the first place," Mike continued, hanging coffee mugs from hooks above the shelf where he'd put the salad bowl. "My part of the agreement was that I'd help with mundane chores." Holding a cast-iron skillet, he gestured at the dishwasher. "Like doing this. Organizing and scheduling are her domain because she's good at it."

"Oh, yes," Judith agreed. "She reminds me of Aunt Ellen—on speed."

Mike looked puzzled. "What's wrong with that?"

Judith sighed. "Nothing, I suppose. Aunt Ellen can hold down three jobs at once, volunteer for every needy cause in Beatrice, Nebraska, serve on I don't know how many committees, manage a gubernatorial campaign, take night classes, raise three kids, attend all the Cornhusker football games with Uncle Win, and make crafts. She's lived away from here for so long that she's forgotten Pacific Northwest-erners rarely wear earrings made out of corn kernels. And did we ask for a photo in a sunflower seed frame showing Aunt Ellen and Uncle Win standing in front of the world's largest ball of twine in Cawker City, Kansas?"

Mike grinned. "I get your point. But Kristin turns out some really cool stuff." He removed the last items from the dishwasher and frowned. "I don't know where the measuring cups and the vegetable peeler and the Tupperware go."

"Just leave them on the counter. Please. My head's spinning."

"You sure?"

"Yes!"

"Whoa!" Mike moved closer to his mother. "Don't you feel well?"

Judith started to answer, but stopped. This would be the perfect time to mention her Sunday departure, but she couldn't. She smiled wanly. "I'm just tired. It's been a hectic year." She saw the concern on his face. Although he'd inher-ited Joe's coloring and red hair, his eyes were brown. As he grew older, he looked more like her own father. "I shouldn't have pried about you and Kristin. To quote Aunt Ellen, it's *N-O-M-B*—none of my business. I'm just so glad that the two of you have resolved your issues." *Oh, good grief,* Judith thought, *I'm spouting psychobabble.* "I mean, meddling motherhood isn't my style."

"Forget it," Mike said, kissing Judith's cheek. "We're fine."

"Good." Her smile was genuine. "Tell your dad I'll be up shortly."

"Sure." Mike started for the back stairs, but stopped short of the hallway. "I'm glad this worked out for us. The boys can't wait to go trick-or-treating in the city after dinner Sunday. It'll be fun to have them meet the neighbors, especially in the cul-de-sac."

"It will." Judith felt her smile freeze. "Night."

She watched her son disappear up the stairs. Before she could pick up the phone to call Renie, the two couples from Alaska returned, laughing their heads off. By the time Judith got to the entry hall, she could see only feet as they headed up to their rooms. The Canadian father and son were still out. As Judith was about to lock the door, she heard someone on the front porch. She saw a man and woman through the peephole. "Yes?" she said, opening the door.

"Hi," the raven-haired woman said. "We heard you have a vacancy. Can we come in?"

The couple looked respectable and had two small overnight bags. "Please do," Judith said, stepping aside to let them enter. Before she could close the door, Sweetums padded inside with a disdainful swish of his plumelike tail. "Did you find us through the state B&B office?"

The man, who Judith judged to be in his mid-thirties, turned to the woman, who looked about the same age. "The . . . what?"

His companion nodded. "Someone with the state," she replied, and gave Judith a self-deprecating look. "I'm awful at names."

"That's okay," Judith said. "Your room is the largest one we have." She paused, waiting for one of the newcomers to inquire about price.

"Sounds great," the man said. "How do we pay?"

"Credit card or cash," Judith replied. "Is this for one night?"

"We're not sure," he said, taking two one-hundred-dollar bills out of his wallet. "Will that cover it?"

"That covers the room," Judith said. "There's tax, of course."

He dug out two twenties. "Does that work?"

Judith accepted the bills. "More than enough. Do you want change?"

He hesitated, watching a haughty Sweetums study him from the parlor door. "Keep it for the cat." The man smiled, revealing a slight gap between his front teeth. "Where's the room?"

"I'll show you." She picked up the registration book from the oak stand next to the credenza and noticed that she'd left her notations about the train trip alongside the visitor information. Not wanting Mike or Kristin to discover her plans, she tucked the travel data inside the registry. "Name?"

The woman burst into laughter. The man looked bemused. "You'd better let me fill that out," he said. "It's hard to spell."

Judith watched him print ZYZZYVA in the appropriate space. "You're right," she agreed. "It is hard to spell. How is it pronounced?"

The woman laughed again. "I told you I was awful with names. It's taken me two years to spell his. It's pronounced Zee-zee-vah."

Judith smiled. "I hope your first names are easier."

"They are," Mr. Zyzzyva said. "I'm Dick, she's Jane."

"That I can do," Judith assured them.

Dick finished the registration form while Jane tried to pet Sweetums, who briefly allowed the attention until he yawned and ambled off to the living room.

"I like cats," Jane said in a rather wistful voice. "House cats, I mean. The undomesticated types are to be avoided."

"Definitely," Judith agreed, handing over the keys and the B&B information packet. "I'll go up with you. Breakfast starts at . . ." She paused as the front door opened to admit the Canadian father and son.

Jane was already on the first landing. "You're busy. We'll figure it out. Thanks!" She continued going upstairs.

Jean-Paul Gauthier and his son, Étienne, were touring the United States to visit parks, gardens, and other outdoor areas designed by Frederick Law Olmsted and his sons. Judith had spoken only briefly to the Gauthiers upon their late check-in. Étienne, who preferred being called Steve, was working on his PhD in landscape architecture. As part of his dissertation, he and his father were touring North America to study numerous sites designed by the Olmsteds.

"Were you able to see much of interest this late in the day?" Judith asked.

"Sometimes," Gauthier père replied in his French-Canadian joual accent, "you see more in the dark. Shapes, forms, how sky and earth mingle. The rain is not so good, but it has stopped now."

Gauthier fils darted an amused look at his father. "Papa has eyes like a cat," he said with only a faint accent. "I'd rather see things in daylight."

The father gave the son an indulgent look. "The young— so literal. We must humor them, eh? Our accommodations are most agreeable, madame. *Merci et bon soir.*" He sketched a little bow.

The pair went upstairs. Judith locked the door and returned to the kitchen. It was ten-thirty, but not too late to call Renie, who was a night owl.

"Oh, good grief!" Renie exclaimed after Judith finished her recap of the situation with Mike's family. "You get rid of one pain in the butt with Willie and then you end up in another mess. You really need to get out of town. It's too bad we can't leave now."

"Can Bill take us to the train a bit later?" Judith asked. "It's a ten-minute drive to the station, and on a Sunday there shouldn't be much downtown traffic."

Renie didn't answer right away. "Well . . . Bill's gone to bed, so I can't mention it tonight. He's like his brother, Bub. They insist on leaving an hour earlier than any normal person would because they want to make sure they have a seat, a pew, a parking place, a . . . whatever. It's got to be a Midwestern thing. I don't think either of them changed their watches after they moved here forty-odd years ago. Or," she added musingly, "do I mean daylight savings time? I hate the idea so much that I try not to think about it. What's the point?" Her voice grew angry—and loud. "What the hell are we saving the daylight *for*?"

Judith never understood her cousin's opposition to the concept, except as an example of Renie's contrary nature. "Relax," she urged. "We change back in the wee small hours Sunday."

"Hmm. That gives me an idea."

"What?"

"Never mind," Renie said. "It involves math. I'll figure it out by Sunday."

"I need answers now," Judith insisted. "What do I tell the kids?"

"Nothing. Don't expend energy making up one of your convoluted lies."

"Fibs," Judith snapped. "I don't lie. I only tell fibs in a good cause."

"You just told another one." Renie sounded impatient with her cousin's attitude toward deception. "Don't say anything. Yet."

There was no choice but to reluctantly agree. Renie might be older, but that didn't mean she was wiser. Besides, Judith admitted to herself as she slowly climbed the stairs, keeping quiet was easier than blurting out the truth.

When she reached the third-floor family quarters, she paused as she often did to rest her hip and take a deep breath. All was quiet in Mike's old room and the den. Joe, however, was still awake and reading a book by one of his favorite crime caper authors. He paused as Judith entered the bedroom. "I should never have tried to watch that Weevil movie," he said. "It's a good cure for insomnia. I must've dozed off for almost an hour, so now I don't feel sleepy."

"I do," Judith replied. "I'm suffering from a moral dilemma. Have you mentioned our Boston trip to Mike or Kristin?"

"Only that I'm heading back there next week," Joe said. "I

knew you were in a pickle, so I didn't mention your plans."
His green eyes twinkled. "I'm anxious to hear how you plan
to wiggle off the hook on this one."

"I'm not," Judith retorted. "Renie's handling it."

"Oh God!" Joe flung an arm across his forehead. "That's
worse than your mega-lies!"

"Don't you start in on me," Judith warned. "Renie's already done that. It's not my fault Mike and Kristin showed
up for the weekend without notice. Mother should've mentioned it sooner, but if I'd had the courage to tell her about
the trip, she might've told them their timing was bad."

Joe snorted. "It'd be like her not to tell them just to be
ornery."

Judith glared at her husband from over the neck of the
sweater she was pulling off. "Mother isn't always mean."

Joe feigned bewilderment. "Maybe it's just me."

"Maybe it is." She placed her sweater on top of the dresser.
"I've given up on either of you making peace."

"You might as well," Joe said. "I figure contention is one
of the things that keeps the old girl going."

"Could be." Judith stepped out of her slacks. "Feistiness
has its benefits."

"I think she's lived so long because God doesn't want her."
Joe closed his book and set it on the nightstand. "Are you
really tired?"

"Yes," Judith snapped. "It's been a long and . . ." She
paused, staring at Joe's mischievous expression. "Maybe I'm
not *that* tired."

He reached out to take her hand and draw her closer to the
bed. "Let's see if I can perk you up."

Moving into the circle of his arms, Judith smiled. "You
always could." She sighed softly. "You always will."

"Good," Joe said, burying his face in the curve of her neck
and shoulder. "After all, we're still making up for lost time."

During the night the rain and wind stopped, but by morning, fog had settled in over the hill. The little boys were sleeping in, having been worn out by the previous day's activities. Mike and Kristin came down to the kitchen shortly before eight. Judith had just returned from taking her mother's breakfast to the toolshed. She'd considered breaking the news about the Boston trip to Gertrude, but changed her mind at the last minute. It wasn't just putting up with the old lady's predictable complaints about her daughter abandoning her for such a long time, but that her mother would blab the news to Mike and Kristin.

The early part of the morning was typically busy. Kristin volunteered to help with the guests' breakfast. Judith accepted the offer, but pointed out that the menu was already planned. Kristin could help by setting up the serving area in the dining room. Judith sensed that her daughter-in-law was put off by the request. Having quickly accomplished the task, Kristin remarked that the curtains in the family quarters needed washing. Judith hadn't argued, but Phyliss pitched a fit.

"Your son's wife should keep her nose out of my business," she griped as the Alaskan quartet and the Tennessee couple were finishing their meal. "I've got a system and a schedule. Those curtains shouldn't be washed until the third week of November. Come next May, everything will be higgly-piggly."

"Let her do it. Kristin isn't happy unless she's busy," Judith said, not without sympathy for Phyliss.

"Then she ought to be all smiles, which is more than I can say for some of your paying guests. From what I've seen of them this morning, they're a grumpy bunch. Too much noise during the night. Maybe Miss Know-It-All was running the vacuum in the wee small hours."

"It was probably the wind." Judith cocked an ear in the direction of the dining room. "The Canadians just came downstairs. I should greet them."

Right behind the Gauthiers was Libby Pruitt, a Northwestern University lit professor on sabbatical. Judith hadn't been able to visit much with Ms. Pruitt, who'd checked in late Tuesday and was due to check out Friday morning. The guests already at the table greeted Judith as they made way for the newcomers.

Gauthier père studied the offerings on the sideboard that had been installed the previous winter by Judith's handyman, the ageless and energetic Skjoval Tolvang. "No omelets?" he exclaimed in something akin to shock.

"Chill, Papa," Gauthier fils said softly. "The scrambled eggs look great."

"Tomorrow," Judith said, "my husband is making his Joe's Special. It's not exactly an omelet, but our guests always rave about . . ."

A blond head loomed over the half doors to the kitchen. "Omelets coming up!" Kristin cried. "Three minutes!"

Judith's smile was strained. "The ham and two kinds of sausage are excellent. Try the blueberry pancakes and the Belgian waffles. Everyone always seems to enjoy them."

Steve Gauthier shot Judith an amused glance. "My father likes waffles. Don't you, Papa?"

The older man uttered a little grunt. "They are fine. Usually."

His son had already filled his plate. "The whipped cream's homemade and the strawberries are fresh, not frozen."

"In October?" Mr. Gauthier was incredulous. "How can that be?"

Judith was flummoxed. She had no idea where Falstaff's got their berries during fall and winter. For all she knew, the store manager grew them in his bathtub. "Australia? Chile? Our grocer flies in items from all over the world."

Mr. Gauthier poured his orange juice. "Ah! Real oranges. *Excellent.*"

Judith started for the kitchen to see what the overzealous Kristin was up to, but a clearing of the throat by Libby Pruitt caught her attention. "Yes?" Judith said, realizing that Ms. Pruitt remained in the dining-room doorway.

"May I have a word, please?" she asked in a low voice.

"Of course," Judith said, noting that her guest's pale face looked worried. "Shall we go into the living room?"

"That's not necessary." Libby Pruitt had moved into the entry hall and stopped by the powder room. She was tall and slim, close to six feet in her low-heeled shoes. "This morning I dropped one of my contact lenses by the window." She made a face. "It was for my left eye, which is considerably worse than my right. I'm farsighted, so I literally had to feel for it. I finally moved the braided rug at the foot of the bed—and found this." She opened her right hand to reveal a plain gold band in her palm. "It's engraved. Perhaps a previous guest didn't realize the ring was missing until after checking out."

Judith plucked up the ring and peered at the tiny markings. "It looks too big for a woman, but you never know. I can't see this without a magnifier."

Libby smiled. "Once I found my contact, I could read what turned out to be initials. They're *RK,* an ampersand, and *JG.* There's also a date—1990."

Judith nodded. "I see that now. The guest who stayed there ahead of you was an Episcopal priest from New Jersey attending a church conference. I don't recall if he wore a wedding ring. His last name was Dobbs. Wrong initials."

"Maybe," Libby suggested, "the ring has been there for some time."

Judith shook her head. "I doubt it. A lost wedding ring—at least that's what it looks like—isn't something you'd forget."

Libby's thin lips curved slightly. "It is if you want to forget the person wearing the matching band."

"Uh . . . that's so." Judith had already noticed the oval garnet ring on Libby's left hand. Maybe it had replaced a wedding band that evoked unhappy memories. "Thanks for finding this. I'll do some research to figure out who may have lost it."

Libby smiled. "Good luck." She walked into the dining room.

Judith put the ring in the pocket of her tan slacks before opening the guest register to check the most recent occupants of room two. It was not only the smallest of Hillside Manor's six rooms, but had a single bed. She searched all the way back to October 1, but found no one with the initials *RK* or *JG*. Stumped, she returned to the dining room just as Kristin entered bearing two big platters.

"Omelets," she announced with a big smile, setting the dishes on the table instead of the sideboard. "This one," she continued, pointing to her left, "is shrimp and mushrooms. Traditional, tasty. The other is hardier as well as healthier. Chopped raisins and nuts. Try it with some of the powdered sugar that's in the small green bowl." She nodded toward the sideboard. "Enjoy!"

Judith smiled at her guests in passing as she followed Kristin into the kitchen. "You didn't need to make the omelets. We have ample food for everyone now that all the guests are seated. By the way, where did you get the nuts?"

"In the pantry," Kristin replied. "Isn't that where you keep them?"

"Usually," Judith said. "I don't cook with them except during the holidays. Aunt Renie is allergic to all kinds of nuts, especially peanuts."

"Peanuts aren't nuts," Kristin said. "They're legumes."

Judith agreed. "She's allergic to both. It's peanuts that can be lethal."

"That's awful," Kristin declared. "How can she not eat nuts and be healthy? Couldn't she be desensitized?"

"She'd never risk it. Renie's always lived with the allergy. She prefers being unhealthy—and undead," Judith said, trying not to sound annoyed. But the attempt failed. Kristin suddenly looked offended. Judith quickly put a hand on her daughter-in-law's arm. "I really appreciate your help. Now that everyone's been served, we can close the kitchen."

Kristin still looked prickly. "Aren't all of your rooms full?"

"Yes, but—" Judith stopped. "Oh, drat! I forgot about the Zs."

"The Zs?"

"A couple showed up last night and I put them in room three. Their last name is unpronounceable. Maybe they went out to breakfast." Judith started for the back stairs. "I'll ask Phyliss. She'll know if they're still in their room."

"Phyliss needs to mind her manners," Kristin said. "Doesn't she understand that you're the employer and she's the employee?"

Judith turned around. "She insists she works only for God. I'm strictly in the middle. Phyliss has her ways, but it's best not to rile her."

Kristin was standing between the hall and the kitchen, her hands braced against the doorjambs. With her Valkyrie-like appearance, she reminded Judith of Samson holding up the pillars of the temple. If, she thought fleetingly, Kristin removed her hands, would the whole house fall down?

"Insubordination is unacceptable," Kristin said. "It erodes self-esteem."

Judith tried to keep her temper in check. "Phyliss has worked for me from the get-go. We have an unspoken understanding. She puts up with my shortcomings and I shrug off her Bible-thumping. She's a fine worker, loyal and never shirking. As for self-esteem, at my age, I don't dwell on it."

Kristin moved out of the doorway and took a few steps into the hallway. The house did not fall down. "That's unwise. Age isn't a factor, I hate mentioning it, but there are times when you seem to be . . ." Her forehead wrinkled as she struggled to find the right word.

Judith braced herself against the wall by the stairs. "Yes?"

Kristin took a deep breath. "You've become a doormat. There. I've said it." She smiled wryly. "You let people run right over you, including Joe, Gee-Gee, Aunt Renie, and even Mike. That's why you should reflect on your lack of self-esteem. It'll get worse with time. Society shuns older people, ignoring their wisdom and experience. We live in a youth-obsessed culture, but by valuing yourself and exuding confidence, you needn't become invisible."

"Thanks, Kristin," Judith said, feeling as if her face had frozen. "I'll think about that. If I agree with you, I'll let you know." *And no thanks for making me feel like a lowly, worthless worm. If, as you suggest, I had more spunk, I'd wring your neck and stuff you in the Dumpster.* "Now I have to look for some missing guests." Before Kristin could respond, Judith started up the back stairs.

Phyliss was coming out of room six, which was where one of the two Alaskan couples was staying. "Are these Eskimos checking out today?" she asked, setting a trash bag down in the hall.

"No," Judith said. "All of the Alaskans are staying another night. And I don't think they're Eskimos."

Phyliss glowered at Judith. "They're from Alaska, aren't they?"

"It doesn't matter what they are," Judith said. "I'm looking for the couple in room three. Are they up yet? Breakfast is nearly over."

"What couple?" Phyliss responded. "I thought that crazy blasphemous sinner was hauled off to the hospital."

"New guests arrived last night. Did they go out to breakfast?"

Phyliss stared at Judith. "I don't know anything about them. The room looks just the way I left it yesterday. Neat as a pin."

"That doesn't make sense," Judith said. "Let me have a look."

"Go ahead," the cleaning woman said. "Have I ever told a lie?"

"No," Judith admitted. "Maybe I'm going insane."

"It happens to a lot of people I know," Phyliss said. "Straight to the booby hatch. I'm taking out the trash. If you see phantom guests in room three, keep it to yourself."

Phyliss was right. Room three was pristine, as if no one had occupied it since the previous day. Judith checked the wastebasket, the bathroom, the closet, and the bureau drawers. There was no sign of the Zs. They seemed to have evaporated into thin air. *Am I delusional?* she wondered. But she recalled putting the $220 cash payment in the strongbox. She also remembered that the Gauthiers had arrived just as the Zs headed upstairs. The vanishing act baffled her, but at least she hadn't been stiffed for the room fee.

Judith closed the door. In her fifteen years as an innkeeper, there had been many strange, puzzling, and even tragic incidents. People were unpredictable. They came and went. She'd probably never cross paths again with Dick and Jane Z. Going back downstairs, Judith dismissed them from her mind. They were gone and might as well be forgotten.

She was only half right.

Chapter Four

The next two days passed in a blur of activity for Judith. That was just as well. There was little time to worry about the Zs' disappearing act or reveal her impending departure to Mike and Gertrude, or to figure out who'd lost a gold band. All the guests who had been staying at Hillside Manor during the week had checked out by Sunday morning, but their vacated rooms were filled with newcomers. Mike and Kristin had taken the boys to the zoo and the aquarium on Thursday, returning Mac and Joe-Joe to their grandparents' care while they dined at a waterfront restaurant. The McMonigles spent Friday visiting a haunted house, a corn maze, and a pumpkin patch. Saturday morning Kristin took the boys to see a play based on "The Legend of Sleepy Hollow" at the nearby children's theater. In the afternoon, Joe and Mike went on a ferryboat ride with the boys to visit the naval shipyard across the sound. Kristin lunched with a friend from her college days and did some shopping downtown. To Judith's relief, there had been no opportunity for another of her daughter-in-law's self-esteem lectures.

"I'd forgotten how bossy she is," Judith said to Renie as the Flynns and the Joneses left Our Lady Star of the Sea's eleven o'clock Mass. "But she has many good qualities and I shouldn't gripe about her," she added, looking up at the cross on top of the church steeple. "I should be more charitable."

"Count your blessings," Renie said. "You get to see Mike and his family fairly often. Our three and their spouses live too far away. Not to mention that we have no grandchildren." She made a face. "I just did mention it. Damn."

The cousins stopped by Joe's MG. "What's our plan for getting to the train?" Judith asked. "I'm almost packed, but I feel edgy. Are you sure you know what you're doing?"

Renie's gaze shifted to Bill and Joe, who were standing by the church's south entrance. "Pretty much. Which reminds me, I'd better get in the car first. Stand by for further instructions." She hurried off to the Joneses' Toyota Camry.

A few moments later Joe joined Judith in his cherished classic red MG. "I could almost put the top down today," he said cheerfully.

"It's nice out." Judith's tone lacked enthusiasm. "Do you know how Renie plans to get me to the parade and the train at the same time?"

Joe frowned before shifting into reverse. "I thought Bill was picking you up at three forty-five. Are you sure Renie's not joking?"

"She isn't. I suppose she'll tell Bill they don't need to leave until four and can pick me up on top of the hill."

"Makes sense." Joe pulled out of the parking place and headed for the avenue. "Bill didn't mention it. We were talking about fish."

"Naturally." The husbands were both avid anglers. Judith remained silent during the final three blocks to the cul-de-sac, trying not to tie herself into knots over how she could get through the day—and out of town—without causing a family rumpus.

After Joe put the MG in the garage and turned off the engine, he gazed at his wife. "So you really don't know what you're doing today."

"No." Judith sounded bleak. "Renie thinks she does, but . . ." She stopped speaking and shook her head. "All I know is that I'm packed except for a few last-minute items. I've tried to keep from worrying, but I can't. Except having you ask the Rankerses to take over while we're gone, I haven't done any of the things I usually do before going away. No trips to the dry cleaners', no balancing the checkbook, no grocery inventory. The three parties who were checking out today left before we went to church, and I asked Arlene to welcome the new guests." She sighed. "I still have to tell Mother I'm leaving. I'm going to do that now before I lose my nerve." She offered Joe a tremulous smile. "Wish me luck."

Joe looked unusually somber. "Don't."

"Don't what?"

"Don't tell her. We'll fake it."

"What?"

Joe took Judith's hand. "It wouldn't be the first time you told your mother a . . ." He grimaced. "An altered version of what actually happened."

Judith thought about trips she had taken to far-off lands, while convincing Gertrude she was only a couple of hours away from Hillside Manor. Her memory tumbled back even further, to when she and Joe had been engaged over forty years ago. "Like the time we drank too much at the Clover Club and drove to the ocean to get married?"

Joe nodded. "Like that."

Judith glanced at the MG's dashboard. "You kept your money in that ashtray. You told me we could afford to drive all the way to California and spend our honeymoon in Carmel. But when we stopped in that little town on our own part of the coast, we couldn't find a justice of the peace at three in the morning."

Joe chuckled. "We walked on the beach at low tide to sober up. You tripped over some driftwood and turned your ankle."

Judith laughed softly. "We slept on the sand until the tide started coming in and woke us up before we drowned. The worst part was ruining my I. Magnifique evening gown with the deep V-neck down to my waist and the slit in back almost up to my rear."

Joe put his hand on Judith's knee. "Great dress. Easy access." The magic gold flecks had returned to his eyes. "When I finally brought you home the next day, your mother believed your tall tale of how we'd been mugged at the salmon derby. She did wonder, though, why we'd gone fishing in evening clothes."

"It was the early sixties," Judith said. "Everybody dressed better then. That was my Jacqueline Kennedy/Audrey Hepburn phase." She frowned. "I'd better finish packing. It's after one."

Joe slid his hand off of Judith's knee and got out of the car. Judith remained in the passenger seat, mulling her options. "Wait for me," she called, finally deciding that Joe was right. Discretion was the better part of cowardice. "I want to ask Renie what she's told Aunt Deb."

The house was quiet when Judith entered through the back door. Mike had pinned a note to the bulletin board by the half doors. *Went to noon Mass at the cathedral. Stopping for lunch at McDonald's, back around two.*

Judith had hoped Kristin would make Gertrude's lunch. That hope was in vain. She hurriedly put together a ham-and-cheese sandwich, sliced pears, chips, and the last two snickerdoodles. When she reached the toolshed, her mother was doing a jumble puzzle in the Sunday newspaper.

"What's that?" Gertrude asked, scowling at the tray.

"It's lunch." Judith moved closer to the card table in front of her mother. Several dirty dishes were stacked haphazardly on one of the elegant frosted glass trays Judith used for guests. "You already ate?"

"'Course," the old lady said. "Kris brought my lunch before they went to church. One of those omelets with all kinds of good stuff in it. She gave me dill pickles, some of her tasty jam, and a real nice quilt. It's on my bed. Take a look—or do you have time before you leave town?"

Aghast, Judith set the tray on the card table. "Where did you hear that?"

"Your aunt Deb. As usual, she talked my ear off, but she told me about your trip." Gertrude glowered at Judith. "What's this boondoggle for?"

Judith sighed as she sat on the small sofa. "It's Renie's idea. You know how she hates to fly."

"I don't blame her," Gertrude said, peeking inside the ham-and-cheese sandwich. "That's one thing about her that makes sense. I'd never get in one of those things, not after what happened to me with Ozzie Popp. Some pilot! He turned that plane upside down and said he wouldn't land until I kissed him. He should've known better than to get fresh with me. That was the end of that."

"And that was the end of Ozzie," Judith murmured, having heard the story a hundred times.

"It sure was," Gertrude declared, her hearing obviously more acute than she let on. "A week later he crashed that cardboard contraption into a barn that had a chewing tobacco ad painted on it." The old lady snorted. "Ozzie bragged that he could land that airplane on a dime. I told him he couldn't hit the broad side of a barn. I was wrong about that. I've never been on an airplane since."

"Flying's changed," Judith said for the hundredth time. "That was 1928."

"So?" Gertrude snatched a snickerdoodle off the plate. "Those planes still leave the ground, don't they?"

"Never mind, Mother," Judith said wearily. "I'm going to Boston with Renie because she has a free ticket. Both Bill and Joe have business there, so we'll meet them and spend a few days sightseeing."

Gertrude had taken a bite of cookie. After pausing to swallow, she wagged a finger. "That part makes sense, which is more than I can say for some of the stunts you and my niece pull off."

Judith leaned forward. "You're not upset because I'm leaving?"

"No. Dumbcluck's going away, isn't he?"

"Well . . . yes," Judith said, wishing that her mother would use Joe's actual name. "He's got Renie's plane ticket and I'll take Bill's place on the train."

"Good," Gertrude said. "The plane might crash."

Judith's shoulders slumped. "Mother—" She stopped. "Skip it. Have you told Mike or Kristin I'm leaving this afternoon?"

"Nope." Gertrude picked up half of the sandwich. "They were in a big rush to get to church when they brought out my lunch and the other goodies." She started to take a bite of the sandwich, but paused. "They don't know, do they?"

"No." Judith stood up. "I may be able to watch some of the costume parade, but I can't trick-or-treat with them in the evening."

"You're in a bind, toots." Gertrude bit into the ham-and-cheese.

"I know." Judith picked up the tray Kristin had brought to the toolshed. "Maybe I can do it with the boys next year."

The old lady put the sandwich back on the plate. "Next year." She stared into space. "Yes, next year. If there is one for me."

"Mother!" Judith exclaimed. "Don't say things like that."

Gertrude shrugged. "I don't kid myself." Her smile was bittersweet. "Nobody's guaranteed next year—or even tomorrow." She picked up the sandwich again. "Enjoy yourselves in Boston. Don't let the Redcoats get you down."

The McMonigle brood didn't get back to Hillside Manor until almost a quarter after two. Mike explained that the McDonald's they'd gone to had a play area. "It was really hard to get the boys off the slides," he told Judith. "Finally we had to tell them, if they didn't stop horsing around they couldn't go to the costume parade. Kris is getting them ready now. We'll leave here about ten to three. See you at Moonbeam's."

"Okay." Judith had second thoughts. Maybe she should tell Mike about her early departure. Before she could speak, he hurried down the hallway to the back stairs. Judith sighed, staring out the window over the sink. The sun had come out, promising good weather for the trick-or-treaters. She sighed again—and gave a start when the phone rang. Judith all but dove to snatch up the receiver from the kitchen counter. "Hello?" she shouted.

"Why are you yelling?" Renie asked. "We're set. We'll pick you up at four-thirty."

"You talked Bill into leaving that late?"

"Sort of. See you."

Joe had already put her luggage in the garage. She decided to wait until after the costume spectacle to break the news to the rest of the family.

Joe ambled into the kitchen. "What now? Last-minute jitters?"

She gave her husband a sheepish look. "Bill and Renie are picking me up here at four-thirty. I can stay for the whole parade."

Joe frowned. "Isn't that cutting it close for a four forty-five train?"

"It should take less than ten minutes. All we have to do is check in and try not to act like terrorists."

Joe shrugged. "I trust Bill's judgment. It just doesn't sound like him." He turned at the sound of raucous high-pitched shouts from the back stairs. "Well!" he exclaimed as two square entities with feet hurtled down the hallway. "What's this I see?" He murmured over his shoulder to Judith. "What are they?"

"Boxes," Judith said under her breath. "Cute," she enthused loudly. "Clever."

The red and the silver boxes nodded assent. "Mom made our costumes," Mac said. "I'm a race car."

"Ah," Joe said. "Yes, I see your number now. It's sixteen for . . . um . . ."

"Greg Biffle's car," Mac said, and ran from the hallway through the kitchen and back again. "Varoom! Varoom!"

The silver box hopped up and down. "Guess me!"

Judith went for the obvious. "Another race car?"

Joe-Joe stomped his silver foot. "No! I'm a robot! Woof, woof!"

"A robot dog?" Judith said.

The silver box swung from side to side. "No. I'm Tekno, the Rheumatic Puppy."

"Shouldn't you have a cane?" Joe asked.

The red box thumped the silver box. "It's Robotic Puppy, dopey."

"Cool," Joe said. "Very good. Why don't you show GeeGee?"

"Why don't you wear signs?" Judith murmured as the boxes scampered out the back door. "Good grief—Kristin really is Aunt Ellen's clone."

"At least those outfits didn't cost big bucks for—" Joe stopped as Mike and Kristin appeared at the bottom of the back stairs.

"Don't they look great?" Kristin asked with a big smile.

"Yes. Yes, very creative," Judith said.

"Did the boys go to the toolshed to show Grams?" Mike asked.

Seeing her in-laws nod, Kristin made a thumbs-up gesture. "We'll get them and start walking," she said. "See you there."

As Mike and Kristin went out the back door, Judith and Joe exchanged bemused looks. "The kids don't mind," she said.

"Maybe that's good," Joe said, retrieving his jacket from the peg in the hallway. "I'll take homemade anytime over the big bucks that rich parents around here spend on extravagant getups for their kids."

Judith sighed. "I suppose. Renie never spent money on costumes for her kids. Every year she'd hand them each a white sheet and say, 'There. You're a ghost. Have fun.'"

"For a graphic designer, she didn't have much imagination," Joe remarked as they headed out the back door.

"She saved the good ideas to earn a living," Judith said. She paused when they entered the garage and glanced at her luggage stacked in a corner. "We can leave that stuff here. The Joneses always park in the driveway." She grimaced. "I hope Renie's plan works. We're not allowing for any unexpected problems getting to the station."

Joe didn't respond until they were both in the MG. "We'll be back by four-fifteen. Why not tell Renie to come a few minutes earlier?"

"I will," Judith said, digging into her purse for the cell that always ended up at the very bottom of the bronze-toned hobo bag that had been a birthday gift from Joe's daughter, Caitlin.

Renie answered on the second ring. "I suppose we could leave a few minutes earlier," she said. "Let me ask Bill. He's talking to Oscar."

Judith groaned. "Please. I'm not in the mood for your fantasies about that stuffed monkey."

"Ape," Renie said emphatically. "Oscar is not a monkey. He's a dwarf ape, dammit. Unlike monkeys, they don't have tails."

"Okay, okay." Judith took a deep breath. "Just ask Bill. Please."

"Fine."

Judith waited impatiently for her cousin's response. Turning out of the cul-de-sac, Joe headed for Heraldsgate Avenue. "Well?"

"Renie's talking to Bill, who's talking to Oscar," Judith said in disgust. "I can't hear what they're saying. It sounds muffled."

Joe frowned. "I hope Oscar hasn't talked Bill into using my plane ticket."

"Stop!" Judith glared at her husband. "Don't ever, ever buy into that bunk about Oscar. Or Clarence, the pampered dwarf lop bunny with an entire wardrobe, much of which he's eaten. Not to mention that they call their car Cammy because it's a Camry. One of these days they'll both go 'round the bend and give a name to their furnace."

Joe didn't respond immediately. "It's not coal, so they couldn't use Stokely. If it's gas, then they—"

"Shut up," Judith said between clenched teeth. "Renie's talking."

" . . . so probably around four-twenty, okay?"

"Yes, great," Judith replied. "See you then." She clicked the phone off. "That's a relief. But I still have to tell the kids I'm leaving."

"Tell them now," Joe said, waiting at the four-way stop on the crest of the hill. "Here they come, right behind Wonder Woman and Batman and Robin."

Sure enough, the red and silver boxes were bobbing and bouncing along in the crosswalk. "What am I supposed to do? Yell at them?"

"Why not? Traffic's so backed up on the avenue that we can't go more than five miles an hour. Get it over with."

Judith shook her head. "No. There are so many people and so much noise that I probably couldn't get their attention. I'll wait until they get to Moonbeam's."

Joe sighed. "Have it your way, but you're going to get one of your god-awful stress-induced headaches before they get that far." The MG inched forward. "Too late. They went into the hardware store."

"All the businesses offer some kind of treat," Judith said. "Did you bring the camera?"

"Damn!" Joe glanced at Judith. "I thought you did."

"No. I saw it . . ." She shook her head. "I don't remember. Maybe I'm thinking of the older one. I don't know how to use the digital camera I gave you for Christmas."

"Never mind," Joe said as they passed the bookstore. "I can take some pictures after the boys get home."

"Okay." Judith tried to enjoy the merchants' outdoor decorations that included artificial cobwebs, witches with steaming cauldrons, giant spiders, and life-size skeletons. It was a struggle to keep the tension headache at bay and ignore her stomach's version of the danse macabre.

At three-fifteen Joe dropped her off by Moonbeam's before he tried to find a parking place. After buying a hot cocoa and a latte, Judith went outside to find a vacant table. There weren't any, but an older couple Judith recognized from Our Lady Star of the Sea motioned to her.

"Do sit with us. We SOTS have to stick together," the sprightly older woman said, using the shortened acronym for parishioners. She nodded in the direction of a lanky teenager in a red suit with horns, tail, and a pitchfork. "Here comes the devil now."

"Thanks, Mrs. Shaughnessy," Judith said, recalling the couple's name. "My husband's parking the car. It's more crowded every year."

Mr. Shaughnessy set his unlit pipe on the metal table. "When this started ten years ago, our grandchildren were teenagers. Now the eldest is married and has a baby girl. Ah!" He stood up. "I see Hannah. She's a pea pod in the checkered stroller with her mother and our grandson, Neal. Excuse us."

Arm in arm, the Shaughnessys left to greet their offspring. Judith sipped her hot chocolate and watched the many-splendored costume wearers walk, weave, wobble, and whoop their way along the avenue. Glancing at her watch, she saw that it was after three-thirty. There was still no sign of Joe or the rest of the family. She sipped more cocoa and waved good-bye to the Shaughnessys as they walked across the street with the pea pod and her parents. The only distraction was the occasional neighbor, shopkeeper, or acquaintance. For once, she didn't try to make casual chitchat. There was less than an hour to go before the Empire Builder was due to leave the station.

At ten to four, Joe came puffing up from the alley behind Moonbeam's. "My God," he gasped, bracing himself on the table, "I had to drive around forever to find a parking spot. It's a zoo around here, and I'm not talking about the lions, the tigers, the bears, and the oh-my-what-the-hell-are-theys."

"Did you see our gang?" Judith asked.

"Often," he replied, slumping into a chair. "They were going into Falstaff's about five minutes ago."

"That's almost two blocks away," Judith said in dismay. "Will they get here by four or should we meet them at the grocery store?"

Joe shook his head. His face was more flushed than usual and his high forehead was damp with perspiration. "I don't know what to tell you." He took a sip from his latte. "This sucker's cold."

"Of course it is," Judith said. "I bought it right after you dropped me off. What did you want me to do? Sit on it to warm it up?"

"Right, okay, I get it." He used a paper napkin to wipe his forehead. "It's your call."

Judith grimaced. "How far away did you park?"

"Halfway down the alley by the pub's Dumpster."

"You've seen the kids," Judith said after a brief pause. "I'll start out for Falstaff's and you can pick me up in the parking lot."

Joe leaned back in the metal chair and expelled a big breath. "This is one hell of a holiday." Before Judith could say anything, he grabbed the paper cups, plastic spoons, and napkins. "Go. I'll see you at Falstaff's."

"Okay," Judith said meekly as Joe stood up and went over to the already crammed trash bin by the curb. He had a right to be annoyed, she thought as she made her way across the street through a maze of costumed celebrants, one of whom was a grandfather clock with the hands pointing to midnight. A peek at her watch told her it was two minutes to four. Judith picked up the pace, ignoring a twinge or two from her artificial hip. By the time she reached the corner of the block where Falstaff's was located, she espied the red and silver boxes straggling behind Mike and Kristin.

"Hey, Ma," Mike called. "We were just coming to see you."

Judith moved out of the way for a trio of boisterous pirates. "Your father's picking me up in the parking lot," she said, gesturing at the grocery store. "I'm afraid I have to get home to—"

The red box tripped over his own feet and fell down. Kristin bent down as Mac let out a howl. "Can't you see where you're driving?" she asked. "Are you hurt?"

Mac's reply was drowned out by Joe-Joe's whining. "I'm tired! I don't feel good! My box is hot!"

"Now, now," Kristin said as some of the other revelers paused to stare at the small spectacle, "don't be spoilsports. You're having fun."

"I'm not!" Mac howled. "My foot hurts! It's broke!"

Joe-Joe tugged at Mike's pant leg. "Daddy! I wanna go home!"

"Me, too," Mac said tearfully. "I have to wee-wee."

"Ur-in-ate," Kristin said sharply. "You're too old to talk like that. Come on, let your grandmother see how brave and strong you are."

"It's okay, Kris," Judith asserted. "They're tired and crabby. Maybe you should—"

A horn honked loudly. Judith recognized it at once as belonging to the MG. Joe had pulled up at the corner. "What's going on?"

Mike hurried over to the curb. "Mac hurt himself and Joe-Joe's worn out. Do you mind taking the boys home? We'll wait here with Ma." He glanced at Judith. "She looks kind of pale."

Joe leaned out the window to study his wife. "Are you okay?"

Judith didn't answer. It was all she could do to keep from screaming at every member of her immediate family.

Kristin leaped into the breach. "The MG has no child safety seats. You know the boys can't go anywhere without them." She paid no attention to her whining, moaning sons or the honking horns from other cars as their drivers tried to get by Joe and the MG. "Here's what we'll do," Kristin went on. "Mike, you go with your dad to collect the Rover.

I'll wait here. Your mom can help entertain the kids until you get back."

Torn by her grandchildren's distress and the relentless march of time, Judith attempted to nudge her daughter-in-law out of the way. It was like trying to move a hundred-year-old Douglas fir. Ignoring Kristin's expression of curiosity, she countermanded the orders to Mike. "I'm going with you, Joe. You can drive the Rover back here. There's room for everybody. Excuse me, Kris. Can you move so I can get in the MG?"

Kristin looked stunned. "I don't . . . well, I guess . . ."

"Move!" Judith shouted.

Kristin obeyed.

"I love you all." Judith cried, ignoring the squalls and the honks and the curious passersby. "I'm leaving town. Happy Halloween!"

If Mike and Kristin were shocked by her announcement, Judith didn't want to know. She was out of breath after she got into the bucket seat and felt her whole body sag.

"That was easy," Joe said. "You see? All that fretting for nothing."

"I feel guilty, though," Judith admitted.

"Don't." Joe had taken a detour to avoid the avenue by driving on side streets to Hillside Manor. "I'll be back for the kids in ten minutes."

"I hope," Judith said as they pulled into the cul-de-sac, "that Bill and Renie take the shortcut, too."

"They will," Joe assured her. "Bill knows what he's doing."

Judith sighed. "I hope Renie does."

Joe drove straight into the garage. "You wait for them here. And let Bill carry your luggage."

Joe and Judith got out of the MG. "See you Tuesday night," he said, putting his arms around his wife. "Have a safe trip. And try to relax. I'll explain everything to Mike and Kristin."

"Thanks." Judith hugged and kissed Joe. "You, too."

She watched Joe hurry to the Rover and get in. Just as he started the engine, Bill and Renie's Camry pulled into the cul-de-sac. Another glance at her watch told Judith it was four-seventeen. Joe called out something to Bill as the vehicles passed each other. A moment later the Camry came to a stop just in front of where Judith was standing.

"Chuga-chuga!" Renie shouted. "Woo-woo!"

Bill got out of the car. "Where's your luggage?"

Judith gestured to the corner of the garage where Joe had stashed the garment bag, the suitcase, and the carry-on. She waited to make sure Bill had everything before she opened the rear door. A loud "yoo-hoo!" caught her attention. Turning around, she saw Arlene Rankers on the back porch. "The first guests have checked in," Arlene said. "Carl's playing cribbage with your mother. Everything's under control. Have fun! You'll love Baltimore."

"It's Boston," Judith called back.

Arlene shrugged. "They both begin with a *B* and they're on the East Coast. As far as I'm concerned, anything on the other side of the Mississippi is a bit peculiar. And old." She blew Judith a kiss.

Bill closed the trunk and shouted his customary word to get going: "Boppin'!"

"What now?" Renie asked after Judith got into the backseat and Bill reversed out of the driveway. "Why is Joe driving the Rover? Don't tell me the MG finally died on him."

"Oh, no," Judith said, explaining the mayhem on top of the hill. "At least," she concluded, "I may have showed my smug daughter-in-law that I'm not a total wuss."

"Kristin hasn't learned that you have to choose your battlegrounds," Renie said. "I hope Mike stands up to her—even if he is only an inch taller." She winced and rubbed her neck. "I'd better stop trying to turn around to listen to you. I've got a kink." She was silent for a moment. "Hey, Bill, why are we taking the viaduct to the station? It's the long way."

"I'm checking for fishing boats out on the bay," he replied as they traveled above the harbor's edge. "I only see a couple, but it's getting late. It turned out nice today. Look at the mountains over on the peninsula."

"This isn't a sightseeing tour," Renie said, sounding agitated. "Turn off by the football stadium."

"You're giving me directions? We'll end up at the ferry dock. Checking in at the station's a snap compared to the airport, and you only have to walk about fifty yards to get on board." He glanced at the dashboard. "The clock says it's three thirty-two."

"No!" Renie shrieked. "It's four thirty-two!"

"See for yourself," Bill said. "You changed all the clocks to standard time."

"Oh, my God!" Renie held her head. "I . . . I . . . did, but I changed them back again."

Bill stared at Renie. "What?" he bellowed. "Are you crazy?"

"Look out!" Judith cried. "That motorcycle's cutting in . . ."

Renie gasped; Bill swore. But the Camry narrowly missed hitting the biker. Judith was shaking; Renie was sitting ramrod straight; Bill stepped on the gas, cut over two lanes, and headed for the stadium exit. None of them said another word until they pulled up in the no-parking zone at the depot's main entrance. The clock tower read 4:43.

Bill got out of the car first and opened the trunk. Renie had her big purse and carry-on with her. She ran inside the station while Bill hauled out the rest of the luggage. Judith tried to help him.

"Don't," he snapped. "Just go."

Judith obeyed, but she didn't dare hurry. She was too unsteady on her feet and her nerves were shredded. By chance, a wheelchair was just a few feet away from the door. A rosy-cheeked young man wearing an Amtrak uniform noticed that she seemed in distress. "Can I help you, ma'am?" he inquired.

"Yes." She collapsed in the wheelchair. "Just push me out to the platform. Or has the Empire Builder left?"

"Not quite," he replied. "Hang on."

As they moved quickly through the almost empty station, Judith looked for Renie. She was at the check-in booth, apparently arguing with someone who looked like a conductor. Bill had already found a trolley, loaded the luggage, and was heading for the platform.

"There," Judith said, pointing to Renie. "She must be checking us in. She has both of our tickets."

Up close, Renie looked as if she were about to vault over the counter and attack the conductor. There was precedent, Judith recalled, grimacing at memories of her cousin flinging herself over obstacles to get at victims of her outrage.

"Coz!" Judith cried as the young man wheeled her up to the counter. "What's wrong?"

Renie swiveled around, her elbow knocking over a display of Amtrak information. "We've been demoted!" she yelled. "This bozo says we can't have either of the downstairs rooms because some other passengers have priority. I'll sue! I'll call Bub! I'll set his suits on the whole damned railroad system!"

Judith's face began to twitch. "Please. Calm down. Please." She turned to look up at the young man and saw his name tag identified him as Walter Robbins. "Thanks, Walter. Can you stand by?"

Walter shot Renie a wary glance. He shuddered slightly. "Yes, ma'am. I can stand by for you."

The conductor, whose name tag identified him as D. C. Peterson, managed to keep his aplomb. Judith figured he was in his fifties. Gray hair showed from under his conductor's cap and his long face was deeply lined. "Your deluxe bedroom on the upper level has its own shower and toilet. It's also closer to the dining and dome cars. I'm sorry for the confusion, but when there's an emergency, we give the lower accessible accommodations to the most severely impaired passengers. A mother traveling with three small children had reserved the family room over a month ago," he continued, moving from behind the counter, but keeping a safe distance from Renie. "Your request for the accessible bedroom stated that neither of you is confined to a wheelchair." Mr. Peterson winced slightly. Judith wondered if he was thinking that Renie should be confined to a cage. "You realize that neither of the lower-level rooms have their own shower facilities. The bedroom upstairs has both."

"Well . . ." Renie looked chagrined. "I forgot about that," she mumbled. "Okay, fine."

The conductor seemed relieved. "The person who requested the accessible bedroom is immobilized." He glanced at his pocket watch. "We're ready to pull out." He paused as his cell phone rang. "Excuse me. It's the engineer. I must answer this."

Renie, whose wrath was usually explosive but short-lived, motioned at Judith. "Let's go before Bill kills somebody if he finds out we've been moved and our luggage has to go elsewhere."

Judith's shoulders sagged. The last thing she needed was to suffer through another Jones All-World Tantrum. Not for the first time, she wondered how Bill and Renie had kept from killing each other.

Bill, however, was standing calmly on the platform two cars down and smoking a cigarette. "You made it," he said above the noise of the train. "It's a good thing they had to wait for some VIP."

"Did they tell you we've been moved?" Renie asked.

Bill nodded. "Same car, though." He gestured at the attendant in the white shirt and black vest standing by the open door. Except for their sleeper, the long line of silver cars were already closed. Only a few Amtrak workers and well-wishers remained on the platform. "Need a hand?" Bill asked Judith.

"I've got Walter." She smiled at the young man as she stood up. "Thanks for your help, Walter."

"No problem," the young man replied.

Bill had tossed his cigarette and ground it out with his heel. He and Renie hugged and kissed. And hugged and kissed again. Judith smiled. No wonder Bill and Renie had stayed married—and alive—for forty years. With her own fifteenth anniversary on the horizon, Judith knew it was a good idea for the Flynns to keep up with the Joneses.

As Walter guided Judith to the step that led onto the train, Bill offered her a peck on the cheek. "Take it easy. See you in Boston."

"Let me go first," Renie said to Judith. "If you trip, I can cushion your fall." She climbed up onto the train and waited.

Walter got Judith as far as the first step. "Oh-oh," he said, looking back toward the station. "I'm needed by the late arrival." He hurried off. The attendant took over, holding Judith steady as she got into the car.

"Another wheelchair," Renie said, looking beyond Judith. "This one's fancier. You got the no-frills model."

Judith gazed out to the platform, where the conductor was leading the way for two people and someone in a sleek, upholstered high-tech wheelchair. The invalid's right arm sported a blue sling; the left leg was in a white plaster cast. "Oh, no!" she gasped. "I don't believe it!"

"What now?" Renie asked in alarm.

The attendant chuckled. "Your friend knows her celebrities. It's always a break in the routine to see famous people in person. My, my—back in the day, I was a big Wee Willie Weevil fan, too."

Chapter Five

Judith and Renie almost fell over each other trying to get out of the way and up the steps to the next level.

"I can't believe it," Judith said as they reached the corridor that led to their bedroom. "As soon as I saw Pepper's red hair, I wanted to jump out on the other side of the train."

"Stop fussing," Renie urged. "Willie's in a wheelchair. He's been rendered harmless by your pyracantha. I'll bet he won't be able to get to the dining room. With any luck you won't have to see him."

Judith narrowed her eyes at Renie. "That's what I thought after he was hauled off by the medics."

"Come on," Renie urged. "Let's get settled before the train starts up. Once Willie gets on board, we're out of here. You should be grateful to him," Renie continued, moving to the lighted number designating their room as A9. "If the train hadn't waited for him, we'd have missed it."

"And whose fault was that?" Judith demanded.

"Oooh . . ." Renie threw up her hands. "Okay, I screwed up." She slid the door open. "This is fine. Two chairs, view window, upper and lower berth that come out at night, goodies basket with snacks, small table, smaller bathroom. I don't mean the bathroom's smaller than the table, I mean it's—"

"Don't change the subject," Judith snapped. "What did you do with the clocks?"

A shout from outside signaled the train's departure. "Sit," Renie commanded. "We might lurch a bit at first."

"You're evading the question," Judith persisted, settling into one of the chairs.

Renie was bending over to look out the window. "Bill probably can't see me, but I'll wave anyway." She paused. "I can't see him. I suppose he left to move the car out of the no-parking zone."

"Let's hope so," Judith murmured. "If he got towed, you might as well keep going straight across the Atlantic after we get to Boston. Talk, coz, before I throttle you."

Renie flopped into the opposite chair just as the train began to move. "It's not easy to explain because I'm not sure what I did."

Judith was confused. "What?"

"It had to do with the change from daylight to standard time," Renie began. "I always change our clocks—all fifteen of them, which is yet another reason why I hate the whole stupid concept. The only timepiece I don't change is Bill's watch, even though he never remembers which way to move the hands. Mr. Science, he's not."

"And you're not exactly Mrs. Science," Judith pointed out.

"Yeah, right. But I do know it's 'fall back' and 'spring forward.'"

Judith nodded. "Go on."

"What I did sounds confusing." Renie shifted uncomfortably in her chair. "Well, it *is* confusing. I reset everything last night before I went to bed so that we'd be on time for Mass. If Bill wakes up before sunrise, he doesn't look at the digital clock on the armoire, but at his watch on the nightstand next to the bed. It glows in the dark."

"The nightstand? The watch? Bill?"

Renie made a face. "You're not being your usual patient self. Now I'm even more muddled." She frowned. "Where was I?"

"Watching Bill glow in the dark?"

Renie made a growling noise. "Stop it. When Bill got up

this morning and went into the bathroom, I changed his watch, just in case he might check it later in the day, which he rarely does."

"Wow," Judith remarked drily. "The things I never knew about you and Bill. Cut to the chase before my head explodes,"

"Cammy's dashboard clock was tricky," Renie said. "I didn't dare change it until Mass was over. Bill and Joe were chatting outside. I hurried to the car and moved the clock just as he was about to get in."

"Can you finish this story before we get to Idaho?" Judith asked wearily.

Renie looked irked. "I'm almost done. After we got home, I realized the clocks should be set back two hours, but I couldn't remember if I'd done that last night." Frowning, she paused. "Let's start over. I'm telling this all wrong."

"That could describe it," Judith murmured.

"The point was to make Bill think we were leaving when he said we would." Renie fingered her chin, apparently sorting through her addlepated scheme. "I knew Bill wouldn't agree to go later," she finally said. "It's not how he operates."

"Right. So what did you do with your clocks at the house?"

"I . . ." Renie scowled. "I'm not sure. You know how confused I get with anything that has to do with numbers."

"Oh, good Lord!" Judith leaned back in her chair and closed her eyes. "Never mind. I wish I'd never asked."

"That probably was a bad idea on your part," Renie conceded. "Don't be so grumpy about it. Whatever I did, it was for you. Frankly, it wasn't worth the effort. Your family adventure sounds like a fiasco."

"It was," Judith admitted. "Mike and Kristin should've made sure we knew they were coming for Halloween. I couldn't change my plans, but I'd have warned them I had to leave this afternoon and spared myself a near nervous breakdown."

"Skip the regrets," Renie advised. "It turned out for the best. You showed Kristin you're not really spineless."

"We'll see," Judith murmured, realizing that they were suddenly in the dark. "Have you got me so confused that I'm going blind?"

"No. We have to go through a tunnel under the downtown area before we take the northern route across the mountains."

Judith shook her head. "I think you've infected this train. Who knows where we'll end up? Alaska? Peru? Jupiter?"

Renie shrugged. "I'm not the engineer. Let's get organized while we're still going slow. What do you want from your carry-on?"

"Nothing now," Judith replied. "Where's the rest of my luggage?"

"Our other stuff's in the downstairs luggage rack," Renie said. "I saw it when we boarded because ours was loaded last."

"Where's Willie?"

"In the accessible room to our left as we got on," Renie replied.

"He needs it more than we do," Judith said, feeling the train pick up speed after its snail's pace through the tunnel. She looked out the window where the setting sun glinted off the bay. "I didn't realize this route goes along the water."

Renie leaned forward as the attendant who'd been standing outside the sleeper knocked softly. "Hi," she said. "When do we eat?"

"Can you wait until the first sitting at five-thirty?" the attendant replied with a smile that revealed perfect white teeth. "I'm Roy Kingsley. We'll announce when the dining car opens in about half an hour."

Judith smiled. "Hi, Roy. I'm Judith Flynn and that's my cousin Serena Jones. Her nickname's Renie. Will you be with us all the way to Boston?"

"I'm afraid not," Roy replied. "When you change trains in Chicago, you get a new crew. Don't worry. Whoever takes my place will be just fine. Meanwhile, don't hesitate to ask for anything. I see you have your bottled water and your snack basket. The newspaper will be at your door in the morning. I'll make up your beds whenever you want. Coffee, hot water for tea, and orange juice are available by the stairwell after six A.M. if you need a jump start before breakfast. I'll show you how to control the temperature, the sound, and the lights."

Judith paid close attention. Renie looked as if she was listening, but as a seasoned train traveler, Judith figured her cousin was enjoying the scenery as the train picked up more speed.

When Roy had finished giving his instructions, Renie finally spoke up. "How about a six-thirty dinner call?"

Roy smiled again. "That sounds just fine. Shall I put you down for the second sitting?"

Renie nodded. "Sure. My cousin and I have to get tanked first so we can stagger to the dining car."

Roy cocked his head to one side. "My, my—I think you ladies will make this trip even livelier. I take it you're a Wee Willie Weevil fan, too?"

"Ah . . . my son is," Judith replied.

"Poor man," Roy said with a shake of his head. "A terrible thing happened to him. Some maniac pushed him out of a sixth-floor hotel window. He broke his leg and his arm. Only Willie could survive something like that at his age."

"Uh . . ." Judith felt her face freeze. "Very resilient," she said after a pause. "Will you be his attendant?"

"Yes," Roy said, looking pleased. "Our conductor, Mr. Peterson, told me Mr. Weevil and his companions are heading for Wolf Point, Montana, to discuss events at the big rodeo held there every year." He shook his head. "Maybe their plans changed since the accident. I'd hate to be the one who put him in such a sorry state."

"Some people enjoy mayhem," Renie said, darting a venomous glance at her cousin. "They like the excitement of big fire engines and ambulances and police cars and medics arriving at their house."

Judith refrained from glaring back at her cousin. Instead,

she changed the subject. "I understand Willie lives in Montana."

Roy nodded. "I know he's originally from Montana—Butte, I think. Someone mentioned he has a home on Flathead Lake."

Judith nodded. "I haven't followed his life and times. I assume the pretty red-haired woman is Mrs. Weevil."

Roy cleared his throat. "You never know these days. A young man is also accompanying Mr. Weevil."

"By the way," Renie interjected, "do you know our next-door neighbors' names? Mrs. Friendly here may want to chat them up."

"There are only two other bedrooms at this end of the train," Roy said. "Next to you is a middle-aged couple named . . ." He made a face. "Kloppenburg. The end bedroom is for two passengers boarding at our midnight stop. The last name is Johnson or Johnston. Don't forget to change your watches. We'll be on Mountain Standard Time after midnight."

Judith shot Renie a prickly glance. "I'll be in charge of that. My cousin has difficulty telling time. She's always been . . . a little backward."

Roy looked sympathetic. "I see." He smiled kindly at Renie. "We'll take good care of her, won't we, Mrs. Flynn?" He gave the cousins a casual salute before returning to the corridor.

"Great," Renie said. "Roy thinks I'm an imbecile because you—"

She stopped as Roy poked his head back inside the roomette. "I'm going to Mr. Weevil's room in a few minutes," he said. "Would you like his autograph?"

"Oh," Judith responded, "that's kind of you, but I'm not a collector."

Renie gave Roy a cockeyed smile. "I'd like his autograph. Could he sign it for 'Teenie Weenie Renie and her not-so-mighty brain'?"

"I'll try," Roy promised, and disappeared again.

"I wish you hadn't done that," Judith said.

"I wish you hadn't told Roy that I'm an idiot," Renie retorted.

"Okay, we're even." Judith leaned forward to look through the window across the corridor. "We're in the suburbs, but still by the water." She checked her watch. "Drat. I forgot we're not on daylight . . . never mind."

"Aha!" Renie cried. "Admit it—you're confused, too."

"No, I'm not," Judith insisted. "It's dark earlier than I'm used to."

Renie smirked. "Right."

"I'm enjoying the sunset."

"Right."

"The last time I took this route was when we went to Canada."

"Right."

"It's certainly more comfortable to go by train."

"Right."

"Stop it!" Judith shrieked. "You're driving me nuts!"

Renie put a finger to her lips and pointed to the sound system, which was turned to its lowest setting. "The bar's open," she said, standing up. "I'll get our drinks. Do you need anything else?"

Judith eyed the gift basket. "I see crackers and cheese. I'm good."

Renie left just as the train slowed for its first stop. The suburban station call was brief. Judith sat back and enjoyed the twilight scenery. Lights had been turned on in most of the buildings along the water's edge. Across the sound she could see scattered homes, some clustered near the beach, others built among the trees on the sloping hills of the peninsula. Renie was right, she thought. Traveling by train was far more pleasant than coping with airports, being treated as a possible terrorist, and getting jammed into a seat designed for midgets. It was quiet, too, with only the muted rhythm of rails on tracks. Renie had left their door open, but no one had come by or spoken since Roy went off on the rest of his rounds. Judith felt so relaxed that she started to nod off.

"Bar service," Renie announced, returning with a cardboard container holding two plastic glasses, ice, water, two small bottles of their whiskeys, a can of 7UP, napkins, and plastic stirrers. "Did I wake you?" she asked, setting the container on the table between their chairs.

Judith felt sheepish. "Almost. I should've opened the snack basket. I guess I'm already feeling liberated."

"I hope so," Renie said, handing the basket to Judith. "You are."

Judith opened the Scotch. "How far away is the dining car?"

Renie sat down. "Just beyond the other sleeper. The dome or sightseer car is on the other side of the diner, with snacks and liquor on the lower level. The coach cars are toward the rear."

Judith nodded. "I can manage walking the length of one car."

Renie held up her glass. "To the cozzes. To relaxing. To being isolated from the rest of the world that always seems out to get us."

"Amen," Judith said, touching her plastic glass to Renie's.

"It beats being crushed between two sumo wrestlers on a plane."

Judith laughed. "I'd forgotten the pleasures of train travel."

"People are in such a hurry," Renie said. "Going from one airport to another, with no sense of the changing countryside. Business travelers often have meetings at airport hotels so they don't . . ." She peered into the corridor. "Speaking of hurrying, Mr. Kloppenburg just rushed by. Did you see him?"

Judith shook her head. "How do you know it was him?"

"I don't," Renie admitted, "but he came from that direction. Roy told us the last compartment's passengers haven't boarded yet and I think the car in front of ours is for baggage or employees."

"What did he look like?"

Renie shrugged. "Blond, six-foot, thirties, trim, average looks."

Judith frowned. "That's not Kloppenburg. Roy described the couple as middle-aged. I hardly consider people in their thirties middle-aged."

"Hey," Renie retorted, "the older I get, the more I think middle age starts at sixty-five. So what if he's not Kloppenburg?"

"Oh . . . it's something nagging at me since I got on the train."

Renie shook her head. "This trip is to get you away from it all. What extra baggage are you hauling along to defeat the purpose?"

"Be honest. The real reason I'm here is to keep you company because you're too chicken to fly without getting soused. I haven't asked how much I owe for my share. I figure it's better that way. I won't have to spend time worrying about paying you back."

"You don't owe me a dime," Renie asserted. "Train travel isn't cheap, but meals are included. Joe gets the price of my airfare reimbursed. Bill flies for free because he's a conference participant. Our hotel bills are covered because I insisted on a suite with two bedrooms, claiming Bill snored. Or that I snore." She frowned. "I guess we both do, but I never hear either of us because I'm asleep. Anyway, there's room for all of us. The only expense is the train, and I won't accept your money." She sipped her drink and eyed Judith curiously. "Well?"

"Your Kloppenburg went by again while you were shooting your mouth off," Judith said smugly. "He's Wayne Fielding, Willie's publicist."

Renie frowned. "You mean the guy who was taking pictures when Willie crashed into the shrubbery?"

"Yes." Judith added more water to her drink. "As I said, something's been nagging at me since we came aboard. I saw Pepper's red hair and Willie in the wheelchair, but I didn't really take in the third person. My subconscious must've recognized Wayne. Why shouldn't I be curious?"

"Curious, yes," Renie said. "Obsessed, no. I never saw the Weevil bunch during their stay at the B&B."

"But," Judith countered, "why did he come down our corridor? The Kloppenburgs are the only other passengers at this end. What's their connection with Wayne?"

Renie groaned. "Maybe he got lost. Who cares?"

Judith sipped her drink. "Isn't the train due to stop before we head east through the mountains?"

Renie glanced out the window. "You're right. We're slowing down." She sighed and stood up. "I'll go look if only to shut you up."

"Thanks, coz," Judith said sheepishly.

"Yeah, right, fine." She stepped into the corridor just as the last call for the first dinner sitting came over the intercom.

Less than a minute later, Renie returned. "No luck," she said, sitting down again. "The Kloppenburgs have their door closed and the curtains pulled. For all I know, Hansel and Gretel may be in there."

"Maybe they're eating bread crumbs," Judith said. "We'd have seen them go to the dining car if they chose the early sitting."

"Let's not discuss this anymore. Let's pretend we're normal people taking a pleasant train trip to an historic and interesting city."

"Okay," Judith said meekly.

"Good," Renie said, though she sounded skeptical. "I'll close our door so we can have some privacy, too."

Judith set her drink down on the table. "Let me. I have to go to the bathroom first. The train's almost stopped."

The bathroom was small, with a shower and toilet, but that suited Judith just fine. There wasn't room enough to fall down. She emerged, washed her hands in the sink, and closed the door to their compartment. Just as she was about to sit, the train suddenly lurched. Judith lost her balance, but Renie grabbed her arm. In the process, their drinks fell off the table.

"Are you okay?" Renie asked, still holding on to her cousin.

"I think so," Judith said.

Renie helped Judith ease into her chair. "Take it easy. I'll clean up the mess." She took several paper towels out of the dispenser by the sink and began dabbing at the floor. "I'll get refills," she said, checking her watch. "We've got a good half hour before the second dinner call."

"I'm sorry you get cleanup duty because I'm a klutz," Judith said.

"Forget it." Renie stuffed the cups and paper towels in the waste receptacle. "I'm no gazelle, but I've got real hip joints."

Judith opened the gift basket. "I'll nibble on crackers and cheese."

"Be my guest," Renie said. "Back in a semiflash." She disappeared into the corridor.

Judith was relieved that she didn't seem to have any lingering effects from her mishap. She ate crackers and cheese while taking in the steady passage of the train. After about five minutes she sensed that something was missing. The realization dawned on her when she heard children's voices that faded after only a few seconds. She assumed they had been coming up from the lower level to the front section of the sleeper. *It's so quiet,* she thought, smiling to herself. No guests going and coming, no phones ringing, no Phyliss Rackley jabbering about God and goiters, no endless complaints from her mother, no doorbells signaling parcel deliveries, no one expecting her to cook meals, not even Joe shouting from some other part of the house. *Maybe I should feel guilty,* she told herself. *Or maybe Renie's right—I need a break to recharge my batteries. Even social animals like me sometimes have to hibernate.* She leaned back in the chair and closed her eyes.

A few minutes later Renie returned with the cocktail

items. "You finally look relaxed," she said, settling into her chair.

"I am."

"Good."

The cousins mixed their drinks. "I wish we were going through the pass in daylight," Judith said. "It must be beautiful this time of year."

"We'll see it on the return trip."

"Maybe there'll be new snow by then."

"Could be."

"Was it busy in the club car?"

"Yes. I had to wait in line."

Judith stared at Renie, realizing that her cousin hadn't made eye contact since returning to their compartment. "What's wrong?"

"Wrong?" Renie finally looked at her cousin. "Nothing. Why?"

"Coz." Judith cradled the plastic cup in her hands and leaned forward. "You seem . . . on edge."

"No." Renie shrugged. "I'm hungry, that's all."

"Have some crackers and cheese," Judith said. "They're good."

Renie was looking out the window. "I'll wait for dinner."

The response bothered Judith. Her cousin's mood had changed after the first hunger pang, but usually she became cranky instead of tense. For the next few minutes they sat in atypical silence, sipping their drinks and watching the train's darkening passage toward the mountain pass.

At six-thirty they heard the announcement for their dinner sitting. "I'll go first," Renie said. "I can open the doors between the cars for you."

"Aren't they heavy? Will that screw up your bum shoulder?"

"If you press the doors in the right place, there's no problem."

The cousins reached the front of their coach, where Roy was standing with a stack of bedding. "There you are," he said in a chipper tone. "Shall I make up your beds while you have dinner?"

Judith glanced at Renie; Renie shrugged.

Roy smiled. "Let's take another vote."

"We may go to the dome car after dinner," Judith said.

"I'll wait a bit, then." Glancing at Renie, Roy's face fell. "Oh, Mrs. Jones, I couldn't get Mr. Weevil's autograph. He was asleep when I went to his room."

"Don't worry about it," Renie said. "It was a whim."

Roy looked relieved. "Mrs. Weevil—I assume she's his missus—told me his condition is worsening. She says his mind wanders and he's delusional. They're suing the party who was responsible for the tragedy. It's so sad for someone like him to end up in such a helpless state."

Judith tried to hide her dismay. "Is Mrs. Weevil serious about a lawsuit?"

Roy shrugged. "I guess so. The attack was criminal. I hope the police were called in."

"Um. Yes." Judith wished she could tell Roy that the police had already been there, at least in the form of a retired homicide detective named Joe Flynn. "I'd better catch up with my cousin," she said, realizing that Renie had drifted off down the corridor. "Thanks, Roy."

By the time Judith caught up with her cousin, there were a half-dozen people lined up ahead of them. "Pepper's crazy," she said under her breath. "If she sues me, she'll be laughed out of court. How can a broken arm and leg put Willie at death's door?"

"Drop it," Renie murmured. "If someone hears you, they'll think you're nuts. Why do you want to go to the dome car after dinner?"

Judith tried to shake off Roy's unsettling account of Pepper's threats. As an elderly couple moved into line behind the cousins, she offered them what she hoped was a cheerful smile before turning back to Renie. "Neither of us likes to go to bed early. Maybe we can find somebody who plays cards."

A tall, lean bald man in front of Renie turned around. "Did someone mention cards?"

"Yes," Judith said. "What do you play?"

The man put an arm around a petite woman with gray streaks in her short black hair. "My wife and I play everything except the hi-lo poker games. You name it, we play it." He squeezed his wife's shoulders. "Don't we, Sharon?"

When Sharon smiled at Judith, her sharp features softened and her oval face lighted up. "If you want a foursome, we're on."

Judith, Renie, and the cardplayers stepped aside as a couple with two young children exited the dining car. "I brought four decks," Judith said. "One set's for pinochle, the other's for bridge or whatever else."

"I'm Jim Downey," the man said, putting out his hand. "We're from Milwaukee."

Noting that Renie hadn't responded to Jim's friendly gesture, Judith hurriedly shook his hand. "Judith Flynn," she said, "and my cousin Serena Jones, nicknamed Renie."

Without enthusiasm, Renie shook hands with the Downeys. "Hi," she said with a strained smile.

"The dome car after dinner?" Jim said.

"Yes," Judith replied, noticing that the line had extended around the corner of the second sleeper. "It looks like you two are next. More of the early birds are leaving at the other end of the car."

"Maybe," Sharon said, "we can sit together. The tables seat four."

"That'd be nice," Judith responded. "Are you heading home?"

Jim nodded. "We got on at that last stop. Our son's stationed at the nearby naval base. We did some exploring in the area. It's really beautiful. The only part of the West Coast we'd been in before was Southern California. This is our first train trip. It's a great way to travel, though I wish the beds were longer."

"Jim," Sharon said in mild reproach, "stop fussing. You're only six-two. Didn't Roy tell us you'd have plenty of room?"

"Roy's five-ten," Jim said. "How could he be sure?"

Sharon's expression was droll. "Face it, Jim. You're all

over the place even in our king-size bed at home." She turned back to Judith. "Are you in this sleeper or the next one?"

"The next one," Judith replied.

"So are we," Sharon said. "The second roomette from the stairwell in the middle of the car." She poked her husband. "We're next," she said, gesturing at the waiter who was beckoning to them.

Jim smiled at Judith. "Let's see if they call you folks, too," he said before following his wife into the dining car.

Judith watched as the Downeys were seated at a vacant table. The waiter reappeared, this time motioning to the cousins. Renie stepped aside, giving the golden agers behind them a phony smile. "Let these folks go first," she said before Judith could move. "We can wait."

The elderly man and woman thanked Renie. Judith glared at her cousin after the couple went into the dining car. "What's wrong with you?" she whispered. "Do you think the Downeys are crooks?"

"No," Renie said. "I don't feel sociable, that's all."

"So you're going to act like you're made of stone? Please—let me have an enjoyable meal. The Downeys seem like nice people."

"They probably are," Renie conceded.

"Now I'll feel embarrassed when I make eye contact with them," Judith complained. "They must think you're a head case."

Renie scowled at Judith. "Be quiet or everybody in line will think we both are. In fact," she went on hurriedly, "go to the bathroom."

"What?"

"Do it." Renie pointed to the restroom across the corridor. "Now!" She virtually shoved Judith against the door.

It was too late. Judith saw Pepper and Wayne Fielding come out of the dining car. Renie dropped her purse in front of Pepper. "Oh!" she cried. "Sorry! Can you grab that mascara wand? It's rolling away. So are my horse chestnuts."

Judith couldn't maneuver fast enough to get into the

restroom, but the waiter was speaking to Renie while Pepper and Wayne retrieved the items on the floor. Realizing what her cousin was up to, Judith managed to squeeze past everyone in the crowded corridor and escape into the dining car. As the waiter showed her to an empty table, she heard Renie call out a loud "thank you!" to Pepper and Wayne.

"I know why you've been acting peculiar," Judith said as a disheveled Renie flopped down next to her. "You didn't want those two to recognize me."

"You're half right," Renie said, rummaging in her purse to see if anything was missing. "Ah! I've still got all my horse chestnuts. Eight big new ones from this September."

Judith smiled faintly at Renie's gathering of horse chestnuts every fall, a tradition started by her father, who'd give some to her and keep the others for himself as a talisman. Uncle Cliff's reason had nothing to do with alleged health benefits, but because he'd picked one up shortly before catching the biggest rainbow trout he'd ever seen. Years ago, Judith had suggested to Renie that her cousin's handbag wouldn't be so heavy if she didn't fill it with so many horse chestnuts. Renie had replied, "It's not heavy, cousin, it's my father."

Renie closed her purse. "I didn't want you to see them."

"Why not?"

Renie groaned. "Because I don't want to spend this trip obsessing about that Weevil bunch. It makes me nervous." She shuddered. "It also scares me."

"Oh, coz!" Judith laughed. "I'm always curious about people."

"Yeah, right. But your interest has gotten you into some dangerous situations."

Judith made a face. "That isn't my fault. I can't help it if—" She stopped as her cousin made a sharp gesture.

Renie's smile was a bit frosty. "We have company. Hi," she said to the two stout gray-haired men who were joining them.

The shorter of the newcomers smiled apologetically. "No English."

"That's okay," Judith said. "I mean . . . we understand."

"Polish," he said, pointing to himself and then to his friend. "Hungarian."

"Ah," Judith said, nodding.

"Lucky us," Renie said with a genuine smile.

Both men smiled back and nodded.

"Tweedledum and Tweedledee," Renie said cheerfully.

The foreigners seemed puzzled. "Sorry?" the other man said.

Renie kept smiling. "No problem."

Judith perused the fairly lavish menu, given the restrictions of what she presumed was a small kitchen. The waiter appeared to take their orders. Judith chose the salmon; Renie asked for the chicken. The foreigners weren't sure.

Renie reached across the table, pointing to the menu. "Cluck, cluck," she said flapping her arms. "Moo, moo," she said, tapping the steak. For the salmon, she made swimming motions, accidentally hitting Judith with her elbow. "Excuse me, coz," she said. "What can I do for vegetarian lasagna?"

Judith pointed to Renie's napkin. "You're the artist," she said. "Draw vegetables, then do your animal imitations again, but shake your head."

"Jeez," Renie murmured. "I can design an annual report expending that much energy." Before she could take a pen out of her purse, both men mooed. "Good work," she remarked. "I might have screwed up the carrot. It could be mistaken for a turnip."

The foreigners were engaged in conversation. Judith couldn't figure out what language they were speaking, but their manner was amiable. "So," she asked Renie, "how did you know Pepper and Wayne were in the dining car?"

"Pepper's red hair is hard to miss," Renie said. "When I went to get our refills, I had to go through the dining car. I saw a redheaded woman with the man you identified as Wayne Fielding. I decided not to mention seeing them for the previously stated reason of making you crazy and you making me even crazier."

Judith understood. "How can I not be interested in that Weevil crew? I was so relieved to be rid of them, but then they showed up here and it unsettled me. I'm even more upset now that they're supposedly suing me. Why shouldn't I be concerned?"

Renie didn't respond until after the waiter brought their salads. "The account that Roy has given us is wildly exaggerated. I'm sure there are other people on this train who know who Willie is. Once gossip starts, it gets twisted after it's passed on—and on. When we got in line for dinner, I noticed Pepper and Wayne were still in the dining car. The two other people who had been sitting with them were just leaving. I was afraid we might get stuck sitting with Willie's cohorts. But then they got up, too. I didn't want them to see you because you know there'd be some kind of scene. That's another reason I wasn't keen on going to the dome car after dinner. Since they came out through the sleeper section, it's possible that they're staying on the lower level with Willie. You'll have to avoid those two until they get off in Montana unless you want to go head-to-head with Pepper and Wayne."

"Damn." Judith sprinkled salt and pepper on her salad. "Maybe you're right—we shouldn't play cards with the Downeys."

Renie shook her head. "I've nothing against the Downeys," she said. "I was just distracted by figuring out how to prevent Pepper and Wayne from seeing you—and vice versa. We can't stay cooped up in our compartment for what may be another whole day. Unless . . . how about a disguise?"

Judith looked incredulous. "Absolutely not!"

"It's Halloween," Renie pointed out.

"But only until midnight," Judith declared. "How would I explain looking like Catwoman or Batgirl tomorrow?"

Renie stirred a lavish amount of dressing into her lettuce and tomatoes. "I was thinking more Darth Vader. But we don't have costumes. Unless," she went on, brightening, "we use the bedsheets and dress up as ghosts."

"Oh, no!" Judith exclaimed. "Not the dreaded bedsheets! Your poor kids never got to be anything else, and they had to use pillowcases for their treats. Meanwhile, I was forced to spend money I didn't have on Luke Skywalker."

"True," Renie admitted. "But our kids had fun. Or did they? Maybe that's why they moved so far away." She stuffed a big helping of salad into her mouth.

"Forget the disguise," Judith said. "We'll watch for Pepper and Wayne sightings. You move faster, so you can be my advance man. Woman, I mean."

"Your scout," Renie said, and frowned. "I've got to explain my odd behavior to the Downeys after dinner. It's a good thing we're not seated near them. It gives me time to explain why I acted like a jackass." She paused, adding more salad dressing. "You do it. You're much better at untruths."

Judith smirked. "The truth is that sometimes you are a jackass."

"Okay. Go with it." Renie shoveled in more salad and chewed lustily.

Judith laughed. "I can be blunt?"

"Suptuyu," Renie replied with her mouth full. "Hifis!"

The cousins slapped hands. The foreigners smiled and nodded.

"America woman, very good," the first man said.

The other man agreed. "Live well. Live long. Much courage."

The cousins smiled at the foreigners. "Let's hope," Judith said, "we don't need too much courage to stay alive and well."

"Amen," said Renie.

Chapter Six

The four-handed pinochle game with the Downeys had gone so well that Judith and Renie agreed to play bridge with them Monday night. When the cousins got back to their room around eleven-thirty, they remembered to set their watches ahead.

"We've lost another hour," Renie grumbled. "By the time we get to Boston, it'll be Thanksgiving."

"You gained an hour today," Judith reminded her.

Renie looked puzzled. "I did?"

It was pointless to argue. "Never mind." She stared at Renie's tiger-striped nightgown. "What zoo did you buy that from?"

"Nordquist's zoo, marked down to less than half price." She reached into her carry-on. "Matching peignoir included," she said, holding up a flowing garment with black boalike feather cuffs. "Bill hates it. I think it scares him."

"It scares me," Judith said. "It's a good thing we're not going on safari. You'd get shot the first day."

"Right," Renie conceded. "By Bill." She twirled the thin satin rope that served as a belt. "I thought he'd find this sexy. Maybe I should've added tassels."

"You should've avoided the lingerie sale," Judith muttered, waiting for Renie to climb into the upper berth before getting into her own bed.

"You okay?" Renie asked a moment or two later.

"I may have nightmares about tigers, but I've settled in," Judith replied.

"Good. 'Night."

There wasn't another peep from Renie, who seemed to have already dozed off in her cozy little nest. Judith, however, was still awake when the train made its last stop before Idaho. Minutes later she heard voices in the corridor and remembered that the third bedroom's passengers must have just boarded. As the train picked up speed, the rocking motion lulled Judith to sleep. When she woke up the sun was out. *Montana,* she thought, wondering where they were in Big Sky country. Pushing aside the curtain, she peeked through the window.

"Coz!" she cried. "I see snow!"

"Wha'?" Renie's voice was muffled.

"Snow. Trees. We've slowed down. Are we near Glacier National Park?"

Renie groaned. "Shuddup."

Judith heard her cousin rustling around in the upper birth. "It's after eight-thirty. When do they stop serving breakfast?"

There was no reply.

"Coz?" Judith felt stiff when she stood up. "Are you conscious?"

"I am now, dammit."

"I'm taking a shower," Judith said. "Don't go back to sleep."

"Eight-thirty," Renie muttered, "mountain standard time, but my body knows it's seven-thirty back home. I never wake up until—"

Judith closed the door, cutting off her cousin's habitual complaints about not being a morning person. By the time she emerged, Renie was up and griping. "I hate showers," she said, "but I have no choice. Move it." She nudged Judith out of the way. "If I don't come out in half an hour, you'll know I drowned."

Judith got dressed. She'd finished drying her hair when the train slowed to a crawl. Brush in hand, she looked out the window again. A group of children were having a snow-ball fight in front of a four-story half-timbered building. As the train picked up speed again, Judith saw a sign that read IZAAK WALTON INN. As the inn disappeared from view she heard Roy's voice in the corridor and opened the door. He was headed in the opposite direction just beyond the stair-well. "Roy?" she called, keeping her voice down in case other passengers were still asleep. "Roy?"

He turned around. "Aha. I see you're up and about, Mrs. Flynn. Did you have a good night?"

"I did, once I got to sleep," Judith said. "Why did we almost come to a stop? Was something on the tracks?"

Roy chuckled. "There's only one flag stop along the Empire Builder's route. That was it, Essex, Montana. Back in 1939, the inn was built to house the Great Northern Rail-road workers. Later it became a tourist attraction on the south edge of Glacier National Park. The inn's historical status allows travelers to get on and off during the summer and winter seasons. Depending on the engineer's whim, we slow down to acknowledge the site's importance."

"Fascinating," Judith said. "Are we late for breakfast?"

Roy shook his head. "The call for the nine-thirty sitting will be announced shortly. You have plenty of time. I'll make up your room while you're gone."

Judith had finished her makeup when Renie came out of the shower. "Did I hear you chatting up somebody?"

"Roy. He was explaining why the train . . ." She stared at her cousin. "You're dressed. What did you do, take a shower with your clothes on?"

"Of course." Renie looked in the mirror over the sink as she applied a light touch of foundation. "You think I want to be naked when my body is found?"

"You're nutty enough to do it," Judith said.

Renie swiftly wielded her mascara wand, added lipstick, and ran a brush through her short hair. "Let's go. I'm starving."

There was no waiting line for the dining car, though only a few tables were vacant. "All clear," Renie said before a waiter motioned for them to be seated. "No red Pepper hair, no Wayne Whoozits."

The cousins had the table to themselves. After making their breakfast choices, they sat in silence for a few minutes, enjoying the mountain scenery as the train cruised along the outer edges of the park.

"I've never been to Glacier," Judith said. "Dan and I couldn't afford pleasure trips. If his mother hadn't paid our way to Arizona, we'd never have seen her. She refused to go anywhere that wasn't sunny and warm. Dan's grandma lived closer to us, but our last visit was sabotaged by the 1980 Mount St. Helens volcano eruption. We were forced to turn back just twenty miles from her home."

"I forget the fun you never had," Renie remarked. "Frankly, I wouldn't have recommended Glacier to Dan. Being four hundred pounds, he wasn't the outdoor type. In fact, Bill and I had our own problems. If you hike in Glacier, you take along bells to warn off the bears. Gallons of insect repellent don't faze the park's bugs. The deerflies were bigger than our kids. We stayed in so-called rustic cabins—translate that as old shacks with no air-conditioning. Spectacular scenery, of course, including the Going-to-the-Sun Road unless you get behind an RV from Minnesota with a driver who's never traversed anything steeper than Loring Hill in Minneapolis. But the lakes and glaciers and meadows are worth it, even for us spoiled Pacific Northwesterners. It's been twenty years since we made the trip, so I—" Renie stopped. "Are you listening? You're staring like a zombie."

Judith shook herself. "What? Sorry. I thought I recognized someone."

"Who?"

"A young woman. Maybe she's from Heraldsgate Hill. So many rich young techies have moved into the neighborhood."

Renie nodded. "Our dirty little blue-collar secret leaked

out after Bill and I bought our house forty years ago. Back then we could afford a view and a double lot. Sometimes when I'm on the avenue, I feel like a dinosaur. Condos, apartments, high-end restaurants, and chichi shops are everywhere."

"Don't remind me, especially after last summer's debacle with Herself and her ill-fated condo venture." Judith glimpsed a trio of deer grazing in a meadow as yet untouched by snow. "Did you see that?" she asked Renie.

"What?"

"The deer. They seem so tame. They didn't even look at the train."

"Their habitat may be shrinking," Renie said. "Remember last winter when a cougar wandered onto a school playground by the city limits? And a bear showed up at an Eastside car lot? I wouldn't want to haggle over price with him."

The waiter arrived with Judith's cheese omelet, sausages, hash brown potatoes, orange juice, and toast. Renie had ordered pancakes, bacon, eggs, and apple juice. Both cousins focused not only on their food, but on the alpine scenery. No one joined them, and by the time they finished their meal, they'd made a brief stop in the small town of Browning.

Renie pointed to a sign for East Glacier. "From October to April, the only stop for this side of the park is here. We're very close to the Canadian border, where Glacier becomes Waterton Lakes National Park in Alberta."

Judith laughed. "Did you memorize all this before we left?"

"No," Renie said, indignant. "I like geography. It drives Bill nuts when we travel. He'd ignore me if I told him we were going over Niagara Falls in a barrel."

"I appreciate it," Judith said, starting to get up. "Is that an elk?"

Renie leaned over to look past her cousin and glimpsed the elk drinking out of a meandering stream. "Wow—those are some antlers."

"I wish I had my camera," Judith said, following Renie into the aisle. "I should've put it in my carry-on instead of in my big suitcase."

"I'll get it from the baggage area," Renie said as they exited the car.

"Thanks," Judith said. "The camera's in a side pocket."

The cousins parted company by their room. The beds had been put away in their absence. Judith opened the newspaper that had been delivered earlier, but decided the scenery was more enjoyable than the daily dose of bad news. They'd crossed the Continental Divide. The landscape was changing as the mountainous terrain sloped downward. Glaciers, meadows, and lakes were left behind. At the edge of the Great Plains, Judith gazed at great swaths of farmland that merged into distant buttes on the far horizon. After a few miles she was surprised to see oil wells. She had forgotten Montana's deposits of oil and gas.

"It looks like Texas," she told Renie when her cousin returned.

"A real change after Glacier," Renie said, handing over the camera case. "The Cut Bank stop is about ten minutes—"

Judith interrupted her cousin. "This isn't my camera."

"What?" Renie looked puzzled. "It was in your suitcase. Did you bring more than one?"

"No," Judith replied. "It's not my camera case, either."

"It was in the pocket you described. How many cameras do you have?"

"Two. Mine's an older model," Judith explained. "I gave Joe a digital camera for Christmas, but it isn't this one."

Renie sat down. "Could it belong to Mike and Kristin?"

"Maybe. I can't recall if they intended to take pictures of the parade."

Renie shrugged. "They might've." She studied the camera closely. "Top-of-the-line. I've been on shoots with pros who use these. They cost several grand. Would Mike pay that much to photograph his kids dressed as cardboard boxes?"

"I doubt it, unless the forest service provides cameras for rangers."

"Call Mike at the next stop," Renie suggested. "If he lost this camera, he'll be frantic." She checked her watch. "We'll get to Shelby in less than an hour."

"I can't use my cell phone on the train?"

"Poor or even no signals in these wide-open spaces." Renie grinned. "Otherwise, my mother would've called me ten times since we left town."

Judith nodded. Aunt Deb refused to believe that the umbilical cord between mother and daughter had ever been severed. "How hard was it to tell your mother you were leaving town for so long?"

"I tried something different this time," Renie said. "I told her Bill and I were going on a 'round-the-world cruise and we wouldn't be back until February. Naturally, she pitched a fit. The next day I let her know that the trip had been shortened by a month or so due to schedule changes. After another day or two, I said we'd decided to take a train trip across Canada for six weeks so we could be home for Christmas. Finally, on Friday I told her we couldn't afford to take such a leisurely vacation, but by a stroke of luck Bill had been asked to speak at a conference in Boston and we'd be gone only a couple of weeks. She was so relieved that she stopped moaning and groaning."

"I lucked out," Judith said. "My mother surprised me by not making a fuss. Frankly, that worries me."

Renie nodded. "That is odd. Is she feeling okay?"

"I think so," Judith said. "She always perks up when Mike's family visits." She glanced outside. "We're stopping. Can I get off to call Mike without going through the lower level in our car?"

"This is Cut Bank. You won't have time. Wait for Shelby. We'll go out through the other sleeper on our way to lunch. That'll save you extra steps."

"Did you bring a camera?" Judith asked.

Renie shook her head. "Cameras are as bad as . . . clocks. Why do you think I hire photographers for my graphic design business?"

Cut Bank was yet another small town. Judith marveled at the vastness of the land—and the absence of inhabitants along the train's route. Less than fifteen minutes after the brief stop at the depot, the train slowed down again. "What's happening?" she asked. "We don't have a stop around here, do we?"

"No," Renie replied. "Maybe there's something on the tracks."

Judith shuddered. "I hope it's not a body."

Renie shot her cousin a disgusted look. "You'd be delighted if it was. It's happened at least twice in broad daylight on my train travels—a spectacular way to commit suicide while screwing up everybody else as a farewell gesture."

"You really are heartless," Judith said.

"No, I'm not." Renie paused. "Well . . . sometimes. I'm also realistic."

The train came to a full stop. Except for more oil rigs and some scattered buildings in the distance, Judith couldn't see anything unusual. She was silent for at least a couple of minutes. Renie had picked up her copy of the Doris Kearns Goodwin book on Franklin and Eleanor Roosevelt. "Should we ask Roy what's going on?" Judith asked.

Renie didn't look up. "No."

"I'll go check the other side of the train," Judith murmured.

"Fine. Bye."

When Judith opened the door, she heard voices in the corridor beyond the stairwell. She recognized one of the speakers as Jim Downey. A quick glance through the window on the opposite side of the train revealed nothing of interest. Judith walked past the stairwell and saw the Downeys talking to a young Asian couple she hadn't yet seen.

"Anyone know why we stopped?" she asked the foursome.

"Hi, Judith," Sharon said. "These folks think we're waiting for a freight to go by. They're old hands at train travel."

"My cousin wasn't concerned," Judith said.

The younger woman nodded. "Freight trains still have right-of-way. Frankly, they should change that. Passengers have connections to make and people meeting them. A brief delay won't spoil food or create panic if new cars are an hour late getting to the dealership."

Jim nodded. "Judith, meet Matt and Laurie Chan from St. Paul."

Judith shook hands with the Chans. "I haven't ridden on a train in ages," she confessed. "I forgot how much fun it is to meet new people when you're traveling. On an airplane you can't mingle with anyone other than your seatmates." Judith turned to Sharon. "Are Matt and Laurie cardplayers? Maybe they could join us tonight after dinner."

The Chans shook their heads. "Matt's obsessed with video games," Laurie said. "The only card game I ever played was Old Maid. Is it still called that? Or did they change it to SWF to be politically correct?"

"Hey," Matt said, "what's with the *W*? How about us?"

Laurie playfully punched her husband's upper arm. "You're right. How about an update called Dysfunctional Families?"

"Speaking of functioning," Jim said, "has anybody seen Roy in the past half hour? Our sound system's not working. We turned the call light on, but he hasn't responded."

Judith and the Chans shook their heads. "Maybe he's on a break after putting the beds away," Laurie said.

"He's very conscientious," Sharon said. "He'll show up."

Judith murmured an excuse and headed back to her own compartment. She realized that she still hadn't seen the Kloppenburgs or the passengers in the adjacent roomette who'd boarded after midnight.

"We're probably waiting for a freight train," she informed Renie upon entering their compartment.

"So I figured." Renie put her book aside. "We'll be late getting to Shelby."

Ten minutes later, the freight rumbled along. Judith gazed at what seemed like an endless passage of every color and type of flatcars, refrigerator cars, ore cars, and closed freight cars. As the train disappeared, she heard voices in the corridor. She got up and moved to the door she'd left open.

"What now?" Renie asked.

"Why aren't we moving?"

"It takes a while," Renie replied. "Maybe the crew went out for cigarettes."

The flippant response didn't satisfy Judith. She went into the corridor, where the conductor was talking to a couple in Western outfits. The woman had curly blond hair under her ten-gallon hat; the man was also fair-haired, judging from the long sideburns Judith could see under his matching hat. "I'll see to it," Mr. Peterson said. "We've had some electrical problems in this car today."

"Thanks," the man responded as the train began to move again.

The couple turned around and nodded at Judith as they moved past her to the end of the car. "Excuse me," she called to the conductor.

He looked up from a small handheld electronic device. "Yes?"

"Are they the Johnsons? Or is it Johnston?" Judith asked, noting that the Western-clad couple had gone into the last compartment.

"Johnston," Mr. Peterson replied. "Is your sound system working?"

"We haven't checked," Judith said. "Should we?"

He smiled. "Only if you want to hear announcements or a spiel about the points of interest along this route. Oh—music, too."

Judith smiled back. "My cousin has taken this train several times, so she knows about the territory. The last time I traveled on the Empire Builder was on our way to New York almost forty years ago. We wanted to spend a few days there before we sailed to Europe."

Mr. Peterson nodded. "You have your own travel guide. Excuse me, Mrs. Flynn, but I have to see what we can do about our electrical problem. Apparently it's only in this car."

"Of course." Judith entered the compartment.

"Well?" Renie said, looking up from her book. "How many people just became your new best friends?"

"Test the sound system," Judith said. "It may not be working."

"Neither am I." Renie resumed reading.

"I'll check it," Judith said. She braced herself on the chair arm, leaning to reach the controls. "Nothing. I should let Mr. Peterson know."

Renie glanced up from her book. "Mr. Peterson?"

"The conductor." She sat down hastily as the train began moving at a much faster clip. "We must be trying to make up time."

"It can be done." Renie looked at her watch.

"I saw the Johnstons," Judith said. "They're next to the Kloppenburgs."

"Good for them. Excuse me, Pearl Harbor just got bombed." Renie continued reading.

Judith sighed. It was a relief not to have to cope with everyday crises and problems. She needed a break from routine. She was seeing parts of the country that she'd either never seen before or couldn't remember. No one—except Renie, of course—could make demands, criticize, argue, or otherwise ruffle her feathers. It was so peaceful on the train. So quiet. So . . .

Judith grimaced. *Am I nuts?* she wondered. *Do I need chaos? Am I missing the often stressful ebb and flow of an ordinary day at the B&B?*

Renie again looked up from her book. "Now what?"

Judith feigned ignorance. "What do you mean?"

"I know that look." Renie closed her book. "I've seen it since you were five. It's the I-don't-want-to-be-here-but-I-have-to-pretend-I-do look. The first time I saw it was during Mass when we were kids. You couldn't sit still, you climbed up on the kneelers, you kept bugging me, and once you literally flew out of the pew and ended up in the center aisle while Father O'Reilly was giving his sermon. You still haven't outgrown it."

Judith was indignant. "That's unfair. I like going to Mass. It restores me. I need the peace and the grace of the sacraments. I haven't fidgeted in church since I was ten."

"Try sixteen." Renie was bemused. "You thrive on activity. After your hip surgery, Joe told me he might have to handcuff you to the sofa."

"I don't like being waited on," Judith asserted. "I feel helpless, and it makes me feel guilty when—"

A tap on the door interrupted her. Renie held up a hand. "Sit and stay," she said. "I'll get it."

Judith saw Mr. Peterson in the corridor. "Mrs. Jones?" he said warily.

"Yes?" Renie sounded benign.

Apparently overcoming his fear that Renie might still be in a combative mood, he smiled in Judith's direction. "Have either of you seen your attendant, Roy, in the past hour or two?"

"Not since before breakfast," Judith said.

"Oh." Mr. Peterson's voice was faint. "Is your sound system working?"

"No," Judith replied. "I meant to tell you," she added, with a reproachful glance at Renie, "but I was delayed."

The conductor nodded. "We're looking into it. If you see Roy, would you ask him to contact me?"

"Sure," Renie said, looking as if she was about to close the door.

Judith got to her feet. "Sir?"

"Yes?" Mr. Peterson's smile was forced.

"When do we get to Shelby? I need to use my cell."

"Ten minutes," he replied. "We've made up time. It's a fairly brief stop, so stay by the train."

"I will," Judith said. "Thanks."

Renie slid the door closed. "Are you hungry?"

"Not really." Judith was still standing, bracing herself on the sink. "It seems like we just finished breakfast."

"We did. I'd rather wait for lunch."

"Me, too." She paused. "Should we head for the other sleeper now? We're slowing down. I don't want to get stranded in Shelby."

"Okay," Renie agreed, her amiable mood restored. "I'll join you. After your call, I'll go to the club car to get some soda or juice."

It took several minutes for the cousins to maneuver through the sleeping cars and reach the lower level. A young female attendant was already positioned by the door. Her name tag identified her as Jax Wells. "Fresh-air fiends or smokers?" she asked with a cheerful smile.

"Neither," Judith said before introducing herself and Renie. "I have to make a phone call."

"Stay close," Jax said. Her voice was soft yet clear. "We're taking on one new passenger and letting two off from the coach section."

The train slowed to a crawl. "Shelby looks small," Judith noted.

"It is," Jax replied, "but it's the seat of Toole County." The sleeper car stopped just short of the station. She opened the door and placed the movable step on the platform. "Be careful. I'm not going anywhere except to have a cigarette and stretch my legs."

After Jax stepped outside, Renie followed. "I always go first on the stairs," she explained. "My cousin's had a hip replacement, so if she falls, she can land on me. I'm a human cushion."

Jax smiled. "Are you a deductible medical expense on her taxes?"

"Not a bad idea," Renie responded as Judith cautiously made her descent. "I don't come cheap, though."

"Big blue sky or not, it's chilly out here," Judith said, dialing Mike's number. "I hope he picks up. What time would it be at home?"

Renie looked incredulous. "You're asking me?"

"Okay, an hour behind . . . Hi, Mike," she said, relieved. "No, I'm fine. We're in Shelby . . . I thought you'd know where it is after your stint in Montana. I have to make this quick. Did you leave your camera at our house? . . . You didn't?" Judith read from the note she'd made. "It's a Canon EOS 5D Mark II . . . Yes, Aunt Renie told me they were pricey . . . Is everything okay with you guys? . . . Good. I still feel bad about having to leave . . . What?" She saw Jax walking toward the train.

"Let's go," the attendant called, putting her cigarette out.

Renie was by the door with one foot on the step. "No," Judith said into the phone. "Did you ask your dad? . . . They must be somewhere. Have to go. Love you." She disconnected and let Jax help her get back on.

"Well?" Renie said as the train started moving again.

"It's not Mike's camera. Otherwise, all's well, except they can't find Willie's old videos they watched at our house. I told him to check with Joe."

Renie's expression was sardonic. "Kristin screwed up?"

"She *is* human," Judith said. "I think."

The cousins climbed the stairs to the upper level. "Can you make it back to our compartment without me?" Renie asked. "I have to go through the dining car to get to the bar on the lower level."

"I think so," Judith said. "Bottled water for me. I finished the freebies."

"Okay. Be careful. It's noon so it may take me a while. Lots of passengers get sandwiches and salads in the club car."

Fortunately, the train wasn't yet at full speed by the time Judith reached their bedroom. Twenty minutes passed before Renie staggered through the door. "Now I'm hungry," she declared, setting down two bottled waters and two Pepsis.

"What's our next stop?" Judith asked.

Renie scanned the schedule she kept inside her book. "Havre, just after one. We're there for twenty minutes. It's the Empire Builder's midway point before the Twin Cities.

When James J. Hill built the Great Northern Railway, he founded the town as a major service center. It's our last stop until Malta just before three."

Judith opened a water bottle. "Shall we head for the dining car at the Havre stop?"

"Sure." Renie poured Pepsi into a plastic glass. "Do you want to me to check your suitcase to make sure you didn't pack your camera?"

"It might be Joe's. He meant to take pictures of the Halloween parade, but left it at the house. Maybe I grabbed it by mistake in my addled condition."

"I should put the Canon back. Can you lock your luggage?"

Judith grimaced. "I could if I knew where I put the key. I haven't seen it since the Scotland trip. It's probably in the suitcase."

Renie nodded. "I'll look for—" She was interrupted by a knock on the door. "Now what? Yes?" she called.

The door slid open. Jax stepped just inside the compartment. "They're working on the sound system, so we're taking dinner reservations now."

"Where's Roy?" Judith asked, standing up.

Jax's smooth, almond skin grew darker. "He's . . . not available. I'm taking on his duties in both sleeper cars, at least for the rest of the day."

"Is he ill?" Judith asked.

Jax clutched the clipboard she was holding and didn't make eye contact. "I can't say. Which dinner service would you prefer?"

Judith looked at Renie. "Six-thirty?" Seeing her cousin nod, she turned back to Jax. "Can we do that?"

"I . . ." Jax dropped the clipboard. "Oh, darn! I'm all thumbs!"

Renie picked up the clipboard. "You're also upside down. Let me switch this around." She unclipped the reservation sheet, turned it right side up, and secured it to the board. "You're trembling. What's going on around here?"

Jax held out her hands and studied them with an anxious eye. "I . . . I'm upset. You must think I'm an idiot."

"No we don't," Judith said with compassion. "You might feel better if you told us what's going on."

Judith and Jax were the same height. The attendant couldn't avoid her passenger's compassionate dark-eyed gaze. "I can't. I mean . . ." She gave herself a good shake. "It's just strange."

Judith nodded. "Roy's not ill, right?"

Jax looked startled. "Why do you say that?"

"I can't explain," Judith admitted. "I don't mean to pry, but—" She stopped. "If he'd come down with flu, you'd say so."

"Mrs. Flynn isn't nuts," Renie said, wearing what Judith called her Boardroom Face. "If you tell her what's wrong, maybe she can help."

Jax bit her lower lip. "Help?" she finally said. "How?"

"I have to know what's wrong first," Judith said quietly.

"Maybe," Jax said after looking out into the corridor, "I should come in and try to pull myself together."

Judith stepped aside; Renie slid the door shut. Jax glanced at the closed door, as if she suddenly had misgivings. "This feels wrong," she said fretfully. "You should talk to the conductor."

"Bad idea," Renie said. "Have a seat. I'll stand."

Jax still looked in doubt. "Why not talk to Mr. Peterson?" she asked.

Renie spoke first. "If there's a problem besides the sound system, he's already got a full plate. My cousin has a reputation for solving problems. You might say she has special powers."

Jax stared at Judith. "You mean she's like a psychic?"

Renie looked aghast. "Oh, no! 'Consultant' describes it best. She has a Web site you can check. Sit and unburden yourself."

Judith was already seated. Renie's sudden about-face was

puzzling. She seemed as ambiguous as Jax, who was frowning as she settled into the other chair. "Go ahead," Judith said. "I've heard it all."

"There isn't much to say," Jax said after a pause. "Roy hasn't been seen since around ten o'clock this morning." Her soft voice had an edge and her limpid brown eyes were moist. "It's not like him. I've worked with Roy for six years. I've heard tales about employees who've jumped ship and disappeared. But Roy's totally reliable. We've had three stops since ten o'clock, not counting the freight train delay. We were ahead of schedule before that."

Renie was perched on the edge of the sink. "I realized that at Essex." She shot Judith a reproachful look. "If we'd kept to the schedule, coz here wouldn't have had to wake me earlier with her excitement over the Izaak Walton Inn."

Jax tugged nervously at the cuffs of her white shirt. "We slowed down by the inn, but Roy wouldn't have gotten off unless we'd come to a complete stop. We searched the train and called Browning and Cut Bank. Mr. Peterson even contacted Shelby, though we were sure Roy was missing before we got there." She pressed her hands together. "I'd better go. My workload's doubled."

Judith recalled her chat with Roy. "He was chipper when we saw him after we slowed down at Essex. He told us about the inn. Our beds were made when we got back from breakfast."

"If," Jax said, "you spoke to him around nine, you were among the last people to see him. Everyone had already gone to breakfast except the couple next door."

"The Kloppenburgs?" Judith said.

"Yes. They wanted to make up their beds themselves, but around nine-thirty, they asked Roy to bring breakfast and leave it outside. They're very private people. Some passengers don't want strangers in their rooms. Maybe they've had a bad experience. It happens."

Judith understood. As an innkeeper, she'd had guests

who'd insisted on complete privacy during their stay. "Let me think on this," she said as Jax got to her feet. "If you hear anything, no matter how trivial, tell me."

Jax frowned. "I suppose it's okay to do that."

"It might help," Judith said, also standing up. "By the way, have you been downstairs since Roy went missing?"

"Yes," Jax replied, edging toward the door. "Mr. Weevil has his meals brought in. I took him lunch just a few minutes ago."

"How's he doing?" Judith asked.

Jax shrugged. "He seems out of it. The poor man rambled. Mr. Peterson said Mr. Weevil was a big TV and movie star, but I didn't recognize him."

Judith figured Jax for late twenties. "You missed his glory days."

"I guess." She opened the door. "Mr. Weevil and his companions are getting off at Wolf Point around four-thirty. If you need to make another phone call, we'll be there at least twenty minutes while we move him from the train."

"Thanks for letting us know," Judith said.

At the doorway, Jax still looked upset. "Do you really solve . . . mysteries?"

Judith grimaced. "I wouldn't put it like that. I've got a logical mind and I understand people. The combination helps me solve . . . problems."

Jax nodded. "That makes sense." She disappeared into the corridor.

"Well?" Judith said, fists on hips as Renie slid the door shut. "What's with you? I thought you were pissed off because I couldn't stand not being caught up in some kind of mysterious predicament."

"I was," Renie said, looking puckish, "until I realized that if I had to listen to you jabber about trivialities all the way to Boston, you might as well have a real problem to chew on. We're trapped on this train, so you can't look for trouble. Thus, the Case of the Missing Amtrak Attendant is right up your alley."

"You made me sound like some crackpot psychic."

"So?"

Judith threw up her hands. "Okay, okay. I'm curious, snoopy, meddlesome, and inquisitive. Anything else you'd like to add?"

"That pretty much covers it," Renie said placidly. "I could've told her how to find your Web site, but after careful consideration I realized that if I did, you might kill me."

"Probably," Judith agreed. "The site's embarrassing. It's flattering to have admirers like the people who created it, but I wish they had a different acronym. 'Female Amateur Sleuth Tracking Offenders' is too easily turned into FATSO instead of FASTO. I don't need any reminders to watch my weight."

"You obsess about it," Renie said. "You always have. Speaking of calories, are you hungry yet? It's going on one."

"Not very," Judith replied, "but let's go to the diner at the next stop. I felt wobbly while I was calling Mike. Riding a train is like being on a ship. Even on solid ground, you feel as if you're still in motion."

Renie agreed. "It takes me a whole day after a train trip to get my bearings. Say—do you want me to put that camera in my suitcase? It's locked."

"Wait until after lunch. I'll take it with me. I don't want somebody swiping it while we're at lunch." Judith unzipped the carry-on, removed the camera, and placed it in her handbag. "We're slowing down. Let's go."

Renie led the way. When they reached the dining car, she eyeballed the other passengers. "All clear," she announced as a waiter beckoned them to a vacant table near the entrance.

Judith recognized the Chans, who were just finishing their meal. "Hi," she said, "this is my cousin Serena Jones, also known as Renie."

Laurie smiled as the cousins sat down on the other side of the table. "Flynn, right?"

"Call me Judith," she said. "How was lunch?"

"Good," Matt replied. "Nothing exotic, but highly edible."

Laurie cuffed her husband's shoulder. "Matt's a doctor, one of the rare MDs under forty who's in family practice."

Matt chuckled. "It's a dirty job, but someone's got to do it."

"I know there's a critical shortage of GPs," Renie said. "Med students want to specialize because that's where the big money is."

"Speaking of shortages," Judith said, "have you seen our attendant, Roy?"

"Not since this morning," Laurie replied. "I saw a young woman dressed like an attendant talking to a couple of kids who'd been running up and down the corridor. She warned them they could get hurt when the train goes fast."

"They could get hurt by the other passengers," Renie said drily. "I'm glad they were—" She stopped as the waiter appeared.

"Hey," Matt said, "we'll leave you in peace. Enjoy your lunch."

The cousins both ordered hamburgers, salad, and chips. Judith was the first to speak after the waiter moved on. "It doesn't sound as if the Chans know Roy's disappeared."

"Word will get out," Renie said. She looked through the window. "We're slowing down for Havre."

"It doesn't seem like a very big town, either," Judith said. "Or is this just the outskirts?"

"It's Montana. The state is huge, the towns are small. Get over it."

"I'm not complaining," Judith protested. "It's fascinating country. Diverse scenery, dramatic landscape, and a sense of the real West. Not just now, but in the past." She lowered her voice. "If someone like Roy decided to quit his job and jump off the train, why here? A stranger would be noticed right away."

Renie paused as their salads arrived. "You think he deserted?"

"No." Judith stared out the window as the train pulled

up beside a life-size sculpture of two military men shaking hands. "What's that?"

Renie studied the bronze figures. "Oh—it symbolizes U.S. and Canadian friendship." She pointed to the Stars and Stripes and the Maple Leaf flanking what Judith assumed was Montana's state flag. "As I mentioned, we're closer to the border than you'd think."

"Hmm." Judith looked thoughtful. "Maybe I should revise my thinking about Roy. What if he had serious personal problems?"

"Criminal or otherwise?"

"Otherwise," Judith said without hesitation. "I've known lots of crooks who can fool the rest of the world, but . . ." She grimaced. "If I have any God-given talent, it's for judging people."

"Definitely." Renie's expression was ironic. "You married Dan."

Judith didn't try to hide her exasperation. "I knew what Dan was like. You know better than anybody that I was in a jam, being pregnant and Joe eloping with Herself in a drunken stupor."

Renie's expression softened, though Judith couldn't be sure if the change was caused by remorse or gratitude for the waiter serving their hamburgers.

"Okay," Renie said, adding onion slices to her patty. "You have amazing people skills. If Roy isn't a felon, I assume you mean he'd head over the border to dodge an ex-wife, a jealous husband, or . . . the IRS?"

"Not the IRS," Judith said in a droll voice. "That spells felony. The last I heard, we still have an extradition treaty with Canada."

"Right," Renie agreed. "I see your point. The middle of Montana has a long, lonely border without patrols."

"It'd be easy to . . . oops!" Judith looked at the floor. "I dropped my tomato. I can't reach it. Can you ask the waiter to get me another one?"

"Sure." Renie leaned out into the aisle. "Here he comes. Let me grab the one on the floor so nobody steps on it and slips."

While Renie ducked under the table, Judith apologized to the waiter and asked for another tomato slice. "I'm clumsy," she said. "By the way, where are the Canadian border crossings on this route?"

The waiter, whose name tag identified him as Earl, cocked his head to one side. "Are you making a connection?"

"Just curious," Judith said, hearing a thud and a cussword near her feet.

"Ah." He nodded. "We passed a connecting point at Cut Bank," he said as Renie clambered into her place and rubbed her head. The waiter offered her a solicitous look. "Are you all right, ma'am? I could've picked up that tomato."

"No problem," Renie said.

The waiter started for the serving area, but stepped aside to let a young woman pass. Nearing the cousins, she smiled, nodded, and kept going.

"There she is again," Judith murmured. "Did you see her?"

"Who?"

"The blond with the dimples that I saw earlier. I've seen her recently, and this time she acted as if she recognized me."

"She may have," Renie said. "We started from home. It's a wonder you haven't run into a dozen people you know. Maybe she's from Heraldsgate Hill."

"Maybe," Judith said vaguely.

The cousins ate in silence for a couple of minutes while the train remained at the Havre station. Three passengers got off and two got on. The conductor and two other crew members huddled together with a trio of Amtrak employees from the station. "Do you think they're trying to find Roy?" Judith asked.

"I hope so," Renie said.

Judith was surprised by her cousin's reaction. "You're serious. You really care. I thought your concern was a ruse to divert me from bugging you."

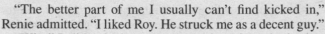

"The better part of me I usually can't find kicked in," Renie admitted. "I liked Roy. He struck me as a decent guy."

"Why," Judith asked, "are you speaking of Roy in the past tense?"

Renie grimaced. "I did?" She munched on a potato chip before speaking again. "Years ago I was on a train coming from L.A. When we stopped in Oakland, I wanted to stretch my legs. An attendant warned me not to. He told me that a month earlier, an employee got off for a short break, but never came back. Days later, his body was found in a nearby Dumpster. His throat had been slit."

Judith grimaced. "Did you tell me about the incident?"

Renie shook her head. "It happened while Dan was still alive. Why add another horror story to the one you were living back then? My next train trip to California was after the 1989 earthquake. The area around the old station had been severely damaged—the collapse of I-880 was right by there. A nice new station had replaced the old one." She looked unusually somber. "I never forgot the poor guy in the Dumpster."

Judith scrunched her napkin. "My appetite's gone. I wish I hadn't asked."

"Sorry. It brings back grisly memories, but I can still eat." Renie gobbled up the last potato chips before pointing to the window. Mr. Peterson and some other Amtrak employees were in deep conversation. "They seem upset."

"You're right," Judith said. "They're shaking their heads. They must not have found any trace of Roy."

Renie checked her watch. "We're due to leave here just after one-thirty. It's one-forty—assuming my watch is correct."

"Dubious," Judith murmured. "Shall we visit the dome car?"

"I thought you wanted me to put your camera in the suit-case."

"That can wait," Judith replied. "It's safe in my purse."

The cousins moved through the dining car with Renie leading the way to make sure that Pepper and Wayne weren't anywhere in sight.

"All clear," Renie announced, "but the place is pretty crowded. I think there may be a couple of seats toward the far end. Are you game?"

"Lame but game," Judith responded.

"Funny, coz," Renie remarked drily.

The cousins sat down just as the train began to move again. Judith poked Renie. "See those two people in cowboy hats sitting near the club car stairs?"

"Yes. Why do I care?"

"They're the Johnstons," Judith said in a low voice. "You know—the couple next to the Kloppenburgs."

"Fascinating. How can I contain my excitement?"

Judith ignored the remark. She also tried to ignore Renie's sudden frenzied back-and-forth foot movement. "What are you doing?" Judith asked.

"Something's stuck to my left shoe," Renie said. "I thought I scraped it off on the way from the dining car, but it's still there."

"Have you considered removing it with your fingers instead of looking like you're having a conniption fit?"

Renie looked indignant. "You want me to actually touch whatever it is? You were not raised by a germaphobe. Yes, Mom's obsessive, but some of her cautions rubbed off on me. I never touch unknown items off of floors."

"So take your shoe off and see what it is. People are staring as if you're some kind of shuffling, scuffling freak show."

"I can't," Renie said, grimacing.

"Why not?"

"I hurt my other shoulder opening the door into this car."

Judith gaped at Renie. "You dislocated your good shoulder?"

"No," Renie replied, finally keeping her feet still. "But it scared me. You know what that's like. You always fear the worst. I want to sit here until I know it's only a twinge, not a disaster."

Judith leaned back in her chair. "I'm sorry," she said

softly. "If I could help you more, it'd be . . ." Her words trailed off helplessly.

"It's fine. It's just annoying," Renie said. "I think it stuck to my shoe when I was under the table retrieving your tomato." She stared at her brown suede flats. "I got these at Nordquist's spring sale. I love buying shoes, but I don't love wearing them." She paused, gazing at the gold-and-brown fields of Montana. "I think I'll stop wearing shoes. At least when I'm home."

"That's very . . . strange," Judith said.

"Not really. Why do we wear shoes in the first place?"

"Coz," Judith said, puzzled, "why are we having this conversation?"

Renie smiled. "The Cowboy Hats just went down to the bar with Pepper and Wayne Fielding. I wanted you focused on me with your back turned so they couldn't see you." She paused as Judith swiveled around in her chair to look where the Johnstons had been sitting. "Would you rather I discussed whether Richard the Third murdered his nephews in the Tower of London?"

"Stick to Dumpster horror stories. Were the couples chummy?"

"No. Maybe it was a coincidence they went downstairs at the same time."

Judith frowned. "So they may not know each other."

"Why do you care other than to avoid the Weevils and their putative hangers-on? Aren't you more concerned about Roy? I told you to concentrate on real life, not some fantasy about Willie and Company."

Judith felt sheepish. "You're right. But Roy's disappearance stumps me. I've no idea what's happened to him. His coworkers have far more to go on than I do—yet they seem dumbfounded."

"I gather Roy's worked for Amtrak quite a while," Renie said. "He's what? Around forty? Did you notice a wedding ring?"

"No," Judith replied, "and I always check. Old habits die hard."

Renie laughed. "It's good to hedge your bets. Speaking of looking, would you mind not turning every ten seconds to see if your nemeses are coming back from the club car?"

"Sorry." Judith forced herself to stop glancing at the stairwell. "Maybe we should go back to our room. I feel edgy."

"Why? Even if Pepper or Wayne recognized you, they couldn't do more than make a scene and embarrass themselves."

"It'd embarrass me, too. It's not just that. You said something a minute ago that reminded me of . . . I don't know, but it made me uneasy."

"We were talking about Roy," Renie said. "You should feel uneasy. You're supposed to find him."

Judith scowled at her cousin. "I'm not a magician. Come on, let's go."

Renie hesitated. "We're moving pretty fast. Shouldn't we wait?"

"For what? Isn't the next stop way down the line?"

"Yes, at Malta, an hour or so away."

Judith pondered her ability to cope with the fast-moving train. "Oh, heck, let's do it. I'm getting a stomachache wondering when Pepper will pop up out of those stairs and attack me."

Renie looked dubious, but finally agreed. "Hang on to my arm," she urged as they cautiously made their way through the dome car.

"How's your shoulder?"

"It hasn't fallen off yet. Don't try to pull it out of the socket, okay?"

The cousins went through the dining car, which was now empty except for the employees preparing the dinner settings. In both sleepers, all was quiet. Judith felt as if they had the train to themselves. It was a pleasant thought, especially compared to airplane travel.

"Give me the camera," Renie said when they reached their room. "I'll take it downstairs."

Judith delved into her purse while Renie removed her left shoe. "It's not gum, but it's sticky," she said, carefully using a tissue to peel off the scrap. "There's some numbers and the word 'ox.'"

Judith was puzzled. "Ox?"

"So?" Renie tossed the scrap and tissue into a waste bin by the stairs.

Judith shrugged. "Nothing. Oh—could you get a pair of my thick wool socks? I imagine it'll get colder as we move east."

"Sure," Renie said, already halfway down the stairs. "Back in a—"

The train suddenly rocked violently. Judith lost her balance. She felt herself falling, opened her mouth to scream, but only heard the sound inside her head. *Have I gone mute?*

That was her last thought before the world faded to black.

Chapter Seven

Judith was aware of nearby shouts and a shriek that seemed to come from a hollow cave. She slowly opened her eyes to see a blank wall. Blinking several times, Judith realized she wasn't lying on whatever was beneath her feet. *I'm disoriented, but not in pain.* Her hands clung to a sturdy waste bin that seemed to be propping up the rest of her body. *Not my home, yet it seems familiar.* She was on a train—in Montana? The train wasn't moving. Gasping for breath, she heard anxious voices, mostly male. A female voice, loud and angry, rose up from the stairwell. *I know that voice. It's Renie.* Relieved, Judith tried to focus.

"Coz!" Renie staggered up the stairs. "Are you okay?"

Feeling stupid, Judith nodded. She was shaking, but found her voice. "You . . ." She blinked a couple of times. "Did you fall?"

"Not quite," Renie replied, also looking unsteady. "I caught myself just in time. But I banged my knees on the luggage shelves."

Jim Downey and Matt Chan had come out of their respective compartments. So had some other people Judith didn't recognize.

"Does anyone know what happened?" Jim asked.

No one responded immediately.

"We've stopped," Renie finally said. "Maybe we hit something."

Matt, with Laurie now at his side, spoke up. "Is anybody hurt? I'm a doctor." His expression turned wry. "If needed, I make train calls."

The cousins looked at each other. "We're fine," Judith declared.

A plump brunette was standing behind the Chans, her hands on the shoulders of the two young boys Judith had seen earlier. "Jason," she said, giving the younger child a slight nudge, "hit his head on the sink. He seems all right, but I'd feel better if you took a look, Doctor."

"I'll check it out," Matt said. "My kit's downstairs. I'll be right back. And," he added, starting for the stairs, "let everybody know I'm available."

Renie intercepted Matt before he reached the first step. "When you finish with the kid, could you check my cousin? She may be in shock."

"Sure," Matt said, and quickly headed down the stairs.

Judith stared at Renie. "You think I'm acting goofy?"

"You're shaken up," Renie said, rubbing her sore knees. "You should sit."

Judith wanted to protest, but saw Jax rush from the stairwell. "Everyone okay?" She noticed Jason and his mother. "We've got a doctor on board."

The Downeys were in the corridor. "What happened?" Sharon asked.

Jax looked grim. "We've been told someone tried to beat the train at the crossing. He made it, but his load of sugar beets is all over the place. There may be some damage to the first of our two engines. We'll be stuck here at least until the tracks are cleared. I'm very sorry."

Laurie spoke up. "We look like we're in the middle of nowhere."

Jax made a face. "That's because it *is* the middle of nowhere. Not many people live around here, which is why the crossing has signs and flashing lights and bells, but no arms that come down. It's a dirt road used mainly by farmers."

Matt returned with his kit. "Okay, Jason," he said to the

boy, "let's go in your room to take a look." He let Jason's mother lead the way.

"Don't forget Mrs. Flynn," Renie called after Matt.

"I won't," he promised just before disappearing from view.

Jax excused herself. "I must check the other sleeper."

Somewhat reluctantly, Judith let Renie herd her into their room. "I'll get us a couple of drinks from the bar car. Meanwhile," she went on, all but shoving Judith into the chair, "let's play Log."

"Log?" Judith didn't think she'd heard correctly. "What's that?"

"Log," Renie repeated, only louder. "It was Bill's game with the kids on long car trips. The point was to see which kid could keep quiet and stay motionless the longest. It worked wonders, at least until they got to be nine or ten and finally figured it out."

"Maybe it was just as well that Dan and I couldn't take vacations like that," Judith said. "Of course we only had Mike."

"Two parents and one kid. Bad idea," Renie asserted. "We did that once when our kids got older and had summer jobs or felt that Mom and Dad were so uncool that they couldn't bear to be seen with us in the same vehicle. We thought we solved it the next time by taking along one of our kids' friends, who always turned out to be ten times worse than our own." Renie slung her purse over her shoulder. "I won't be long. Stay quiet."

Judith stared out the window. There was no sign of the wreckage from her vantage point. Instead, she saw ominous gray clouds moving across the vast horizon. Maybe it'd rain. Her mind drifted, wondering why anyone with half a brain would try to race a train. Maybe the wide-open spaces that reminded her of the Old West still stirred a sense of adventure and risk. The great openness of the land must rouse a primal urge to challenge the elements. Or, in this case, an iron horse, symbolic of the movement to the last frontier.

"Hi."

Judith gave a start. "Matt! I was daydreaming."

"How do you feel?" he asked, entering the roomette.

"Better."

His dark-eyed gaze had a piercing quality. "You sure?"

"I think so," she said, aware that her tone wasn't as convincing as she'd hoped. "I guess I blacked out for a minute."

"Let me have a look."

Judith followed the movement of Matt's fingers this way and that. "Okay," he murmured before looking into her eyes with a bright light. "Now I'll check your pulse, heart rate, and blood pressure."

Judith didn't say a word as they went through the medical ritual. "Have you been under a lot of stress lately?" he asked.

"Well . . . yes."

Matt closed his kit. "Your blood pressure's elevated and your pulse rate's a bit fast." He smiled wryly. "I hope this trip's a vacation for you."

"It is," Judith assured him. "My cousin told me I needed to get away."

"Good idea—except for this wreck." Matt paused and raised his voice. "Anyone else need a doctor?"

No one responded.

"Is the little boy okay?" Judith asked.

Matt chuckled. "He could use a dose of discipline, but I don't have any with me. He and his brother are growing up in the School of Rampant Self-Expression. Every time Laurie and I run into brats like that we rethink our decision to start a family of our own."

"It's not the children's fault," Judith pointed out. "It's the parents'."

Matt made a face. "That's what scares us. You think having kids is a wonderful idea, but there's no way to practice parenting. Maybe Jason's mother gave up before her boys could walk and talk." He shook his head. "I have a family practice, but I don't know how to practice having a family."

"It's hard, but it can be done. I had only one child, but he turned out fine. By the way, do you know how Mr. Weevil survived the wreck?"

Matt looked puzzled. "Mr. Weevil?"

Judith realized Matt might not know Willie was on board. "The movie and TV daredevil." She paused to smile at Laurie, who'd just entered the bedroom. "He's in this sleeper."

"Wow!" Matt's eyes lit up. "My brother, Luke, and I worshipped him. Willie was incredible, especially with martial arts. We begged our folks to let us take classes in kung fu, karate, judo, aikido, or anything Willie did. Mom and Dad finally gave in, but it was a waste. We were the only Asians in the class, but the worst students. The only sport I can play without embarrassing myself is tennis."

Laurie snickered. "The last time we played I beat Matt six–one and six–two."

Matt frowned at his wife. "I turned my ankle."

"What about your brother?" Judith asked before an argument could start.

Matt hesitated before answering. "Luke's much more athletic. He played hockey and was on the wrestling team in college. Then he took up kayaking, motorcycling, mountain biking, and I don't know what all. With a last name like ours, he thought he could be the next Jackie Chan. Instead, he's an auto mechanic—but a darned good one."

"Lucky us," Laurie said. "He works for free." She squeezed her husband's arm and laughed. "Matt still had Willie's comic books when we got married."

"I sure did." He made a face at Laurie. "She tossed my collection on one of her cleaning rampages. Laurie was into Wonder Woman."

"My son admired Willie, too," Judith said. "He's about your age."

"I wouldn't mind seeing Willie," Matt said. "Where is he?"

Judith was reluctant to reveal too much information. "I think he wants to stay incognito." Seeing Matt's look of disappointment, she rushed on. "He's not feeling so good. By chance, I saw him come aboard in a wheelchair."

"How sad," Matt murmured. "Maybe I'll spot him along the route."

"Maybe," Judith said. "Thanks for checking on me."

"Sure. Take it easy, okay?" Matt smiled before he and Laurie exited.

Several minutes passed in silence. There were no raised voices, no footsteps, no sounds from outside—just a calm that somehow unnerved Judith. She wished she knew what was going on outside. But she'd have to use the stairs. That wasn't merely foolhardy, but dangerous.

Judith started to nod off, but kept trying to stay awake. She was almost asleep when Renie's arrival startled her. "Coz!" Judith gasped, shaking herself. "Good grief, I guess I'm more worn out than I thought."

"I don't doubt it," Renie said, placing their drinks on the small table. "Pepper, Wayne, and the Cowboy Hats weren't in the bar or dome cars. Everybody's milling around, talking about Mr. Beets." She added ice to the Scotch and handed the drink to Judith. "Did Dr. Chan pay you a call?"

Judith nodded. "He thought it was stress. I think he's right."

"You've been running on fumes too long. Chill." Renie settled into her chair. "Before I got to the bar, I wanted to view the wreckage, but Jax was by the other sleeper's door and told me to get back on the train. They were rounding up passengers who were already having a look-see."

"Did they arrest the truck driver?"

"No. I suppose they have to wait for the sheriff or the state patrol."

"That could take a while," Judith said.

"That's not all," Renie said. "We have to replace the front engine. It should come from Havre, but Jax says there's too much track damage. We'll switch to another spur, then crawl to Williston, our first stop in North Dakota. Even on schedule, we wouldn't get there until tonight."

"That's a pain in the butt," Judith remarked. "Oh, well. At least we're not stuck sleeping on an airport floor with small children stepping on our heads."

"Nor are we dead," Renie said, "which is what happens when planes crash."

"True." The cousins were silent for a few moments. "Oh," Judith finally said, "did you find my wool socks when you put the camera away?"

Renie's brown eyes widened. "Damn!" She set her drink down and stood up. "We crashed before I could do anything. I landed against the luggage shelves and—" She stopped, frowning. "I rushed up here. Did I still have the camera?"

"I don't think so," Judith said, "but I was muddled."

Renie moved to the corridor. "I must've dropped the camera between the stairs and the luggage racks. I'll look for it and get your socks." ·

Judith hoped the expensive camera wasn't lost. It might belong to a B&B guest. If so, the owner would be upset. Maybe she should ask Joe if there'd been any inquiries. Sipping her drink, she tried not to anticipate trouble. But there wasn't much activity outside to divert her. Small dark birds hopped among thimbleberry vines. A rusted farm implement lay against a ramshackle split-rail fence. The gray clouds continued to gather. Would rain hinder the accident cleanup? To her knowledge, she'd never seen a sugar beet.

Judith checked her watch. It was two-thirty, mountain standard time. They'd change to central time in North Dakota, losing another hour. Sipping more Scotch, she heard voices nearby. One belonged to Renie, but she didn't recognize the others until the Cowboy Hats walked by. The Johnstons, she reminded herself as Renie appeared a moment later looking chagrined.

"I couldn't find the camera," she confessed, handing Judith a pair of dark green wool socks. "I'll ask Jax if anyone's turned it in."

"Damn," Judith murmured.

Renie sat down. "I found the socks, but a couple of people

from the downstairs roomettes were using the restrooms, and the Cowboy Hats were searching their own luggage. I didn't have much maneuvering space."

"Did you talk to the Johnstons?"

Renie frowned. "Who? Oh—the Johnstons. Or the Bobbsey Twins. Couples who dress alike look alike. Mrs. Johnston heard we were moving on. She asked if I knew where we'd get another engine. I told her at Williston."

"We need a change of scenery," Judith said. "I'm bored watching birds try to eat thimbleberries that probably dried up a month ago."

Renie gazed out the window. "Are those thimbleberries or salmonberries?"

"I don't suppose they'd let me off to call Joe and ask if anyone's lost a camera at the B&B."

"I think two of those birds are some kind of warbler."

"If we start moving, I'll have to wait until we get to . . . Williston?"

"Not warblers—more like buntings. We rarely see them at home."

"I don't remember if Joe had any appointments today," Judith said. "He and Bill leave tomorrow, so he may be wrapping up loose ends."

Renie's nose was all but pressed against the glass. "Or some kind of thrush? It has to be a bird that doesn't go south for—"

Both cousins jumped as someone shouted, "All aboard!"

Judith stared into the empty corridor. "Where'd that come from?"

"Ah!" Renie pointed to the intercom. "The PA system works." She poked a button to lower the sound. "We're moving." She waved good-bye to the birds.

Judith sank back in her chair. "I wonder if Roy will ever be found."

"Work on it," Renie coaxed. "You don't want to disappoint Jax."

"I can't do what I can't do," Judith said, and paused. "I

suppose I could start by talking to other members of the crew, such as the conductor. We don't know anyone else except Mr. Peterson and Jax."

"You know the waiters," Renie reminded her.

Judith looked uncertain. "The one who served us lunch was Earl, but I don't remember the other names. He's the only one I've actually talked to."

"Earl seems nice," Renie said.

"Yes, he does. Since we're going slow, it'd be a good time to visit the dining car. The waiters are between sittings."

"They're getting ready for dinner or taking a break," Renie said. "Why don't you play Log? Want to go for our kids' record? It was nine minutes and . . ." She frowned. "I forget."

"Just as well," Judith said wryly.

"Williston, here we come. Leave the light on, but don't wait up."

Judith opened the novel she'd brought along, a mystery set in Victorian England. The book had been recommended by a former coworker from Judith's day job at the Thurlow Public Library. Before leaving on the trip she'd tried to get into the story, but Prince Albert as a time-traveling sleuth seemed implausible.

She got to page 46 and started yawning. Renie looked up from her Roosevelt saga. "Are you going to sleep again?"

Judith sat up straight. "I hope not. Prince Albert just ran into Charlemagne at a local convenience store in Scappoose, Oregon."

"No kidding. Let me know if FDR and Eleanor show up, especially if they're wearing togas." Renie went back to her own book.

Judith was trying to figure out how the time travel novel had gotten published in the first place when Jax poked her head into the doorway. "Everything okay?" she inquired.

"Just ducky," Renie said. "How long will it take us to get to Williston?"

"There's been a change in plans," Jax said, stepping inside the roomette. "We're only going as far as Scuttle, twenty miles west of Malta. It's not a regular stop, but the new engine is being brought from Williston because it can go much faster than we can. We shouldn't be more than a couple of hours behind schedule once we're under way. We'll reach Chicago in plenty of time for your connection."

"Say," Judith said, "did anyone turn in a camera?"

Jax looked puzzled. "Not that I know of. Did you lose yours?"

"It's not mine," Judith explained. "I packed it by mistake. It got lost in the luggage area downstairs when we collided with the truck."

"I'll ask around," Jax said, and hesitated. "Any ideas about Roy?"

Judith shook her head. "Not so far. Was he married?"

"Divorced," Jax said. "He married very young. It didn't last long and there were no kids. Roy went to work for Amtrak after the split-up. He wanted to get away. His father and grandfather both worked for the railroads, though Roy never intended to make a career of it. But once he started, he discovered he liked it." Jax looked sad. "I can't understand what happened to him. Mr. Peterson says it's as if Roy vanished into thin air."

Feeling guilty for not following through on what had happened to Roy, Judith changed the subject. "Has the man who caused the wreck been arrested?"

Jax seemed uneasy. "Not yet, but Amtrak's police have been notified."

"I know trains have police," Judith said, "but do they ride along?"

"Not as a rule," Jax replied. "On this route, both Amtrak and Burlington Northern Santa Fe have their own law enforcement officers."

Judith indicated the wide, empty vista. "They're not based nearby?"

"No," Jax said, "but they reach trouble spots quickly to start investigating the collision. Local authorities will take the driver into custody and charge him."

Renie shot Jax a sharp look. "You mean the lunatic's still on the loose?"

Jax smiled wanly. "I think the troopers were chasing him earlier."

"I don't get it," Judith said. "You mean he was left on his own?"

Looking pained, Jax stepped inside and lowered her voice. "The pickup wasn't damaged. It was on the clear side of the tracks, so the driver kept going. There is something odd, though."

"Isn't the collision odd enough?" Renie remarked drily.

Jax bit her lip. "I shouldn't discuss this with passengers, but I can't keep my mouth shut around you two."

"A common problem with my cousin," Renie said, nodding at Judith. "Don't fuss. She knows when to keep her mouth shut."

Jax looked relieved. "It's like I've always known you," she said to Judith. "You do have special powers."

"Not at all," Judith said. "I'm not overly self-centered. I like people. I like to listen to them." She smiled encouragingly. "What's so odd?"

"A crew member from this area said sugar beets are harvested in October, but he couldn't think why a load of them would show up here. They're grown around Missoula in western Montana, then shipped to Idaho refineries."

"That is odd," Judith agreed. "I have a logical mind that has to make two and two equal four. When that doesn't happen, I ask why."

"I know. Things should make sense." Jax turned to leave. "My beeper went off. Somebody needs me." She hurried into the corridor.

"This is the real Wild West," Judith said. "Or am I off base?"

Renie smiled. "We live farther west, but I don't equate

our region with popular Wild West concepts. Maybe it's our temperate climate. Or that the pioneers and the natives got along okay." She shrugged. "Or the seafood."

"What?"

"You know—the fish and crabs and clams and oysters. Our Native Americans didn't struggle to find food. Neither did the early settlers. Who wants to kick the crap out of somebody else when you're eating Dungeness crab or rainbow trout? And don't forget our state motto, 'Alki,' Chinook jargon for 'by and by' or 'don't bother me while I eat these oysters.'"

"You have the most peculiar ways of interpreting—" Judith stopped. "What was that?" she said, getting up.

"That what?" Renie asked.

Judith was already at the door, peering out into the corridor just in time to see Jax and Matt Chan hurry down the stairs. "Come here," she said to Renie. "Somebody needs a doctor. Go see who and why."

"I'm your lackey?" Renie snapped. "I like my book, though I still can't believe the DAR wouldn't allow Marian Anderson to sing at Constitution Hall. I want to cheer every time I read how Eleanor Roosevelt arranged for Anderson to sing at the Lincoln Memorial. My God, the greatest contralto of the era—"

"Stop!" Judith cried. "Something's happening downstairs. Please—could you find out? I'd go, but I don't dare."

"Okay." Renie sighed, closed her book, got up, and exited.

Judith went into the corridor to wait by the stairs. She could hear nothing further from below. Moments later, Laurie emerged from her roomette. "Any news?" she asked.

"Renie's checking," Judith said. "Who's got the medical crisis?"

"Matt's hero, Wee Willie Whoever," Laurie replied. "The redhead who's with him insisted someone tried to kill him earlier in the week."

"Oh, no!" Judith turned away from Laurie to hide her dismay.

"Are you all right?" Laurie asked, sounding alarmed.

Judith quickly composed herself. "I'm still rattled after passing out."

"Tell Matt," Laurie suggested. "Maybe there's a clinic nearby."

Judith was aghast. "I'm sure Matt's right that it's just stress." *And more stress,* she thought, staring down at the empty stairs. "Where's my cousin?"

"I'll check," Laurie volunteered, but paused on the first step. "I didn't mean for you. I meant if Mr. Superhero needs to be checked more thoroughly."

"Oh." Judith watched Laurie disappear from view. Faint voices floated up the stairs, but none of them belonged to Renie. A woman sounded upset, though her words were inaudible. Whoever had been talking stopped. Judith decided to tackle the stairs. On the second step she was startled by a voice behind her.

"Sorry, Mrs. Flynn," the conductor said. "I didn't mean to scare you. Are you waiting for someone?"

"My cousin," Judith replied. "She went downstairs to find out what was happening to Mr. Weevil."

"That's what I'm doing," Mr. Peterson said grimly. "We're lucky to have a doctor on board. And don't mention the word 'jinx.' It's already crossed my mind." He forced a thin smile before hurrying downstairs.

Judith knew the feeling.

Indistinct voices again floated out of the stairwell. Thankful that the train was moving at a crawl, Judith took her time going down the steps. The lower level was deserted. The doors to both of the larger bedrooms were closed, as were the four roomettes between the luggage shelves and the accessible bedroom. Without checking each of the Vacant/Occupied signs, Judith couldn't tell if anyone was using the shower and toilet facilities.

"Coz?" Judith called in a low voice. "Coz?"

She heard a noise in the corridor, but wasn't sure where it came from. A moment later, she heard another sound, human and high-pitched. Whoever it was must be in one of the restrooms. As she moved closer, the last of the doors opened, and a little girl emerged. She was entangled in a roll of toilet paper that trailed behind her as she struggled to the family room.

Renie staggered out of the same restroom. "Serves you right, Emily," she yelled. "When you learn to read, your first word should be OCCUPIED."

Emily glared. "Shubbub!" A curly-haired young woman opened the door and grabbed the tot. "Bab lady!" Emily said, with a final dirty look for Renie.

Judith turned to Renie. "Which of you took the best two out of three?"

"It was a draw. The kid's quick on her feet. I almost got caught listening outside the accessible bedroom, so I ducked into one of the stalls. Then someone banged on the door. I hadn't shoved the latch all the way closed, so in comes Emily, who had to wee-wee. She managed that but had problems with the fifty yards of toilet paper she'd unrolled." Renie gestured toward the family room. "Now I suppose her parents will finger me as a pervert."

Judith tried to look sympathetic. "I doubt it."

"No? My own kids reported me to CPS after I booked all of us into a motel with only two stars. They insisted it was cruel and unusual punishment. How could I help it if there wasn't another motel within a hundred-mile radius? Then they argued that Bill was an unfit father for not driving three more hours to a motel that had at least four stars."

"The more I hear about your family vacations . . ." Judith shook her head. "Never mind. Did you hear anything about Willie?"

"How? I was trapped in the bathroom with a two-year-old virago."

"Maybe Emily's on the case," Judith murmured, studying the area. The stairs were in the middle of the car and the luggage rack was next to an outside door. Her suitcase and foldover were on top of several others on the middle shelf. Two facing roomettes flanked the accessible bedroom. The family room was at the opposite end. "Have we met any of the passengers from the other rooms down here?"

"Don't ask me," Renie said. "You're the social animal."

Judith moved closer to the stairs. "I shouldn't be down here. I keep expecting Pepper to fly out of their compartment and hand me a subpoena." She paused, tapping a finger against her cheek. "Do you know who's in their room?"

"Willie, Pepper, Wayne, Jax, the Chans, Mr. Peterson, and Mrs. Hat."

"Mrs. Hat?"

Renie nodded. "She's a nurse. I think she was checking her luggage when Matt was called. Now what?"

Judith stared at the accessible bedroom's door. "It's not my fault Willie's in bad shape. He's spent a lifetime damaging his body with crazy stunts. I begged him not to jump out the front window and Joe tried to stop him when he was on the roof. Willie wouldn't listen."

Renie looked annoyed. "Are you really feeling guilty?"

Judith grimaced. "I shouldn't, but Pepper could still sue me." She checked her watch. "It's three-twenty. Going this slow, it'll take a half hour to reach Malta—or is it Scuttle?"

"That's where we get the new engine," Renie said, turning toward the stairs. "Let's go. I'm tired of standing here."

Before the cousins could move, the door to Willie's room opened. Mr. Peterson came out first, followed by Jax and Laurie Chan.

Judith realized she'd been holding her breath. Her shoulders slumped as the grim-faced trio approached. "What is it?" she asked.

The conductor cleared his throat. "Mr. Weevil is ill, so an ambulance is meeting us at Scuttle. Phillips County Hospital is in Malta, just minutes away."

"What a shame," Judith murmured. "Did he have complications?"

"I've no idea," the conductor replied, sounding faintly surprised. "Excuse me—I have to use the stairs." With a heavy step, Mr. Peterson made his way to the upper level. A subdued Jax followed him.

"Poor old guy," Laurie said under her breath. "Matt's doing his best to keep his game face on, but he really admired Willie."

"Is Matt staying with him until we get to Scuttle?" Judith asked.

Laurie nodded. "I'm useless when it comes to patients. At least my MBA qualifies me to run the business side of Matt's practice."

"We're no help either," Renic said. "I suggest a trip to the bar."

"Sounds good," Laurie responded. "It's cocktail time in the Twin Cities."

A female voice called from behind the trio. Judith, Renie, and Laurie turned around. Two young women had come into the corridor from a roomette.

"A passenger's sick," Laurie said. "Don't fret. It's not contagious."

Judith couldn't help but stare at the newcomers. She suddenly recognized the short, dimpled blonde and her taller, dark-haired companion. The young women stared right back.

"I know you," the blonde said. "Not from seeing you on the train, but . . ." She turned to the dark-haired girl. "Tiff? Help me out here."

The dark-haired Tiff looked puzzled for a moment. "Um . . ." She glanced at the blonde. "Nordquist's shoe department, Maddie."

Maddie paused before nodding enthusiastically. "Oh, yes! You bought those to-die-for black strappy shoes."

Both young women giggled. "Thanks!" Maddie called over her shoulder as they scurried back to their roomette. "We're glad whatever is wrong with that guy in the accessible room isn't catching."

Neither cousin said a word, but continued up the steps. Judith decided there was no point in expressing doubts about the young women's veracity in front of a virtual stranger. When the trio reached the dome car, Laurie held up a hand. "My treat. I like to feel useful. Stay here and get us some seats. What'll it be?"

The cousins gave their standard orders. Laurie headed downstairs. Renie pounced on three chairs toward the end of the crowded car, two of which had just been vacated by a couple of teenagers. For the first time since leaving the lower level of their sleeper, Judith noticed that a heavy rain was falling.

"Fitting gloom-and-doom weather," she murmured as she sat down. "I actually feel sorry for poor old Willie."

"Of course you do," Renie said. She gave her cousin a sly glance. "Okay—what was that conversation with those two girls all about?"

"You noticed?"

Renie looked exasperated. "Of course. I'm not brain-dead. Yet."

Judith kept her voice to a whisper. "Those two showed up at the B&B right after Willie fell in the pyracantha. They asked about Herself's rental. I told them they had the wrong address and to see Mrs. Rankers next door. Her daughter was the rental agent. I was anxious to get rid of them because the usual rescue crew was due to arrive. I didn't notice if the girls went to see Arlene—I just assumed they did. Now I wonder if it was a ruse connected to Willie."

Renie was skeptical. "Like what? Asking for his autograph? How about an honest mistake and couldn't remember where they'd seen you?"

Judith narrowed her eyes at Renie. "Do you believe that?"

"I'm not sure," Renie admitted. "But I can't think why they'd lie. More to the point, why would they need to?"

"Yes," Judith agreed. "That's one of the questions."

Renie looked wary. "Oh?"

"Two, in fact. How did they happen to be on this train

staying in a roomette only a few yards from Willie? And how did they know that the sick passenger was in the handicapped room? Laurie didn't tell them."

"Because a person in the aforementioned room is there because he or she has poor health?" Renie threw up her hands. "Here we go again!"

Judith was affronted. "What?"

Composing herself, Renie began her reasons for ignoring Willie and his hangers-on. "A crazy old coot jumps off your roof, breaking an arm and a leg. You and Joe told him repeatedly it was against B&B rules. By chance, he arrives on the same train we're taking. Fractures rarely prove fatal, and over the years Willie's probably broken every bone in his aging body. Since you got on board, you've tried to figure out a connection with him and some other passengers, including the no-show Kloppenburgs, the Cowboy Hats, and now the ditzy girls who inquired about Herself's rental. Maybe you think Emily is a midget spying on you for Pepper, and forget her threats—that's all they are. A judge would toss out a lawsuit against you faster than you could say, 'If he do jump, you can kiss my rump.'" Renie paused for breath.

"Coz," Judith said quietly, "you don't need to—"

Renie held up a hand. "I'm not done. Willie has a competent doctor and concerned Amtrak employees attending him. Yet you think Willie's knocking on the Pearly Gates because you helped him get there." She rechecked her watch. "It's three thirty-five. Willie gets off in less than half an hour. You'll never see him again, you probably won't ever hear from Pepper. Try needlepoint as a hobby instead of envisaging potential corpses or killers among your B&B guests."

"I used to needlepoint," Judith said. "It got too hard on my eyes."

"Try turning on a light," Renie snapped. "Here's Laurie with the drinks."

The next half hour was spent in pleasant chatter, what Judith called "The Getting to Know You Show." The exchanges with guests and other strangers tended to be one-sided, with Judith learning ten times more about newcomers than they found out about her. Renie was so used to her cousin's adroit queries and encouraging comments that she sat back and kept quiet. As often as she'd played a supporting role, Renie appreciated Judith's conversational prowess. The Chans had met in L.A. while Laurie was in grad school at UCLA and Matt was interning at Cedars-Sinai Medical Center. Laurie had gone on a blind date with her roommate's brother, who turned out to be a jerk.

"I told this creep I was coming down with flu," Laurie said, her dark eyes full of mischief. "He didn't understand no meant no. Finally I said I was going to throw up. We happened to be a block from Cedars-Sinai, so he pulled into the ER entrance and virtually shoved me out of the car. I staggered inside and fell over a walker. My so-called date roared off, and there I was, lying on the floor with a sprained ankle. I looked up to see this good-looking guy in a white coat. He asked if he could help. I was so rattled that I said he certainly could, adding he could even marry me. Which he did exactly one year later."

The cousins laughed. Over halfway through her martini, Laurie grew wistful. "That was eight years ago. We're still wondering about having kids. We've considered adoption— I was adopted. My mom and dad got me through a Hong Kong–based agency. Taking an unwanted child instead of having our own appeals to us, but Matt's parents are very traditional. They were born in China before the Communist takeover. When the subject comes up, they have a fit. I hope we figure it out before we're old enough to be grandparents."

Their glasses were drained when the train stopped. "This must be Scuttle," Laurie said, looking at a cluster of buildings. "Maybe I can help Matt get Mr. Weevil off the train."

"Thanks for the drinks," Judith said. "We'll return the favor before we get to the Twin Cities."

After Laurie had hurried off, Judith noticed that there was no train station, or even a sign designating the town as Scuttle. The commercial section featured a motel, a café, a gas station, and a hardware store on one side of the street, and two taverns, a drugstore, a variety store, and a post office on the other.

"Not a thriving metropolis," Renie noted. "The word that comes to mind is 'shabby.' No wonder it's not a regular train stop."

"I don't see an ambulance," Judith said. "It must be parked out of sight, probably by the sleeper. Should we go back to our compartment while we're not moving? It shouldn't take long for Willie's transfer."

"I'll make a quick run to the bar car for Pepsi," Renie said, standing up. "Bottled water for you?"

"Sounds good."

After Renie left, Judith stared through the rain-streaked window. Only one car and a pickup drove down the street in the next couple of minutes. A man came out of the hardware store. A woman went into the drugstore. The rain looked as if it was turning to sleet.

A teenage girl in the chair next to the one Renie had vacated addressed Judith. "'Scuse me," she said. "What's going on? My stop's at Malta."

"A sick man is being taken to the Malta hospital," Judith replied.

The girl seemed puzzled. "But Scuttle's only twenty miles from Malta. Why couldn't they wait until we got there?"

"The man's very ill," Judith said. "At the rate we're moving, it may be faster to drive him to Malta." She saw Renie at the head of the stairs. "Excuse me. My cousin's waiting for me."

"Bummer," the girl murmured. "Who's sick? Maybe I know him."

Judith had risen from her chair. "Then you'll hear about it when you get home." She forced a smile as she moved on to join an impatient-looking Renie.

"That would be New Friend Number Twenty-eight?" Renie murmured.

"Not really," Judith replied. "She wanted to know why we stopped here. She lives in Malta and knows the entire population."

"Hmm." Renie juggled the Pepsi, bottled water, and a bag of pretzels. "She sounds like a Judith Flynn wannabe."

"Skip the sarcasm," Judith retorted. "Have you heard any sirens?"

"No," Renie said as they moved between the dome and the dining cars. "But the boozers in the bar were pretty loud."

Judith noticed that three of the waiters, including Earl, were putting the table settings in place. She smiled at him. He smiled back.

"Not now," Renie said softly. "I'm not a circus performer. I'll be lucky if I don't spill the ice. Interrogate him about Roy at dinner."

By the time Judith and Renie reached the entrance to their room, the train hadn't moved. "I still can't see the ambulance," Judith said, checking both sides of the car. "Maybe they've come and gone."

"Probably." Renie put the carrier on the table and sat down.

Judith remained standing. "I'll see if Laurie and Matt are back in their roomette. They'll know what's going on."

"Go for it. You won't be satisfied until you find out."

Judith went back down the corridor to the Chans' compartment. The door was shut. She rapped twice. Laurie slowly slid the door open. Judith saw at once that the younger woman looked upset.

"Mr. Weevil died before the ambulance arrived." Laurie stepped aside so Judith could enter the roomette. "Matt's still downstairs. I've never been with him when a patient died. I don't know how he copes."

Judith's knees turned weak. She had to sit down. Her reaction wasn't caused by shock or even surprise. But she felt a strong sense of guilt. No matter how hard she'd tried to discourage Wee Willie from jumping off of Hillside Manor's roof, Judith was convinced that somehow she was responsible. A dozen what-ifs raced through her mind.

"Judith," Laurie said in alarm, "are you okay?"

Judith wasn't sure. "It's . . . terrible news."

Laurie hovered over her. "Can I help? Should I get Matt?"

Taking a deep breath, Judith tried to collect herself. "I'll be all right," she said hoarsely. "I feel . . . sad."

Laurie's expression was sympathetic. "Did you know him?"

Judith hesitated, wondering if she should be candid. She decided on discretion. "Like Matt, my son was a big fan of Willie's," she hedged.

Laurie nodded. "I understand. Matt never met Willie, but he felt as if he knew him from all those movies and TV shows."

The unasked but inevitable question refused to stop nagging Judith. "Does Matt know the cause of Willie's death?"

"He assumes it was a cardiac problem," Laurie said. "Not knowing the patient's history, Matt can only guess."

"Was Willie still alive when Matt went down to see him?"

"Yes." Laurie looked outside and shivered. "What's taking the ambulance so long? We're close to Malta. Is it colder or am I having a nervous reaction?"

"It is chilly." Judith also glanced outside. "It's getting dark early."

Laurie moved to the sink, where she stared into the mirror. "I look ghastly. What's wrong?" she demanded shrilly. "I'm a rational person, but I feel uneasy, as if a big dark cloud's hanging over my head."

Judith stood up. "You watched a man die. Being upset is natural. In the presence of death, we're reminded of our own mortality."

Laurie uttered a harsh laugh. "A doctor's wife asks a nonpractitioner to diagnose her? That figures. The whole world's skewed."

A tap on the door prevented Judith from responding. "I'll get it," she told Laurie. "Maybe you're the one who should be sitting down."

Mr. Peterson, still grim, addressed Laurie. "Mrs. Chan, could you please come downstairs?"

Laurie was taken aback. "Why? What's wrong? Is my husband okay?"

"Yes," the conductor replied. "It's a formality. Dr. Chan can explain."

Laurie straightened her shoulders. "Okay. Let's do it."

With a heavy step, Judith returned to her room. Renie looked up from her book. "Well?"

"Willie's dead."

Renie crossed herself. "Sad." She gestured at the window. "It's snowing."

Judith moved closer to see for herself. "It's colder in here, too."

"What now?"

Judith frowned at her cousin. "What do you mean?"

"Has the body been removed? Is the widow grieving? Will the train start up? Should we wait for the spring thaw?"

Judith's expression was reproachful. "You can't be sympathetic for more than sixty seconds, can you?"

Renie remained stoic. "I can if I know the person. I'll pray for him, but I won't mourn. Willie and I were strangers on a train."

Judith didn't say anything. She was frustrated, sad, and for some reason she couldn't fathom, she was scared. Maybe Laurie's traumatized reaction had fueled her own fears. Watching the snow fall in big, wet flakes that obscured most of Scuttle's homely little main street, Judith thought back to the past few days' events. The previous Monday had been ordinary. Willie hadn't yet arrived at Hillside Manor. Renie hadn't begged Judith to accompany her on the train trip. Joe hadn't known that he, like Bill, was going to Boston. Willie hadn't yet made his leap off of the B&B's roof. There had been no inkling that Mike and his family would show up for the Halloween weekend. *If only,* she thought, *I could obliterate the past few days—just like the snow hides the squalor of this little wide spot in the road. But I can't. The snow will melt, the town will still be drab. I can't change anything.* "I'm tired," Judith murmured.

Renie had also been watching the snow. "I know." She smiled cynically. "Here we are, stuck in the middle of nowhere on a train that can't move, snow coming down, with a corpse for a fellow traveler. What could possibly go wrong?"

Judith didn't respond. She saw the book she'd been trying to read and shoved it into her carry-on. "I don't want to sit here. It's too quiet. Why don't we go to the club car?"

"You're spooked, aren't you?" Renie's serious expression indicated she wasn't teasing. "Sorry, coz," she said before Judith could speak, "but you're not acting like yourself. Do you feel all right?"

"Physically? Yes, except for still feeling tired."

"You're not given to mood swings that smack of gloom and doom," Renie asserted. "Aside from Willie taking that final leap into eternity, why—"

Mr. Peterson stood in the door that Judith had left open. "Mrs. Flynn? Would you come downstairs with me?"

Judith was puzzled. "Of course," she said, standing up. "But why?"

The conductor looked pained. "Someone wants to speak to you."

Judith's anxiety intensified. "Who?"

"Please." Mr. Peterson's usual air of calm authority had deserted him. Backing into the corridor, he beckoned to Judith. "Please?"

Renie had also stood up. "Not without me she can't."

The conductor tried to look conciliatory. "Don't worry, Mrs. Jones. I'll make sure that Mrs. Flynn gets down the stairs safely."

"You bet your butt you will," Renie snapped, barging in between him and Judith. "I'm coming, too. Let's hit it."

Mr. Peterson led the way. At the bottom of the stairs, Judith saw Jax in the corridor with the Chans. The trio looked uneasy as a tall man in a state trooper's uniform came out of Willie's room. He moved toward the newcomers with long, deliberate strides. "Which one's Mrs. Flynn?" he asked in a deep voice.

"I am," Judith said, surprised to hear her voice crack.

The trooper gestured to an open roomette on his left. "Would you mind stepping inside? The occupants are in the dome car."

Warily, Judith walked to the doorway. Renie was right behind her, but the trooper held out an arm to bar her way. "Sorry, ma'am. This is a private conversation. You'll have to wait outside." He deftly stepped in front of Renie, backed into the roomette, and shut the door.

Judith sat down on the small sofa. The trooper remained standing. There was nowhere else for him to sit in the small compartment. As he loomed over her, she focused on his ID badge. J. L. Purvis was in his mid-thirties, plain of face, but with skin weathered by Montana's hot summers and cold winters. His only notable feature was a pair of shrewd, glacial blue eyes now fixed on Judith.

"We've got an awkward situation, Mrs. Flynn," he said calmly. "I hear you knew the deceased Mr. Weevil."

"Who told you that?" Judith asked—and realized that she sounded defensive, even hostile.

"That's not important," Purvis said. "Is it true?"

Judith was tempted to say she wouldn't answer any more questions until the trooper revealed his source. But that would be a mistake. She knew from Joe that a witness's lack of cooperation was adversarial. "He was a guest at my B&B last week," she finally said. "It was the only occasion I ever encountered him."

"Excuse me," Purvis said, "but didn't you see him at the depot?"

"I saw him being wheeled to the train. I haven't laid eyes on him since."

Purvis looked faintly skeptical. "Your reservation was made under another name—Jones. Why didn't you use yours?"

"The reservation was made by my cousin," Judith replied. "I had no idea I'd be traveling with her. And yes, Jones is her real name."

"But at the last minute you decided to join this Mrs. Jones."

"She begged me to come. She doesn't like airplanes. Our husbands both have business in Boston this week . . ." Judith shut up. It was never smart to babble when cops asked questions.

Apparently Purvis read her mind. He waited almost a full minute before speaking again. "When did Mr. Weevil leave your B&B?"

"Um . . ." Judith wished her brain worked faster, but it seemed as tired as the rest of her body. "He arrived Tuesday about six and left Wednesday afternoon."

"Was that according to plan?"

"I don't know what you mean."

"Their reservation at your B&B," Purvis said, still impassive and composed. "I assume it wasn't open-ended."

"That's true." Judith raised her head and managed to stare defiantly at the trooper. "Mr. Weevil insisted on jumping off our roof, despite warnings from my husband and me. He misjudged his landing, which is how he fractured his leg and his arm. We had to call 911. The medics took Mr. Weevil to a hospital and he never returned to Hillside Manor. By the way, my husband is a retired police detective. If you doubt my word, I'll give you Joe's phone number. Surely you wouldn't consider that a fellow law officer might lie."

"That depends on the situation," Purvis replied. "Even in domestic disputes, spouses often take sides against the officers who show up at the scene of what has obviously been a no-holds-barred fight."

"I know. But," she added, "Mr. Weevil violated innkeeping rules for guests. He'd jumped out a window earlier, but landed safely."

Purvis nodded slightly. "I understand that first leap was the result of a wager your husband had made with Mr. Weevil. Mr. Flynn had, I'm told, more or less dared Mr. Weevil to jump."

Judith briefly closed her eyes. *I know where this is going,* she thought with a sick feeling. "Untrue," she asserted. "My husband made a glib remark that Mr. Weevil took seriously. Joe wasn't home when Willie made his first jump." Anger had replaced Judith's earlier fears. "Why are you asking these questions?"

Trooper Purvis looked uncomfortable. "Comments have been made by Ms. Gundy. She's expressed qualms about Mr. Weevil's death."

Judith barely heard Purvis's last few words. "Who?"

"Dorothy May Gundy, Mr. Weevil's companion."

"Do you mean Pepper?"

Purvis did his best to maintain his aplomb. "Who's Pepper?"

"The redhead that I assumed was Willie's wife."

"I don't think so," Purvis said. "Her given name is Dorothy—"

"Please," Judith broke in, "what's this person saying about me?"

Purvis cleared his throat. "She insists you got on this train to finish what began at your B&B. Ms. Gundy accuses you of murdering Wee Willie Weevil."

Chapter Eight

Good God!" Judith cried, staggering to her feet. "Is Pepper crazy?"

Purvis looked faintly puzzled. "You mean Ms. Gundy?"

"You know who I mean," Judith retorted, looking up at the trooper, who had a four-inch height advantage. His regulation hat's high crown made him even more imposing. She visualized Joe in that kind of headgear, recalling that he'd once tried on Mike's forest ranger hat. Wearing jeans and with his slight paunch, Joe had looked like Smokey the Bear. Judith and Mike couldn't keep from laughing. The memory made Judith giggle.

And giggle some more. "Ma'am?" Purvis said in an uncertain voice.

Judith couldn't stop giggling. She had to lean against the trooper to keep her knees from buckling. "So . . . funny," she gasped. "Everything . . . funny!"

A sudden noise caused Judith and the trooper to stiffen. She couldn't see around Purvis's broad form, but realized that the compartment door had been slid open. She also recognized Renie's outraged voice.

"What the hell . . . ?" A pause followed. "Is this an interrogation or an assignation?" Renie demanded, almost drowning out Mr. Peterson's loud protests.

Judith stopped giggling. Purvis cautiously took two backward steps.

"Mrs. Flynn is somewhat hysterical," the trooper said in a strained voice.

Renie stood with fists on hips. "And would be because of . . ." She paused for an instant. "Police venality? Sexual harassment? Cop bafflement?"

Mr. Peterson had been poised to grab Renie, but froze. Jax's eyes were shut tight as she leaned against the wall. Matt and Laurie were clinging to each other. Emily was climbing onto the luggage rack. A cell phone rang nearby.

Purvis glanced at Judith. "We'll finish this conversation later." He reached inside his jacket, took out his cell, and stalked off into the corridor. As he went past the luggage rack, Emily's foot slipped, dislodging a big duffel bag. It fell against the trooper's legs. Emily fell on top of the bag, letting out a bloodcurdling scream. Jax's eyes flew open. Emily thrashed wildly in the bag's denim folds. Purvis scooped her up—and dropped his cell phone.

"Mama!" Emily screeched, kicking at Purvis. "Mama!"

The curly-haired woman ran out of the family room. "Put my baby down!"

Purvis loosened his grasp. Emily broke free, snatched the trooper's cell, and showed it to her mother. "Can I have thith?"

"No," her mother replied. "Give it to the policeman."

Emily stamped her foot. "No! Mine phone!"

Purvis joined mother and child. "I need that," he said, pointing to the cell Emily was holding behind her back. Getting down on his haunches, he offered a strained smile. "I have to catch some bad guys, so I need the phone . . . Emily."

"Wha' bab guy?" Emily asked.

"I don't know yet," Purvis explained quietly, "because you have my phone. I have to find out who the bad guy is."

Emily surveyed the other adults. "I thee a bab lady," she said—and pointed at Renie. "Pub her i' da jail."

Everyone stared at Renie, who looked like she wanted to

throttle the kid. Emily took advantage of the lull, broke away from her mother, and skittered back to the family room. At the open door, she turned for a last look at the grown-ups. "I gots a phone, 'n camerth, 'n bibeo gamth, 'n a iPab." She stuck out her tongue. "Pl-uff-hpt!" Emily went inside and closed the door behind her.

"Darn," her mother said. "Now she'll wake the twins."

"Oh, God!" Renie cried softly. "There are two more like Emily?"

"They're babies," Jax said.

Renie snorted. "Not for long. I bet Emily used to be a baby, too."

Judith watched the exchange between Purvis and Emily's mother. They were both speaking in low voices, but enough of the conversation could be heard to indicate that the trooper wanted his cell phone ASAP.

"What's Mom's name?" Judith asked, sidling over to her cousin and Jax.

"Courtney Mueller," Jax replied. "She's traveling with her children to visit relatives in North Dakota. Her husband's in the Middle East."

"Sounds safer than around here," Renie said, turning to Judith. "What's with the trooper?"

Judith shook her head. "I'll explain later. He's going into the family room." She turned to Jax. "Where's the so-called Ms. Gundy?"

Jax pointed to the handicapped room. "She's still there, with the . . . body. So is Mr. Fielding." She winced. "Gruesome."

Mr. Peterson, who had been speaking quietly to Matt and Laurie, broke off the exchange as a red-faced Purvis strode out of the family room. "Does anyone have a spare cell?" he asked. "Emily hid mine and won't say where."

Nobody responded. Purvis sighed heavily. "Then I'll have to wait until her mother can coax her into telling where she ditched it."

Mr. Peterson took out his own cell. "You can borrow mine."

"Thanks," the trooper said.

The conductor handed the phone to Purvis. "Meanwhile, can Dr. and Mrs. Chan return to their roomette?"

Purvis, whose leathery face was growing less flushed, scrutinized the pair. "Yes. But," he went on, "don't go anywhere. I need formal statements."

Matt looked resentful; Laurie still seemed on edge. Judith smiled at the couple as they started up the stairwell, but neither Chan noticed.

Renie addressed Purvis, who seemed to be having trouble using Mr. Peterson's cell phone. "Are you finished grilling Mrs. Flynn?"

"For now," Purvis mumbled. "I have to contact my superiors."

"Good luck with that," Renie said, watching the trooper fumble with the device. "Try smoke signals. We're not far from Little Big Horn. Blow a big *C* for Custer and wait to find out who blows back." She grabbed Judith's arm and headed for the stairs.

Inside their roomette, Judith collapsed into her chair. "The so-called interview with Purvis was so incredible that I can hardly talk about it."

Also sitting down, Renie waited for her cousin to continue, but Judith was staring into space. "Say something," Renie demanded, "or I'll have to hurt you."

To her own surprise, Judith laughed. "I realized I suddenly feel better—emotionally, I mean. It's as if I knew this was coming, lurking like some kind of stalker. Now it's out in the open, so I can deal with it."

Renie leaned her head back and stared at the ceiling. "Gosh. It'd be helpful if you'd tell me what lurked. And stalked. Or is it a secret?"

"Of course not," Judith said. "Apparently the woman we know as Pepper has accused me of killing Willie."

"That's absurd," Renie declared. Why 'the woman we know'? Fill me in so that when the butterfly net guys come, I can explain why you're nuts."

Judith related her interview with Purvis. "That's as far as we got when you barged in. I assume his phone call was from a superior."

"Probably wanting to know if Purvis was on the right track." Renie let out a weary sigh. "We're on the tracks, but going nowhere."

"True," Judith agreed. "The question is why Pepper would accuse me of trying to kill Willie. Does she—or Matt Chan—think Willie's death is suspicious? Something unusual must've occurred just before or just after Willie died. Why else would Mr. Peterson have asked Laurie Chan to come downstairs? She was with Matt when Willie expired. She has no medical expertise. Maybe it had to do with what Laurie saw or heard."

"Publicity," Renie said. "When a celebrity dies, sales memorabilia skyrocket. It's as if the public wants a piece of The Deceased. Pepper must be very angry at Willie for dying in a place where there's no big media coverage."

Judith considered Renie's words. "You mean she's frustrated because he died in a remote area, so she's resorting to foul play for publicity?"

"Very likely," Renie said. "That angle prolongs the sad saga until she can get besieged by eager reporters. Her best bet is probably the Twin Cities, but I wouldn't count out Fargo. Except," she added after a pause, "I think we go through there in the wee small hours."

"Why me?" Judith demanded. "Why not somebody more . . . colorful?"

"Well . . ." Renie seemed perplexed. "The only reason I can think of is that . . . you're here."

"How did Pepper know that? She hasn't seen me on board."

"She probably saw your luggage on the rack downstairs. The tag has your name, address, and phone number."

"True." Judith thought for a moment. "That's just plain bad luck."

"I agree." Renie rubbed her eyes. "Damn. Something set

off my allergies. I'll bet Emily wears peanut butter under her clothes."

Judith was familiar with her cousin's lethal reaction to peanuts. "I've got tissues." She delved into her tan slacks' pocket, but Renie shook her head.

"I've got my own." She took out a travel packet of Kleenex. "Remind me to make a sign I can wear saying 'Off-Limits to Emily.' The kid's . . ." She paused, noticing that Judith was staring into the palm of her hand. "What now?"

"It's a ring one of my guests found in room two. I forgot it was there."

Renie downed the pill with a swig of Pepsi. "Any idea who lost it?"

"No," Judith replied. "I went back through the guest register as far as October first, but couldn't find a match for the engraved initials. The ring was under a rug that may not have been moved recently. That was . . . Friday? I've lost track of time in all the confusion, but I was wearing these slacks."

Renie took the ring from Judith and studied it closely. "Engraved with *RK* and *JG,* 1990. Anything odd about the guest who found it?"

Judith shook her head. "Her name is Libby Pruitt, a Northwestern University professor on sabbatical."

"Very suspicious," Renie murmured. "You can't imagine how many peculiar colleagues Bill ran into at the U." She rubbed her eyes again and suddenly let out a little shriek. "I forgot to ask Bill what Oscar's going to do without him. Maybe he can leave the TV on so that—"

"No!" Judith cried. "Talk about loony professors! And their wives. Don't say another word about Oscar."

Renie looked miffed. "You're a poor sport sometimes. I should've brought Clarence along instead of you. Oscar doesn't like to travel. We've had some awkward experiences with him in the past."

"Yes, yes, I know all about that," Judith said impatiently.

"It's a good thing Mom was willing to have Clarence stay with her," Renie went on. "They enjoy each other. She can talk his lop ears off. Of course he can't roam free at her apartment, but she does let him out so they can cuddle."

"Double gack," Judith said. "I hope Aunt Deb puts pants on him when he sits on her lap. Bunnies have poor hygiene."

"Mom has a special towel for him to shi . . . to sit on. It's green, his favorite color. Like lettuce."

"I don't want to think about it," Judith declared. "You aren't really going to call Bill, are you? He hates the phone."

"Well . . ." Renie's ruminations were interrupted by Jim and Sharon Downey, who were standing in the open doorway.

"Do you know what's going on?" Jim asked. "We came back from the dome car and overheard some people talking about a man who died. Was it the truck driver who raced the train?"

Judith half rose from her chair. "Hi. Sorry we can't offer you a seat."

Sharon laughed as the couple stepped inside. "Hosting get-togethers in the sleeper is awkward. We've been sitting for a long time anyway."

"The dead man is Wee Willie Weevil," Judith answered without any show of emotion. "He came straight from the hospital after a bad fall."

"Oh," Jim said. "The daredevil. That's too bad. He couldn't have been any spring chicken."

Sharon's face grew somber. "Poor guy. It must be extra hard for his family to cope with the logistics in this situation."

"You're so practical," Jim said with a teasing glance at his wife. "If it'd been me, you'd have made sure I stayed alive until we got home."

Judith was about to speak when Jax appeared in the corridor behind the Downeys. "Excuse me," she said, still looking upset. "I'm double-checking dinner reservations. You're all six-thirty, right?"

The cousins and the Downeys confirmed their sittings.

Jax smiled faintly, but before she could move on, Sharon asked a question. "We've been sitting here for over an hour. Are we still waiting for the new engine?"

"Um . . . yes," Jax said, avoiding eye contact. "The body has to be removed, but there are complications. And the snow is causing delays."

"Why?" Renie asked. "Can't they keep Willie on ice?"

Only Jim showed any sign of amusement. Jax looked appalled; Sharon appeared embarrassed. But Judith was resigned to her cousin's insensitivity. "I understand," she said, "that someone has suggested foul play. I assume that's why the trooper is aboard."

Jax stared at Judith. "I thought he was trying to find out about Roy."

Judith had already considered a possible connection between Roy's disappearance and Pepper's accusations. "Maybe."

"I hope so," Jax said softly. She squared her slim shoulders. "I have to check with my other passengers."

As Jax went out of sight, Sharon put a hand on Jim's arm. "Let's go, Jimbo. Maybe I can take a quick nap before dinner." She waved at the cousins. "See you in the dining car. Is it bridge or pinochle tonight?"

"Your call," Judith said.

"How about a game of Clue?" Renie muttered after the Downeys left. "With real weapons and real bodies."

Judith shot her cousin a sour look. "Has it occurred to you that the only person accused of foul play in Willie's death is me?"

"Maybe you can solve this case by announcing you did it, and then you can arrest yourself."

"Get serious. What do we know about Willie?"

"Hmm." Renie fingered her chin. "He's dead?"

"Stop acting like a twit. I mean his life and times. Mike and Justin talked about Willie quite a bit—at least when they were younger."

Renie shrugged. "So? I don't recall hearing them. Why would I?"

"Justin's been at our house for several holiday and birthday dinners," Judith said. "He's candid and a good conversationalist. Sometimes he'd talk about his family, including his famous uncle."

"Infamous," Renie murmured. "I only remember some of the anecdotes about Willie's zany stunts or how he treated other people like dirt. Justin and his mother couldn't stand to be around him."

Judith waited for Renie to continue. "Well?" she prodded.

"Coz," Renie said with an exasperated expression, "it's been ages since I heard any mention of Willie. Mike and Justin met twenty-odd years ago. They outgrew any hero worship long before they reached the legal drinking age."

"Justin never worshipped Willie," Judith said. "Oh, he saw some of his uncle's movies and TV shows, but being a nephew, he knew the real person, not the celebrity image. Mike was still a fan, though. Looking back, I realize that Justin's negative attitude only added to Mike's interest in Willie. He could enjoy the Willie he saw on the screen while feeling like an insider because he knew what the guy was like in real life."

"That's understandable," Renie conceded. "I know Justin's parents divorced when he was a baby, but what became of his dad?"

"Willie's brother?" Judith tried to recall what she knew about Justin's father. "He was younger than Willie. His first name was . . . oh, damn, I can't think of it at the moment. Justin never talks about him. I don't think they had any real relationship. The dominant male figure in his life was his maternal grandfather."

"I met his mother once," Renie said. "Germaine may be from Butte, but when it comes to fashion and looks, she's strictly Avenue Montaigne, Paris. I felt all homely and small and dumpy."

Judith laughed. "I was there. I figured I'd gone wrong at birth."

The cousins turned as the Chans came to their door. "Ah," Matt said. "You're laughing. I take it the trooper isn't going to arrest you?"

"Not yet," Judith replied. "Do you know what that was all about?"

Laurie still seemed nervous. Matt looked pained. "Kind of," he said. "Is it okay if we come inside and close the door?"

"Sure," Judith said. "Do you want to sit down? We can stand for a bit. The train's not moving."

"We heard we're stuck here for a while," Matt said, refusing Judith's offer to sit in her chair. "Between the snow, the dead body, and Roy's disappearance, we're stuck until more cops, including the railroad detectives, show up."

Renie groaned. "Great." Having given up her seat to Laurie, she leaned against the wall by the door. "We'd better not miss the Chicago connection. It's a five-hour wait for the train that goes to the East Coast, but this debacle could eat up more time than that."

Judith's concern, however, was more immediate. "Why," she inquired of Laurie, "did Mr. Peterson ask you to come downstairs after Mr. Weevil died?"

Laurie flushed. "It was silly." She glanced at Matt. "You tell her."

He shook his head. "I don't think I should. It may not be ethical."

Laurie's dark eyes flashed. "Oh, for . . . ! It wasn't the patient who said it. It was that Pepper woman."

Matt held his ground. "Keep me out of this. I smell trouble."

"Don't be such a stickler," Laurie admonished. "If you won't say anything, I will. Somebody has to speak up because it sounds so preposterous." She glanced at Judith. "You have no idea how it feels to repeat this in front of you."

"I wondered if that might not be the case," Judith said quietly.

"Go for it," Renie urged. "Coz here has heard it all."

Laurie folded her hands in her lap as if she were going to recite in school. "When I went to see if I could help Matt, Pepper—the woman I thought was his wife—was there and so was a man about my age named Wayne. Pepper was upset, but coherent. I never spoke to her—she and Wayne were huddled together. Pepper said something about 'that old fool' and nodded at Willie, who was writhing in pain. His speech was garbled—something about 'it shoulda been him. Talk about a fall . . .'" She looked at her husband. "Was the next word 'guard'?"

Matt shrugged. "I didn't catch it. He'd mumbled before Laurie came downstairs. The only word I understood was 'ring.' He repeated it several times."

"Interesting," Judith murmured. "So he was in considerable pain?"

Laurie deferred to her husband, but Matt hesitated. "He was agitated. It was tricky to take his vitals. I assume he was hurting, because his efforts to move were hampered by the casts on the fractured leg and arm. I was reluctant to give him a sedative. Pepper thought he'd taken some diazepam. I asked for a list of his meds, but she couldn't find them."

"Conveniently misplaced?" Judith suggested.

Matt grimaced. "I don't know. She finally did show them to me, but that was a few minutes later and poor Willie was literally at death's door. I tried to revive him, but . . ." He shook his head. "That's when doctors feel helpless."

"Hey," Renie said, "if patients get sick, there's a good chance some will die. You can't beat yourself up over that. In this case, you didn't know the guy."

"I felt like I did," Matt said. "He was one of my heroes."

"Even heroes die," Renie said.

"I know. That's why watching Willie hit me so hard. I remember the younger Willie, all buff and bravado. This was like seeing a stranger."

"A shell of a man," Judith murmured. "How did Pepper react?"

"She cried," Laurie said. "That Fielding guy seemed upset, too, though he tried to comfort her."

"This all sounds very natural," Judith said, puzzled. She turned to Laurie. "Why were you asked to come down after Willie died?"

Laurie looked at her husband. "There was some confusion. The conductor or maybe the attendant—Jax?" She saw her husband's helpless shrug and continued. "Anyway, one of them thought I was a nurse because Matt had mentioned I worked with him. Whoever it was didn't realize I managed the business side of his practice."

Matt put an arm around Laurie. "Mrs. Johnston—the woman in the bedroom at the end of our sleeper—is a nurse. She'd offered to help, though there wasn't much she—or I— could do." He grimaced. "I'm no prude, but I could smell liquor on her breath and all I could think of was if Willie died and I'd had an inebriated nurse assisting me, a malpractice suit could be in my future."

Laurie nodded. "It's a good thing I'm not a nurse. I smelled like vodka."

"So you stayed on," Judith said.

"I was about to leave," Laurie responded bleakly, "but I felt awkward, just walking away. Pepper was pulling herself together. Then she got angry, yelling at Wayne. She told him they should never have left Montana, that somebody-or-other shouldn't or wouldn't see Willie, and the trip was a mistake. Wayne insisted it wasn't his idea, it was Willie's. Pepper started crying again and blamed . . ." Laurie paused, looking apologetic. "She mentioned someone's mother."

"Somebody named Mike?" Judith said helpfully.

Looking relieved, Laurie nodded. "His name meant nothing until Pepper started talking about the B&B where Willie had his accident. She said Mike and Willie's nephew were close friends. It was a conspiracy between Mike's mother, who owned the B&B, and Willie's relatives to benefit monetarily from Willie's death. What was most upsetting to Pepper was that—I quote—'the Flynn woman' had the nerve to travel on the same train to make sure Willie didn't survive."

Renie grinned at Judith. " 'The Flynn woman.' I like that. It makes you sound glamorous and notorious, like the Dragon Lady."

"Knock it off," Judith warned. "So I engineered the plot to kill Willie?"

Laurie lowered her gaze. "That's what she said."

"It's ridiculous," Judith declared. "Okay—what happened next?"

"Nothing," Laurie replied. "Mr. Peterson and Jax left to give Pepper and Mr. Fielding some privacy. I felt useless, so I came upstairs." She looked at Matt. "You tell the rest of it."

"I tried to calm Pepper," Matt said. "Fielding had given up. I asked her if she needed a sedative. She said no and calmed down almost immediately." He gave Judith a bleak look. "I thought it might help to ask some low-key questions about Willie's accident. Her response was a little disjointed, but she claimed that Mrs. Flynn had coaxed Willie into doing one of his stunts. It would be good for the B&B's publicity to show him staying at her inn."

"Oh, good grief!" Judith said softly. "That's absurd! The last thing any innkeeper would want or even permit is to endanger a guest."

"Yes," Renie agreed with a straight face. "It'd be unthinkable for a mishap to occur at or even near my cousin's establishment."

Judith refused to look at Renie for fear of succumbing to an urge that would qualify as a very serious mishap. "An understatement," she said calmly. "Mrs. Jones is such a source of comfort."

"You're lucky," Matt said, and made a helpless gesture. "That's all we can tell you. Mr. Peterson returned to tell us that the authorities had been summoned."

"Authorities?" Judith echoed. "Such as train officials and police?"

"I don't know," Matt admitted.

There was nothing more Judith could say. The accusations were bizarre. Matt shifted his stance. Laurie looked embarrassed. Renie wore an expression that Judith recognized as *Okay, coz, what now?*

Judith was thinking the same thing. Finally she spoke. "There's a method to this madness. I have to ask," she went on, addressing Matt, "if there was anything suspicious about Willie's death. I assume there'll be an autopsy."

Matt nodded. "Probably."

"Pepper knows that," Judith said softly. "Do you know her real name?"

"No," Matt replied. "I heard someone call her Ms. Gundy."

"I did, too," Judith murmured, trying to remember how Willie had signed in at Hillside Manor. His handwriting was cramped, but it matched his credit card signature. "I think he wrote 'Willie Weevil and Pepper' in the guest register. I thought she was his wife or girlfriend. Adding her name as an afterthought didn't seem so odd. I figured it was ego. It's happened before with a couple of allegedly famous guests."

Renie looked surprised. "It has?"

Judith shrugged. "I'd never heard of them. One was an aging rock star, still full of himself." She turned back to Matt. "Whoever she is, she'll have to sign the death certificate, right?"

"I assume so," Matt replied.

"What," Judith inquired, "are you stating as cause of death?"

Matt looked uneasy. "I'm not sure."

Judith stared at him. "You mean it could be foul play?"

His whole body stiffened. "Yes."

"Gosh," Renie said drily, "what a shock."

Chapter Nine

Why," Judith asked, "do you think Willie's death is suspicious?"

Looking lost in thought, Matt stared at the window, where the snow was still falling. "I'm not sure," he finally said. "Maybe it was Pepper's allegations. Or that a broken leg and a broken arm aren't usually fatal. There had to be complications, but without Willie's medical history, I'm helpless. The autopsy should show what killed him."

Judith nodded slightly. "He did jump from my B&B. Twice."

Laurie looked flabbergasted. "So part of Pepper's claim is true?"

"Yes. That's what makes the situation awkward. My son, Mike, and Willie's nephew, Justin, have been good friends since they were kids. Willie had made himself persona non grata at our city's major hotels. Justin asked if his uncle could stay for a few days. I couldn't refuse. Mike had been a Willie fan, and he wanted his two little boys to meet him. That never happened because Willie got hurt in his second jump, the one off our roof. There was no way to stop him. I tried to dissuade him from the first jump, but luckily, he made a safe landing. The second time, my husband and I both warned him not to jump. He wouldn't listen. The other man you saw with Willie and Pepper was Wayne Fielding, who was urging him on and taking pictures. He's Willie's publicity guy."

Laurie seemed to have regained her aplomb. "Where was Pepper?"

"She was in the house when he made both jumps. I didn't see her after the accident until I went inside."

Laurie glanced at her husband. "Owning a B&B must be fun. I mean, when you don't have guests like Willie."

Judith smiled. "It is. I'm a people person. I've met so many interesting types from all over the world. Watching them interact during the social hour is enjoyable. Educational, too. I often hate to see them leave."

"Especially in a body bag," Renie said under her breath.

Apparently, the Chans didn't catch the remark. "Of course," Judith went on rapidly, "we get a lot of return visitors."

"Returned from the dead," Renie murmured.

Laurie frowned. "What did you say?" she asked, staring at Renie.

Judith responded before her cousin could open her mouth. "They return for the bed. Guests often praise our mattresses. They're top of the line," she went on, talking faster to prevent Renie from making any more caustic remarks. "It's a bed-and-breakfast. I serve heartier breakfasts than most B&Bs offer. And there's nothing like a good night's sleep to make for a perfect day."

Laurie stood up. "Sleep sounds good. Come on, Matt. I need a nap." She waved halfheartedly. "See you later."

"What suddenly turned Laurie off?" Renie said after the Chans had departed. "Or turned her on? Maybe Dr. Chan's first name isn't Matthew, but Mattress."

Judith shook her head. "Maybe she *is* worn out. 'Delicate' could describe more than her looks."

"Maybe." Renie turned toward the open door. "Shall I close that?"

"Oh—no," Judith said. "Don't bother."

"You think you'll miss something?"

The comment irked Judith. "Miss what? It's quiet out there—" She was interrupted by loud voices just out of sight in the corridor. The cousins leaned sideways to listen.

"Don't remind me," a woman's strident voice said. "I'm not stupid."

"No," a man responded angrily, "but you can be damned careless. After all we've been through, do you want to ruin—" He stopped abruptly. The corridor was eerily quiet.

The cousins straightened up, opening their books as the Cowboy Hats walked quickly past the open door.

"Heading for the bar?" Judith said after a long pause.

"Or the dining car. It's going on six." Renie looked out the window. "Still snowing, still sitting. When do we move on?"

"Don't ask me," Judith said. "I see only occasional head-lights on the main street. They don't seem to have rush hour in Scuttle. If Malta's the county seat and has a hospital, maybe Willie's body has been taken there for the autopsy."

Renie scowled at her cousin. "You mean we have to sit here until they find out why he died? That's crazy."

"You know we won't." Judith stood up. "Let's go to the dome car for a preprandial cocktail. I can walk normally when the train isn't moving, though you're right about the sea-leg sensation."

Renie, who realized she'd opened her book upside down, closed the volume. "You'll get over it." She set the book aside and regarded her cousin with a puckish expression. "What comes first on your wish list? Seeing if the Cowboy Hats are in the dome car? Being able to see both sides of the tracks? Or just a stiff shot of Scotch?"

Judith was already on her feet. "All of the above."

"At least you're honest," Renie said, slipping off her chair.

Passing along the corridor, Judith noticed that the doors were closed to the Downeys' and the Chans' roomettes. In the next sleeper a couple of teenagers were by the open space near the door, moving silently to the beat coming from their iPods. The dining car was almost full. Judith scanned the passengers, recognizing only the foreign men who'd sat at their table the previous evening. Despite the delay, everyone seemed in an affable mood.

The dome car was jammed. Apparently the cousins' fellow travelers had the same reaction as Judith and Renie. If the scenery wasn't changing, they'd alter their view by moving to a different part of the train. Judging from the noise level, being near the bar was an added attraction. Several passengers had gone from pleasant to raucous.

"Everybody's bored," Renie said, craning her neck to see if she could spot an empty seat. "I hope they don't run out of booze. Wait here while I see if there's any liquor left. If somebody gets up, sit. I can lean."

Before Judith could protest, Renie moved quickly to the stairwell that led to the club car. Judith strolled down the aisle, searching for a man, woman, or child who might be about to leave. Just past the stairway she saw a plump middle-aged woman with upswept peroxide blond hair trying to shush an equally plump, middle-aged bald man as he belted out an off-key rendition of "City of New Orleans": "'Good mornin', America . . . How are ya? Doncha know I'm your native son . . .'" He hiccuped and began to cough.

"That's it, Rowley," the woman hollered, standing up and tugging at one of his rolled-up shirtsleeves. "It's not morning, it's supper time, and we're going to eat that nice fried chicken I packed. Move it!"

Rowley coughed again, but didn't get up. "G'way, Irma," he muttered. "I'm almost to the best part." He began to sing again. "'I'm the train they call the City of—'"

Irma picked up her knitting bag and smacked it against Rowley's bald head. "Get up, you old fart!"

Rowley stopped singing, but was unfazed. Some of the nearby passengers, however, looked faintly alarmed. Irma wound up for another whack at Rowley, but before she could follow through, Judith tapped her shoulder. "Can I help?"

Irma glared at Judith. "If you're a lawyer, you can get me a divorce."

Judith smiled. "I can't do that, but maybe I can get your husband to give up his seat. I may not look it, but I'm handicapped and my . . . nurse is bringing me something to drink."

"It better not be what this bozo's tossing down," Irma said, shrewd blue eyes scrutinizing Judith. "You're really a cripple?"

"I've had a hip replacement," Judith said quietly.

Rowley attempted a leer. "Want to show me your scar?"

"Don't talk like that," Irma barked. "Shut up and get up!" With her bright golden hair curled up into little peaks atop her head, she reminded Judith of a cockatoo. "My sis got one of them artificial things a while back. She's doing all right, but she didn't walk so good in the first place with those bowlegs of hers. Couldn't catch a pig in an alley."

"Never wanted to see *her* scar," Rowley mumbled, his head having sunk onto his chest. "Homelier than a gopher, whiskers and all."

"Never you mind about my sis!" Irma yelled. "Move your butt!"

"Huh?" He squeezed his eyes together and wiggled his nose several times. "A gimp?" Rowley said, focusing on Judith. "She looks pretty good to me." His lopsided grin revealed a couple of missing teeth.

"Just get up," Irma ordered. "C'mon, Rowley. You need to walk. You want them blood clots coming back?" Slinging her patent leather purse over one shoulder and a knitting bag over the other, she reached out to help pull her husband from the chair.

Rowley heaved a big sigh before grasping Irma's hands. "I already walked today," he muttered. "All the way to that creek. They got some peculiar notions about fishing around here. One of them fellas couldn't stand up on his own two feet, let alone cast a line."

"A damned-fool stunt on your part," Irma said as Rowley grunted a couple of times before he finally stood up. "That was hours ago. You're lucky the train didn't leave you stranded."

"Pshaw!" Rowley sputtered, narrowly missing Judith with a spray of saliva. "We wasn't going anywhere with all that mess on the tracks." He leaned on Irma, but didn't move. "We ain't going anywhere now," he said, peering out the window. "Where the heck are we?"

"We're still in this one-horse town, waiting for that engine."

Rowley frowned. "What Injun? Is this where Custer had his last stand?"

Irma shook her head and turned to Judith, who was making sure Rowley wasn't leaving any undesirable evidence of his occupancy on the seat. "Thanks, hon," Irma said. "Pay no mind to him. He's been seeing things even before he started swigging down that damnable liquor." She punched her husband's upper arm. "Let's go. Walk!"

As the couple moved awkwardly toward the coach car, Judith sat down and placed her handbag on Irma's vacant chair. Only a couple of minutes passed before Renie appeared with their drinks.

"You did it," she said with a big grin. "Nice work, coz. Did you have to arm-wrestle somebody for these chairs?"

"I didn't, but the wife of the husband who was blotto practically had to put him in a headlock to get him back to their coach seats." Judith accepted the already poured Scotch from Renie and laughed softly. "Irma—the wife—had made fried chicken to eat on board. What does that remind you of?"

Renie laughed. "Our family picnics with Grandma and Grandpa Grover. We never went anywhere without our own food because we couldn't afford restaurants. Grandpa insisted on eating in cemeteries because he hated hot weather and wanted to sit on the cold tombstones. There was always running water nearby and big shade trees."

Judith nodded. "He insisted graveyards were much quieter than picnic areas. It was easier for Grandma to set everything on the flat stone markers. We always had fried chicken, unless we were on the road long enough to eat two meals. Then it was sandwiches and whatever fruit Grandma and Grandpa had in season from their trees in the backyard." She paused, thinking of how much fun the family had managed to have, even on the cheap. "The only surviving tree in the backyard is the cherry. After our grandparents and my father died, Mother couldn't take care of the others on her own."

"I know." Renie's smile was bittersweet. "Apple, pear, peach, apricot, plum—and cherry. There was an exotic one, too. What was it?"

"Figs," Judith replied promptly. "Don't you remember how Mr. Tweedy would steal them when he lived on the other side of the back fence? Grandpa almost killed him."

"Mr. Tweedy could run faster," Renie said after taking a sip of Canadian whiskey. "So? Aren't you going to ask the inevitable?"

"That walk down memory lane distracted me." Judith cocked her head at Renie. "Well?"

"Not much to report. The Cowboy Hats were there. So were those two young women we saw in the dining car. They came down just as I was coming back up. I don't think they recognized me."

"That's it?"

"What did you expect?" Renie retorted. "A police lineup?"

Judith shook her head. "Hardly. But I figured the state trooper would ask me more questions. I wonder what happened after he talked to his superiors."

"Maybe he tried to find you, but we weren't in our room. Gosh, he might show up here and arrest you in front of all these respectable people."

"Not funny." Judith noticed that the snow was letting up. "We can finally see something outside."

"Such as?" Renie asked, looking outside. "There's nothing to see."

Judith pointed at the tavern. "A couple just came out."

"Wow. Shall I take notes?"

Judith ignored the remark. "The woman is going in one direction and the man in the other. What's the shortest way around the train?"

"Is this a math puzzle? You know I never got beyond long division. In fact, I never *got* long division."

"To cross the tracks," Judith said, exasperated.

Renie assumed a thoughtful look. "I like riddles. Why did the drunkards cross the tracks?"

"Would you please stop—"

Renie held up a hand. "Wait. I've got it. To get to the other side." She feigned a triumphant expression, but sobered quickly. "I see your point. As I recall, we're toward the front of the train. Two engines, but the damaged one probably has been detached. Then maybe some kind of support car, baggage car, crew car, two sleepers, dining car, dome car, maybe three or four coach cars, and one at the end that's used as a view and snack car for coach passengers. The residents of Scuttle would probably have to walk at least a city block to get across the tracks. Dare I ask why you want to know?"

"Can we can get off the train instead of sitting here like lumps?"

Renie looked taken aback. "With snow on the ground? Maybe ice? Why would you do that?"

"I want to find out if Joe and Bill are set for tomorrow's flight. I'd also like to make sure everything's okay at home, including Mother. Will you call Bill?"

"Are you insane? Bill's worse than Aunt Gert about phone calls."

"True," Judith allowed. "Maybe they won't let us off." She checked her watch. "It's after six. We don't have much time before dinner."

"If you must phone Joe, go between the cars and ask somebody to open a door so you can at least stick your head outside."

"That's a good idea," Judith said. "Where's the best place to do it?"

Renie motioned toward the diner. "Somebody there can open it."

Judith handed Renie her drink, took out her cell, and set

her handbag on the seat. Between the cars, she peered into the diner. Earl was serving desserts at the nearest table. When he finished, Judith opened the door and called his name. "You may not recognize me," she began, "but at lunch you—"

Earl smiled. "The tomato lady. Did you miss your dinner call?"

"Ours is six-thirty," Judith replied. "Could you open the door between these cars? I want to call my husband to ask about my elderly mother. I assume we're not allowed to get off the train, is that right?"

Earl made a face. "Yes, but that's not stopping some folks. We may be moving on in the next half hour or so. If they aren't back by then, they've got a long wait for the next Empire Builder."

Earl led the way. It took only a moment for him to open the outer door. "Thanks," Judith said. "I appreciate your extra effort."

"No trouble. I'll set the step outside, but don't stray, Mrs. . . ."

"Flynn," Judith said.

"Got it, Mrs. Flynn." He was putting the step down when the Cowboy Hats entered from the dome car. They glanced at Judith before speaking to Earl.

"Are we too early for the six-thirty dinner?" the man asked.

The waiter turned around. "Five minutes," he said cordially. "One couple didn't want dessert. You can wait here until the table is cleared."

"Thanks," the woman said, with another glance at Judith. "Aren't you in the same sleeper we are?"

Judith remembered that their name was Johnston. "Yes. My cousin and I are on the other side of the Kloppenburgs."

Mrs. Johnston seemed amused. "Is that their name? We haven't seen or heard anything out of that roomette. I thought it was empty."

"They keep to themselves," Judith said. "They must have food sent in." She turned to Earl, who was starting back into the dining car. "Do you know anything about the Kloppen-burgs next to our compartment?"

Earl frowned. "Kloppenburgs? Oh—Conrad and Lily in A10. Easier to remember their first names. Yes, they've had meals delivered. Some folks like to stay put."

Jack Johnson pointed at the door. "Smoke break?"

"Not officially," Earl replied. "But don't wander off." The waiter continued on his way.

Jack took his wife's hand. "Come on, Rosie. Let's go."

Rosie hung back. "It's still snowing. I can wait."

Jack shrugged. "Okay. You can get us seated." He doffed his ten-gallon hat to Judith, smoothed his sideburns, put the hat back on, and stepped onto the ground.

Earl returned to the diner. Judith cautiously descended onto the step. The cell informed her that she'd missed a call from Mike. Maternal panic set in. Her fingers were stiffen-ing from the below-freezing temperature, so it took her four tries to retrieve the message. "Ma," Mike's recorded voice said, "you may not get this right away, but Pa said none of my Willie stuff is at your house. Did you put it somewhere he wouldn't check? No rush, but the boys are sulking."

The call had come through at 3:25 P.M. Judith didn't know if that was Pacific or mountain time. She wondered how thoroughly Joe had looked for the missing items. It was a big house, and she knew that with Joe, as with most men, if something wasn't tweaking his nose, he wouldn't find it.

Shivering from the cold, she had trouble calling Mike back. She misdialed twice, wiped snowflakes off her cheeks, and noticed that Mr. Cowboy Hat—or Jack Johnston—was strolling around while he smoked and seemed to have his gaze fixed on the motel across the street.

After finally punching in the right number, she got voice mail. Heaving a sigh, Judith suggested that if Kristin was coming into town soon, she could stop by and look for the lost items. If anyone could find them—or the Rhinemaid-ens' lost gold—it'd be Brunhild McMonigle.

Judith hesitated before calling Joe. Maybe she'd try his

cell. It was almost five-thirty at home, guest check-in time and social hour preparations. She didn't want to bother Arlene. She entered Joe's number. He answered on the third ring.

"Just touching base," Judith said. "We're stuck in Montana."

"What?" he asked. "You're breaking up."

She spoke louder. "We're stuck in Montana. The train was hit by a truck."

"Stuck? Truck? You're stuck in a truck?"

Joe's voice was coming through loud and clear. Frustrated, Judith shouted. "The truck struck the train." She winced. "Never mind. How are you?"

"Fine," Joe said, though Judith wasn't sure if he'd actually heard her. "Hey," he went on, "I'm pulling into the driveway. You okay?"

"Yes. And Mother?"

"A murder? Oh God, please don't tell—"

"No! No! *Mother.* How is she?"

"Fine," Joe said repeated. "Bill and I are all set for take-off. By the way, Justin phoned you this morning. When you get a better signal, call him, okay?"

Judith wondered if Justin had heard about Willie's death. Then she realized that if he'd called in the morning, his uncle would've still been alive.

"I'll try," Judith said.

"Fine."

Judith's teeth were chattering. "D-d-do you have J-J-Justin's number?" she asked, realizing that she hadn't brought it with her.

"Jumper? Sorry. I can't hear you. Here comes Carl. He's taking some brownies Arlene baked to Gruesome Gertie. See you soon." Joe rang off.

Judith angrily snapped the phone shut. At least the snow had stopped. She'd started back inside when she realized Jack Johnston was nowhere in sight. The only sign of life in any direction was a man in a parka walking by the motel. *To hell with Mr. Hat,* she thought, and stepped into the train.

"Aha!" Renie exclaimed. "I was starting to worry. They called us for dinner. It's after six-thirty. I'm starving."

"Oh." Judith took her drink and handbag from Renie. "Thanks."

"What's wrong?" Renie opened the diner's door. "You look traumatized."

"I'm just cold," Judith insisted as Earl beckoned them to a table in the middle of the car.

"Did that work for you?" he asked as Judith and Renie sat down.

"The reception on my husband's end was poor," Judith replied, "but at least I got to talk to him."

Earl nodded. "You can't predict how the signals work, especially in bad weather. I'll be back after you've made your meal choices."

"Duck!" Renie exclaimed, looking at the list of entrées. "Yum!"

"Sounds good," Judith said, putting the menu aside.

Renie scowled at Judith. "You haven't looked at the menu. What now?"

"Mrs. Hat." Judith nodded discreetly across the aisle and down one table.

"She came in just ahead of me. Why do you care?"

"Mr. Hat—Mr. Johnston—is Jack," Judith whispered. "She's Rosie. He got off to smoke while I was outside. I never saw him get back on."

"So?" Renie said. "He's probably stretching his legs."

"Maybe," Judith said grudgingly, "but he kept staring at the motel."

Renie peered outside. "What else could he stare at? I don't see the Statue of Liberty or the *Mona Lisa*. Except for a couple of kids making a snowman—check that, a snow woman—by the motel, I don't see any riveting sights."

"Okay, okay," Judith said, with a discreet look at Rosie Johnston. "She doesn't seem worried."

"Nor am I," Renie said, suddenly wide-eyed as she stared out the window. "I think those kids are making a snow hooker. Double-D boobs and everything but a beaded bag."

Judith glanced outside. "Kids these days. But appropriate for a motel."

"This town's too small for hookers," Renie said. "I'll bet they're all amateurs. A pimp in Scuttle somehow doesn't seem . . . uh-oh," she said under her breath. "We may have dinner partners."

Judith leaned around Renie to see the newcomers and did a double take. "The Zs," she gasped, recognizing the mysterious thirtysomething couple who'd arrived unexpectedly at the B&B. "They're here, too!"

But the Zs were ushered to the table across from Rosie Johnston, who acknowledged the new arrivals with a brief greeting.

Renie was puzzled. "The Zs? Where are the Zuiders? Oh, I know—they're outside with Mr. Cowboy Hat. When traveling, the Zuiders Zee everything along the way, like that zeedy motel."

"Really," Judith said earnestly, "I may kill you before we get to Boston. You're acting like a ditzy sixth grader. What next? You turn into potty-mouth?"

"It's my defense mechanism," Renie replied. "It shifted into gear the moment you saw Wee Willie Weevil wheeling his way to the twain." She groaned and shook her head. "You see? I can't help it, no more than you can stop obsessing about homicides."

Judith's shoulders slumped. "You're right. Sorry."

The cousins were silent for a few moments, though Judith had to forcibly restrain herself from looking at Rosie and the Zs. Renie finally spoke. "Go ahead, tell me about the Zs before you implode."

"Did I tell you they stayed at the B&B?"

Renie shook her head. "Not that I recall. Nor have you told me what Joe said. Are the husbands ready to fly, fly away?"

"Yes. Joe came through fine, but he couldn't hear me very well."

"He's a husband. They never can. So what?"

"I mean there was a problem with—"

"Skip it. Here comes Earl." Renie grinned at the waiter. "Quack, quack." She pointed to Judith. "That means for both of us."

Earl smiled obligingly. "Shall I start you with salads?"

Judith spoke up before Renie could make another wacky response. "Yes, with blue cheese dressing." She hesitated, but couldn't refrain from inquiring about the Zs. "Do you know where the couple across from Mrs. Johnston got on?"

Earl eyed the pair discreetly. "They were here for lunch, but not for breakfast. That doesn't mean they couldn't have come aboard earlier. Some folks skip breakfast. I'd better see to my other passengers."

As Earl moved on, Renie seemed bemused. "I might find this more interesting if I knew how you know the Z-zeers."

"I tried to," Judith said, "but you interrupted asking about Joe and Bill."

"I know our husbands. I don't know the couple across the aisle."

"Fair enough," Judith allowed, still speaking quietly. "They checked in . . . Wednesday night? I've lost track of time. Too hectic. They didn't have a reservation." She paused to find a pen in her purse and spelled the name on a napkin: ZYZZYVA. "It's pronounced Zee-zee-vah."

Renie scowled at the name. "And?"

"They were vague about how they knew we had a sudden vacancy," Judith explained, slouching just enough so that Renie blocked the Zs' line of sight. "First names, Dick and Jane, paid cash, and were also vague about how long they'd be with us. The next morning they were gone."

"Wow." Renie pretended to yawn. "That really got me all atingle."

"Are you being dense on purpose?"

Renie waited until Earl brought their salads. "No," she finally said. "If you're thinking what I think you are, maybe we should think about it together."

Judith sipped the last of her Scotch. "Well, thank you very

much. I was beginning to believe that you hadn't packed your brain."

"Right." Renie ditched her sarcasm and put on her Boardroom Face. "Too many coincidences. Weevil and Company on the same train. Ditto the ditzy girls who came to your house and then insisted they'd seen you at Nordquist's. And now the Zs." She paused to glance at the couple, who were chatting with each other while Rosie Johnston stared out the window. "It doesn't seem as if the Zs know Mrs. Cowboy Hat. Oops," she went on, "I mean Mrs. Johnston. And here comes Mr. Johnston. Maybe he had two cigarettes."

"Does he seem to know the Zs?"

"No. He just nodded at them."

"So," Judith said, after eating a bite of salad, "what do you surmise?"

"I'm not sure," Renie replied. "There's one common denominator in all this." She gave her cousin a bleak look. "You."

"And Willie."

"You have no connection except his stay at the B&B because of Mike's friendship with Justin," Renie pointed out.

"That reminds me," Judith said. "Joe told me Justin tried to reach me this morning. It can't have anything to do with his uncle's death. Wayne, as Willie's publicist, may have given out a press release."

"Here's breaking news," Renie said. "Jim and Sharon are joining us again. Hi, guys. What's up?"

"We're bored," Jim said, sitting down across from Judith. "The view on this side of the train is the same as the one in our roomette."

"That's right," Judith said. "You're on the opposite side of the corridor from us. We have the tavern."

Sharon made a face at her husband. "The motel view isn't all that bad. Despite the snow and the early evening, there's enough activity to cause speculation about the vagaries of human nature."

Jim snorted. "If you enjoy watching adulterers and druggies. What else is there for small-town excitement? And how do you keep a secret? I don't see the point in parking your pickup on the side street, going in the back way, and coming out the front twenty minutes later."

"Spoilsport," Sharon murmured. "I thought it was funny when the one guy knocked on the door and it was opened by a naked man. He must've been cold standing there chatting."

"He's probably nuts. By the way," Jim went on, "is there any news about Roy, our missing attendant?"

Judith shook her head. "It's worrisome, isn't it?"

"It is," Sharon said. "We heard there was a state trooper on board. Maybe he knows something about Roy. Have you seen him?"

For an instant, Judith wondered if Sharon was probing. But the other woman's face was devoid of guile. "No," she replied, "not lately."

Jim glanced at the table across the aisle and lowered his voice. "Aren't those people wearing Western getups in our sleeper?"

Judith nodded. "They're next to the reclusive Kloppenburgs."

"What's with those Kloppenburgs?" Sharon asked. "Jax said they prefer keeping to themselves. I'd think they'd atrophy from boredom."

Renie laughed. "Coz here is about to explode with curiosity. The two of you should concoct a plan to flush them out in the open."

"I've got a puzzle for you girls," Jim said, his voice still low. "Not about the Kloppenburgs, but the Western couple. I talked to the husband briefly this morning when we were waiting to be seated for breakfast." He turned to Sharon. "See for yourself and tell me if I'm crazy."

Sharon uttered an impatient sigh. "Fine, but I'll need my glasses." After rummaging through her brown suede hobo bag and putting on her glasses, she asked what she was supposed to see.

Jim, who was sitting in the seat next to the aisle and facing the Johnstons, nodded slightly. "Him, not her."

Judith and Renie exchanged puzzled glances.

"I feel like a spy," Sharon murmured, pretending to read the menu. "This is a blur. I'm shortsighted." She smiled, even as her eyes veered toward Jack Johnston. "He looks fine to me."

"No sideburns," Jim said.

"So what?" Sharon removed her glasses. "He must've shaved them off."

Judith poked Renie. "Drop the pepper shaker."

"What?"

"Drop the pepper shaker. Then retrieve it."

"Oh." Renie picked up the shaker—and dropped it in the aisle. "Oops! Clumsy me." She slipped from her seat, crouched to retrieve the shaker, picked it up, and sat down again. "Well," she said to Judith, "did that help?"

"Yes." But Judith didn't sound pleased. "You're right," she said to Jim, who looked as bewildered as his wife. "He had sideburns when he went outside."

"That's crazy," Sharon said. "He gets off to smoke and shave?"

Jim looked irked. "Jeez, Sharon, how do I know? Why don't you ask him? Go ahead, we talked to him this morning. We're old chums."

Sharon hesitated. "Oh, hell!" She jumped up from the seat, grabbed her purse, and shoved her way past Jim.

Startled, Judith watched her stomp out of the dining car.

Jim held his head. "My wife can be so damned—" He stopped, a sheepish expression on his face. "I'm sorry. It was a stupid argument. They usually are."

Judith smiled. "How long have you been married?"

"Twenty years," Jim replied. "Right now it feels like a hundred."

Renie shrugged. "My husband and I've been married twice that long. Not," she added hastily, "two hundred . . ."

She paused, eyeing Judith. "I don't do numbers. What would that come to?"

"Blows," Judith retorted, "as in me punching you in the nose." She was immediately apologetic. "Cousins argue, too, Jim. Don't worry about feeling bad. Half an hour ago I was annoyed with my husband. I'm over it already."

Jim nodded. "Sharon's fairly good-natured, but something about this trip has her on edge. Maybe it's the daredevil guy who died." He shrugged. "I hope the body's been taken off the train. That could give anybody the creeps."

Earl appeared with the cousin's entrées. "Duck and more duck," he said, putting the plates on the table. "And you, Mr. Downey?"

Jim sighed. "I'm not sure if my wife's coming back. I'll wait—unless there's a big lineup for this dinner setting."

Earl looked at both entrances. "More than usual. The coach passengers are passing the time by eating dinner in here, but you've got reserved seating. If you want to check on your wife, I'll hold your places."

Jim nodded. "If I'm not back in ten minutes, give our seats away." He excused himself and made his exit.

The cousins concentrated on their meal until Judith broached the subject that had preoccupied her. "Sideburns or no sideburns?"

"Mmm," Renie murmured. "Duck good, duck tender, duck ducky."

Judith scowled. "Try to focus on something else at the moment. You saw the Johnstons by the luggage rack earlier. Did he have sideburns?"

Renie licked her lips. "I didn't get a good look at him. Mrs. Hat was doing the talking. I honestly didn't notice anything unusually hirsute about Mr. Hat's appearance under his hat."

"Hmm." Judith craned her neck to look at the Johnstons and the Zs. "You're blocking my view. What's going on with our persons of interest?"

Renie glanced across the aisle. "All's quiet on the opposite front. The Zs are talking to each other. The Johnstons are focused on food. They all watched Sharon storm off but didn't seem overly interested."

"So I noticed. I also noticed you have duck sauce on your chin."

"Oh." Renie wiped her mouth with a napkin. "Thanks."

Judith ate some rice pilaf before speaking again. "I saw Jack Johnston fairly close when we were waiting to go outside. He definitely had sideburns. He doffed his hat to me."

"A Western gentleman," Renie murmured.

"Or devious." Judith winced. "Sauce now on upper lip."

Renie used a second napkin to wipe away the sauce. "What do you mean by 'devious'?"

"If whoever is across the aisle isn't the real Jack Johnston, maybe there's a reason for the first one to make sure somebody noticed. But I can't think why."

Renie cut off another slice of duck. "You have the logical mind. Put it to use. Oops!" More sauce went awry, dripping onto Renie's bosom. "Damn! I'm running out of napkins." She yanked at the tablecloth, dipped part of it in her water glass, and tried to mop the sauce off of her brown sweater. "At least it matches," she said lamely.

"Have you thought about wearing a bib? Really, coz, you're such an untidy eater. A rain slicker would work better than a bib."

"Maybe. This sweater's cashmere. I don't want to ruin it. I can change—"

The dining car erupted with sound and motion. Several people across the aisle were on their feet, voices raised in excitement.

"What the hell?" Renie said, jumping up and trying to see around the Johnstons and the Zs. Earl and another waiter were at either side of the serving area, caught in midstep and trying to balance their serving dishes. "Move it!" Renie yelled at Mr. Z. "I'm small but mighty!"

"You're mighty small," Mr. Z said. "But okay," he added, stepping back just enough so Renie could see what was going on outside.

Judith couldn't help herself. It was pointless to avoid her mysterious B&B guests and the putative Jack Johnston. At five-nine, she could see over Renie. It looked to Judith like a drunken brawl that had started in the tavern and spilled out onto the sidewalk. A half-dozen people were exchanging blows, pushing and shoving while they slipped and slid on the snowy pavement. A pair of newcomers approached the mayhem, but stopped at a safe distance.

"The Wild West," Renie remarked. "Maybe this is Scuttle's version of live entertainment."

Judith tried to recognize the people involved, but the sole streetlight illuminated only a patch of pavement by the hardware store. Their identities were further obscured by the snow that encrusted their clothes. "Pig pile," she murmured as the jumble of combatants wallowed around on the pavement.

"Just another night at the saloon in Smalltown, Montana," someone said. "After they recover from their hangovers, they'll all be best buddies again when the tavern opens up tomorrow."

Judith realized that the speaker was Dick Z, who flashed a peace sign and sat back down. His words apparently had a reassuring effect. A few other diners also stopped gawking as the sound level diminished.

Until they heard a shot.

"What was that?" a woman cried from somewhere toward the rear of the car. "A backfire? A firecracker? A gun?"

The cousins knew a gunshot when they heard one. The passengers erupted with screams, gasps, and shouts. Judith, who'd started back to her seat, shoved Renie toward the window. "Quick," she said. "See what's happening."

Skirting around the Zs and stepping over two young men who'd ducked for cover, Renie squeezed past an older couple who seemed transfixed. "No harm done," she shouted over the din of panicky voices and the clatter of crockery. "It must've been a warning shot."

Sidestepping a fallen cup and some silverware, Judith

joined Renie at the window. "Everybody's standing up out there—more or less," Judith murmured. She counted the bedraggled brawlers, but didn't include the growing number of curious onlookers. "Seven, plus a state trooper who probably fired the shot."

"Purvis?" Renie murmured.

"I think so. Right size. Unless Emily stole his gun."

"Recognize anybody?"

"Besides Purvis?" Judith noticed that the older couple's eyes were glazed and their skin was ashen. "Hey," she called to Earl, who was trying to calm a hysterical young woman, "can we get Dr. Chan in here?"

Earl didn't respond right away. The young woman was leaning against him, sobbing noisily. Before he could disengage himself, Mr. Peterson entered the dining car. "Attention!" he shouted. "There's no cause for alarm. I repeat, there's no danger to anyone on this train. Please resume your places."

Judith waved at Mr. Peterson. "We need a doctor." She indicated the oldsters. "They're in shock."

The conductor nodded abruptly even as he scanned the distraught passengers. "Anyone needing medical attention should come to this end of the car. If you're not certain you can walk, let me know. I'm calling for Dr. Chan. If there are other medical practitioners aboard, let me know. Thank you." Mr. Peterson exited the car.

Earl had calmed the hysterical young woman. He stood in the aisle, banging a metal spoon on a cast-iron skillet. "Ladies and gentlemen," he said, "please be seated except for the last two tables at the end of the car. We need room for the doctor. We're sorry for the inconvenience, but there's no cause for concern. Some locals got into a dispute that turned ugly. It has nothing to do with us. Be easy."

Renie made her way back to their table, but Judith couldn't leave the elderly couple. As an innkeeper, she was required to periodically take a Red Cross refresher course in first aid. Gently, she lifted the woman's thin arm, carefully pulled back the sleeve of her Fair Isle cardigan, and felt for a pulse. "Don't be frightened," she said soothingly. "Nothing bad is happening."

"Hey!" A man's voice broke her concentration on the pulse count. "I was a medic in the First Gulf War. I can help."

Judith turned around. Dick Z was right behind her. He stared; she froze. "You're the B&B lady," he said, looking astonished.

"You're Dick Z," she retorted, realizing that it sounded like an accusation. "I mean . . . skip it. We can talk later. You take his pulse while I take hers."

Even without interruptions, it was difficult for Judith to focus. There was too much noise and too much movement in the dining car as passengers and crew tried to regroup. Just as she was about to try again, the woman blinked and attempted to speak. "Am . . . is . . . what?" she gasped.

"Nothing's wrong," Judith assured her. "We're safe here on the train."

The old lady turned to the old man. "J-J-Julius?" she said.

"He'll be fine," Dick Z said. "Won't you, Mr. . . . um . . . Julius?"

Julius's color was improving. He nodded.

"Take a sip of water," Dick Z said, handing a glass to the old man.

Judith saw Matt Chan enter the dining car. "It's okay," she said to the woman. "There's a doctor here if you need him."

The old lady tapped the window. "Is this Wolf Point?"

"We're in Scuttle," Judith said. "A trooper fired his gun to break up a tavern brawl."

Her faded blue eyes brightened. "A real brawl?"

"It looked real," Judith said.

"Oh." The old woman seemed disappointed. She turned to the old man, who was being eased into his seat by Dick Z. "Julius? Where's Chester?"

Julius frowned. "Wolf Point. Where else would he be, Bessie?"

"I don't know." She looked sad. "I don't know anything anymore."

Judith steered Bessie back to her seat next to Julius.

Dick Z moved out into the aisle. "Queer old duck," he muttered when Judith joined him. "His brain's scrambled."

"He must be close to ninety. He's entitled to be daffy." She got out of the way as one of the waiters moved meals from the end of the car where Matt Chan was talking to the young woman who'd had hysterics. "So you're a fellow traveler. How did you enjoy your stay at my B&B?"

"It was fine," Dick Z replied. "We decided to take off early and drive over the pass. Pretty time of year with all the autumn foliage."

"Yes," Judith agreed, "though a bit late in the season. We came through the pass after dark, so we couldn't—"

"Excuse me," Jane Z said, nudging Judith and moving next to her husband. "Do you need help? Maybe a walk in the brisk air would clear their heads."

Dick Z smiled at his wife, revealing the gap between his teeth that Judith recalled from their first meeting. "Good thinking, hon. The clouds are lifting. There's supposed to be a full moon tonight."

"Let's do it," Jane Z said, moving to join the old couple.

Judith, however, was dubious. "They aren't dressed for cold weather. Shouldn't you consult Dr. Chan?"

"He's busy," Jane Z retorted. "We'll get their coats. Let's go, Dick."

The oldsters seemed to protest. Judith couldn't hear what they were saying, except for something about Wolf Point.

"We won't get there until tonight," Dick Z said, nudging the old couple toward the sleepers. "You have to get your circulation going. I was a medic in . . ."

A woman with two little girls was trying to get past Judith. The older girl was sulking and the younger one was sobbing. "Please," the mother said, "I must let the doctor see my kids. They're scared to death."

Judith realized that there wasn't anything else she could do to help. Sitting down next to Renie, she noticed that her cousin had almost finished eating. "How could you?" she asked incredulously.

"How could I not?" Renie responded, wiping her mouth with a napkin. "I hate cold food, and I'm useless in a crisis. I'm creative, not practical."

"Oh, stick it!" Judith snapped. "You can also be utterly selfish."

Renie was unmoved. "You know I get crabby when I don't eat." She twirled her fork. "You're the helpful type. I see you and Dick Z are now best friends. How 'bout that?"

Judith kept her gaze on the Zs and the old folks. "Mr. Z insists they drove through the pass to see the fall colors, but I don't trust him. Look."

Renie saw the younger couple escorting the oldsters from the dining car. "They're taking them . . . where?"

"For a walk," Judith said. "I don't like it."

Renie shrugged. "The golden agers may be tarnished, but they're not made of tin. If they don't want to go, they can say so."

Judith surveyed the dining car as order was restored. Only two adults and the mother with the little girls were clustered around Matt. "Can they?"

Renie looked puzzled. "You think the Zs cast a spell over them?" She pointed at Judith's plate. "Are you waiting for your duck to fly south for the winter?"

"I've lost my appetite." Judith picked up her purse. "I'm going to call Justin to see what he wanted. It's after five at home. He should be off work. I'll go out through the other sleeper."

"Oh Lord!" Renie held her head. "Shall I come with you?"

Judith was on her feet. "No. Eat your dessert. I'll be back before you finish whatever you add to your trough."

Renie shrugged. "Peach cobbler, maybe. Sounds good with duck."

Judith started to walk away, but changed her mind about

which way to go. "I'll do what I did before," she said to Renie. "I'll see if Earl or somebody can open the window so I don't have to go outside."

"Peachy keen," Renie said, but gave her cousin a hard look. "Please—don't do anything dumb and come right back, okay?"

"I'm not in a risk-taking mood."

"Five minutes." Renie was still solemn. "Then I send the posse."

"Got it," Judith said, and left on her mission.

She was immediately at a disadvantage. There was no one available to help between the dining and dome cars. Earl and the rest of the dining crew were busy, catching up on orders and working under cramped conditions. Standing between the cars, she considered opening one of the windows herself, but was afraid she might trigger an alarm and give the passengers yet another scare. The areas on both sides of the train were clear of human traffic, drunk or sober. Before she could decide what to do, a tall figure came out of the tavern. As he moved from the shadows and closer to the light, she recognized Trooper Purvis. He paused by the train, looking up at her and waving his arms. She pointed to the window; he nodded impatiently. After a brief struggle, she slid the glass pane up. "Are you locked out?" she called to him.

"Just open the danged door," he yelled back.

"How?"

His instructions weren't complicated. In less than a minute, Judith unlocked the door. Purvis took one long leap onto the train.

"Thanks," he said grumpily. "You get a free pass for now."

Judith was surprised. "Why?"

"I couldn't get back on the train and I still don't have a cell. While I sorted out the drunks, Emily jammed the sleeper door. I don't think that kid likes me." He took off his hat and smoothed his rumpled auburn hair. "We'll talk later." Purvis put his hat back on and stalked off to the dining car.

Judith didn't mention that the hat was on backward. She dialed directory assistance for Justin's number. Moments later, her call was put through. Justin answered on the fifth ring. "Hello," he said breathlessly.

"Hi," she began, "it's Judith. Joe told me you'd called, but my phone hasn't been on. Am I coming through okay?"

"You're a bit faint, but I can hear," he replied. "How do I sound?"

"Fine. The problem's at this end. Before you tell me why you called, I'm afraid I have some bad news. Your uncle—"

"I know," Justin broke in. "That's why I tried to reach you this morning."

Judith wondered if she'd heard Justin clearly. "I don't get it. Your uncle didn't pass away until later in the day."

A pause was followed by crackling on the line. "No," Justin said. "Mom told me this morning that Uncle Willie died . . ." His voice faded completely.

"What?" Judith shouted.

"I said," Justin answered, also shouting, "my mother says whoever is on that train isn't Uncle Willie. He's been dead for five years."

Chapter Ten

Judith almost dropped the phone. "Could you repeat that?"

Justin's voice had grown faint. "Sorry—I'm losing you."

The stepstool was by the opposite door. If she could set it outside and get off the train, the reception might be better. Cradling the cell with her chin, Judith tried to lift the stool, but it was heavier than it looked. "Hang on," she shouted to Justin. "I'm going to see if I can . . ."

A harsh buzzing noise assaulted her ear. Judith cringed and moved the phone away. The buzz stopped. "Justin?" There was no response. "Justin?" she repeated louder. The line was dead. Judith redialed his number, but heard only silence. She was wondering what to do when Renie came out of the dining car.

"Any luck?" she asked.

"No." Judith turned the phone off. "I mean, yes."

Renie sighed. "Are you having another fit?"

"No. I need some answers. Let's get out of here."

"Okay," Renie said, opening the dining-car door. "I ordered you some peach cobbler, too. While we eat dessert, you can tell me about your questions."

"No," Judith snapped. "I don't have time for that. Let's go."

"Where?" Renie asked, annoyed. "You look like bird doo. Sit down until you pull yourself together." She opened the door to usher her cousin inside. The dining car seemed back to normal except for Matt Chan, who was tending to a stout man by the other door. The Johnstons were ordering dessert. There was no sign of Jim and Sharon. Apparently, they'd given up on dinner.

"Well?" Renie said when they reached their vacant table. "Are you going to sit or stand there like a stuffed moose?"

Judith slid over to her previous place by the window. Renie sat down beside her. "Okay, what's got you in such a tizzy?"

It took a moment for Judith to respond. Maybe she was mistaken; maybe she had misunderstood. But she had to confide in Renie. "Justin told me Wee Willie Weevil has been dead for five years."

Renie was scowling at her leftover cobbler crumbs. "Why didn't I ask for à la mode? Their ice cream . . ." She gaped at Judith. "What?"

"You heard me," Judith snapped. "Dead Willie isn't the real dead Willie. Justin wanted us to know that."

Renie stared in disbelief. "But Justin called you this morning before Willie . . . I mean, the Willie we knew as Willie . . ." She tossed her napkin aside. "Never mind. You know what I mean."

"I do," Judith said, careful to keep her voice down. "But why did Justin apparently learn about his uncle's actual death from his mother earlier today? Neither of them could've known that the bogus Willie was dying. Unless . . ."

Renie regarded her cousin with a perceptive gaze. "Are you implying that Germaine Weevil was involved in this mess?"

Judith grimaced. "No, but her timing is odd. Justin's mother was so annoyed with her former in-laws that she left town for a few days to avoid seeing them."

"Germaine and her ex weren't close. Why would she stay in touch with his family?"

Judith tried to piece together what little she knew about the Weevil family's relationships. "She didn't, not in recent years. But her ex's father—and Willie's—was a World War

Two veteran and a semi-invalid. He'd been a dive-bomber pilot in the Pacific. Justin told us his grandfather's plane had been shot down during the Battle of Midway. Despite being injured, he managed to stay afloat until he was rescued. Germaine and Justin enjoyed hearing Grandpa Kermit's war stories. The old guy was a daredevil in his day, especially flying. He'd been a crop duster before the war and flew in air shows. Willie inherited his dad's lust for thrills. The old man died some twenty years ago, soon after Justin graduated from college. Willie's real name was Wilbur. His brother is . . . Winston."

Renie smiled. "If Gramps loved airplanes so much, I thought it might be Orville. But what's with this impostor? He had to be a daredevil, too, or he wouldn't have jumped off your roof."

Judith nodded. "He also ran up and down the Counterbalance. Joe saw him doing it. The non-Willie had to be in terrific shape."

"You don't think . . ." Renie stopped. "Never mind."

"I know what you're wondering," Judith said. "Could the dead man be Winston Weevil? But Justin described his father as completely opposite from Willie. Winnie was more artistic. He's the one who got Germaine interested in becoming an interior decorator."

"Germaine ended up with two good things from that marriage—a highly marketable skill and a wonderful son," Renie said. "But she obviously has talent when it comes to taste and design."

"Definitely. She's a natural, but her ex must've recognized that—" She stopped as movement outside caught her eye. Four people were walking slowly in front of the motel. There was something familiar about them. The tallest person seemed to be holding up someone who was barely shuffling along the sidewalk. They moved past the weathered motel sign with its single floodlight. Judith thought she recognized the Zs with the elderly couple from the dining car. "Coz," she whispered in an urgent voice, "do you see what I see?"

Renie leaned around Judith to look outside. "The tavern drunks? A couple of them look wobbly."

"No. Try again."

Inching closer, Renie watched the foursome move on to the parking lot. "I can't make out much except that one couple's elderly and the other isn't."

"It's the Zs with the old folks I was helping. They were going for a walk."

Renie shrugged. "That's what they're doing. Why do we care?" She jabbed her fork at Judith's cobbler. "Eat. It's good, even without ice cream."

"I'm not hungry," Judith said, her gaze still fixed on the quartet as they neared the motel's tiny office. "I'm too upset. I want to talk to—"

A sudden jolt of the train jarred both cousins. "What the hell?" Renie said, bracing herself on the table edge. "Ah." She laughed in relief. "We're moving."

"We can't be!" Judith looked out where the motel view had been replaced by a decrepit water tower. "What about the oldsters and the Zs? Where's Earl?"

Renie turned to search for their waiter. "He's talking to Matt, who seems about to leave. The doctor's office hours must be over."

"Let's go," Judith urged. "We can talk to Earl on our way out."

"What about your cobbler?"

"No. All I want is some answers from Pepper and to let Earl know about the Zs and the old coots we left behind. Move!"

"Sheesh," Renie said under her breath. "Okay, okay, I'm moving."

As they headed down the aisle, Judith saw Matt leave the dining car. Earl, who was about to reset the table that had served as the doctor's consultation area, had his back to the cousins. He turned when Judith called his name.

"Ah!" the waiter exclaimed with a smile. "Did you want your dinner, Mrs. Flynn? I saved it for you."

"Thanks, but no," Judith said hurriedly in a low voice. "I think we've left some passengers behind."

Earl looked startled. "What do you mean?"

"The couple who were sitting across from the Johnstons whose last name begins with Z," Judith said, "and that older couple, the ones Mr. Z and I were trying to help after the gunshot panic."

"Oh, of course." Earl's expression was kindly. "Nice folks," he said, "but up in years and very frail." He sobered quickly. "Are you saying Mr. and Mrs. Gundy have been left behind?"

"Gundy?" Judith said, surprised.

Earl nodded. "They've made this trip several times when I've been working. They live in Wolf Point, but one of their children is in Kalispell." He had lost his usual bonhomie. "I don't understand. Why did they get off?"

"The Zs thought the fresh air would do them good," Judith replied, trying not to let nearby passengers listen in. "Did you say 'Gundy'?"

"Yes." Earl was trying to acknowledge another waiter, who apparently needed backup. "Sorry, I have to go. I'll pass on what you thought you saw to Mr. Peterson about the Gundys and the other pair."

"He thinks I'm nuts," Judith murmured after they left the dining car.

"You're not," Renie said. "If that foursome got left behind, we're going so slow that if they could get a ride, they'll be in Malta before we will. What I don't understand is the Gundy connection. Are they related to Pepper?"

"That's another question," Judith said grimly. She glanced out the window of the first sleeper as the train crawled eastward across desolate, snow-dusted terrain. "Purvis called her Dorothy May Gundy. By the way," she added as Renie opened the door to their sleeper, "did you see the trooper in the dining car?"

"Yes," Renie replied. "He was in a rush. I meant to ask if you'd talked to him. He must've passed by while you were talking to Justin."

"That's a long and stupid story in itself," Judith said. "He'd come out of the tavern, where I assume he was trying to find out who or what started the brawl. The bottom line is that Emily had locked him out of the train and I had to help him get back on."

Jax was coming out of the roomette next to the Downeys. "Oh—hi," she said, looking frazzled. "I'm doing bed checks. When do you want yours ready?"

The cousins exchanged glances. "Later," Judith replied. "Around ten? By the way, which sleeper are the Gundys in?"

Jax looked puzzled. "Ms. Gundy is still in the bedroom downstairs. She insisted on taking Mr. Weevil's body to Wolf Point, rather than into Malta."

"No, not that Gundy. I mean the elderly couple who came from Kalispell. Were they in this sleeper or the other one?"

"Sorry," Jax said. "I didn't realize there were any other Gundys on board. The only Gundy I know is the one downstairs. Are you sure about the name?"

"That's what Earl told us," Judith said. "He knows them because they travel frequently between Kalispell and their home in Wolf Point."

Jax nodded. "Now I understand. The other Gundys would've gotten on at Whitefish early this morning. There are connecting buses between Kalispell, Missoula, and Whitefish. If we were on time, we'd have been in Wolf Point around four-thirty this afternoon. They wouldn't book a sleeper for a day trip."

"I should've known that," Renie said, disgusted. "I've taken this route several times, but I didn't realize Kalispell and Whitefish are so close together."

Jax smiled faintly. "Montana's a big state. It's hard to know distances between the towns and cities." She started to turn away, but Judith stopped her.

"Wait." She saw Jax tense. "I hate to burden you with bad news, but the Gundys—the old folks—and another couple may've been left behind in Scuttle. I've told Earl, the waiter, and he was going to alert Mr. Peterson, but just in case, I thought you could make sure the conductor knows."

Jax looked horrified. "Oh, no! How could such a thing happen?"

"They got off to get some fresh air," Judith explained. "I saw them outside—just as we started to move again. Do you know where Mr. Peterson is?"

Jax took a moment to compose herself. "Probably with the engineer now that we're under way again." She shut her eyes tight and pressed her lips together. "This trip has been a disaster," she finally said. "First Roy disappears, then there's the collision with the pickup truck, poor Mr. Weevil dies, and now we've got four passengers stranded in Scuttle. I feel as if we're hexed." She looked close to tears.

"I understand how upsetting this must be to you," Judith said.

Jax waved a dismissive hand. "I shouldn't blab. This route is usually uneventful." She smiled weakly. "As a rule, the problems are minor, like the people next to you who wouldn't open the door when I asked about their beds."

"The Kloppenburgs?" Judith asked.

"Yes," Jax said. "They yelled at me to go away, they'd do it themselves." She squared her shoulders. "Sometimes passengers have strange little ways. That's fine. It's one less chore for me." She shrugged and moved on.

After Jax disappeared, Judith poked Renie. "Let's see the other Gundy. If Pepper wants to go nuclear again, that's fine, but she better have some answers."

Renie took her time to reach the stairs. "Is viewing of the body optional?"

"It wouldn't be a first, would it?" Judith snapped.

Renie shrugged. "Seen one dead body, seen too damned many."

There was no sign of activity downstairs. Renie had qualms. "Keep on guard. Emily may be lying in ambush. What's your opening line for Pepper?"

"Truce for truth." Judith rapped on the accessible room's door, but there was no response. Listening for any sound inside, she heard nothing. "Too quiet?"

"Well," Renie said, "the dead guy probably can't hear you."

"I suppose it wouldn't be pleasant to spend the day with a corpse," Judith said, more to herself than to Renie. "Pepper and Wayne could be in the bar or the dome car." She stared at the door. "Dare I?"

Renie sucked in her breath. "You wouldn't!"

"I shouldn't."

But Judith opened the door anyway.

There was no one—dead or alive—in the accessible bedroom.

"Where's the body?" Renie asked.

"I've no idea." Judith was surprised to see that the accessible bedroom was so small. Two beds—both unmade—and a sink and toilet were the only furnishings. "Where's the wheelchair?"

"Maybe," Renie suggested, "they put the phony Willie in it and wheeled him to the baggage car."

"I wouldn't want to spend time in here with a corpse." Judith studied the room. It was neither tidy nor trashed. "Watch for anyone coming downstairs. I wonder where Wayne slept. There's only room for two."

Renie took up her sentry post by the door. "Did someone say Wayne was in one of the roomettes down here?"

"Makes sense." Judith peeked inside a big green tote bag filled with cosmetics, hair products, apparel, and other travel accessories. "Pepper must have her purse and wallet with her. I don't see any ID."

"I do," Renie said, gesturing at the window by the lower bunk bed. "That looks like the same train info I keep by our window."

Judith went across the room, but paused at the side of the bed. "This must be where Willie died. He couldn't have used the upper berth."

"Berth and death," Renie remarked. "Can you reach the packet?"

"Yes," Judith said, "but I feel like a ghoul."

"Oh, coz," Renie said with a sigh. "You're used to it. If you had to, you'd crawl over Willie's dead body to get at what you think is some kind of clue. Heck, you'd make your way through dozens of fatalities in a bus crash or plow over a couple of hundred earthquake victims or—"

"Ooof! I dropped the damned packet." She stuck her hand between the bed and the wall. "Got it. Hmm . . ." Judith murmured, feeling some sort of thick folder. "What's this?"

"Got me. I'm still on guard duty."

Judith removed the train info packet first before tugging at the larger item. She finally dislodged a thick, dog-eared manila envelope that bore the logo and name of Back Bay Insurance Company, Boston, Massachusetts. Holding on to the envelope and the train packet, she slid off the bed.

"Jiggers," Renie said under her breath. "I hear voices on the stairs. Sounds like those young women." She slid the door almost closed, but peered through the open half inch as Tiff and Maddie came into view.

Judith joined Renie. The two young women were still talking, their voices subdued and serious.

"I'm at a loss," the blond Maddie said. "What do we do with him?"

Tiff shook her head as she opened the door to their roomette. "Beats me. We never should've gotten mixed up in . . ."

They disappeared and closed the door behind them.

"They're not yakking about Nordquist's," Renie said. "Who's 'him'?"

"Good question." Judith gave the room another once-over. "Maybe we should get out of here."

"What's with that stuff you got by the bed?"

"I don't know yet. There's only one way to find out." Judith opened the door. "Let's go."

"You're stealing that?" Renie asked, taken aback.

"I'm borrowing it," Judith said. "We'll put it back later."

"Okay," Renie said, "but as sometimes happens, your curiosity makes me nervous. What do you expect to find?"

"If I knew," Judith responded as they walked past the luggage racks, "I wouldn't have to swipe—I mean *borrow it,* would I?" She stopped just short of the stairs. "Luggage. Camera. How the heck did that camera get into my suitcase?" She stared at the door to the family room. "What else did Emily brag about having collected when she ran off with Purvis's cell?"

Renie frowned, trying to remember. "She mentioned a game—a video game, I think. It's been so long since I had to buy the latest high-tech toys for our kids that I don't know what's hot these days. Do you?"

"I leave that up to Mike and Kristin," Judith said. "They have computer games, handheld games, video games, and for all I know, a microchip you can insert in your head and make up your own."

"Gee, maybe you just invented the next generation of gaming technology," Renie said. "If we could put microchips in our heads to solve mysteries, we wouldn't be standing here like a couple of obsolete fogies. I'm still wondering what happened to those old Speed Graphic cameras reporters used."

"Ah!" Judith exclaimed. "Emily had a camera. I'll bet it's the one you dropped when the pickup collision occurred. Let's buddy up to her."

Renie gasped. "Who else? Hitler? Attila the Hun? Vlad the Impaler?"

Judith headed for the family room. "Why didn't we look at the photos?"

"Because we didn't know how to do it?"

"We should've tried. I'll bet its owner is connected to the Weevil bunch."

"There may not be a Weevil bunch," Renie noted, "or at least no Willie."

"Doesn't matter. They wanted us to think Willie was alive." Reaching the family room, Judith motioned for Renie to step out of sight. "You don't want to get us off on a bad foot, do you?"

"About now, I'd like to get off, period." But Renie moved away toward the shower and toilet stalls.

Emily's mother opened the door a bare inch. "Yes?"

"I'm Mrs. Flynn," Judith said. "I'm sorry to bother you, Ms. Mueller, but I think your daughter has my camera. It has the last photos I took of my dear mother before she passed away."

The curly-haired young woman looked puzzled. "It has?"

"Yes." Judith suddenly realized that Courtney Mueller might have already looked at the photos. "Mother's in the background in her wheelchair. You might not have noticed if you checked the pictures to see who the camera belonged to. It was a present from my uncle Al before he was run over by a cement mixer."

"I . . ." Courtney paused. Judith saw Emily creeping up behind her mother.

"Yes?" Judith coaxed. "Those photos mean the world to me."

"Call me Courtney," the woman said, and turned to Emily. "Darling, could you get the camera you found? We don't want this lady to cry, do we?"

"Why not?" Emily retorted. "I can cwy, too." Proving the point, she erupted into high-pitched sobs.

Judith winced. Renie's obscene comment was drowned out by the earsplitting shrieks.

"Howth dat?" Emily asked, pleased as punch.

"Very nice," Courtney said, "but you're a big girl. Big girls don't cry."

Emily peered at Judith through the narrow opening. "She's a big girl. A reawee big girl. Can I thee her cwy?"

"She might cry for being happy after you give her the camera."

Emily's violet-blue eyes studied Judith. "You gob bibeo gamth?"

"Video games?" Judith shook her head. "You like video games?"

"I wove ThmackBown. Ith wethling with goob and bab guyth."

Courtney forced a smile. "Emily enjoys wrestling. Her dad wrestled in high school and college."

"That's nice," Judith said hastily. "About my camera . . ."

To Judith's surprise, Emily trotted off out of sight. One of the twins started to fuss. Courtney opened the door another inch, but Judith still couldn't see Emily or her siblings. Their mother looked to her right. "Don't do that to Dylan, Emily. He doesn't need changing . . . oh! Oh! What a clever hiding place for the camera! Maybe we should wipe it off before we give it back to Mrs. Flynn."

"Yes," Judith said, trying to remain patient. "It would be kind of you to make sure the camera's . . . tidy."

"Of course," Courtney agreed. "I'm sure it's—no, no, Emily! Stop! Don't run it under the water!" She rushed off in the direction of the sink.

Hearing Renie groan, Judith warned her to shut up. "If Emily sees you, it could be a deal-breaker and we can kiss off the camera."

Both twins were bawling by the time mother and daughter returned to the door. "Here," Courtney said, holding the camera out on a damp facecloth. "Is this one yours?"

Judith took a good look. "Yes. Does Emily have more than one?"

Courtney nodded. "She's quite the little collector when it comes to technology."

"Thanks," Judith said, taking the camera from Courtney. "And thank you, Emily."

Manners weren't Emily's strong suit. Her gaze was combative. "Wanna wethle wif me?"

"Not now," Judith replied. "Bye-bye."

With one last sour look, Emily shut the door.

Judith carefully wrapped the camera in tissues and put it in her purse. "Want to guess who the other camera belongs to?"

"You?" Renie asked as they moved on.

"Maybe. But this model looks a lot like the one Wayne used to take pictures of Willie's ill-fated leap, though how it ended up in my luggage baffles me."

"Not 'how,'" Renie chided. "But 'who.' You admitted you misplaced the key after our trip to Scotland. Did you ever look inside your suitcase to see if it was tucked away someplace?"

"No," Judith admitted. "Maybe I should do that now."

"I thought you wanted to confront Pepper."

"I can't do that when I don't know where she is."

"She can't be far. She's got to be in the club or dome cars or . . ."

Judith waved the manila envelope at Renie. "I can hardly start a conversation with her when I've got this in my hand, can I?"

Renie kept a straight face. "Probably not. Though it'd make a good opening gambit if you want to get arrested."

"Unfortunately, Pepper is postponed," Judith declared. "I'm taking this to our roomette. If you want to look for the key, go ahead. When you're done and I've checked out the train tickets and what's in this envelope, we can try to view the pictures."

"Wow," Renie said sardonically. "Have we got entertainment or what?"

Judith ignored the comment and headed upstairs. She almost ran into Jax, who was hurtling around the corner.

"Oh!" Jax exclaimed. "Sorry. Mr. Peterson just told me he's letting the trooper off so he can find the passengers we left behind in Scuttle."

Judith involuntarily clutched the manila envelope and the train information packet closer to her chest. "That's a relief. I felt sorry for the old couple. I hope they've been inside all this time." She stopped speaking as a sudden thought struck her. "They were in coach, right?"

"Yes," Jax said, regarding Judith curiously. "Is something wrong?"

Judith wanted to say everything was wrong, but held her tongue. Jax had enough problems. "No, though I wondered if the senior Gundys could be related to Ms. Gundy downstairs. By the way, do you know where she is?"

Jax shook her head. "The last time I saw Ms. Gundy was about an hour ago when Mr. Weevil was moved."

"Moved?" Judith said.

"Ah—in a way," Jax said, looking ill at ease. "We have a standard policy to abide by the survivors' wishes, which means transporting the body to the nearest funeral home or, if that's inconvenient, to keep the deceased on board until we reach the final destination." She grimaced. "I'm not saying that right, but often the deceased is going home." She grimaced again. "I mean, to where the person lives. Lived." Jax put a hand to her head. "I'm doing a poor job explaining it, but usually family members or close friends make the decision."

Judith decided it would only further upset Jax to ask where the body would rest while still on the train. "I understand," she said sympathetically. Cold-storage car, baggage car, or propped up in a vacant coach seat, Judith thought—it'd make no difference to Willie . . . or his alter ego. "Then I assume the other Gundys aren't related to Pepper—I mean to Ms. Gundy."

"I don't know." Jax checked her watch. "I have to dash. I'm way behind."

Entering her room, Judith heard Jax greet Renie on the stairs. Their exchange was brief. When her cousin arrived, Judith had settled into her chair.

"You're the only person I know," Renie said, tossing a luggage key on the table, "who'd hide this in a slight gap between the inner lining and the exterior."

"Oh." Judith offered her cousin a sheepish smile. "I put it there after we got home from Scotland. Sometimes the pocket zippers get stuck and I can never remember which one I put the key in. I figured it'd be easier to find it that way."

"It would," Renie agreed, "if you recalled where you put the damned key."

"Okay," Judith admitted. "But you do weird things, too. What about a few weeks ago when you put your phone in the microwave?"

"That," said Renie, glaring, "was a mistake."

"It sure was. I didn't realize you could defrost a phone— or call somebody on a frozen chicken drumstick."

"I get it," Renie snapped. "What's with the insurance and the tickets?"

"I haven't had time to look." The train's slight jarring movement caught her attention. "We've stopped. They're letting Trooper Purvis off so he can find the other Gundys and the Zs."

Renie looked out the window. "I can't see anything except a lonely old clapboard church. It's not snowing here, though."

"We must be close to a highway," Judith said. "Another trooper is probably waiting for Purvis in a patrol car."

"A patrol car? They're going to need a patrol *bus* to bring four people to our next stop at Malta."

"Let's assume they know what they're doing."

"Let's not. Most people don't."

"I don't see any action, either," Judith said. "Purvis must be getting off on the other side. That's probably where the highway is."

The train began moving again. Renie pointed to the manila envelope and train packet. "Well?"

"I haven't looked yet. I got sidetracked by Jax." Briefly, Judith filled Renie in on Amtrak's policy regarding an on-board passenger death. "But," she went on, "Jax mentioned something else that bothered me. Were the Gundys wearing coats when we saw them by the motel?"

Renie realized what Judith meant. "Maybe jackets, but not coats."

Leaning back in her chair, Judith nodded. "I heard Jane Z tell the old folks to bundle up and then she hustled them toward the sleeper cars. But the Gundys weren't traveling by sleeper, and the coach section is at the other end of the train. Mr. Gundy had on a jacket and Mrs. Gundy was wearing a cardigan sweater. Not the sort of outerwear for a couple of old codgers in cold weather."

Renie frowned. "You think they wanted to freeze the Gundys?"

"No, but they were in a big hurry to get them off the train. Looking back, I wonder if the Zs knew the train was about to move again." Judith sighed. "Maybe I'm making too much of these so-called coincidences. They do happen."

"That's why there's a word for it—'coincidences,'" Renie said. "But I have a hunch that something else is going on here. I also trust your judgment."

"Thanks," Judith said, and meant it. "Okay, let's see if the Weevil tickets are in this packet." She found the schedule where Wolf Point's arrival time was circled. So were Havre and Malta with question marks next to them. She handed the schedule to Renie. "What do you make of these marks?"

"Wolf Point was their destination. Are the tickets in the packet?"

"Yes," Judith said, taking her first look. "The tickets were issued to Wilbur Weevil and two other adult passengers whose names aren't listed. First class, accessible bedroom, and a roomette, A3."

Renie looked thoughtful. "That's downstairs. I think all four of those rooms are for two people. If Wayne is in one of them, I wonder why he didn't ask for a single—unless they booked so late that he couldn't get one."

Judith flipped through the remaining information. "Just what you'd expect, same as ours. Any ideas about the circle and question marks?"

Renie stared at the schedule. "It was between those two stops that the pickup hit the train." She looked curiously at

Judith. "It could be an innocent notation concerning the delayed arrival at Wolf Point. But . . . ?"

Judith nodded. "It could also indicate something more
ominous. The pen that was used to circle those two stops is
the same as the one for Wolf Point, but that only indicates
the same person probably used it."

"Pepper?"

"My first guess," Judith said. "But Wayne's a possibility."

Renie nodded. "I assume we're thinking the same thing—
one of them knew there was going to be an accident."

Judith took the schedule from Renie and looked at it again.
"Not exactly," she said grimly.

"What do you mean?"

"That there was no accident. The collision with the train
was planned to cover up a murder."

Chapter Eleven

Renie looked only mildly surprised. "That almost makes sense. But what happened with the pickup driver? Was he ever caught?"

Judith sighed. "We've never heard a word about him. You'd think there'd be a certain buzz on the train if he'd been arrested."

"Maybe the state patrol or the Amtrak cops won't make an announcement until they're sure they've got the right perp."

"Yes, yes," Judith said impatiently. "But . . ." She shook her head. "I've got to have some time to think this through—logically, of course."

Renie smiled. "Of course."

"Let's check out this envelope." Judith studied it for a moment. "It's not new; it's dog-eared and the little metal clasp tabs are worn off." She removed a thick sheaf of paper. "It's a life insurance policy."

"Do I win a prize if I guess it was taken out on Willie?"

Judith scanned the first page. "Bingo. It's a term policy, dated February thirteenth, 1977." She noticed there seemed to be a second policy, separated from the first by a red flag. "Whoa! This is for Willie, too. The payoff is thirty mil to a company called WWF, covering accidental death, disability, and dismemberment."

"Sounds right for Willie," Renie said. "What do they call it? The Piecemeal Plan?"

"Not funny," Judith said.

"Hey—I'm not kidding. Years ago I designed an employee benefits guide for the phone company. The insured got so much for losing a finger, so much for an arm, a leg, a—"

"Stop. I'm trying to concentrate."

"Losing your mind wasn't included in the dismemberment section."

Judith glowered at her cousin. "I'm losing my temper. Do you want to lose consciousness?"

Renie shut up.

"The term policy," Judith said after a long pause, "is five mil, beneficiary, Richard Elmo Weevil." She frowned. "Willie's son?"

Renie shrugged. "How would I know?"

"Ricky," Judith murmured. "Justin's mentioned him, but not favorably. Ricky's a jerk, according to his cousin." She stared hard at Renie. "There are times when cousins feel that way about each other."

Renie stared right back. "Indeed."

Judith was puzzled. "If Willie died five years ago, Ricky would've gotten five million dollars."

"What do you mean? Ricky received the money when Willie died, but nobody else knew he was dead?"

Judith looked confused. "No . . . I mean . . ." She shook her head. "I understand what you're saying. If Willie died back then, but was supposed to be alive until this afternoon, the policy would never have been paid to Ricky. This sheds new light on things, doesn't it?"

"In a dim and mystifying way," Renie conceded. "How do we know if Ricky collected the money?"

"We don't." Judith's eyes were fixed on the first page of the policy. "Why would anyone carry this paperwork around if the insured is already dead?"

Renie's expression was wry. "I'll bet you have a few ideas."

"They're off the wall," Judith said, gazing out into the

pitch-black night. No longer could she see a building, a light, a car, or any sign of life. "If I'm right about the truck driver racing the train, then this whole situation has been a setup. But why? And where did it all begin?"

Renie scowled. "I'm not sure I understand."

"Neither do I," Judith said. "What's the point of keeping insurance policies after the person dies? If Willie has been dead for five years, did Ricky Weevil collect? He must know the truth."

"They sound like a fractured family. Are you sure Ricky's alive?"

"Justin would've mentioned if he wasn't," Judith said. "They were about the same age. There were a couple of other children from Willie's second marriage, but I think they're girls. Justin's never talked about them much."

"How many times was Willie married?" Renie asked.

"Twice?" Judith guessed. "Or maybe a longtime live-in girl friend." She uttered a rueful laugh. "I assumed it was Pepper."

"You don't think so now?"

"I don't know what to think." Judith reached into her purse and took out the camera. "Let's figure out how to view these photos." She removed the damp tissues and put them in the waste receptacle. "Here," she said, handing the camera to Renie. "You've worked with photographers who use cameras like this."

Renie's jaw dropped. "Are you nuts? That's why I work *with* photographers. You know I can't operate high-tech gizmos."

"Poke something. There's a little screen."

"Oh . . ." Renie turned the camera over and pressed a button. "It's a front view of your house. You're standing on the walk, looking up."

"Let me see." Judith studied the frame. "Yes, I was trying to dissuade Willie from jumping out of the window." She poked the button. "Here he is, landing in the rhododendron bush." She moved on to the next picture. "I'm arguing with

Willie—I call him that because I don't know him by any other name."

"Understood," Renie said, getting up to move so she could look over Judith's shoulder. "There's Willie rushing off. Did you scare him?"

"No. That's when he ran up and down the Counterbalance. Joe saw him doing it. Here's Arlene talking to me." She looked at Renie. "Who took these? Wayne didn't show up until later."

"Why take the pictures at all?" Renie asked. "The only reason I can think of is that it shows Willie's first jump."

"I agree. Let's see what's next."

The next photos started with Judith and Phyliss arguing on the back porch; Phyliss making the sign against the evil eye behind her back; Gertrude wheeling herself out of the toolshed; and an angry, red-faced Joe in profile. "Joe's warning Willie not to jump," Judith said before pointing to the shot showing Willie about to take off. "There's Mother again, looking fit to spit."

"Gee," Renie said, "I'm sorry I missed all this."

"I'll bet." Judith pressed the button again. "Ah! See— Willie's sailing through space. Oh, dear—here's his crash landing." She couldn't suppress a shudder. "It's really kind of awful."

"Right." Renie's sounded unsympathetic.

"Wayne's trying to help Willie, but Joe tells him to back off because he could do more harm than good. That's after Joe called 911."

"Stop," Renie said. "Go back a few frames."

Judith had no problem reversing the process. "How far?"

"Right there," Renie replied. "Look at Willie's face before he jumps. He seems scared. Also, note the leaves in the air. Was it windy?"

"Yes," Judith said. "A big gust came along just as Willie jumped, sending him off course, so that he landed in the pyracantha instead of the lily-of-the-valley bush." She peered more closely at the picture. "He does look startled."

"Check out the next two shots after he lands. Not," Renie went on, "at Willie and Wayne and Joe, but to the left at the back door. That's not Phyliss—she's standing on the porch steps almost out of the frame."

"You're right," Judith said. "That red hair belongs to Pepper."

"That's not all," Renie said. "Go back to Joe before the jump, where he looks irate. It's a profile. Now look again at the three guys by the bush. What's wrong with this picture?"

Judith frowned as she studied the frame. "If you mean how Willie's grimacing and grinding his teeth in pain or Pepper knowing something bad has—oh! I get it. Wayne has the camera around his neck, so he didn't take these pictures."

"That's not all," Renie said. "This shot had to be taken from at least thirty feet away to get the area from the driveway to the back door."

Judith was mystified. "The only person who was further back in the yard was Mother. She hasn't used a camera since her old Kodak got run over by our Model A Ford during World War Two."

Renie nodded. "Wayne's camera is probably very good, but he didn't use this one to take these pictures. Let's see the rest."

The next two frames showed Judith heading into the house, followed by a shot of Wayne and Joe looking at Willie, who was still entangled in the bush.

"That's it," Renie said. "Whoever took the photos stopped here. There could be a hundred or more unused frames in the camera."

Judith didn't respond at once. "I'm trying to piece together what happened after the EMTs arrived, but I'm muddled. It was a bad day."

Renie sat in her chair. "What happened after you went inside?"

Judith sighed. "I had a headache from all the commotion. I wanted to avoid the EMTs. I recall wondering where Pepper was and how she could miss the chaos. She wasn't in the kitchen, but she must've been there a few moments earlier since she's at the back door in the shot after Willie took his dive."

"When did she confront you?"

Judith recalled taking Excedrin, but blanked out on what came next. "I didn't see Pepper until after the EMTs arrived. She must've gone outside to see what happened and talked to the medics because she knew Willie had broken his leg and his arm. She didn't come from the kitchen or I'd have seen her when I came indoors. Maybe she used the front door or the French doors off the living room." She made a helpless gesture. "I can't remember."

Renie laughed. "You're a good sleuth, but a damned poor witness."

"You don't need to mention that," Judith said ruefully, and paused to concentrate. "I heard sirens and then saw the medics approaching. I couldn't bear facing them for the umpteenth time, so I went into the parlor and watched from the window as they pulled in."

"Very good, coz." Renie's ironic expression changed abruptly. "Wait—you saw and heard the EMTs? Where were you before you went into the parlor? You couldn't see them from the kitchen."

Judith clapped a hand to her forehead. "Good grief! That's the part I forgot. I was on the front porch. Those girls—Maddie and Tiff—came to ask about Herself's rental. I sent them to see Arlene. After they left, I rearranged some of my holiday decorations that had gotten blown over by the wind."

"Well, well." Renie's brown eyes twinkled. "The missing links."

"But where do they fit in?" Judith asked, leaning forward and lowering her voice. "When we were downstairs a few minutes ago, what did they say about wishing they hadn't gotten involved with . . . a man?"

"I don't recall the exact words," Renie admitted. "They alluded to a man, but it was more like . . . how to deal with him?"

"Maybe." Judith paused. "Can you remove those pictures?"

"Ah . . ." Renie grimaced. "It's a memory card. You can take it out, but we can't look at the pictures without a computer."

"Doesn't matter. I want to return the camera to its rightful owners—assuming it belongs to Tiff and Maddie."

"And you will next say, 'There's only one way to find out.' "

Judith nodded. "They must still be downstairs. We haven't heard anybody in the corridor since we got back here."

"Okay," Renie agreed reluctantly. "Shall I remove the card?"

"Yes."

"Hoo boy," Renie said under her breath. "This could be ugly."

"I trust you," Judith assured her. "What could possibly go wrong?"

Renie shot her cousin a withering glance. "Let's put it this way—the damned thing probably won't explode and kill us."

While Renie fiddled with the camera, Judith tried to organize her thoughts. She felt as if her brain was working on overload. There was Pepper, who might know the bogus Willie's identity and explain why she had an insurance policy on a dead man. There were Dick and Jane Z, who seemed to have abducted the elderly Gundys. There were the Cowboy Hats, with Mr. Hat apparently morphing into someone else after getting off the train to smoke. There was Wayne Fielding, who might or might not be who and what he claimed to be. And there was the missing truck driver, who could be anyone, anywhere.

"Got it!" Renie exclaimed, holding up a small computer memory card. "Where do you want to put it?"

"My purse," Judith said. "If the camera belongs to Maddie and Tiff, how could they take the pictures and not be seen?"

"Easy," Renie responded. "A telephoto lens. They might've shot the front of the house from a car by the entrance to the cul-de-sac. Out back, your yard slopes up the hillside. You've got all kinds of shrubs and bushes there, just like we do. I trim our evergreens by using them for Christmas decorations."

"Pruning's an endless job," Judith said. "I enjoy gardening, but it's hard for me to . . ." She stared at Renie. "Maybe Mother isn't crazy."

"Maybe not, but I've no idea what you're talking about."

"She called Willie Santa Claus because he was by the chimney wearing a red jumpsuit," Judith explained. "She also mentioned Santa's elves. Thinking back, I visualized Maddie and Tiff. They were wearing red and green jackets— Christmas colors. Remember when we took our kids to see Santa? His helpers were always pretty girls dressed as elves."

"Sure. One Santa was a lecher who got too chummy with our Anne. Of course, she was seventeen and drop-dead gorgeous, if I do say so myself."

"When did your thirtysomething offspring stop believing in Santa?"

Renie looked affronted. "Who told you they stopped?"

"Forget it," Judith said, with a pitying expression. "Okay, Maddie and Tiff probably took the photos." She stood up. "Let's go see them."

Two minutes later the cousins were at Maddie and Tiff's roomette door. Renie had volunteered to take the lead, assuming that the young women wouldn't recognize her voice. She rapped twice on the door.

"Yes?" The response was unidentifiable.

Renie looked inquiringly at Judith, who shrugged.

"Tiff? Maddie?" Renie said in an unnaturally chipper voice. "It's Mrs. Jones. I have good news."

"What is it?" the voice asked warily.

Renie looked at Judith, who mouthed, "Maddie."

"It's a surprise," Renie said. "Think Nordquist, Choo shoes."

After a brief pause, Maddie opened the door. Her blue eyes sparkled until she saw Judith behind Renie. "What is this?" the young woman demanded. "I don't see any Jimmy Choo shoes from Nordquist."

Renie managed to sidle inside the roomette, leaving room for Judith to follow her lead. "Jimmy Choo?" Renie said in surprise. "You must not have heard correctly. Choo-choo, as in train, Nordquist's shoe department, as in where you claim you saw Mrs. Flynn. But," she went on, ignoring the suspicious look on the faces of both Maddie and Tiff, "we do have a surprise. Show them, coz."

Judith slowly removed the camera from her purse. "I believe you left this at Mrs. Rankers's house."

Tiff actually recoiled. "Mrs. Who?"

"The mother of the rental agent who's handling the house in the cul-de-sac by my B&B," Judith explained calmly.

"Awesome!" Maddie cried, snatching the camera from Judith. "I never thought we'd see this again." She looked at Tiff, who seemed bewildered. "Don't you remember how we thought we'd left it in the restroom on the ferry?"

Tiff forced a laugh. "Yes, yes. I completely forgot we'd planned on taking pictures of the rental, but Mrs. . . . Rankers told us to wait for her daughter."

"We couldn't," Maddie babbled on, "because we were meeting a high-school chum for dinner." She looked again at Judith. "Our trip was so hectic. There wasn't time to squeeze everything in. Thanks so much. Come on, Tiff. Let's get a drink and look at our pictures in the dome car. We saw so many great sights during our visit that I've forgotten what we photographed."

The cousins blocked the young women's exit. "Sounds like fun," Renie said, nudging Judith. "Why don't we join these girls to get an idea of how tourists view our fair city?"

"That's a great idea!" Judith exclaimed. "I hear some B&B guests' reactions, but often they check out before we can really chat."

Renie sketched a little bow for the young women. "After you."

Maddie and Tiff looked as if they'd been invited by Nero to face off with a bunch of hungry lions.

"What's wrong?" Judith asked, feigning concern.

"Nothing," Maddie said.

"Everything," Tiff said at the same time.

The young women exchanged glances. Maddie forced a giggle. "We took some . . . weird pictures. I mean . . . goofing off, and then there was this guy we met and . . ." She made a face. "One thing led to another. You know how it is."

"Huh," Renie said. "I'm too old to remember." She turned to Judith. "Let's relive our misspent youth with these frisky chicks."

"Good idea," Judith agreed. "Let's do it."

Any trace of Maddie's insouciance disappeared. "No," she said, putting the camera behind her back. "We're not sharing personal pictures with people we don't know." She looked at Tiff. "We'll go through the photos here, okay?"

The other young woman's angular features had hardened. "That's right." Her coal-black eyes looked threatening. "You'd better go now."

Sensing her cousin's bellicose reaction, Judith spoke quickly. "Fine. We just thought it might be fun. See you." She turned around and started down the corridor to the stairs. Renie followed a moment later, but neither of them spoke until they were back in their own room and had closed the door.

Renie and Judith sat down. "I waited to see if they shut their door," Renie said. "They sure did, and damned near caught my rear end with it."

Judith nodded. "I figured they'd do that."

"You changed tactics," Renie said. "I thought we were going to watch them open the camera and discover the missing memory card."

"Not a good idea after all," Judith said, shifting around in her chair to get comfortable. "When they started to balk, I realized that wasn't necessary. The original point of our visit was to make sure the camera belonged to Maddie and Tiff. If they try to look at the photos, they'll realize the memory card's gone and assume we took it. Or," she added slyly, "they may not."

Renie frowned. "Who'd want the photos? They were in your suitcase."

"But who put the camera there? Maddie and Tiff weren't surprised we had it, so they knew it was missing. The thief ditched it in my luggage. We now wait for their next move."

As the train crept along, Renie gazed out the window into the deep, vast darkness. "I sense you know why those girls took the photos. Connecting the dots, we might assume that the man they referred to when we overheard them in the corridor might be the link. Maybe he stole the camera."

"It's possible," Judith replied, "but I'm considering that the man asked them to take the photos. If so, all he had to do was get it back from them. That brings up another point. So why didn't Maddie and Tiff deliver the camera before boarding the train? Was it because the man wasn't in town? Maybe he got on later. That leaves out Pepper, Wayne, and the bogus Willie."

"What about the Zs?"

"They claim they drove out of town to go through the mountains, which means they would've gotten on the train around midnight when the Cowboy Hats did." Judith made a face. "Yet the Cowboy Hats and the Zs didn't act as if they knew each other when we saw them at the same table this evening."

"And Mr. Cowboy Hat changed his appearance after he went out to have a cigarette. Curiouser and curiouser, as Alice would say."

"Definitely," Judith agreed. "I feel as if I fell down the rabbit hole. I wish I could peer into the looking glass and see something helpful. At the moment, we're playing a waiting game."

"Do you know what we're waiting for?"

Judith sighed wearily. "No, but we'll find out when it happens. And it *will* happen. I can feel it."

The cousins sat in silence for a few minutes. Renie picked up her Roosevelt book, put it down, and took out a crossword puzzle magazine she'd brought along.

"I'll work on my own brainteaser. What's a six-letter word for 'baffle'?"

"How about 'Judith'?"

"Oh—it's 'puzzle,'" Renie said. "I got it by going the other way."

"Good for—" Judith stopped. "Maybe that's what I should do—look at this mess from another angle. What if the dead man really was Willie?"

Renie set her puzzle aside. "Justin's mother is lying?"

"No," Judith said. "Maybe someone told her Willie died five years ago. What if he'd left his estate to Justin or Germaine? We know the Weevils were quarrelsome. Willie may've changed his will whenever he got mad at a legatee. Whoever was disinherited might produce an older version to claim the estate."

"It wouldn't be a first," Renie allowed.

Jax ran by, heading for the end of the car. Judith saw her through the window in the door. "What now?" she murmured, getting up and going to open the door. "Jax?" she said, leaning into the corridor as the attendant knocked on the Kloppenburgs' door.

Jax pointed up at the glowing call light. "I don't know." The door opened and she disappeared inside.

"Well?" Renie said.

Judith shrugged. "The Kloppenburgs' call light's on," she explained, leaving the door open before returning to her chair. "It must be important or they wouldn't summon Jax."

"Maybe they poked the wrong button," Renie said. "Or they're—uh-oh!"

The cousins both turned toward the corridor as Jax again raced by.

"My turn," Renie said, getting up to see where Jax was going. "She's knocking on the Chans' door. A medical emergency?"

"Ah!" Judith exclaimed. "Maybe we can help."

"Coz," Renie began as Judith joined her, "for once, could you rein in your rampant curiosity?"

"I'm serious," Judith said, trying to edge past Renie, who was blocking the doorway. "I am accredited for first aid by the Red Cross."

"And I'm Nurse Ratched," Renie said, barring Judith's way. "Stay put. You can find out later what's going on."

As if on cue, Matt Chan entered the corridor carrying his medical kit. He nodded curtly as he moved past the cousins with Jax at his heels. She looked anxious, but didn't take her eyes off of Matt's back. Laurie exited the Chans' roomette and passed the cousins without a glance in their direction. As the trio entered the Kloppenburgs' room, Judith peered around Renie to see Jim and Sharon Downey coming out of their compartment.

"What's happening?" Jim asked.

"Somebody next door needs a doctor," Renie said. "Matt could open up a practice on this train."

Sharon shook her head. "Honestly, if we have any more crises on this trip, I'm never leaving our house again."

A moment later, Laurie suddenly burst into the corridor.

Judith edged around Renie, putting out a hand to detain Laurie. "Who's sick?" she asked.

Laurie's face was white and her hands shook. "Does it matter? It's all my fault." She took a single step and collapsed at Jim Downey's feet.

Chapter Twelve

Jim Downey knelt next to the unconscious young woman. "Good God," he cried, "what now?"

Sharon Downey's manner was detached as she studied Laurie's motionless form. "That woman's a head case. I've thought so from the start. I think I'll enjoy being a hermit and avoiding further contact with the rest of the world."

Jim shot his wife a sharp look. "Knock it off. What should we do?"

Judith could see that Laurie was breathing. "We could wait for Jax or Matt, but if she simply fainted, we ought to move her where she can lie down." A quick glance into the Downey and Chan roomettes indicated that neither had been made up for the night. Judith looked at Sharon. "Do you have any brandy?"

"No," Sharon replied, her tone less harsh. "I'll get some from the club car."

Laurie's eyes slowly opened. "Ohhh . . ." She grimaced and closed her eyes again. "I'm . . . so . . . sorry."

Jim put his arm under her shoulders. "Can you sit up?"

The only response was a soft, kittenlike moan.

Sharon sighed. "Brandy or no brandy?" she asked of no one in particular.

Jim looked at his wife. "Your call. But we can't leave her here."

With obvious effort, Laurie finally spoke. "Sorry. I'll be okay."

Jim studied Laurie's face. "You sure?"

Laurie nodded. "Just help me get up."

"Hang on." Jim easily lifted Laurie into a standing position. "It's a good thing you can't weigh more than a hundred pounds."

"A hundred and six," Laurie said, sounding more like herself.

Sharon and Renie were still in the doorway. "I'll get the brandy," Sharon said. "If Laurie doesn't need it, I'll drink it myself."

"I'll go, too," Renie volunteered. "Coz and I could use a pick-me-up."

"Let's get drunk," Sharon said, "and pretend we're in a peaceful place, like Iraq or Afghanistan or . . ." Her voice faded as she and Renie headed for the bar.

Judith followed Jim and Laurie into the Chans' roomette.

"Do you want to lie down?" Jim asked.

"I'll be all right," Laurie said softly. "Thanks."

"Do you know who had the medical emergency?" Judith asked.

"Mrs. Kloppenburg."

"Oh." Judith gazed at Laurie, who had curled up into a ball. *Fetal position,* she thought, *escaping to the sanctuary of the womb.* "Do you want one of us to stay with you until Matt gets back?"

"No," Laurie said, her voice more emphatic. "I'm fine."

"Okay," Judith said. "You know where to find us." As she exited the roomette she asked Jim if he'd keep an eye on Laurie.

"Sure," he said, from his roomette doorway. "Sharon's speaking to me again. I hope she brings back food. I'm starved."

"You got shortchanged at dinner," Judith said. "See you later, Jim."

Jax exited the Kloppenburg room, looking as if she'd

recovered most of her composure. "What's the problem?" Judith asked.

"Dr. Chan thinks Mrs. Kloppenburg may've had a mild heart attack."

Judith felt relieved. "That doesn't sound too serious. Maybe that's why the Kloppenburgs wanted privacy. The wife might've felt ill when they boarded."

"I don't know," Jax replied. "I didn't get a chance to talk to her husband. Mrs. Kloppenburg could barely speak, and I don't mean to criticize, but her English is . . . um . . . limited."

"German?"

"No, some kind of Asian language." Jax looked apologetic. "It's especially frustrating in a crisis to deal with people who don't speak English."

"I understand," Judith said. "I've had some difficulties with foreign B&B guests. By the way, Mrs. Chan had a . . . a kind of spell. You might want to tell Dr. Chan if you see him before Laurie does."

Jax looked startled. "Is she sick, too?"

"I don't think so," Judith replied. "More like nerves. It's a good thing she's married to Dr. Chan. He must have her medical history memorized by now." But, she reflected, maybe not her birthday. After forty years, Joe still thought his wife had been born in September instead of October. "How's Mr. Kloppenburg?"

"He's okay."

Jax's apathetic response piqued Judith's interest. "You mean in terms of his reaction to his wife's heart problem?"

"It's hard to say," Jax said, looking as if she was anxious to end the conversation. "I suppose he was upset. He was bossy and almost rude with Dr. Chan." She made a face. "No, not rude—more like arrogant."

"Odd for a man whose wife's having a heart attack," Judith said.

"He acts like he's used to giving orders and expects to be obeyed. A CEO or ex-military, maybe." She paused. "We're stopping. Got to go."

Jax ran down the stairs. Judith looked at her watch. It was almost nine-thirty. Jim Downey had stepped into the corridor. "This must be Malta," he said.

Judith felt a sense of panic. Dare she get off to call Justin or his mother? Would the Zs and the elder Gundys return to the train? And where was Pepper?

Keeping her voice down, she moved closer to Jim. "What side are they loading and unloading from?"

"The other side," he responded, nodding in the direction of the Chans' roomette, where Laurie was still resting.

"Thanks." Judith started to walk away, but turned back. "Is Laurie okay?"

"She's asleep," Jim answered. "What about your neighbor?"

"A mild heart attack. I assume she'll be taken to the county hospital here."

" 'Mild' sounds encouraging." Jim paused. "I think I hear Sharon and your cousin coming."

Sure enough, the two women appeared at the far end of the corridor, both loaded down with food and drink. "Good timing," Renie called, awkwardly balancing the cardboard carrier containing plastic glasses, ice, travel-size liquor bottles, and assorted snacks. "I almost dropped this stuff when we stopped."

Sharon was carrying sandwiches, chips, and tea. She glanced at the Chans' roomette. "How's she doing?"

"Just resting," Jim said, stepping back so Renie could get by. "Matt should be back soon."

Judith followed her cousin. "Did you hear the new engine is meeting us here?" Renie asked, setting the snack items on the table.

"No," Judith said. "I thought it'd been sent to Scuttle."

"Change of plans." Renie studied her cousin. "What's with you?"

"Nothing," Judith snapped. "Hand me a Scotch. I'm getting off."

Renie passed Judith a small Jameson's. "It's freezing outside. Don't go far. Be careful on . . ."

Grabbing her hooded coat, Judith didn't pause for the rest of Renie's advice. She forced herself to descend the stairs slowly. Jax was already standing outside, her breath visible in the cold night air.

"Who's getting off here?" Judith asked.

"Just the Kloppenburgs," Jax replied, giving Judith a hand to reach the snow-dusted ground. "Someone said the ambulance has arrived."

"The station's kind of small," Judith remarked, careful of her footing. "Malta isn't very big, especially for a county seat."

"That's Montana," Jax said. "Plenty of land, not many people. It's stopped snowing, though."

"Good." Judith had her cell in one hand and the Scotch in the other. Moving away from the train toward the blue-and-cream wooden station, she unscrewed the bottle cap and took a quick sip, not caring if Jax might wonder about her drinking habits. A backward glance showed no sign of the attendant. Maybe, Judith thought, she'd gone inside to help the Kloppenburgs. Two men were moving a gurney toward the sleeper.

Although she'd memorized Justin's number, Judith's cold fingers misdialed the first time. On the next try, he answered on the third ring.

"It's Judith," she said. "I'm in Malta. Can you hear me okay?"

"Yes. You're in Malta? You should be almost in North Dakota by now."

"There was a problem," Judith said, not wanting to go into details. "We lost an engine. I have an important question for you, Justin. When your uncle died, did you or your mom inherit anything?"

Justin laughed. "Are you kidding?"

"No, but if Willie's been dead that long, why wasn't it known?"

"You mean how come Mom and I never knew?"

"Not just you," Judith said, watching Mr. Peterson and the

ambulance attendants put down a ramp for the gurney. "The public."

"We wouldn't know now if Mom hadn't gotten the anonymous call today."

"An anonymous call? How odd. What did this person say?"

"Mom sets the alarm for seven, and the phone rang about six-thirty. The caller told her Willie died of a heart attack five years ago and was buried in Wolf Point under another name. Then the line went dead."

"No caller ID?"

"The screen showed 'security screen.' Mom doesn't know what to think. It could be a hoax—but why?" Justin said, obviously skeptical. "On the other hand, if my uncle died a long time ago, why was his death kept a secret? And how could that be since Uncle Willie seemed to be still in public view? If whoever stayed at your B&B wasn't Willie, who the heck was he?"

"Good point," Judith said, walking along the platform to keep warm. "If whoever died today had impersonated your uncle, he did a plausible job. He also had to have help, so somebody knew he wasn't the real deal. Has your mother called the cemetery or the funeral home in Wolf Point? They'd have burial records."

"I know, but Mom started a new project today for a mega-mansion on the Eastside. She may still be there. I haven't heard from her since this morning. Besides," Justin continued, "she confessed that despite wanting to avoid Willie while he was in town, she felt sorry for him when she heard about his accident. She didn't want to get me involved, but she went to see him at the hospital Sunday afternoon. Visitors weren't allowed, and in any case, he was being discharged. Nobody told her he was leaving town. If whoever stayed with you was the real Willie, she's guilt-tripping because she lost her chance to say good-bye."

"Why . . ." Judith paused as she saw the gurney being lowered onto the platform. Mr. Peterson and Jax were standing by, but there was no sign of Mr. Kloppenburg. "Why does your mother feel guilty if she believes what the person told her this morning on the phone?"

"She doesn't know what to think or who to trust."

Judith's gaze followed the gurney's progress. Jax and the conductor remained by the sleeping car. "Would your father know?"

"I haven't a clue," Justin admitted. "The last I heard he was painting in some small Mexican town."

"I didn't realize he was an artist," Judith said, trying to get a closer look at the patient from some twenty yards away. An oxygen mask concealed everything except some dark hair. Bringing up the rear was a tall, broad-shouldered man with rigid military bearing. *Mr. Kloppenburg?* she wondered. Carrying two pieces of luggage, he strode purposefully behind the ambulance attendants. Judith turned her attention back to Justin. "Is your father successful?"

"He survives," Justin replied. "He doesn't sell much art, but the town is an enclave for Americans. I think he does okay painting their houses. I don't know much about him. I don't care much, either. Sorry," he added with a lame laugh.

"No need," Judith said. "If you haven't yet contacted anyone about this Willie confusion, you should. A crime may've been committed."

"A crime? How so?"

"Concealing the identity of a deceased person, for one thing." Judith hesitated. She didn't want to mention murder. "Fraud, maybe. Pepper brought along an insurance policy for Willie. Doesn't that strike you as suspicious?"

Justin laughed. "Wow! That's crazy. Did she show it to you?"

"No. I stole it."

"You what?"

"I stole it. But we won't classify that as a crime. I intend to give it back when I get the chance. The beneficiary is Willie's son, your cousin Ricky. Do you know where he is?"

"Ricky?" Justin was silent for a moment or two. "He got married several years ago. Mom and I got an invitation to

the wedding, but we didn't go. We did send a gift. I think
the ceremony was in Missoula. That's the last time we ever
heard from him. Actually, I suppose the invitation was sent
by his bride. We got a thank-you from her, but it went to
Mom. I didn't bother to read it."

"What about his sisters?"

"I haven't seen them since they were kids. They were
at that awkward age, somewhere around twelve, going on
thirty."

"Do you remember their names?"

"No. Mom called them Gidget and Widget. Not much
class with that part of the family. I'm not a big help, am I?"

"I'm more interested in Ricky than his sisters," Judith
said. "I'm wondering if—assuming Willie died five years
ago—his son got gypped out of his inheritance. This whole
mess smacks of deceit—or worse."

"It sounds serious. I know you," he went on, "and I sense
you're on the trail of something grim. Be careful."

"I will," Judith promised. "We leave here shortly. We'll
make better time with the new engine. If we get to Wolf
Point early enough, I'll call to see if your mother has any
news, okay?"

"Sure, though I doubt she can learn much tonight."

"Every little bit helps. I'd better go, Justin." She rang off
and walked toward the station. Looking up into the eaves
above the entrance, she noticed a carving of a black bird.
The sculpture looked familiar. She'd seen it before—more
than once, she thought. But where?

A few flakes of snow drifted to the ground. Judith was still
shivering as she moved across the platform. Mr. Peterson
was gone, but Jax stood in the doorway, hugging herself to
keep warm.

"We should be leaving in about fifteen minutes," she informed Judith. "I hope so. It must be down into the low twenties around here." Jax helped Judith into the train. "I saw you
admiring the bird over the station door. Cute, isn't it?"

"Cute?" The description didn't fit Judith's reaction. "How do you mean?"

"The story is that when the old Great Northern Railway was built, this had to be one of the stops, but it had no name," Jax explained. "So somebody in the main office closed his eyes, spun a globe, and pointed. His finger landed on Malta—the island in the Mediterranean. Years later, somebody carved that bird and put it over the station door." She shrugged. "I've always thought it was cute. Or maybe clever?"

"Ah." Judith tried to smile, but her face felt stiff. "Yes, it's clever." The shiver that crept along her spine had less to do with the cold than with a sudden apprehension. In both book and film, the Maltese Falcon had led to multiple murders in a case so complicated that even Sam Spade was baffled. If seeing the bird was an omen, Judith hoped it wasn't meant for her.

Renie was standing by the luggage rack. "You're still alive," she said. "That's good."

"Have you been spying on me?" Judith asked, exasperated. "I'm an adult."

"A risk-taking adult. I worry." Renie turned toward the stairs. "Let's relax and have a drink. You go first. I'm watching your back."

When they got to their compartment, Judith stopped. "Wait. I want to see something." She kept moving and opened the door to the Kloppenburgs' sleeper.

Renie followed Judith inside. "I should've known. What are we looking for?"

"I'm not sure. Lock the door and start with the storage cabinet," Judith said, checking out the bathroom. "What's odd about this compartment?"

Renie looked around. "It's very tidy. I saw Mr. Kloppenburg with a couple of suitcases. Maybe he needs to keep busy in a crisis."

Judith shook her head. "It's too tidy. He had luggage, but

there wasn't time to be this thorough. If you had a heart attack, would Bill have the presence of mind to pack everything and make sure he didn't leave any items behind?"

"That'd depend on whether or not he and Oscar took their eyes off the TV long enough to notice that I was on the floor fighting for my life."

"You have a point," Judith conceded, wondering if Joe would react any differently—unless by accident, her collapse had knocked the remote out of his hand. "How do I pull the bed down?"

Renie stared at the top bunk that was tucked against the ceiling. "I think you press that buttonlike thingy. Want some help?"

"No," Judith said. "I don't want you dislocating your shoulder. What about the storage space?"

"Nada," Renie replied. "The trash is . . . trash, and not much of it."

"I wonder how recently it was emptied. We should check those bins in the corridor," Judith said as she opened the bunk. "Ooof!"

"You okay?"

"Yes. It's heavier than I thought." She carefully lowered the bunk. "There's bedding, but no pillows. Are they in the storage unit?"

"Yes, but I didn't take them out," Renie said. "Maybe I should. There might be something written in code on them. Gosh, I wish I still had my Jack Armstrong decoder ring from the old radio show."

"Why? The only message you could get was 'Eat Wheaties.'"

"Right," Renie agreed, tugging at the pillows, "and I couldn't do that because I was allergic to wheat along with . . . well, well!"

Judith turned around. "What?"

Renie held up one of the pillows for Judith's inspection. "Blood?"

Judith studied the brownish spots at the pillowcase's edge.

"Could be. But whose?" She shrugged. "Pull off the pillow-case for a . . . souvenir."

Renie shot Judith a sly glance. "Or evidence?"

"Maybe." She closed the top bunk. "Skip the lower berth. Let's go."

"Want me to go through the trash bins?" Renie asked.

"Okay," Judith said, entering the corridor. "I'll ditch the pillowcase." She saw Matt come out of his roomette. "Go downstairs," she murmured to Renie.

The cousins were on the same wavelength. "Got it," Renie said under her breath, and headed for the steps.

"How's Laurie?" Judith asked, tucking the pillowcase under her arm. "She gave us a scare."

"She'll be fine," Matt replied, closing the door behind him. "I'm getting her some juice from the bar car. Laurie's high-strung."

Judith nodded. "I understand. Will Mrs. Kloppenburg be okay?"

"She should be." Matt seemed noncommittal. "Her husband insisted she should be hospitalized. They'll run some tests and keep her overnight for observation. If they don't find anything serious, the Kloppenburgs can catch the next Empire Builder tomorrow."

"Was she ill when they came on board?" Judith inquired.

"Apparently not," Matt responded. "I'd better go. I don't want Laurie to get dehydrated." He smiled faintly before moving on.

Judith was musing on both the Chans and the Kloppen-burgs when her cousin's voice startled her. "That was a washout."

"The bins?" Judith turned as Renie reached the top of the stairs.

"There's only one and it was almost empty. I'll check the two on this level." Renie started off to the other end of the car, but had to step aside for a small, older man who seemed lost inside a red-and-black hunting jacket with a matching cap that had earflaps sticking almost straight out from his head. Judith watched with curiosity as the newcomer spoke to Renie. After a brief exchange, the man moved stealthily toward her, as if he were stalking prey in the forest. Renie, looking puzzled, followed him.

"Judith Anne Grover McMonigle Flynn?" he said in a deep rumbling voice that contrasted with his slight frame.

"Yes?"

The man reached inside his jacket and removed a white envelope. "You've been served," he said. Without another word, he turned on his heel, almost collided with Renie, and moved back down the corridor.

"What was that all about?" Renie demanded.

Judith opened the envelope, scanned the first page, and found herself speechless. Renie waited a moment before snatching the papers and envelope from her cousin. "Oh, no!" she cried. "You're being sued!"

"Got to sit," Judith murmured. On feet that felt as if they were encased in cement, she plodded into their compartment. "Pepper," she said, collapsing into the chair. "Damn!"

Engrossed in her reading, Renie misjudged her chair's location. "Oops!" She grabbed at the table to regain her balance. "How much?"

"I didn't get that far," Judith said, taking the small bottle of Scotch from her pocket and almost draining it in a single gulp. She winced, choked, and leaned back in the chair. "I didn't think she was serious."

"Do you want to read the rest?" Renie asked.

"You do it. I'm tapped. How much?"

Flipping through the pages, Renie found the sum. "Thirty million bucks for causing the death of Wilbur Kermit Weevil? That's . . . insane!"

Judith rocked back in her chair. "What?"

Renie shook herself. "This is ridiculous. It's time to call Bub."

Judith didn't bother reading the lengthy description. "Don't involve your brother-in-law yet," she said. "I can't believe this. What's the date on it?"

Renie looked at the last page. "November first. It's been filed, so it had to be earlier today."

"Hold on. Who's suing me?"

"You said it was Pepper. Isn't she really Dorothy May Gundy?"

"That's what we heard. I don't understand. She's on this train. How could . . . did she sign it anywhere?"

"I can't read the signature," Renie replied, "but it's not hers—too short. Somebody else filed this on her behalf. Maybe it was a lawyer or a proxy in Malta. It's the county seat, so there's a courthouse. I don't know the actual process."

"I don't either." Judith downed the last sip of Scotch. "Let's find her. Was she in the club car?"

"I didn't see her when I was down there," Renie replied. "It was really crowded. She could've been in the dome car upstairs or even the dining car. They're serving late because of the extra customers who got bored sitting on their dead butts in Scuttle. Anyway, Sharon was in the lead and she's a fast walker."

Judith stood up, took off her jacket, stashed the pillowcase in her carry-on, and put the lawsuit filing in her purse. "Let's go."

"Are we armed?" Renie asked, following Judith into the corridor.

"No, but we're dangerous," Judith retorted. "It'd help if you'd get mad. Then we could be almost lethal."

"I'll work on it," Renie promised.

When they got to the end of the sleeper, Judith saw the trash bins. "Let's check those out while we have the chance. Maybe you'll find something infuriating as you dig and delve."

"You think I'd put my hand in one of those things? Downstairs I pulled out the liner bag and shook it so I could get an idea of what was inside. I'd advise you to do the same."

"Good thinking," Judith agreed.

Before the cousins could begin their task, Wayne Fielding entered the car. He took one stunned look at Judith and opened his mouth to speak, but nothing came out.

"What?" Judith demanded. "You didn't know I was on board?"

"I . . ." Wayne swiped at his fair hair with one hand. "No." He glanced at Renie. "I've seen her before. You're traveling together?"

"Yes," Judith said. "Mrs. Jones is my cousin."

"Oh." Wayne regained his composure. "That's a coincidence."

"What is?" Renie asked. "That we're cousins? That we're both on a train? Or that you and your fellow travelers decided at the last minute to leave town on the same eastbound Empire Builder I'd already booked?"

"No, no." Wayne made a feeble attempt to smile. "It's just a—" He stopped, apparently searching for the right word.

"Coincidence," Judith finished for him. "Skip it. Where's Pepper?"

The question seemed to freeze Wayne. "I'm not sure."

"You can do better than that," Judith said, fists on hips. "Don't act dumb. You must know she's filed a lawsuit against me."

Wayne's stunned expression appeared genuine. "No. Is it true?"

"Would I kid about that?" Judith demanded. "Where is she?"

"I don't know," he insisted. "She was in the dome car earlier, but when I came up from the club car, she was gone. Did you try the accessible bedroom?"

"Not lately," Judith replied with a straight face. "In fact, when we tried to see her, she wasn't there."

"Maybe she is now," Wayne said, increasingly ill at ease. "Pepper could've gotten out from a different car and returned later to the sleeper."

"Perhaps." It also occurred to Judith that Pepper could have gotten off and not come back at all. "We'll try again."

Wayne went on his way, presumably to the sleeper's lower level. "Is he lying about Pepper moving on and off the train?" Renie asked.

"Off, yes—on, no. Maybe." Judith's voice betrayed her frustration. "If she's not aboard, we don't have much time to find her in Malta or we'll get left behind. After we leave, how long will it take to get to Wolf Point?"

"I think there's a stop in between . . . a Scottish name like Aberdeen or Dundee or . . . Glasgow. That's it." Renie looked pleased with herself. "As I recall, it should take an hour or so to get to Wolf Point, the last stop before North Dakota, where we set our watches back an hour."

"Back?"

"Yes, they're . . ." Renie made a disgusted face. "Right. We set them ahead. Most of the Midwest is on central standard time, not central day—"

"Stop! You're driving me nuts. I get it."

Renie scowled. "I'm trying to make sure I'm in the right time zone." She pulled out a plastic bag and shook it vigorously. "I have to deal with a bunch of morons' half-assed attempts to tell God and Mother Nature they didn't know what they were doing when it comes to the sun, moon, and stars. If it's true that daylight saving time started to help farmers . . . or the war industry . . . or to save energy . . ." She paused, studying the third bag she'd taken from the waste bin. "The original idea was Ben Franklin's. In his old age in Paris, he partied into the night, so he wrote a whimsical piece on why we should have more sun in the evening so he wouldn't miss several hours of daylight. I understand the concept, but it's even more impractical than the one-hour change. Years ago, the Twin Cities were on different times. St. Paul went to daylight saving, Minneapolis didn't. Confusion ensued for the dysfunctional twins."

"Fascinating," Judith said drily. "Did you see anything odd in this junk?"

"No. This is a perfect example of wasting, not saving, time."

"True," Judith agreed. "Let's find Pepper."

Renie groaned, but trudged behind Judith to the dining car, where only a handful of passengers were still eating.

The waiters, including Earl, seemed to be moving in slow motion.

Judith stopped at the serving area, where Earl was picking up bowls of ice cream. "A long day," she noted. "I sympathize. You must feel jinxed."

Earl's dark eyes were sad. "It's not just the delays and the extra work—we get used to that. It's Roy's disappearance that's got us down. We get like family after a while. His going off like that isn't right. I keep thinking I'm going to see him walk through here and cheer us up. He was always upbeat, that cheerful kind of brother, and I don't mean just for black folks. Roy was color-blind about race, but those eyes of his took in plenty. He was the noticing kind. He could tell when somebody was down or sickly by just looking at them. Excuse me, Mrs. Flynn, I'd better deliver this ice cream before it melts."

Earl went to the far end of the car. The cousins followed at a discreet distance. As soon as he'd served his customers, Judith asked a question. "Have you seen the redhead who was traveling with Mr. Weevil?"

Earl thought for a moment. "Pretty lady, but kind of sour? I saw her pass through a while back."

"Going this way?" Judith asked, pointing toward the dome car.

Earl nodded. "Haven't seen her since, though it's hard to notice when we're busy."

"I understand. Thanks." She smiled and moved on.

The dome car was crowded, but Pepper wasn't among the noisy passengers. "Everybody seems to have lifted their spirits by lifting spirits from the bar car," Renie noted. "I'll see if Pepper's getting a refill."

"Okay. I'll check the coach cars in case Pepper's hiding out."

There were several empty seats in the first coach. Judith figured their occupants had gravitated to the club and dome cars. Many of the remaining passengers were asleep. Judith kept going. The other coach sections followed the same pattern. Giving up, she made her way back to the dome car. The train began to move just as she stepped inside. Stopping by the stairwell, she wondered why Renie was taking so long. Before she could decide about going to the club car, two cowboy hats appeared before their owners came into view.

"Hi," she said cheerfully as Jack and Rosie Johnston stepped into the dome car. "We're finally on our way."

Jack tugged at his hat brim in a courteous gesture and mumbled hello. Rosie offered a toothy smile. "That's right," she said. "You're a sleeping car neighbor. Mrs. Flynn, isn't it?"

"Call me Judith. You missed some excitement from the room between us."

"What kind?" Rosie asked.

"Mrs. Kloppenburg had a heart attack," Judith said. "They took her to the hospital in Malta."

Rosie gasped. "Really?" She turned to Jack. "We wondered why that ambulance was by the station, didn't we?"

"You did," Jack said, moving into the aisle. "Let's go. I'm beat."

"It has been a long day," Rosie murmured. "G'night, Mrs. . . . Judith."

The Johnstons hurried off. Before Judith could see if there were any vacant seats, Renie emerged from the stairwell.

"It's still a zoo down there," she said. "But no Pepper. I did see the Cowboy Hats while I was at the back of the line, but they left."

"I know," Judith said. "They were in a rush. At least he was. I couldn't get a good look at Jack to see if he was the same guy we saw earlier. His hand covered most of his face when he made a halfhearted attempt to tip his hat and then he hustled Rosie out of here."

"That sounds a little suspicious," Renie said.

"Yes." Judith sighed. "Let's see if Pepper's in the accessible bedroom." She gestured at the soda cans, pretzels, and packs of gum Renie was holding. "You replenished our snacks—again," she said as they started for the car's exit.

"You know me," Renie said as Judith opened the door. "I see a line of people with food at the other end, and I have to join it."

"Sad but true," Judith allowed.

The train had picked up speed, trying to make up for lost time. The cousins didn't speak again until they got to their compartment.

"Are you sure you want to go downstairs?" Renie asked, setting the snack container on the table. "It's risky while we're traveling this fast."

"Confronting Pepper is risky if we're standing still," Judith noted.

"But it's harder to hit moving targets." Renie ripped open the pretzel bag and stuffed a handful in her mouth. "Lethgo."

Judith scowled. "You sound like Emily with your mouth . . ." She stopped at the top of the stairs. "Where did Emily find the camera?"

Renie swallowed before she answered. "Where I dropped it when the truck crashed into the train."

"You didn't see the camera there?"

"I wasn't looking for it," Renie admitted. "I thought we'd derailed. Meanwhile, you were having some kind of fit."

"It wasn't a . . . skip it. I want to know exactly where Emily found it."

Renie clapped a hand to her head. "Don't tell me we have to see that brat again. Emily. Pepper. Charles Manson. Jack the Ripper. Torquemada. Anybody else on your visiting list?"

"Stop. You're going to make me crazy before we get to Boston." Judith gave Renie a shove. "Go. Down. Stairs."

With a huge sigh, Renie began her descent. "Abandon hope, all ye—"

"Stop! Even I can go faster when you're dragging your butt."

At the bottom of the stairs Judith poked a finger at Renie's chest. "Stay out of sight. Sound, too. Hide in one of the bathrooms."

"Gee," Renie said innocently, "I wish I'd brought my crossword puzzle. If you don't come out in an hour, I'll organize a search party."

Ignoring the remark, Judith headed for the family room. She made sure Renie was out of sight before knocking. Courtney responded almost immediately.

"Oh, hi," the younger woman whispered, looking frazzled. "I just got the children settled. Was your camera okay?"

Judith cursed herself for not realizing that even Emily would be sleeping by ten o'clock. She figured the adventurous little girl was like a windup toy or else she ran on batteries—the heavy-duty variety.

"I won't come in," Judith said, also whispering. "Yes, the camera's fine. Thanks again. But do you know where Emily found it?"

"I'm not sure, but somewhere near the stairwell. Or maybe the luggage rack," Courtney said, looking uncertain. "She's so full of high spirits that I can hardly keep up with her. I think she's explored every inch of this part of the train. Curiosity is a wonderful thing in children, but I caught her pretending the duffel bag in the storage area was a pony and she was galloping around on it up and down the corridor. I'm afraid I . . ." Courtney was interrupted by a voice calling for mama. "Emily, go back to sleep, sweetheart."

"I'll leave," Judith said, but before she could move, Emily bounded into sight wearing a pink nightie that at first glance appeared to have a boxing gloves motif. Up close, Judith realized the brown items were chubby gingerbread boys.

"I wanna thee the big lady," Emily said, staring up at Judith with critical eyes. "You go' thomding for me?"

"I'm afraid not," Judith said, forcing a smile.

Emily stomped her foot. "You took my camer." She pouted briefly before tugging at her mother's slacks. "No pwethenth. Can I thee the corpth?"

"Want to *be* the corpse?" Renie came through loud and clear.

"Whath dat?" Emily asked, zipping into the corridor. "Ith

dat mean lady. I thaw her kill dat man wif a big gun, jus' like da Theel Athathin." Emily pantomimed shooting. "Bang! Bang! Bang!"

Courtney grabbed her daughter and hauled her back into the family room. "You shouldn't watch those violent video games, darling. They could give you nightmares. Sorry," she murmured to Judith. "I have to go now."

"That's . . ."—the door closed—". . . okay."

Renie came out of the bathroom. "Serves you right."

Judith shook her head. "You couldn't keep your mouth shut, could you? Why hasn't Bill killed you during the forty-odd years you've been married?"

"Some of those years *were* pretty odd, now that I think about it."

"That happens," Judith said, heading for the accessible bedroom. "Try not to screw up this encounter." She knocked three times and waited. "Pepper must be in here, unless she got off at Malta." She knocked again. There was still no response. "Damn! Dare we go in?"

A male voice from behind the cousins made them both jump.

"Still looking for Pepper?" Wayne asked from his room-ette's doorway.

"Yes," Judith replied. "Is she down here?"

Wayne stepped into the corridor. "She must be. The door's locked. She was really drained by what happened today. Maybe she took something for sleep and she's dead to the world." He winced. "So to speak."

"So to speak," Judith echoed, and hoped it was only a turn of phrase.

Chapter Thirteen

"If," Judith said to Wayne, "you're worried about Pepper, we could ask Jax to unlock the door."

Wayne briefly considered the suggestion. "No. It's after ten. Pepper needs her rest. The last few days have been so hard on her. And then today . . ." He looked helplessly at Judith. "It's a shock. Willie was really tough. I figured he'd rally like he always did. But he . . . didn't."

Judith felt gauche. "I must see her before she gets off at Wolf Point."

Wayne cleared his throat. "She's going on to Chicago. Pepper decided against having Willie's body removed in Malta. The weather and our late arrival complicated things. I notified the undertakers to meet the train in Wolf Point. Final arrangements will be made after Pepper consults with family members."

Judith was surprised. "They're in Chicago?"

Wayne flushed slightly. "Not all of them. It's . . ." He shook himself. "Sorry. I shouldn't talk about this, since you told me about the lawsuit."

Judith put her hand on Wayne's arm. "Please hear me out. There's more at stake than a frivolous lawsuit. How long have you worked for Mr. Weevil?"

The question surprised Wayne. "Four years. Why do you ask?"

Judith pointed to Wayne's roomette. "Can we speak privately?"

Wayne appeared to be considering how much danger two ordinary middle-aged women might present. Judith had assumed a solemn yet kindly expression. For once, Renie looked almost amiable.

"I suppose we could," he finally allowed, "as long as you don't intend to get me into trouble with Pepper. She's my liaison with Willie."

Judith nodded. "That's fine. We're trying to figure out what's going on, and not just because of the lawsuit. There are some things about Mr. Weevil's death that don't make sense."

Wayne looked surprised. "I don't understand. His heart failed."

"I know," Judith said. "Can we talk about that in your roomette?"

"Okay," Wayne responded, stepping aside so the cousins could precede him. "There's only room for two on the couch. I'll stand."

"I'd rather stand," Judith said as Renie sat down. "One of the drawbacks of train travel is too much sitting." Noting Wayne's wary expression, she quickly reassured him. "Don't worry. I won't ask any awkward questions. I'm interested in how well you knew him—and Pepper. Is her last name Gundy?"

"Yes," Wayne answered readily. "Pepper's a nickname." He uttered a faint chuckle. "Her red hair, her temperament. She's a bit of a pistol."

"Did you know there were other Gundys on this train?"

"No," he said, seemingly surprised. "It's not a common name. Does Pepper know? They could be related."

"I wondered, too," Judith said. "She never mentioned them?"

Wayne shook his head. "Pepper never talks about family. She's all business. Willie was like a father to her. I figure her own dad is dead or he walked out. Pepper's mom died years ago."

"Why's Pepper going to Chicago?"

"Her sister, Lynne, lives there. They keep in touch, but I don't know her."

Frustrated, Judith cast tact aside. "Were Pepper and Willie lovers?"

Wayne burst out laughing. "No!" His face flushed again before he grew serious. "Oh, I see what you mean. They shared that big bedroom in your B&B. They often did that because Willie had been banned by so many hotels. For many years, he had a bodyguard who acted as his double and stand-in. But the guy died of an aneurysm or something. Willie was paranoid about people trying to take him on and show him up. That went back to his early days in Butte. Being a tough, macho guy was a big deal. Willie was always kind of small, so he got picked on even in grade school. To make up for his size, he started working out and learning martial arts, then moved on to cars and planes and motorcycles. But that made some locals jealous. On any given night in Butte's taverns, there was a drunk who'd challenge Willie. It got worse when he became famous. No matter where he went, there were plenty of macho types who'd pick a fight. But when he was making movies, he had to avoid taking on tough guys in case he got bruised or cut. That could delay filming, and time was money, so he hired a bodyguard."

Judith was incredulous. "Can Pepper fend off an attacker?"

Wayne nodded emphatically. "Oh, yes. She's trained in various martial arts. Pepper could put anybody out of action."

Renie jumped up from the couch, staring daggers at her cousin. "I quit! Go see Pepper by yourself. I didn't sign up for combat duty."

Judith was also disconcerted. "Maybe we can skip it."

"That's the spirit," Renie said, sitting down again.

Wayne seemed mildly amused. "Pepper wouldn't get

physical, unless Willie was threatened. Basically, she's not a violent person."

"You're saying Pepper never left Willie alone?"

Wayne nodded. "Only if she was certain there wasn't any kind of potential danger. I doubt they ever shared a bed. She brought along a sleeping bag."

"Loyal," Judith murmured. "Devoted."

"Psycho," Renie muttered. "Send her to Bill."

Wayne looked puzzled. "Pardon? What bill?"

Judith ignored Renie. "My cousin and I are bowled over by Pepper's dedication. Was the original bodyguard as steadfast?"

"As far as I know," Wayne said. "I never knew him, except that he was another Montanan. I'm from Denver. I'd never been to Montana until I got my job with Willie. I don't remember his name, but he probably got a credit in the movies he worked on." He scratched his head and frowned. "It was a short first name, something that made me think of somebody on TV. Hank? No, that's not it. Dave?" He waved a hand in disgust. "It'll come to me."

"It's not important," Judith said. "The bodyguard must've been reliable as well as tough. Willie evoked strong feelings from people, both good and bad."

"Definitely," Wayne responded. "Willie inspired hero worship. I saw some of his movies when I was a kid, but I wasn't a big fan. I took the publicist job because I felt it'd look good on my résumé."

"You must be handy with a camera," Judith remarked.

"I'm workmanlike," Wayne said. "I'm more into promotion and the media. I'm working on how to handle Willie's death in the media. Pepper won't talk about it, but it's big news. We've got to move on it ASAP."

"Yes," Judith agreed. "By the way, did you ever find your camera?"

Wayne's hazel eyes opened wide. "How did you know I lost it?"

"It's a long story," Judith said, not giving away what had been a wild guess. "It involves Emily and the camera she found."

"Emily." He chuckled. "She's a little cutie, isn't she?"

"Ah . . ." Judith didn't dare look at Renie. "Very . . . spunky."

"The camera she found was a different model," Wayne said. "I used it last at your B&B." He made a face. "Sorry. That must be a sore subject with you."

Judith let the comment pass. "You didn't leave it there, I assume."

"I thought I took it back to the hotel where I was staying. You were booked by the time I got around to making a reservation."

A tap at the door was followed by Jax's voice asking if she could make up Wayne's bed. He looked at Judith. "Do you mind? Jax probably wants to finish her chores. She's had a rough day."

"Go ahead," Judith said, getting up. "Thanks for your time."

Jax was surprised to see the cousins. "Oh—hi." She smiled weakly, but fatigue was obvious in her face and movements. Even her usually crisp white shirt seemed wilted. "Shall I do your beds after I finish here?"

"Sure," Judith said. "I hope you're almost done for the night."

"Yes, thank goodness." She leaned against the doorjamb. "I couldn't find anyone on my first pass down here except for the mother with her kids, so I made up the other rooms anyway. See you shortly."

"When do we get to Glasgow?" Judith asked.

Jax looked at her watch. "Probably before eleven at the rate we're going, then Wolf Point around midnight. Don't forget the time change."

"We won't," Judith said, nudging Renie to move on before she could start yet another harangue about daylight saving time.

Mr. Peterson was at the top of the stairs studying his clipboard. "Greetings, ladies," he said. "Have you survived today's events?"

"We're okay," Judith said. "It's harder on you than it is on us."

"It's better than flying," Renie declared. "If we'd been hit by a pickup at thirty thousand feet, we wouldn't be around to talk about it."

"Um . . ." Mr. Peterson looked bemused. "I've never thought about that. This isn't a typical Amtrak trip. Still, we've had some passengers who left us."

"Oh?" Judith said, bracing herself against the corridor wall as the train hit a rough section of track. "How many?"

Mr. Peterson studied his clipboard. "Not counting the Kloppenburgs, a family in coach whose children were panicky, a woman who thought she was having a stroke, and an elderly couple who apparently left the train in Scuttle. That's odd. I know them from other trips. They were going home to Wolf Point."

"The Gundys?" Judith said.

Mr. Peterson's expression was curious. "You know them?"

"We were in the dining car when the tavern fight broke out," Judith explained. "They left with a younger couple who'd stayed at my B&B. Their last name starts with Z."

"Oh, yes." The conductor studied his clipboard. "They're in B5, the other sleeping car. Jax made up their room, but didn't mention they'd gotten off."

"They did," Judith said. "I saw them with the Gundys in the motel parking lot when the train pulled out of Scuttle."

Mr. Peterson looked flummoxed. "How peculiar." He slid the clipboard under his arm. "Is Jax downstairs?"

"She was making up Mr. Fielding's bed when we left," Judith replied.

Mr. Peterson nodded. "I'll ask her about the Zyzzyvas."

"Excuse me," Judith said before the conductor started down the stairs. "What happened to the state trooper?"

"Purvis? His superiors told him to get off in Malta."

As the conductor continued on his way, Judith wondered why the trooper had been called away. Renie read her cousin's mind. "At least Purvis can't grill you again," she said. "You look beat. Let's sit and wait for Jax."

Judith didn't argue. "I need more resources," she declared as they entered their room. "Wayne's background on Pepper strikes me as strange. It doesn't suit Willie's macho image to have a woman as a bodyguard."

"Read your book," Renie said, taking out her crossword puzzle. "Play solitaire."

Judith sat down. "Want to play cribbage? Maybe I could beat you. Mother always wins when I play with her."

"I've forgotten how," Renie said. "Besides, we don't have a cribbage board. I suppose we could put a small one together with the rest of the cheese and use toothpicks for pegs, but that seems so wrong." She got a pen out of her purse and studied the crossword. "What's a six-letter word for 'fiasco'?"

"'Debacle'? No, that's seven."

"I'll go the other way," Renie said. "Ha! Got it. 'Striped hyena-like animal' must be an aardvark." She started putting in the letters.

"I didn't know aardvarks were striped," Judith said.

"They must be because it fits." Renie wrinkled her nose. "You're right. Something's wrong here. The *v* doesn't work. 'Aard' . . . what?"

"I don't know. What kind of puzzle is this?"

"The theme is 'A TWO Z.' That indicates all the clues with question marks after them are words with two of the same letters in them."

"Good luck." Judith opened her time travel book, but after two pages, she slammed it shut when Prince Albert and Elvis went skiing with Julius Caesar. She'd found a P. D. James novel in her carry-on when Jax arrived.

"Sorry to bother you," she said, still looking as if the next bed she made up should be her own, "but it won't take long."

"We'll wait in the corridor," Renie said.

The cousins stepped outside just as Matt came out of the Chans' roomette. He looked almost as weary as Jax.

"How's Laurie?" Judith asked.

"She's okay," Matt replied woodenly. "I'm going down to the club car again to see if I can get her a sandwich."

"Maybe," Judith said, "she had a delayed reaction to the train collision."

Matt looked ill at ease. "Maybe."

Judith waited for him to elaborate, but he didn't respond. "I'll let you go on your way," she finally said.

As Matt continued down the corridor, Renie sidled up to Judith. "You flunked a grilling session. You must be tired."

Judith's shoulders sagged. "I guess." Except for the clatter of steel wheels on iron tracks, it was quiet. "The Johnstons must have settled in for the night. If Jim Downey says he first saw Mr. Johnston with sideburns and then without, there's a reason for the men changing places. But what?"

"I've no idea," Renie admitted.

Jax exited their room. "Is there anything else you need?"

"We're fine," Judith said. "I'll set my travel alarm, so you can skip the wake-up call. Oh—did Mr. Peterson ask you about the Z couple?"

Jax frowned. "That's beyond weird. If they got off, they left some belongings behind. Maybe they got back on without anyone noticing."

Judith kept her doubts under wraps. "I hope they weren't left behind. Did Mr. Peterson mention they'd stayed at my B&B last week?"

Jax was surprised. "No. So you know them. I can see why you're concerned. They seem like nice people."

"Yes." Judith tried to sound sincere. "Oh—I forgot that Mr. Peterson told us Trooper Purvis had been called away. Do you know if it had anything to do with the tavern fight in Scuttle?"

"No," Jax replied. "It was about the pickup truck that caused the crash. Maybe they found the driver."

"Good," Judith said. "I assume he had to get away on foot."

Jax frowned. "Not if the pickup wasn't damaged. Excuse me, I still have to do paperwork." She hurried off to the crew car.

Renie was leaning against the corridor wall. "Well?"

"What?" Judith asked.

"When do we break into the Zs' compartment?"

Judith tried to look innocent. "Do you really think I'd do that?"

"Of course," Renie said. She stared at the ceiling. "We've already hit Pepper's room, the Kloppenburgs', and had a once-over-lightly of the Chans', the Downeys', and Wayne's roomettes. That leaves only . . ."

Judith glowered at her cousin. "We're going to sit, remember?" She marched into their room and settled down on the lower bunk.

"I'm shocked," Renie said facetiously, starting to close the door.

"Leave it open." Judith picked up her P. D. James book. "We can't act until Matt gets back from the bar car and everybody's settled in."

"Whew!" Renie passed a hand across her forehead in mock relief. "I almost believed you."

"Funny coz," Judith murmured, opening her book and pretending to read while she kept her eyes and ears open.

For the next five minutes the only sound besides the train was an occasional "hmm" or "huh?" from Renie as she worked her crossword. "Aha! Aardwolf, that's what it must be, not aardvark," she said in triumph. "That gives me an f for the first letter of the 'sputter' clue."

"Good," Judith remarked, trying to block out Renie's commentary while listening for activity in the corridor or the stairwell.

"Okay," Renie said after a pause, " 'sputter' is 'fizzle.' " She tapped her ballpoint pen against her chin. "The word going the other way starts with zy and has another z in the middle. That's weird. These repeated letters are driving me nuts. 'South American insect pest.' I've no idea. I need my dictionary to—"

"What?" Judith asked, finally focusing on her cousin.

Renie slid off the bunk. "My dictionary. It's in my overnight bag."

"How big is it?"

Renie stared curiously at Judith. "My overnight bag? See for yourself."

"No. Your dictionary."

Still mystified, Renie searched her belongings before finally pulling out three thick paperbacks.

"Why," Judith asked, "did you bring along a small lending library?"

"Three pleasure books, three for crosswords. I need sources for puzzle clues like 1936 Nobel Prize winner for physics and the currency of Botswana. Here." She held up a thick, well-thumbed paperback. "Big enough to suit you?"

Judith held out her hand. "Let me see."

Renie shoved the dictionary at Judith. "You want the puzzle, too?"

"Not yet." Judith flipped to the dictionary's last few pages. "Good grief, the print is so tiny!"

"I know," Renie said, still annoyed. "Serves you right. Sometimes I have to use a magnifying glass."

"Have you got one with you?" Judith asked. "I can't read this."

Renie heaved a heavy sigh. "Yes, it's in my wallet." She dug into her purse, yanked out her wallet, and unzipped it with an angry gesture. "This is so damned stupid that I . . . Here," she said, flipping the small, flat plastic magnifier to Judith. "Would you like some of my credit cards or just the cash?"

"Shut up," Judith said, placing the magnifier on the page. "Oh, yes! This is interesting. Let me see the puzzle."

Renie sat down again next to Judith. "Here. Keep it." She tossed the pen to Judith. "Go ahead, finish it. You seem to have taken over."

Ignoring the remarks, Judith carefully filled in the empty spaces and handed over the puzzle. "Well?"

Renie gave a start. "What's a 'zyzzyva'?"

Judith's dark eyes danced. "Remember? The Zs' surname."

Renie shrugged. "So? I still don't get it."

"Look." Judith pointed to the word in the dictionary. "Your clue was 'South American insect pest.'" She paused as Renie read the definition.

"Oh!" Renie grinned at Judith. "No wonder you wanted to look it up. A zyzzyva is a weevil."

Judith nodded. "That's a huge clue to the puzzle—and I'm not talking about the crossword variety. Now all we have to fill in are the rest of the blanks."

"Assuming the Zs aren't the Zs," Renie said, curling up on the bed, "who are they? Why did they take off with the Gundys? Are they connected to Pepper? Did they know Willie's stay was cut short by the accident?"

"I barely saw them," Judith said. "I was surprised when they arrived because we should've been full, but the Zs implied they knew we had a vacancy." She made a face. "I asked if they'd gone through the state association. The question seemed to catch them off guard, but I let it pass. They paid cash, so I didn't ask for ID, and they left early the next day."

"Why choose such an odd name? It only calls attention to them."

Judith didn't answer right away. She sat with her head down, unseeing eyes fixed on the floor. "Because their last name really is Weevil?"

"Wow! A relative?"

Judith nodded. "Ricky, maybe, Willie's son. But it doesn't make sense. If Willie wasn't Willie, why would Ricky and his wife show up at the B&B? Surely Ricky knew his father died five years ago. They wouldn't visit an impostor."

"Because they wanted to prove he was an impostor?"

"Maybe, if Ricky was cheated of his inheritance. But why wait five years?"

"Good point," Renie said. "Didn't you tell me the Zs

called themselves Dick and Jane? Maybe Willie's son went by Dick. Ricky is a kid's nickname."

"True." Judith reached into her pocket and took out the wedding band that Libby Pruitt had found in room two. "The initials are *RK* and *JG*. The *J* could stand for 'Jane.' But what does the *G* stand for? 'Gundy'? Old Mrs. Gundy called her husband Julius, but the date is 1990, and her name is Bessie, which I assume would be for 'Elizabeth.' "

"Or a variation," Renie murmured. "When did Libby Pruitt find the ring?"

Judith grimaced. "She found it the same morning the Zs left. But I can't imagine why they'd go into room two."

"Nobody suspicious stayed there during Willie's visit?"

"No. I checked the guest register after Libby showed me the ring. There's only a single bed and everybody who's stayed there lately seems innocent."

"So," Renie said, "someone who shouldn't have been in the room lost the ring or deliberately dropped it. Exactly where did Libby find it?"

"Under the braided rug by the window," Judith replied. "Phyliss moves the rug fairly often. If . . . oh, oh. I just thought of something. That window looks over the front yard—where Willie made his first jump. I wonder if Pepper went into room two to watch. It would've been unoccupied during midday."

"*RK* and *JG* don't fit Pepper's given first name or nickname."

"They don't fit anyone connected to Willie or whoever died today. The *K* could be for 'Kloppenburg,' but his first name begins with *C*. Except for being reclusive and what might be dried blood on a pillowcase, there's no connection." A sudden thought hit Judith. "Or is there?"

"What do you mean?"

"Matt Chan diagnosed Mrs. K as having a mild heart attack. How hard would it be to fake one when the doctor has limited resources? What if the Kloppenburgs wanted to get off the train? What if they needed a legitimate reason for going to the hospital in Malta?"

"Not for the food. I get suspicious when they give patients a flyswatter instead of a fork." Renie shuddered. "I give up. Why?"

"Wayne told us the body was being sent to Wolf Point for burial," Judith said. "There's no rush, since Pepper was going to make arrangements later. Originally, the body was supposed to be taken off in Malta. Maybe the Kloppenburgs didn't know she changed her mind. They might figure the body would be at the morgue."

"Why bother?"

Judith shook her head. "Maybe they wanted to make sure the body on the one-way train known as the Big Adios really was Willie."

Renie yawned. "Maybe we should forget it for now and go to bed."

"Not yet," Judith said. "It's only nine-something at home."

"We're not at home and we move into our next time zone soon, which means it'll be . . . what? Almost midnight?"

"Correct—for once." Judith stood up. "Let's check the Zs' roomette."

"Ohh . . ." Renie sighed. "Sure, why not?"

The vacant corridor conveyed an eerie silence. Only the last two rooms were still lit up. Judith didn't know who occupied them, but wondered if the passengers were still in the dome or club cars. Maybe they'd made friends, an added pleasure of train travel. Unless, she reflected, you ended up getting sued for thirty million bucks by someone in your sleeper car.

The overhead lights had dimmed as the cousins moved on to the next sleeper, where the Zs had been staying. "B5," Judith whispered.

The roomette was dark and the door wasn't locked. Apparently neither Jax nor Mr. Peterson had yet verified the couple's whereabouts, on or off the train.

Renie switched on one of the roomette's lights. The beds were as pristine as Jax had left them. Judith found three magazines, but none with names or addresses. The two overnight cases were the same ones the Zs had brought to Hillside Manor. Both were unlocked. The cousins didn't hesitate to open them and inspect the contents.

"Clothes," Judith said. "Toiletries. Makeup. Nothing of interest."

Renie had the same result with Dick Z's case. "I can't find anything about the cases' owners. It's as if the Zs made sure nobody could trace them."

"They had a reason," Judith said, putting the case back where she'd found it. "Did the Zs know the Gundys were on this train? Dick Z told me they'd boarded on the other side of the mountains because they drove over the pass for the scenic view. Did they learn the Gundys were on board?" She looked around the roomette. "I don't see any Amtrak info. They must have it with them. No outerwear either. When the Zs hustled the old folks out of the dining car, they came back here, supposedly to get the old folks' coats. But the Gundys were in coach—the opposite direction from the dining car. I barely glimpsed the foursome by the motel. Everything happened so fast. Maybe the Zs took their own outdoor gear for themselves and the oldsters. Nothing incriminating was left behind."

"Maybe there wasn't anything," Renie said. "They couldn't predict the brawl and the gunshots, which is why the Gundys were so upset they let themselves be taken off the train."

Judith thought for a moment. "What if the Zs knew there'd be an incident? The brawl might've been a setup."

Renie was dubious. "You've speculated that the pickup wreck was contrived. I can buy that, but no one knew how long we'd be in Scuttle."

"Why not? There aren't many towns on this route." Judith leaned against the wall. "If I'm right about the accident being planned, who'd be able to drive the pickup and time it so the truck wouldn't be damaged, but the trailer would?"

Renie smiled slyly. "Willie or someone of that ilk." She suddenly tensed, peering through a slit of open space between the closed curtain and the corridor window edge. "Shhh! I hear someone," she whispered, turning off the light.

Judith moved to the bed. "Lock the door, get under the covers."

Renie complied with the first order, but balked at the second. "I can't get the ladder in place that fast."

"Then hide under the bed." Judith slipped under the covers.

"Oh, for . . ." With a big sigh, Renie got on all fours and crawled out of sight. "We don't know who's out there. It could be anybody."

"Shut up. I can hear them talking . . ."

The door slid open. Judith tensed.

"What the hell?" Wayne Fielding said under his breath.

"Close it," Pepper said, also in hushed tones.

Peering out from under the bedclothes, Judith saw the couple beat a hasty retreat—and quietly close the door behind them. She caught only a few words before they passed out of hearing range.

"I don't get it," Pepper said. "What did they do?"

"Don't ask me," Wayne replied. "Maybe we don't want to know . . ."

Judith got out of the bed; Renie crept from underneath it.

"I thought I told you to lock the door," Judith said, disgusted.

"I did," Renie asserted. "Did you lock it after we came in?"

"No. Are you sure you didn't?"

"Ah . . ." Renie made a face. "Maybe. I assumed you didn't want anyone barging in on us."

Judith's shoulders slumped. "You unlocked it when I told you . . . never mind." She remade the bed before speaking again. "Is anything out of place?"

Renie scrutinized the roomette. "No."

"Don't move," Judith said sharply.

"What?"

"You've got a Post-it note on your butt."

"Why would I do that? I know where my butt is. I can actually tell my ass from a hole in the ground."

"You must've gotten it stuck to your slacks under the bed," Judith said, removing the small piece of paper. "Well, well. Take a look."

Renie read the hand-printed words aloud. "'Chester Gundy, b. 04/07/36.'" She looked at Judith. "Who's he?"

"I'll tell you who I think he is when we get back to our room."

Despite the train's rocking motion, both cousins hurried through the sleepers until they reached their compartment.

Judith sank onto the lower bunk. "I suddenly recall Mrs. Gundy asking her husband where Chester was. Mr. Gundy said he was in Wolf Point, where else?"

"As if Chester never went anywhere?"

Judith considered Renie's comment. "I'm not sure. The Gundys, especially Mrs. Gundy, seem muddled."

"Okay," Renie said, "if Pepper is a Gundy, she must be related. Why else would she be checking on the Zs?"

"Right. She and Wayne were surprised to find the roomette occupied. Therefore, they must've known the Zs took off—with the older Gundys." Judith studied the Post-it. "Chester, born in 1936. He may be her father and the senior Gundys' son. Where do we go from here?"

"If only we had a laptop, we could check it on the Internet."

"Somebody must have one," Judith said. "I'll bet Matt does, but their roomette was dark when we went by."

"Too bad Emily didn't swipe one of those." Renie leaned closer to the window. "The clouds are moving away. You can see the full moon."

Judith was surprised that she could also see some of the softly rolling landscape. "It's beautiful. Is this farming country?"

"I think so," Renie said. "Wheat and cattle ranches. There's a grain elevator. And a house. No snow." She studied her Amtrak guide. "The Fort Peck Dam is around here. There used to be an air base, but it was closed several years ago. The Milk River runs through the town. Lewis and Clark thought it looked like a cup of tea with milk poured into it, but it's that color because of glacial—"

"Shut up," Judith snapped. "We're slowing down," she noted. "This must be Glasgow. How long will we be here?"

"Not long. It's another small town on what's called the Hi Line that the Great Northern built through virtually unpopulated territory a hundred—"

"Shut up! All I want to know is how long we'll be in Glasgow."

"We're almost stopped," Renie said. "The station must be on the other side of the train. I can't see anything but more grain elevators."

Judith stood up. "I'm going outside to call Joe. He'll still be up."

"You won't have time, you could get a bad connection. He might be going to bed early. Their flight tomorrow morning is at eight . . ."

Judith didn't hear the rest of Renie's protests. She grabbed her jacket and moved into the corridor. When she got to the bottom of the stairs, no one was in sight. The outer door was shut, but she was undaunted. As she grasped the handle, the train began to move again.

"Damn!" Frustrated, Judith felt the train pick up speed as it passed a closed farmers' market, a vacant baseball field, and the serpentine curves of a murky river. Cursing herself for not moving faster and wishing Renie had stopped blabbing, she headed for the steps. Female voices floated down the stairwell. Judith recognized Maddie and Tiff before she actually saw them.

"You!" Maddie exclaimed from the next to the last step. "What did you do with our pictures?"

Judith took a deep breath, regaining her aplomb. "I kept them."

"You're a thief!" Maddie moved closer, her expression menacing. "We're calling the cops."

"Go ahead." Judith remained calm. "You trespassed. I have a witness." *If Mother can remember who I am, let alone the so-called Santa elves.* "It'd help your cause if you told me why you lied about the rental and came onto our property to take photos without permission."

Maddie and Tiff exchanged quick glances. "You have no proof," Maddie finally said. "We wanted pictures of the neighborhood before we talked to the rental agent. People in real estate do that all the time."

"Then," Judith said, "let me see the other photos, especially the ones of the rental and the rest of the cul-de-sac."

Maddie's blue eyes flashed with anger. "We don't have them here."

"You don't have them at all," Judith countered. "You shot the front of our house, but nothing else in the cul-de-sac. Let's cut a deal. Tell me why you took the pictures of Willie and I'll drop the charges."

"Screw you." Maddie nodded at Tiff. "Do it."

Judith and Tiff were the same height, but the younger woman had a lean, willowy body and no apparent physical flaws. As Maddie stepped aside, Tiff grabbed Judith's upper arms and shoved her back toward the outer door. Maddie was already there, trying to turn the latch.

Judith dug in her heels and screamed at the top of her lungs.

"Hurry up!" Tiff urged. "Somebody might hear her."

Judith screamed again, but her struggle to loosen Tiff's viselike grip was doomed. All sorts of hopes and fears raced through her mind. The door must be locked. Her fierce resistance could dislocate her hip. Someone would hear the commotion. Pain ate away at rational thought. Judith began to feel weak, even light-headed. Maddie swore a blue streak.

Another scream echoed in Judith's ears. *Is that me? I can hardly breathe. How could I scream?* A scuffle. A shrill cry. A loud thud. Judith crumpled to the floor.

"Hey!" a woman shouted. The voice was familiar. "What's this?"

The pain was ebbing, but someone close by was making odd, bleating sounds. Judith slowly opened her eyes.

"You want to take me on?" the not-quite-recognizable voice asked.

Another woman spoke. "Not me, Pepper."

Renie. Relief surged through Judith's battered body. She concentrated on focusing her vision and her brain.

"You sure?" Pepper demanded. "What's in that sock?"

"Horse chestnuts," Renie replied. "They make a nice weapon."

A man called out. "Pepper!"

Judith recognized Wayne's voice. She raised her head. Tiff was rolling around on the floor, groaning. Maddie froze in place, her back against the door.

Pepper confronted Maddie. "Who are you? I thought you were partners in crime with Mrs. Flynn."

"Never!" Maddie cried. "She's a crook!"

Pepper lunged at Maddie, viciously twisting her arms. "Talk!"

Renie and Wayne helped Judith to her feet. "Easy does it," Renie said. "She's got an artificial hip."

The words stabbed at Judith's mind. *But I don't hurt, at least not in the unbearable way I feel when I dislocate. Thank God.*

Tiff had stopped her groans and moans, but stayed on the floor, catching her breath as she tried to sit up.

"Which team are we on?" Renie asked Wayne.

He didn't answer. Judith leaned against the luggage rack and shook herself. "Good question," she mumbled.

Wayne also seemed confused. "Don't ask me. Maybe Pepper can tell us."

Pepper, however, was waiting for Maddie to say something. When the younger woman didn't speak, Pepper twisted her arm again. "You want me to put you in traction?"

"Okay, okay!" Maddie was in obvious pain. "Can we go someplace else?" she asked in a quavering voice.

Pepper nodded at Wayne. "Haul the other one to my compartment. It'll be crowded, but we can sit on these little twits."

Before anyone could move, the family-room door opened.

"What's happening?" Courtney asked as Emily raced to the scene of the disaster. "Darling, don't—" her mother called out, but stopped as she took in the carnage. "Oh, dear! Has there been an accident?"

"Nothing to see here!" Renie shouted. "Go 'way, Emily."

Emily was fixated on Tiff. "You dead?" the little girl asked eagerly, probing Tiff's backside with the yellow bill on her ducky slipper. "You like tickleth? Tickleth make me laugh. Like dis." She let out a series of high-pitched giggles.

Pepper glared at Courtney. "Get the kid out of here. Now."

Obviously frightened, Courtney quickly scooped up her daughter. "Don't kick Mommy again," she begged Emily, who was protesting loudly and waggling her ducky feet. "We need night-night time."

Judith was recovering. "I'm okay, but I need to sit," she admitted. "How can we all do that in any of the compartments?"

Pepper was watching Maddie and Tiff with a wariness that would have made a prison guard envious. "If," she said, "I close the beds in the accessible bedroom, some of us can sit on the floor. Like this pair," she added, indicating the two young women by pointing with her foot.

"I can stand outside," Wayne volunteered.

"Whatever," Pepper said. "Let's do it."

Wayne pulled Tiff to her feet. Pepper shoved Maddie toward the accessible bedroom. Renie picked up Judith's purse where it had fallen during the fray and took her cousin's arm. "I warned you," she said under her breath. "You're damned lucky you didn't dislocate."

"I know," Judith replied meekly. "Thanks for saving my life."

"Sure," Renie said. "I went into the corridor and saw Maddie and Tiff heading downstairs as the train started. I deemed it prudent to arm myself."

"Genius," Judith said under her breath.

Wayne held on to the young women while Pepper moved the beds with Renie's help. Moments later, the cousins were sitting down, Pepper was standing, Maddie and Tiff were on the floor, and Wayne was on guard outside. Taking charge, Pepper addressed Judith. "You're not conspiring with these two?" she asked, gesturing at the forlorn girls.

"Hardly," Judith said. "They've been playing nasty games with me since last week. I've got pictures to prove it."

To Judith's surprise, Pepper seemed impressed. "Maybe I pegged you wrong from the get-go."

"Maybe we both made that mistake," Judith said. "Ask them who they're working for. They're not the mastermind type."

Maddie uttered a faint growl. Tiff rubbed the back of her head. Pepper sneered at both of them. "Well?"

"No matter what Mrs. Flynn says, we didn't do anything illegal," Maddie insisted with a hint of her usual verve. "We took pictures at the B&B she owns." She paused, with a quick glance at Tiff. "It was all harmless—like a stunt. In fact, that's what it was—a stunt. Right, Tiff?"

Tiff grunted in apparent assent.

"Some stunt," Renie remarked. "Does 'harmless' mean you'd push my cousin off a moving train?"

"She threatened us with the cops," Maddie said. "That scared us."

Pepper shook her head. "Save the lame excuses. Who hired you to—" She stopped, turning to Judith. "What kind of pictures? X-rated?"

"No," Judith said, "unless you mean the hospital X-rays taken later. They shot the front of our house when . . ." She paused. "When Willie made his first jump out of the upstairs window. The rest were taken from the backyard, including his accident and the aftermath."

Pepper looked puzzled. "Are you sure?"

"Of course." Judith removed the memory card from her purse. "I returned their camera, but kept this. See for yourself."

Pepper frowned at the card. "I will." She looked again at Maddie and Tiff. "Were you the ones I saw in that silver car at the corner of the cul-de-sac?"

Maddie's defiance resurfaced. "So?"

"Who asked you to take the pictures?" Pepper demanded.

Maddie and Tiff stared at each other. Tiff finally spoke. "His name was John Smith. We met him on the train a week ago going the other way."

Pepper was incredulous. "John Smith? Are you serious?"

Tiff nodded—and winced. "My head hurts."

"Tough," Pepper said under her breath. "What did he want?"

"We got to talking in the club car," Maddie said. "He told us he was a private detective, doing surveillance on some daredevil guy staying at Hillside Manor. Mr. Smith couldn't risk being seen too often, so he asked us to drive by on Wednesday and Thursday. If the guy did anything unusual, we were to take as many pictures as we could. When we got to the cul-de-sac Wednesday morning, we saw a rental sign on a house near the B&B. That'd be our excuse for being there. We left the car by the curb on the through street after we took the first pictures." Maddie stopped to clear her throat. "I need water. I'm parched."

Pepper looked suspicious. "Pretend you're in a desert. Go on. Or can't your accomplice speak?"

Tiff shook her head. "I feel woozy."

"That's a shame," Pepper retorted. "Finish your story. Then you can have some water and maybe I can find an aspirin."

Judith, however, had some questions of her own. "Hold on,

Pepper. I want to know why these two came to my B&B's door."

After a moment of silence, Maddie responded. "We were scared that we'd been seen taking pictures of Willie's accident. We hid on the slope in your backyard, but people were all over the place, in and out of the house. We figured someone had called 911. Cops might show up. We went around that big hedge and came to your front porch. There weren't any sirens yet, so we rang the bell and told you we were looking for the rental agent. You didn't seem to recognize us, so we pretended to go next door. After you'd gone inside, we hurried to the car we'd parked by the cul-de-sac entrance. We left just before the emergency vehicles arrived." She cleared her throat again. "Our job was done."

Judith recalled Arlene's remark about cars cruising the neighborhood. No doubt one of them belonged to Maddie and Tiff.

Pepper wasn't interested in the recital. "I don't give a rat's ass how the pictures were taken. Tell me who wanted them and why." She moved closer to Maddie and Tiff. "Unless you want to be put permanently out of action, cough up a better name than John Smith."

"We can't," Tiff said miserably. "It was the name he used as a private eye. He said he'd be on the same train going east Sunday. All we had to do was leave the camera and the pictures in a duffel bag on the luggage rack in this sleeper." Tiff stopped to catch her breath. "When we got to Williston there'd be a locker at the station with twenty grand in cash as our payment. He gave us the key."

Pepper was incredulous. "This crook is on the train? Have you seen him?"

Maddie shook her head. "No. I mean, I thought I did, but it was from a distance. When I saw the guy closer up, I knew it wasn't him." She looked at Judith. "She's the one who got us all messed up in the first place. She tricked us."

Judith was taken aback. "You mean because I took out the

film . . . or . . . because," she went on as the light dawned, "you dropped your camera when you fled the backyard and had to come back later that night. Where did you find the camera you thought was yours?"

"By the side of the house," Tiff said, finally finding her voice. "Not where the hedge is, but by the driveway. At least it looked like ours. But the more Maddie and I looked at it, the more we realized the model numbers were different."

Judith turned to Pepper. "Did Wayne ever find his camera?"

"No." She sucked in her breath. "I don't get it. If you've got Wayne's camera with the pictures he took in it, I want it back."

"I don't have it," Judith said. "You'll have to ask Emily. I think she swiped Wayne's camera from that duffel bag on the luggage rack. She likes to collect cameras, among other things."

"That kid!" Pepper briefly closed her eyes and shook her head. "Never mind that for now." She leaned even closer to Maddie and Tiff, her face contorted with malice. "Describe John Smith. Now!"

Maddie and Tiff shuddered. "He was maybe forty?" Maddie said, talking fast. "Brown hair, five-ten, nice-looking, but no stud. Denim jacket, jeans, dark shirt." She glanced at Tiff. "Can you remember anything else?"

Tiff was unresponsive for so long that Judith thought Pepper was ready to pounce. "Yes," she finally said. "He had sideburns."

Chapter Fourteen

Tiff's detail didn't seem to mean anything to Pepper. "Sideburns?" She threw her hands in the air. "I surrender. You two aren't just stupid and greedy, but utterly worthless. I'm turning you over to the conductor. He'll know what to do. Unless," she went on, looking at Judith, "you have a better idea."

Judith had some ideas, but she wasn't going to air them. "Go ahead. I'll press charges. Keep me posted. Let's go, coz. I'm beat—in more ways than one."

"Take it easy," Renie said, standing up first. "Here, grab my hand."

Getting to her feet, Judith definitely felt wobbly. "Thanks." She turned to Pepper. "Are you still suing me for thirty million dollars?"

Pepper stared at Judith. "Thirty million . . . are you kidding? If I sued you, I wouldn't ask that much."

Judith opened her purse and took out the legal papers. "See for yourself."

As she flipped through the pages, Pepper's jaw dropped. "I don't get it. I didn't do this. How could I?"

Judith snatched the document from Pepper. "We'll sort that out later. Shall we tell Wayne to get Mr. Peterson down here?"

Pepper didn't answer right away. She seemed genuinely flummoxed. "What? Oh—yes. ASAP."

Wayne was leaning next to the door. He looked half asleep. "Is Pepper okay?" he asked as the cousins closed the door behind them.

"Pepper's fine," Judith said. "She's one tough woman. Get the conductor to deal with the double-trouble pair."

"Poor Pepper." Wayne sighed as he turned to open the compartment door.

Neither of the cousins spoke until they reached the stairwell. "One at a time," Renie cautioned. "You've been through the mill."

Judith saved her breath until she'd collapsed on the lower bunk in their room. "I wonder what would've happened if the outside door hadn't been locked or you hadn't come along with a sockful of horse chestnuts."

"They come in handy if I'm attacked by aggressive squirrels. I sensed you were in trouble even before I heard you scream."

"Thank God for your intuition, coz."

Renie curled up at the foot of the bunk. "You'd do the same."

"True." Judith was quiet for a few moments, trying to recover both physically and mentally. "Have I misjudged Pepper?"

"That's not like you, but it's possible. As Wayne said, she's a no-nonsense type. I've no idea what's going on with the lawsuit and her denial of being part of it. I almost believe her. The only thing I'm sure of is that she makes one heck of a bodyguard. If I needed one, I'd hire her. I wonder if she'd take a bullet for me?"

Judith regarded Renie curiously. "That's interesting."

"What? That somebody might want to shoot me?"

"No. I mean, I don't think anybody would want to shoot you. At least not anybody who—" She stopped, fumbling for words.

"Quit while you're ahead," Renie said drily.

"I've been thinking about Pepper's devotion to Willie—or not-Willie," Judith said. "What inspires that kind of dedication?"

"Admiration? Money? A need to be needed?"

Judith shook her head. "I don't think so. How about love?"

Renie wrinkled her nose. "Wayne insisted there was no romance."

"I'm not referring to that kind of love," Judith said. "I mean the more visceral kind—as in parent and child."

Renie gaped at her cousin. "Father and daughter?"

"Do you remember what Wee Willie Weevil looked like?"

Renie took her time responding. "I didn't pay attention to him. Neither did our kids. I saw news photos and TV clips, but he often wore a helmet in close-ups or it was a long shot of a crazy stunt. Willie might as well have been wearing a suit of armor—not a bad idea, really. Bill had seen one of his movies and said the guy couldn't act his way out of a paper sack. Willie never changed expressions, not even an occasional smile. But his fans saw him in person. They'd recognize an impostor."

Judith stifled a yawn. "Willie hasn't made a movie recently. Whoever was at the B&B looked like Willie, but older. According to Justin and Wayne, the original bodyguard was also Willie's stand-in, so they must've had a resemblance. Justin said the guy doubled for some of Willie's stunts in his last movie."

Renie nodded. "Did Willie die five years ago while his last film was in production? When that Hollywood crew stayed at the B&B, Bill told us about insurance for movie stars. If a lead actor can't complete his scenes, the company collects big-time. Imagine what insurance for a guy like Willie would be worth."

Judith was suddenly wide-eyed and alert. "Thirty mil? The beneficiary was a company called WWF. Wee Willie Films?"

"Maybe," Renie replied. "What doesn't make sense is that if Willie died during filming, why didn't the company collect?"

"Good point," Judith said. "That is strange."

"The only reason I—" Renie held up a hand. "Shhh. Somebody's in the corridor." She got up to take a peek.

"What's happening?" Judith asked after Renie moved back to the bed.

"Wayne and Mr. Peterson went downstairs. It's going on midnight. I hope the cops are waiting for Maddie and Tiff in Wolf Point."

"Good riddance," Judith murmured. "Now, if we could only figure out if John Smith and Jack Johnston are one and the same—or two different people, with and without sideburns." She leaned back and sighed. "It's so frustrating not having resources other than our fellow passengers. How many are involved, how many are who they say they are, and how many are lying through their teeth?"

"It's too bad Wayne hasn't worked longer for Willie—or should I say Pepper? How would he know if Willie wasn't Willie?"

"He wouldn't. How will Wayne react if he learns he's been duped?"

"He's probably out of a job," Renie said.

"Not just that. I think Wayne's in love with Pepper."

"I wondered," Renie conceded. "I can't tell if she returns the feeling."

"No. Her emotions are focused on Willie or whoever the dead man is."

A knock on the door startled both cousins. Renie got up. "Yes?"

"It's Wayne. Can I talk to Mrs. Flynn?"

Renie glanced at Judith, who nodded. "Sure," Renie said, opening the door. "Has Mr. Peterson got everything under control?"

"Yes," Wayne replied, entering the compartment. "The

state troopers are meeting the train at Wolf Point. Are you pressing charges?" he asked Judith.

"Probably. I should speak with the police first."

"I'll mention it to them," Wayne said. "Ironic, isn't it? Maddie and Tiff will be taken off the train along with Willie's body." He shook his head. "What a mess. I don't know how Pepper copes. She keeps her feelings under wraps."

"Yes," Judith agreed. "But suppressing emotions can be self-destructive."

Wayne looked defensive. "She's upset, of course, but . . ." He paused. "People are hard to understand."

"True," Judith said. "Thanks for telling us about Maddie and Tiff."

"There's one other thing." Wayne seemed embarrassed. "Pepper would like copies of those pictures. Could you make some for her?"

"I'll do it when I get back home," Judith said. "It'll be almost two weeks. Where do I send them?"

"There's a PO box in Kalispell," Wayne said. "I'll get it for you. But there's one other thing." He paused again.

"Yes?" Judith encouraged him. "What is it?"

"By any chance, did you find a gold wedding ring at your B&B?"

Judith did her best to sound casual. "Yes, I did. Is it yours?"

"No. It belongs to Pepper."

Judith feigned surprise. "It does? I didn't know she was married."

"She isn't," Wayne said. "Never has been, as far as I know. But it's a family keepsake."

"Oh." Judith took the gold band from her pocket. "Someone found this," she explained. "I put it in my slacks and forgot to take it out. I couldn't fit the initials to any recent guests, but I assumed whoever lost it would contact me eventually." She handed the ring to Wayne. "See what I mean?"

"*RK* and *JG,*" Wayne murmured. "Pepper's last name is

Gundy. If it's for an anniversary, the 1990 date might be for her parents, but I think they're dead."

"Yes," Judith said, and wished she hadn't.

Wayne seemed perplexed. "Oh? Did she talk to you about them?"

"Uh . . . no, it was just an impression." Judith smiled. "Maybe she'll tell you when she gets the ring back."

"Maybe." Wayne sounded dubious. "Hey—we're slowing down. We must be in Wolf Point. I have to help Pepper and Mr. Peterson with those two crooks."

After Wayne left, Renie looked sternly at Judith. "Don't you dare."

"I'm gone," Judith said, grabbing her purse and zipping up her jacket.

"Oh, hell!" Renie threw on her coat. "What's the plan?" she asked.

"To get off," Judith said, starting down the steps ahead of Renie.

On the lower level, an unnatural silence struck Judith. The only sign of life was Mr. Peterson, hands clasped behind his back, standing near the door to the accessible bedroom. He took a few steps forward when he saw the cousins.

"What can I do for you ladies?" he asked.

Judith spoke just as the train's whistle blew and the signal crossing bells clanged. "How long will we be in Wolf Point?"

"I'm not sure," the conductor replied. "Two passengers are boarding, three are getting off. Those young women will be taken into custody and"—he paused delicately—"the removal of Mr. Weevil."

"I see," Judith said. "Is the station open?"

"Yes." While the train slowed to a crawl, Mr. Peterson went to the door. "We'll be here at least fifteen minutes, but we can make good time before the Williston stop. Excuse me. I have to get off."

"So do we," Judith said. "Promise you won't leave without us?"

The conductor didn't seem to hear. He was opening the

door as the train stopped. Setting the footstep on the platform, he hurried to the station.

"Go," Judith ordered Renie. "And give me a hand."

On the ground, the cousins moved briskly to the blue and
white building. A state patrol car, a city police vehicle, and
a hearse were parked nearby.

"See the wolf statue?" Renie murmured. "It's a reminder
of the trappers' heyday. Fur is good. Why did I toss out my
fox-lined raincoat?"

"Keep moving. It should be warm inside."

Mr. Peterson had entered the station, but came back out as
the cousins reached the door. "You're right," he said grimly.
"The Gundys aren't on the train. Their great-grandson's
waiting for them. He's worried. We're checking with Scuttle
to see if they got stranded."

"Don't forget the Zs," Judith said, hugging herself to keep
warm.

Mr. Peterson looked chagrined. "We assumed they were in
the club or dome cars. After long delays, passengers tend to
party and lose track of time." He looked to his left. "Excuse
me. Here come the men from the funeral home."

Judith glimpsed the newcomers, but Renie tugged at her
arm. "Stop gawking," she said. "You've never seen funeral
directors in parkas before? It's not snowing, but it feels way
below freezing."

An anxious-looking young man with longish blond hair
and a scraggly beard opened the door for the cousins.
"Thanks," Judith said—and stopped in her tracks. "Are you
waiting for Mr. and Mrs. Gundy?"

"Yes," the young man said. "Do you know where they
are?"

"No," Judith replied, noticing the plump, dark-haired
woman eyeing them from behind the service counter. "They
got off at Scuttle."

"Scuttle?" The young man was incredulous. "Why?"

"I don't know. I'm Mrs. Flynn and this is Mrs. Jones. Are
you the Gundys' great-grandson?"

"Yes, ma'am." He smiled shyly. "I'm Randy. I know the train got into a wreck. Did they get hurt in the crash?"

"No," Judith replied. "A younger couple was with them. Their first names are Dick and Jane. Do you know them?"

Randy looked dubious. "You putting me on?"

It took a moment for Judith to realize what the young man meant. "You're too young to have read the Dick and Jane primers. They were dropped by most schools' curriculum before you were born."

"My granny helped raise me," Randy said. "She saved some of her old schoolbooks. When I was a kid, I'd look at them. Kind of old-fashioned, but I liked that dog, Spot." He shrugged diffidently. "So The Greats are okay?"

"Yes, I think so. You're certain you don't know Dick and Jane?"

Randy wrinkled his nose. "Maybe. What's their last name?"

Judith took a chance. "Weevil."

"Oh!" He looked embarrassed. "Sure. My grandpa worked for his dad. You know—Wee Willie Weevil. Willie's coming to town. He helps plan our rodeo. Come summer, it's a big deal around here."

"So I've heard," Judith said. "You must've seen Willie at last year's rodeo."

Randy shifted from one booted foot to the other. "No. I dropped out of school. Been working at East Glacier the last few years. Got my GED in June, but my girlfriend and I broke up." He fidgeted with the silver chain around his neck. "Better track down the old folks. Thanks." He started to turn away, but stopped. "Oh—got anything to write on? I should leave my number with the train dude."

Judith reached into her pocket. "I may have . . ."

The plump woman at the counter spoke up. "I'll take care of it, Randy."

"Thanks, Marsha," he said. "Here." He scribbled something on a tablet she'd put in front of him. "Want me to write my name on it?"

Marsha's black eyes twinkled. "You think I don't know

how to spell it after all those years I helped your granny raise you?"

Randy looked sheepish. "It's a habit. Lots of folks screw it up." He hurried out the front door.

The cousins exchanged curious looks. "How hard is it to spell 'Gundy'?" Renie murmured.

Judith nodded. "Not that hard. Stay put." She went to the counter. "Hi, Marsha," she said. "How do you spell Randy's name? I should probably have it along with his cell number in case we hear anything from the train staff."

Marsha studied Judith and Renie for a moment. "Oh, why not? You look like good-hearted souls." She printed the information on a separate piece of paper and handed it to Judith. "There you go."

Judith tried not to look surprised when she saw what Marsha had written. She realized the Gundy parent might have been his mother, but she'd never guessed that his father's last name was Kloppenburg.

Marsha was on the phone. The cousins had stepped away from the counter and were standing on the opposite side of the station. Judith put her purse down in one of the chairs for ticketed passengers and people meeting new arrivals.

"Now what?" Renie asked in a low voice.

"Okay, so I'm baffled," Judith admitted. "We need to talk to Marsha. She looks like the chatty type."

"Hold it," Renie said, looking skeptical. "Marsha was not in your original plan. Marsha didn't exist in your mind until five minutes ago. Why are we here, risking a long, cold walk to Williston, North Dakota?"

"It's like war," Judith said softly but firmly. "Battle plans change. Strategy, and all that. Come on, she's off the phone."

The cousins went to the counter. "Marsha," Judith said, wearing a tired version of her friendly expression, "or should I call you Mrs. . . . ?"

Marsha chuckled. "Birdspeak, but call me Marsha. I'm a member of the Assiniboine tribe. You're on the Fort Peck Indian Reservation."

"I knew that," Renie said, as if she was the brightest kid in third grade.

Judith shot her cousin a baleful glance. "Ignore her. She's a member of the Asinine tribe. You must know Randy's great-grandparents. I'm worried about them. They were taken off the train by a younger couple."

"I overheard what you said to Randy," Marsha said. "Don—Mr. Peterson—I've known him forever—was pretty upset." Her dark eyes suddenly filled with tears. "Poor man. He doesn't know the worst of it. Excuse me." She turned away, removed a tissue from a small box, and dabbed at her eyes. "Train crews become friends after a while. I've worked here for fifteen years."

Judith waited for Marsha to collect herself. "You mean Mr. Weevil?"

Marsha shook her head. "No, though that's sad, too." She sniffled and looked toward the front door. "Here's one of the state troopers. Ask him."

Judith turned around. J. L. Purvis trudged into the station, the long day's weariness weighing him down so heavily that he looked shorter and leaner since Judith had last seen him in Scuttle.

"Jake," Marsha called to him. "Can you tell these ladies what happened? I'm going to put on a fresh pot of coffee."

Purvis didn't act surprised to see the cousins. "Why are *you* here?"

"Why are *you* here?" Judith retorted. "Is this part of your territory?"

"No," he replied, "but we've got lots of miles to cover in Montana. I'm no stranger in Wolf Point." He gestured at the vacant chairs. "Sit. I'm beat."

"Aren't we all?" Renie murmured, but she was the first to comply.

Purvis took his time settling his tall body into the chair.

Judith noticed that his uniform and boots were dirty and a bit damp. She couldn't help but feel sorry for him. He was, after all, a member of Joe's law enforcement fraternity.

"I've done some checking," Purvis said, removing his hat and speaking quietly. "You're more than what you seem to be, Mrs. Flynn."

"Oh." Judith sighed. "Are you referring to the FASTO Web site?"

"Yes," Purvis replied. "You should've told me."

"I don't advertise," Judith said. "Nor did I create the site. Frankly, I find it embarrassing, especially when people refer to me as FATSO."

Purvis didn't seem to find the acronym humorous. "You aren't fat," he said, eyeing Judith up and down. "Skinny women are kind of creepy."

"What did you want to tell me?" Judith inquired. "Is it the Gundys?"

Purvis moved his head, stretching his neck. "No." He swallowed hard. "The body of Roy Kingsley, the missing train attendant, was found earlier today by a creek near the train crash."

Chapter Fifteen

Judith's worst fears for Roy were confirmed. "Was he murdered?"

Purvis nodded. "Afraid so. That's why headquarters sent for me."

Marsha seemed to have her emotions under control. "I can hardly believe it," she said, leaning across the counter. "Roy was a fine man."

"That doesn't keep people from getting murdered," Purvis said.

"How was he killed?" Judith asked.

The trooper hesitated before answering. "Stab wound, up close and personal. He was your sleeping-car attendant, Mrs. Fat—Flynn. Sorry. I mean . . . I'm sorry about a lot of things about now."

"Of course," Judith said. "Do you think it happened on the train?"

"Probably, but wc can't be sure," Purvis replied. "He was found late this afternoon by some kids who were horsing around near the train wreck site."

A memory gnawed at Judith. "How far was that creek from the tracks?"

Purvis looked up at the ceiling panels. "Not far, but out of sight from the train. It was almost dark when the kids found him. They live around there. The other attendant, Jax Wells, told us you were one of the last people who saw him."

"True," Judith said. "That was around nine. He seemed quite chipper."

"You didn't hear or see anything suggesting trouble?"

Judith shook her head. "No. Though . . ." Whatever reference she'd heard or seen about Roy remained elusive. "If he wasn't seen after nine or even nine-thirty, he must've been killed on the train. We were ahead of schedule at Essex. Did Jax agree with the time of his disappearance?"

"Yeah, she did." He reached inside his jacket. "After ten A.M., the train made stops at Browning, Cut Bank, Shelby, and Havre. Except for Havre, they were quick ones. But Roy wasn't seen outside at any of those places. He might not have gotten off if he didn't have to assist passengers in your sleeper."

"I got off at Shelby to use my cell," Judith said, "but Jax was the only attendant on the platform. We didn't go out through our sleeper because we were going to get some snack items from the bar." She paused as Marsha announced that the coffee was almost made.

"Black," Purvis said. "Strong."

"That's how I do it," Marsha said as Mr. Peterson returned.

"Are we leaving?" Renie asked, getting up from her chair.

The conductor gave a start. "Excuse me? Oh—no. We have another problem." He turned to Marsha. "Do you know the Rowleys?"

Marsha looked disgusted. "From way back. What now?"

"We can't find Mr. Rowley," the conductor said. "His wife swears she doesn't know where he is and doesn't much care."

"I don't blame her," Marsha said, "though I can see why she'd drive a man to drink. Uh-oh—here she comes. Watch out. She's on the warpath."

Irma Rowley stomped through the doorway, loaded down with belongings. "Go ahead," she said to the conductor. "If that drunken skunk of a husband is still on the train, take him all the way to Chicago and dump him off in that big lake they got back there."

"Ma'am," Mr. Peterson called to her, "come back. Please."

"Please yourself," Irma said over her shoulder, opening the other door. "I'm half froze and I'm going home to build me a fire."

The door swung closed behind her. Marsha shook her head. "The last time Irma did that, she burned down half the house. It's a bad idea to set off a fire in the living room when you don't have a fireplace."

Mr. Peterson looked helpless as he spoke to Marsha. "Do you think Mr. Rowley got off ahead of Mrs. Rowley?"

"Who knows?" Marsha responded. "Nothing they do surprises me."

Purvis had gotten to his feet. "If she reports him missing, I can put out an APB, but he has to be gone forty-eight hours before we do it."

The conductor seemed at a loss. "I've had them on this route before. They have family in Missoula, so they board around seven-thirty A.M. That gives Mr. Rowley a long time to drink himself into a stupor, especially on this trip with the delays. I hate to think of him wandering around in the dark. He could get hit by a car or fall in a creek. The Amtrak police can find him faster than I can."

The elusive remark suddenly came back to Judith. "Get them on it ASAP," she said, standing up. "Mr. Rowley may be in danger."

Both men eyed her curiously. "I agree," Mr. Peterson said. "It's cold—"

"No." Judith interrupted. "The threat to Mr. Rowley is from Roy's killer."

Mr. Peterson and Purvis gaped at her in astonishment. Renie spoke up. "I don't know exactly what she means, but you better believe her."

The conductor balked. "I'm employed by Amtrak and follow company rules. I'll have to get clearance before proceeding with a search by our police."

"Hold on," Purvis said. "I agree with Mrs. Flynn." He turned to Judith. "Did you see Mr. Rowley on the train?"

"Yes," Judith replied, "but earlier in the day. If he got off along the route, Mrs. Rowley should know. Check with her first. And," she went on somberly, "make a thorough search of the train before we leave Wolf Point."

Mr. Peterson was turning red. "Now just a goldarned minute, Mrs. Flynn. Who are you? A major stockholder in Burlington Northern Santa Fe?"

"No." She glanced at Purvis. "You explain to Mr. Peterson. I never promote myself as a sleuth. It just happens. Encountering bodies, that is."

Purvis reluctantly gave in. "Let's talk in private." He gestured at Marsha, who'd been watching with fascination. "Is the restroom unlocked?"

"No," she replied. "I'll get the key. You know all about the vandalism we have around here." She shook her head. "Kids!"

As Marsha went to fetch the key, Purvis scowled at Judith. "If you know who killed Roy Kingsley, you'd better say so right now."

Judith felt uncomfortable. "I can't. I'm not quite sure. There are at least three possibilities, but I need more information."

"This better not be some kind of humbug," Mr. Peterson muttered. "Thirty years with the railroads, and I've never been in a mess like this."

Purvis didn't comment on the conductor's rueful sentiments. Instead, he had a question for Judith. "It'd help if you'd give us a hint."

"I can't. Not yet." Her expression was contrite. "I'm sorry."

Marsha brought the key and handed it to Purvis. "Here you go."

"Thanks." The trooper looked again at Judith. "Well? What's your next move? I can't cut you a lot of slack at this point."

Judith, in turn, looked at Marsha. "Let's put it this way,"

she said, her gaze shifting back to Purvis. "Marsha may have the key in more ways than one."

C offee?" Marsha asked.
    "No caffeine this late for me," Renie responded.
    "No, thanks," Judith said. "I'd get wired, too."
Marsha picked up the mug she'd placed on one of the empty chairs. "I need to stay alert." She settled in between the cousins, shrewd black eyes fixed on Judith. "So you think I know something about who killed Roy. That sounds unlikely—but interesting. Are you really a detective?"
    "No," Judith replied, "but my husband is. He's a retired police officer who works part-time in the private sector." She smiled ruefully and glanced in the direction of the restroom, where Purvis was filling in Mr. Peterson about FASTO's track record as an amateur sleuth. "Skip my background. Purvis will vouch for me."
    Marsha nodded. "Okay."
    "Good," Judith said. "What I need is background on people you may know. Let's start with Randy Kloppenburg."
    "Randy?" Marsha was aghast. "That boy wouldn't hurt a fly."
    "You're probably right," Judith said, pausing as Purvis and Mr. Peterson came out of the restroom.
    The trooper tossed the key at Marsha; it landed in her lap. "Thanks. We're giving the train another look." The two men hurried out of the station.
    Judith didn't miss a beat. "Marsha, who's Randy's father?"
    If the query surprised the other woman, she didn't show it. "His pa's dead, has been for years. That's why his granny, Ella, raised him. She's gone; so's her husband, Chet." Marsha shook her head. "That family's suffered way too much."
    Renie spoke up for the first time. "Chet? As in Chet Huntley?"
    Marsha nodded. "Another Montana native son."
    Renie nodded. "Wayne said the name of Willie's original

bodyguard reminded him of someone on TV. *The Huntley-Brinkley Report,* I'll bet."

"Chet," Judith echoed. "Chester. Mrs. Gundy asked her husband where Chester was. Mr. Gundy told her he was in Wolf Point."

Marsha frowned. "He is—in an urn at the cemetery. Chet passed away about five years ago. He worked for Willie. Now they're both gone."

Judith played along with the charade. "You must've known Willie quite well if he came here for the annual rodeo."

"Well . . ." Marsha hesitated, apparently choosing her words carefully. "Now don't go around saying I didn't admire Willie. I did, for all the risks he took. He made something of himself. But once he got rich and famous, he forgot the so-called little people. Oh, I know celebrities have to protect themselves from crazy fans, and of course he wasn't young anymore. The rodeo's the biggest in the state, maybe the best in the country, if you ask folks around here. Willie's name sold tickets, even if he didn't do the crazy stunts like in the old days. He'd mostly ride out on his horse and wave at the crowd." She shook her head and chuckled. "The past few years he got to dressing up like old Western heroes— Buffalo Bill Cody, Wild Bill Hickok, the Earp brothers. I figured he'd show up next as Calamity Jane."

"So," Judith remarked, "he didn't mix and mingle with his fans?"

"That's right." Marsha made a face. "Like so many big shots, he forgot who helped him get to the top. Plenty of us were fed up with him. But," she went on more softly, "now he's gone and I'll miss him. He might've acted like he was some kind of god, but he was all Montana, larger than life, risking his neck, daring the weather, racing against the wind. There may not be many people living in this state, but the ones who do got more grit than anybody in the other forty-nine. They have more heart, too." Again, she paused. "The problem with Willie was his heart got smaller when his head got bigger. It's a crying shame."

"That's a very perceptive description," Judith said. "It must've been hard for Chet Gundy to work with him."

Marsha sipped her coffee. "Chet could hold his own, a real feisty guy, willing to take risks, too. Not as daring as Willie, but who is? Brave, too. As a bodyguard, he took on all comers." She nodded to herself. "But underneath, Chet had a bigger heart. That's how it got broken. They told us it was an aneurysm, but I don't believe it. Just like Ella, he couldn't live with the heartbreak that finally blew him down like a Chinook wind roaring over the prairie."

Judith continued putting pieces together. "What broke his heart?"

Marsha leaned back in the chair. "Let me go back to Randy. His mama, Lynne, was Chet and Ella's younger daughter. Lynne and Rob had Randy a few years before they tied the knot." She sipped more coffee and cleared her throat. "Rob worshipped Willie. He dreamed of being the next daredevil champ, and like lots of folks around here, he drove like a maniac on our long, empty stretches of road. Ten years ago come February, Rob and Lynne were driving home from Dripping Springs. It was dark and Rob didn't see the black ice. He skidded, crashing head-on into a semi. Rob was killed outright and Lynne was left a helpless invalid. The only good thing was that Randy wasn't with them."

Judith was moved by the tragedy, but her priority was the living. The gold band's *RK* could be for Robert Kloppenburg, but *JG* didn't fit Lynne Gundy.

After a long pause, Marsha continued. "Chet's wife, Ella, didn't last long. She never had good health. Within a year, she withered away. I still marvel at how Dottie's coped. I'd like to see her, but I won't be a pest."

Judith felt she'd lost the story's thread. "Dottie?"

"Oh!" Marsha looked embarrassed. "You don't know who I mean—Chet and Ella's older daughter. When she went to work for Willie she called herself Pepper. More showbiz-like, and that red hair. Her real name's Dorothy May."

Judith nodded. "Sorry. 'Dottie' didn't click right away."

"It wouldn't if you met her recently," Marsha said. "I heard she was getting off with Willie's remains, but Don— Mr. Peterson—told me she's going on to Chicago. That poor girl has been through so much. She'll always be Dottie to me, though I never saw much of her after she went off to the police academy."

Judith gaped at Marsha. "She's a cop?"

"She was, but she quit after her pa died to take over as Willie's bodyguard."

Judith noticed movement and sounds outside. "The train may be about to leave," she said. "Was Rob's grandfather a local?"

Marsha turned sour. "Another one with big ideas and a head to match. He and Willie . . . oh, skip it. You'd better go."

All three women rose from their chairs as Mr. Peterson entered, holding his railroad watch. "Five minutes, ladies," he said before speaking directly to Marsha. "We found Mr. Rowley. He was out cold in a vacant sleeper." His gaze veered in Judith and Renie's direction. "The local police are taking him home."

"Wait!" Judith cried. "Did Purvis talk to him?"

"Given Mr. Rowley's almost mummified condition, it was impossible," the conductor said tartly.

"Somebody had better sober him up quick," Judith declared. "Or don't you care about what happened to Roy Kingsley?"

"Of course," Mr. Peterson snapped. "I leave that up to the police. I have a train to run." He turned on his heel and went back outside.

"We have to go," Judith said, turning back to Marsha, "but can you tell me about Randy's paternal grandfather?"

Again, Marsha seemed unfazed by the question. Judith figured that as stationmaster in a small town, she kept close watch on her fellow residents. "I'll try," she said, speaking faster than usual. "His real name is Conrad Kloppenburg. Now there's a mouthful—we called him Kloppy. He got a notion to go to Hollywood, but it wasn't what he expected.

You had to know people, have connections. Kloppy returned to Montana and settled in Butte. Maybe he was ashamed to come back to Wolf Point. By then, Willie had made a name for himself, so he and Kloppy formed a partnership to make movies." She shrugged. "They got rich, famous—and snooty. The only time I see Kloppy—and that's from a distance—is when he comes back with Willie for the rodeo."

Renie looked curious. "So Kloppy's a producer?"

Marsha set her coffee mug on a chair. "And a director, I think. Willie was always the hero and his movies were kind of silly. Villains getting trounced, upside-down airplanes, motorcycles flying through the air. For kids, I suppose, who like the action and don't care about the story or the characters. At least there wasn't much gore. I hate that."

Renie nodded. "I don't blame you. My husband's a movie buff, but I've never heard of anyone named Kloppenburg. It's a name you'd remember."

"Kloppy changed his movie name to Liberty Whitlash," Marsha said. "It was Chet Gundy's idea. Whitlash is a tiny place nowadays, but during Prohibition it was a bustling hot spot in Liberty County just this side of the Canadian border." She chuckled again. "The county seat is Chester."

"Ironic," Renie remarked, standing up. "We'd better go." She shook Marsha's hand. "Nice meeting you."

"Same here," Marcia said. "A pity it wasn't a happier occasion, Mrs. . . . ?"

"Jones, but call me Renie. It's a nickname for Serena."

Marsha nodded. "Like the Gundys, with all their nicknames. Dottie for Dorothy May, Ella for Marcella, and Lynne for Joycelynne." She shook Judith's hand. "How come you don't go by a nickname?"

"Uh . . . I never had one," Judith said, distracted by Marsha's list of names and nicknames. "I appreciate your time to enlighten me about the locals."

Marsha shrugged. "Can't see that I helped much."

"But you did." Judith heard the train's whistle. "Maybe I can tell you how when we come back this way."

"It'll be a short stop just before noon," Marsha said, disappointed.

"We'll work it out," Judith said, following Renie. "I promise."

She caught up with her cousin by the stepstool. "Breaking news," Renie shouted. "Mrs. Flynn has another new best friend. The total now comes to—"

"Shut up!" Judith hissed. "You'll wake the dead."

"Then you could solve the case," Renie said, helping Judith get aboard.

"Marsha filled some big gaps, but I'm missing something," Judith admitted.

The train got under way just as the cousins reached their room. Judith gasped when she saw the disheveled bed. "Oh, no! It didn't sink in when Mr. Peterson said they'd found Rowley in a vacant sleeper."

"I caught that. We'll get the Kloppenburgs' fresh sheets."

"They're not fresh," Judith noted, stripping off bedding and tossing it into a corner. "They wouldn't let Jax make up their beds."

Renie looked puzzled. "Didn't Roy change the sheets earlier?"

"If he—" Judith clapped a hand to her head and led the way to the adjacent room. "Why," she muttered, "didn't I think of this sooner?"

"What?" Renie asked, still mystified.

"Help me open this lower berth."

"We're trading rooms with the Kloppenburgs?"

"Come on, do it."

With a resigned expression, Renie gave in.

"Well?" Judith said. "I checked the top bunk, but not this one."

"No bedding." Renie grimaced. "I have a sick feeling I know why."

Judith nodded. "I don't recall Roy saying he made up these beds today." She stared at the bare bunk. "If he did, something bad happened here."

"That something forced the Kloppenburgs to kill him," Renie murmured. "Then they wrapped his body in the bedding and . . . what?"

"They removed Roy after the train wreck," Judith said as she tried to reconstruct what had happened. "It must've been total chaos outside. Nobody was paying attention to the sleeper passengers." She looked at Renie. "After we originally searched this room, you checked the bin on the lower level and said it was almost empty, but the ones up here were full. The crew probably chucks the trash only at night. Those bins are big. Roy was average-sized. I think it played out like this—the body was wrapped in sheets and put in the downstairs bin. Then the killer—or killers—got off and dumped poor Roy away from the train by that creek. It'd be risky, but everything about this horror story involves risks."

"I don't quite get it," Renie admitted. "But I am getting the creeps."

"Don't." Judith eyed the upper bunk. "We need a clean sheet."

Renie tugged at her cousin's arm. "Let's go. Take mine. I prefer sleeping without sheets rather than on one last used by a murderer."

"Sleep sounds impossible," Judith said as the cousins went into the corridor. "Even without Marsha's coffee, I'm wired."

At the door to their room, the cousins were surprised to see Trooper Purvis leaning against the sink. "Where've you been?" he asked in a querulous tone.

"Making our rounds," Judith said. "I didn't know you were joining us. Aren't you supposed to be chasing Roy's killer?"

"I can't do it from Wolf Point," Purvis retorted. "The local cops are trying to sober up that drunk so he can tell them what he saw by the creek. I'm waiting for the Amtrak police to come aboard. They'll flag us down somewhere along the way." Glancing in the mirror, he groaned at his reflection. "This is the worst day I've had since I was a rookie."

"Get the pillows from the Kloppenburgs' room so you can sit," Judith suggested. "I assume you want to talk. And," she continued as Purvis started to leave, "put up some crime-scene tape on your way out."

Purvis turned so quickly that he knocked off his hat. "What?"

"I'll tell you when you come back," Judith said.

Purvis looked dubious, but retrieved his hat and made his exit.

Renie sighed. "It's after midnight. It's a good thing I always stay up late. Of course it's not yet eleven-thirty at home. Or is it only ten—"

"Please stop." Judith sank onto the bunk and turned toward the window. "Total darkness. The moon's gone down or it's clouded over."

"I like looking out the window when I'm snug in my berth," Renie said. "Even in less populated places, you see a lone house or headlights. In small towns you pass through the entire community, getting an idea of how people live."

"And die," Judith murmured as Purvis returned with two pillows.

"What's with the bed next door?" he asked. "It doesn't have covers. There's a missing pillowcase, too."

"That's why the room may be a crime scene," Judith said. "The occupants were there until they got off in Malta when they claimed the wife had a heart attack. Does the name Kloppenburg ring a bell?"

Purvis sat down on the pillows. "Kind of," the trooper replied. "They must be on the passenger list I got from Peterson. What's this about a heart attack?"

"Mrs. Kloppenburg allegedly had one," Judith said. "Dr. Chan checked her out, and that was his diagnosis. She was taken to the Malta hospital. You might want to follow up on that."

"Don't get pissed," Purvis said, trying to stretch out his long legs, "but a civilian telling me how to run an investigation sticks in my craw."

"Get over it," Renie snapped from her place next to Judith on the lower bunk. "You're not the only cop who's taken her advice, including her husband, who's no slouch as a 'tec, either."

Purvis gave Renie a dirty look before he reluctantly took out his notebook. "I should have a computer for this," he mumbled. "I should have my head examined. Okay, give me your best shot."

"One step at a time," Judith said. "I have a logical mind, and frankly, I'm still putting this together. Are you a Wee Willie fan?"

"Used to be," Purvis said. "He was a big deal around here."

"Did you ever meet him?"

"Yeah—in Wolf Point at the rodeo. It wasn't long after I joined the state patrol. I was working crowd control."

"What did you think of him?"

Purvis shrugged. "He seemed okay. I talked to him for a few minutes." He paused, fingering his chin. "Willie was smaller than I figured. Guess that's why they called him 'Wee.' He looked huge on the screen. I don't remember what we said, just 'how's it goin'?,' 'like your movies,' 'doin' some new stunts' stuff."

Judith nodded. "Of course. He was friendly?"

"Yeah. Not palsy, but okay." Purvis laughed softly. "Before Willie walked off, he gave me a thumbs-up sign and a big grin. I'd never seen him smile, so I thought he was missing a front tooth. No surprise, the way he'd get banged up with his stunts. Then I realized it was just a gap. I've heard that a space between front teeth is good luck. I guess that's why Willie never fixed it. He needed all the luck he could get."

Renie smiled. "Our uncle Corky has that gap. It's hereditary. I had it as a kid, but eventually my teeth closed together. Uncle Corky served in World War Two. The French told him he'd survive because of his lucky teeth. And he did."

"There were plenty who didn't," Purvis said. "We've got a memorial in Great Falls that honors all the—"

"That's it!" Judith exclaimed.

"What?" Purvis asked.

"Skip it," Judith said. "Let's back up. Were the elder Gundys in Scuttle?"

"Yeah—they're staying overnight at the motel," Purvis said. "The couple with the weird last name thought the geezers should take it easy."

"How did you hear that?" Judith asked.

"From headquarters," Purvis replied. "They went to the motel where you saw the two couples. The old folks are safe and sound. A relative is coming to drive them to Wolf Point tomorrow."

"What relative?"

"I don't know." Purvis was obviously annoyed. "A grandson?"

"Are the Zs staying with them?"

"I don't know that either and I don't give a rat's ass." The trooper suddenly tensed. "We're stopping. Got to go. The Amtrak cops must be here." He exited before Judith could say another word.

"Damn!" Judith cried. "Now I have to start all over with the train cops. There's no time for that." She rubbed frantically at her forehead. "Worse yet, I've no proof, except for that damned pillowcase and the missing sheets. Unless . . ." She stood up. "I have to make a call."

"Oh, no!" Renie protested. "You won't have time. The cops will hop on board and we'll move out."

Judith reluctantly heeded the warning. "You're right. Instead, I'm going to see the doctor." She was on her way before Renie could say another word.

As Judith knocked on the Chans' door, Renie caught up with her. "Whatever you're doing, I'm doing it with you," she said.

"Fine." Judith knocked again. The door was opened by a sleepy-eyed Matt Chan wearing striped pajamas.

"What's wrong?" he asked in a foggy voice.

"Do you have a laptop that can be used on board?"

"Yes," he whispered. "I don't want to wake Laurie. Do you need it?"

"Can I do that in our sleeper?"

Matt nodded. "It's a Mac, wireless. Hold on."

The train started moving again. Renie gave Judith an I-told-you-so look. Matt produced the laptop. "Did we just stop?" he inquired.

"I think the Amtrak police flagged us down," Judith said. "They're investigating . . . the train wreck. Do you want this back tonight?"

Matt shook his head. "It's already morning. Keep it for now."

Judith and Renie walked back to their room. "I hope," Renie said, "you realize I don't know how to use a Mac."

"Mike showed me how to use his when my old PC expired," Judith said, sitting on the bed. "Maybe I can remember how a Mac works."

Renie opened her book. "Let me know how it all turns out. FDR just died. Try to get back to me before Eleanor joins him in that big New Deal in the sky."

It took a few minutes for Judith to get online, but the Phillips County Hospital site offered only the barest information. "I give up," she said in frustration. "Why did I think I could find out who'd been admitted today? I mean yesterday. It'd be a violation of privacy."

Renie stared at Judith. "You didn't realize that going in?"

"No," Judith admitted. "Malta's so small, I figured they'd be more user-friendly. I can't call them and it's too late to send an e-mail to their office."

"Hmm. Guess you'll have to get into Matt's professional records. If he was the doctor who sent Mrs. K to the hospital, he'd have noted it."

"You're right," Judith said, reenergized. "That's the reason I wanted to check with the hospital. Now how do I . . . ?" She squinted at the screen. "Ah—it's easier than I thought. Matt has patients, diagnoses, records, surgeries . . . the whole gamut. I'll start with dates." She typed in *November 1* and read out loud: " 'Wilbur Weevil, worsening condition after hospital discharge, expired at three forty-seven P.M., MST. Cause of death possibly related to myocardial infarction.' "

"Mmm," Renie murmured, absorbed in her book.

"The only other entry is for Li Y. Kloppenburg. Matt notes shortness of breath, light-headedness, possible history of heart problems, and then 'stress' followed by a question mark. That's it. Nothing about sending her to the hospital. What does that mean?"

Renie closed her book. "Didn't Matt imply it wasn't necessary? Kloppy must've called the ambulance. Maybe Matt couldn't spell 'hypochondria.' "

Judith tried to remember all of the seemingly innocuous remarks related to the multiple tragedies. "I'm checking the Internet," she said.

"I'm checking into bed," Renie said, getting up and starting to undress. "Take one of my sheets."

"Thanks. Don't forget to move your watch one hour ahead."

"Ahead? Oh. Sure."

Judith changed her watch before starting the search for WWF, the insurance policy's beneficiary. The browser's first page showed only sites for the World Wildlife Fund and the second one was devoted to the World Wrestling Federation, now World Wrestling Entertainment. "WWE Smack-Down!" she murmured, rubbing her eyes. "Emily's favorite video game." *I'm tired, maybe exhausted. I can't focus. I should get some sleep.* The discarded bedding included the blanket, but it was probably soiled, too. Judith decided to get rid of the whole set and take a blanket from Kloppy's room. For all she cared, Al Capone could've slept under it.

She opened the door, realizing that Purvis hadn't secured the room as a crime scene. The Amtrak police had diverted him—or else he hadn't bought her theory. She dumped the bedding on the floor before summoning up the dregs of her energy to open the lower berth.

But the berth didn't budge. Judith considered her options.

Maddie and Tiff's roomette was empty, but that meant going downstairs. The Zs' room was vacant in the other sleeper. She'd take her time. Back in the corridor she saw a night-light glowing in her room. Renie must be in bed. Judith kept walking.

The train's movement was steady. The door to B5 was unlocked. She slipped inside, relying on the corridor's dim light to strip the lower bunk. Luckily, she was the only person who'd used the bedding. The Zs were long gone.

Or so Judith thought until she saw the threatening faces of Dick and Jane Z looming in the doorway.

Chapter Sixteen

What the hell are you doing?" Dick Z demanded.

"Borrowing a blanket and two sheets," Judith said, after recovering her breath. "I thought you got off with that old couple in Scuttle."

"We did," Jane replied. "We reboarded later."

Judith refrained from asking more questions. "I'll leave the bedding."

The Zs moved closer, forcing her to backtrack. "Do that," Dick said.

"Sure." Feeling hemmed in, Judith awkwardly dumped the bedclothes on the lower bunk. "I heard Mr. and Mrs. Gundy were spending the night at the motel in Scuttle. Are you the relative who's picking them up in the morning?"

Jane flipped on a night-light. "We're not related to the Gundys."

"I know," Judith said, aware that Dick still barred any attempt at flight. It was now or never, she thought, even if what she was about to say could cause her bodily harm—or worse. "You're related to the Weevils, not the Gundys."

Dick laughed, revealing the telltale gap between his front teeth. "Want to put that in writing?"

His response startled Judith. Despite her fears, she couldn't stifle her curiosity. "I know your phony last name means 'weevil.'"

Dick glanced at Jane. "She's smarter than I thought." He grew somber as he stared at Judith. "How did you figure that out?"

"Coincidence," Judith admitted. "It was in my cousin's crossword puzzle. You don't look much like Willie, but you have the same gap between your teeth. I only got the connection a little while ago."

Dick seemed skeptical. "Why do you care?"

Judith wasn't sure how to answer. "It dates back to your stay at my B&B. You didn't fit the profile of my average guests. And then you suddenly showed up on the train. It seemed odd."

"I don't believe it," Jane said angrily. "You're in league with the rest of them. They'll go to any lengths to hurt Dick."

" 'They'?" Judith repeated. "Who do you mean?"

"When you opened your cash box at the B&B," Dick said, "we saw your IOU note from Willie's nephew. The whole family's against me. I don't know how you got involved. You should've minded your own business."

For a moment, Judith had no idea what Dick was talking about. "Oh, good grief!" she exclaimed. "That was a . . . a sort of joke! Justin's going to make a holiday dinner for us. Call him. I realize you two aren't close, but he says you've kept in touch over the years."

Dick's expression was bitter. "That's a lie. Justin wouldn't recognize me if I showed up on his doorstep. He doesn't know I exist. But at least he and his mother know someone's figured out that Willie died five years ago. That should put a scare into all of them."

Judith wondered if Dick Weevil was unhinged, but Jane echoed her husband's sentiments. "He's like all the Weevils, refusing to acknowledge Dick."

"Whoa!" Judith held up a hand. "Maybe I do understand."

The couple stared at Judith. "What?" Jane demanded.

"Don't play us," Dick warned.

"I won't," Judith insisted. "You're not Ricky Weevil."

"Rick the Prick?" He sneered. "Hell, no."

Judith nodded. "So who are you? Another son of Willie's?"

Both Zs had stepped back a couple of paces. "Yes," Jane said, still embittered. "But Willie never got around to marrying Dick's mother."

"I see." Judith thought for a moment. "Who's your mother?"

Dick's resentful expression didn't change. "An actress. Nobody you'd know. She played small parts in a couple of Willie's movies. Her name is Donna Evans. She's an alcoholic who lives with her third husband in Arizona."

Judith's fears were diminished by sympathy. She wasn't sure what to say. "I guess you didn't mourn your father's death."

Dick looked puzzled. "Why should I? I never met the man. I've spent most of my life in Southern California."

Trying to figure out where this new piece fit into the puzzle and unsure of the Zs' intentions toward her, Judith stalled for time. "Working in movies?"

Dick made a face. "God, no. I'm an urban planner in San Diego. Jane's a freelance writer."

The Zs seemed like solid citizens, but so had other people Judith had come across who were ruthless killers. "Do you go by Weevil?"

"No," Dick said. "But my father's name is on my birth certificate. My mother always used Weevil as my last name, but when I got older I rebelled and went by her maiden name of Evans. Jane uses it, too."

"Why," Judith asked, "didn't you register as Evans at my B&B?"

"We're on a quest," Jane replied. "I came across Zyzzyva when I was searching Internet submission sites. It's the name of a West Coast writers and artists journal. It's the last word in unabridged dictionaries. On a whim, we decided to use it because . . ." She bit her lip. "We're hell-bent on Dick's family recognizing him as Willie's son."

Judith nodded. "Is that why you took the Gundys off the train?"

"Yes," Dick said. "We wanted them to authorize a DNA test."

Judith hesitated. "You mean . . . on the deceased?"

"Of course," Jane said. "When we sneaked out the back door of the B&B that night after everybody else had gone to bed, we had to use a flashlight. We stayed close to that big hedge and something shiny caught Dick's eye. It was a camera under a shrub in your yard. We wondered if the publicist left it behind after the accident, so we looked at the first two photos. Sure enough, there was the so-called Willie about to jump out the window. Dick was certain he was an impostor. We didn't take the time to look at the rest of the pictures then, but after we'd driven off, we went through the rest. That's when we realized the Weevil duo had checked out early because phony Willie had gotten badly hurt. Then we couldn't figure out why the publicist was in some of the shots, so we thought maybe you'd taken them. When we got on the train, we saw your name on a suitcase downstairs and remembered noticing something in your cash box that looked like travel information. The coincidence seemed incredible, but Dick decided to put the camera in your luggage and blame you if any of the Weevil gang insisted on a search."

"I wasn't thinking straight," Dick admitted. "I called the Wolf Point funeral home. There'd been no viewing of Chet Gundy's body after he died five years ago, and he'd been cremated. But we need a DNA test showing that the man who died on the train wasn't my father, Willie Weevil." He suddenly tensed. "We've stopped. Are we in Williston?"

"Maybe," Judith allowed, trying in vain to see her watch in the dim light. "Or it could be another delay for a freight train."

Jane leaned against the wall. "These last few days have been hell."

Judith agreed. "Did you come to my B&B to see Willie?"

"Yes," Jane said. "We didn't know he'd checked out until after we arrived. We finally learned which hospital he was in, but visitors weren't allowed. Sunday afternoon we heard he'd been discharged and was on this train, so we caught a flight to catch up with the Empire Builder around midnight."

A brief silence was broken by Judith. "I'm truly sorry for you both. I'll be on my way."

"Okay," Dick said wearily, "I'll talk to the conductor in the morning. He might tell us who could authorize a sample from the body."

Jane put a hand on her husband's arm. "After all these years, what difference—" She gasped as Trooper Purvis loomed in the doorway.

"Richard Lewis Evans," Purvis said solemnly, "you're a person of interest in the murder of Roy Kingsley. Please come with me."

Dick looked stunned. "Who's Roy Kingsley?"

Purvis didn't try to hide his impatience. "Don't act dumb. Cooperate or I'll have to cuff you."

"Wait!" Jane cried. "Are you talking about the attendant who disappeared? We never saw him. Our sleeper attendant is a woman named Jax."

"Nice try," Purvis said drily, never taking his eyes off Dick. "Let's go."

Dick seemed to have lost his nerve. With a heavy step, he moved toward the trooper. Jane, however, was seething. "This is crap! I'm coming, too," she said, grabbing Dick's arm.

"Fine," Purvis said. "Keep it down. We're getting off the train."

Judith spoke up. "Where are we?" she asked. "This can't be Williston."

"Yes, it is," Purvis replied. "We made up time."

"Stay put, Jane," Dick muttered. "This is a farce."

"You're not going without me," Jane declared, tightening her grip on Dick's arm. "Let's get this over with."

Judith was dumbfounded. *Maybe,* she thought, *I've been wrong about more than Dick being Rick. Why would the Zs—or the Evanses—murder Roy?* Fighting fatigue, she left the roomette and headed for the stairs. By the time she got to the lower level, Purvis had gotten off with Dick and Jane. Judith could barely see them walking toward a patrol car parked a few yards away.

But that was all she could see in the almost pitch-black night. If this was Williston, there should be lights, buildings, crew and passenger bustle. Maybe the train was on the outskirts, waiting for a freight to pass. They seemed to be in the middle of nowhere . . . and there was plenty of that in Montana.

Montana. Williston wasn't in Montana, Judith suddenly remembered. It was in North Dakota. Trooper Purvis had no jurisdiction across the state line. She stood in the doorway, wondering what to do. Before she could make up her mind, Dick and Jane had been hustled into the parked vehicle. The stepstool wasn't on the ground, but in its usual spot by the sleeper's door. Purvis had gotten into the driver's seat and was driving off at a fast pace.

"Damn!" Judith swore out loud. "Damn, damn, damn!"

"Damn you," said an irate voice from behind her. "I really thought you were a goner this time. It would have served you right."

Judith moved away from the open door and turned to see Renie in all her wild tiger-striped fury. "I went to the Zs' roomette to—"

"Yes, yes, yes." Renie stood with her fists on her peignoir. "I figured that's what you'd do. But how did you get down here without ending up dead? I know you wouldn't have volunteered."

"But I did," Judith said. "Coz, we've got to act fast. Trooper Purvis just took off with Dick and Jane. Let's find Mr. Peterson."

Renie started to object, but was stopped by the urgency in her cousin's voice. "Okay. You go first."

Judith summoned up enough energy to keep from flagging. Adrenaline, she figured as they moved through both sleepers to the crew car. Renie pounded on the door. She was about to knock again when Mr. Peterson appeared, looking surprised to see the cousins. "What is it?" he asked, stepping onto the space between the two cars and closing the door behind him.

"Purvis has driven off with the Zs," Judith said. "You know—the couple in B5. He's taken Dick Z—I should say, Dick Evans, which is his real name—for questioning in connection with Roy's murder."

Mr. Peterson looked flabbergasted. "That's very odd," he said, blinking in the light—or perhaps at Renie's sleepwear. "Are you sure?"

Judith nodded. "I was there when it happened. Where are we?"

"Just outside of Williston," the conductor replied. "There's a problem with the tracks by the station. Someone left a car parked on them."

"Did you know Purvis was bringing in Mr. Evans?" she asked.

"Mr. Evans? Oh—the Z people. Why would they call themselves . . ."

"Please!" Judith interrupted. "They had their reasons. Can you find out from the state patrol what's going on?"

Mr. Peterson frowned. "I know you're some kind of amateur sleuth," he said, as much to himself as to Judith, "but I don't want to interfere with the state's operation. Maybe I can check with our own police."

"Do that," Judith said.

"I'll have to go outside." The conductor frowned again. "I'd rather not contact them from the crew car and wake up everyone."

"We'll go, too," Judith said, turning to Renie. "Can you fetch our coats?"

Renie rushed off in a flurry of tiger stripes. Mr. Peterson, who wasn't wearing his jacket, excused himself. Judith waited at the top of the stairs. Renie reappeared, handing over her cousin's jacket. "I'll go first."

The conductor joined them, opening the door and putting down the stepstool. "This trip isn't typical of Amtrak," he said, helping Judith descend.

"I know," she assured him. "We're no stranger to . . . mishaps."

"We're hexed," Renie blurted out. "Think nothing of it. Check out the little cloud of doom and death hanging over Mrs. Flynn's head."

Mr. Peterson didn't seem to take in Renie's irony. "Very discouraging for you, Mrs. Flynn." He moved away, apparently seeking privacy for his call.

To Judith's surprise, the weather seemed warmer than it had been in Wolf Point. There was no snow or ice underfoot. She surveyed what little she could see of their surroundings. The landscape seemed flat—and empty. "If," she said, "we're just outside of Williston, I don't see any sign of habitation. And who'd be crazy enough to leave a parked car on the train tracks?"

"A drunk," Renie said. "I saw it happen in Oakland. We were leaving the station and going slowly. An empty beater was parked across the tracks. There was a tavern about twenty yards away, and a crew member got off to make the idiot move his car. It wasn't the first stop on the jerk's night of beer-soaked revelry. He insisted the tracks were part of the parking lot."

Judith shook her head. "You should avoid Oakland. It's bad luck for you."

"Oh, no. Once we stopped next to a circus train. There were all sorts of—" Renie stopped as Mr. Peterson walked back toward them.

"An Amtrak police officer sobered up Mr. Rowley," the conductor said. "After the collision, Mr. Rowley got off to look around. He strolled to the creek where Roy's body was found. A man who fit Mr. . . . Mr. Evans's description was kneeling by the creek. A woman was there, too. He thought they were camping."

Judith quickly sifted through Rowley's account. "That's shaky information. Did he give details, such as clothing, age, size?"

"Fortyish," Mr. Peterson replied. "What he called 'typical' clothes—casual. I suppose. He'd seen them earlier."

"Where?"

"When he and his wife got on the train, and later, going to the bar car."

"Did he see them coming back?"

"Which—" Mr. Peterson stopped, looking puzzled. "You mean from the creek—or the bar car?"

"Either," Judith said. "Or both."

"That wasn't mentioned."

Something about the account was off-kilter, but Judith couldn't put her finger on it. "Has the pickup driver been found?"

"No," the conductor said, not meeting Judith's gaze.

A silence fell upon the trio. Mr. Peterson kept looking at his watch. Renie shifted around in her feather-trimmed satin mules. Judith stared into space. The night seemed empty except for a few dim lights on the train. There was no wind, no moon, no stars—only the vast moribund plains in every direction.

"Where are we?" Judith finally said.

Mr. Peterson gave a start. "The outskirts of Williston."

"So we're in North Dakota?"

"Well . . ." The conductor made a face. "I didn't check the precise location, but we're very close to the state line." He forced a chuckle. "One of us may be in Montana and the others could be in North Dakota."

Judith persisted. "Then which state's cops should we call?"

"For what?" Mr. Peterson inquired, puzzled. "I already spoke with our Amtrak law enforcement people."

"Talk to them again," Judith urged. "Purvis has the wrong suspect."

The conductor was incredulous. "I don't understand."

"I didn't either," Judith said, "until now."

"Mrs. Flynn," he began in his sternest voice, "my first responsibility is our passengers. I have total confidence in the railroad's police and can't interfere with their investigation or that of the other law enforcement agencies. I'm getting back on the train. And," he added over his shoulder as he started to walk away, "I'd advise you to do the same. We should be leaving momentarily."

"Damn," Judith said under her breath. "Now what do I do?"

"Obey Mr. Peterson," Renie said. "It may not be freezing here, but it's still chilly. Do you really want to spend the night stranded on the Great Plains?"

Judith sighed heavily. "No." Reluctantly, she turned back toward the train—just as it began to move.

"Oh, my God!" Renie shrieked. "Stop! Stop!"

"They can't hear you," Judith said, her body sagging. "We're screwed."

"We can't be!" Renie yelled. "Mr. Peterson knows we're out here. Surely he'll make the engineer stop." She stared at her cousin in horror. "We don't have our purses. We don't have cell phones. What the hell do we do now?"

"Walk?"

Renie stuck out a mule-covered foot. "In these? I'm lucky I got this far."

Judith didn't know what to say. The train had picked up speed. Both sleepers and the dining car passed by. The dome car seemed empty, and not a single head could be seen in the coach cars. A moment later, the Empire Builder disappeared into the night.

"If," Judith finally said, "we're on the edge of Williston, we can't be far from some kind of civilization. Should we find the road that Purvis drove off on or should we stay by the tracks?"

"Tracks," Renie said after a long pause. "We've no idea where the road goes, except north. We could end up crawling on our hands and knees, seeking political asylum in Canada."

"All we seek is a phone and a roof. Let's move. It'll keep us warm."

Renie was swearing under her breath as she trudged behind Judith. After the first fifty yards, they still couldn't see any sign of civilization. "On a scale of ten," Renie griped, "this is a twenty as the worst mess you've gotten us into."

"Hold it." Judith had stopped. "There's the road Purvis

must've taken with Dick and Jane. Look closely. Do you see a light in the distance?"

Renie squinted into the darkness. "Maybe. It's pretty dim. But so are you for not getting back on the train."

"Let's skip the blame game," Judith said. "I'm not the one dressed like a low-rent hooker. And why didn't you grab our purses along with our coats?"

"Sorry. You're right." Renie peered into the gloom. "The light's moving this way. Or . . . not. Now it's gone. No, it's turned red. It's a car backing up."

Judith could also see what appeared to be taillights. "It's turning again. What's going on? Do you think they could hear us if we yelled?"

"We can try," Renie said, and started bellowing. "Help! Yo! Help!"

To Judith's amazement, the car kept coming in their direction. "Thank God. Maybe it's Purvis." But as the sedan purred to a stop, Judith saw that it wasn't a law enforcement vehicle, but a sleek silver Porsche.

"Not quite what I expected," Renie murmured.

Judith didn't respond. The car stopped some ten yards away and the headlights went out. A moment later, a man wearing a red-and-black hooded rain suit emerged. He paused before walking toward the cousins.

"Whoa!" he cried. "Who are you?"

"Does it matter?" Renie asked impatiently. "We need a ride to Williston. We've got a train to catch. Again."

"The train's there now," the man said, moving closer. He stared at Renie. "What the hell . . . ?"

"Never mind," Renie shot back. "Can you give us a ride or not?"

The man laughed. "Are you kidding?"

Judith suddenly tensed. "Who were you waiting for?"

"Not you," he replied. "Did you get off the train?"

"Yes," Judith said, keeping her tone neutral, even as she heard Renie's sharp intake of breath. "We're stranded. Did you expect Maddie and Tiff?"

The man looked wary. "You know them?"

Judith paused. "Give us a ride and we'll tell you where they are."

"Why," Renie said, "share with those dim bulbs? We did the real work."

"True," Judith said. "But the pictures are on the train. Let's go."

"Nice wheels," Renie noted. "I'll sit in back. Coz needs more legroom."

Judith got in the front, wondering if this was the stupidest thing she and Renie had ever done—and realized it was the *only* thing they could do. "How far is the station?" she asked as their chauffeur slid into the driver's seat.

"Five minutes," he growled. "We better make it in time. No pics, no deal. Got it?"

"Got it," Judith said.

The Porsche seemed to fly along the dirt road before smoothly veering onto a two-lane highway.

"Whee!" Renie cried from the backseat. "I think I lost my mules."

"What're you doing back there?" the man demanded, looking in the rearview mirror. "I can't see you."

"Trying to find my mules," Renie replied in a muffled voice.

"Your mules? What the hell are you talking about?" he asked, turning to look in the backseat.

"Hey," Judith cried, "watch the road. You must be doing ninety."

"A hundred and four," the man retorted. "There's no traffic this time of night. We're almost in Williston."

Sure enough, Judith could see lights on the town's outskirts. A moment later, the Porsche whizzed by the city limits sign. After a few blocks, the car slowed to a mere sixty. Judith realized that her clenched fists were literally white-knuckled. "Where are we?" she asked. "I don't see any train tracks."

"The station's on the edge of downtown," their driver said.

"Hang on." He hit the gas, racing through a blur of mixed commercial and residential buildings. When he slowed again, Judith saw lighted motel signs and an arrow pointing to Sloulin Field International Airport. What she couldn't see was any sign of a police presence. Her nerves were frayed by the time they pulled up by a sturdy brick building that bore the Amtrak logo.

"Where's the train?" she asked.

"You can't see it from here. Get out and walk straight ahead."

Judith moved to open the door. Renie moved, too, so swiftly that the man yelled out. "What the hell . . . Hey!"

Judith gaped at their driver. His arms were tied to the back of the seat with a tiger-striped rope. "Grab the keys, coz!" Renie cried, and yanked off the rain suit's hood. "Aha! Side-burns!" As her victim tugged at his satin bonds, Renie clobbered him with the heel of one of her mules. He screamed in pain as his head fell forward. "Go!" she ordered a transfixed Judith.

Judith snatched the keys out of the ignition and opened the door. Renie was already outside, running to the station on bare feet. By the time Judith caught up, her cousin was already inside, arguing with a startled middle-aged man wearing an Amtrak uniform.

"Ma'am," he said, "the Empire Builder left three minutes ago. It's already way behind schedule. I can't stop it."

With flying tiger stripes, Renie hurled herself onto the counter, eyeball to eyeball with the Amtrak employees. "Do it or I'll have to hurt you."

Judith had stopped halfway between the door and the ticket counter. "Call the cops!" she shouted. "That woman already attacked a man in the parking lot. I know how to deal with her. I'm from the home where she escaped."

Renie growled and made clawing gestures as if to go for the man's throat. He backed away and picked up the phone.

"It's okay, Petunia," Judith said soothingly as she approached Renie. "No one will harm you. The nice man's phoning for help. You'll be back in your cozy room with a bowl of porridge in no time."

Renie stopped clawing but growled at Judith, who glimpsed the man's name tag. "Barney is a very sweet guy. Let me help you get back on your feet. You've lost your slippers."

Renie slid off the counter. "They're not slippers, they're mules," she said, sounding almost normal. "I love my mules. Hee-haw."

Barney hung up. "The pol—the *people* are on the way."

Judith smiled warmly. "May I use your phone? I must call the home."

Still shaken, Barney handed the receiver to Judith, who dialed 911. "This is in regard to the call from the train station. A silver Porsche's in the parking lot. The man inside is a murder suspect. Have him taken him into custody ASAP. If you don't believe me, check with the Montana Highway Patrol and Amtrak's police. This is no joke. I'll stay on the line until your officers arrive."

The female 911 operator didn't respond immediately. "Are you sure?" she finally said. "Is this something to do with the missing train attendant?"

"Yes. Do it." Exhausted, Judith leaned against the counter, the phone still at her ear. She heard the operator click off.

Barney was bug-eyed. "I don't get it. What's going on?"

"It's a long story," Judith said wearily. "Be patient. You'll find out later. I have to sit, but the phone won't reach the chairs bolted to the opposite wall."

Renie dragged a packing crate over to Judith. "Use this," she said. "I lost my mules when I jumped out of the car. I want them back. They tie the whole outfit together."

"That belt certainly tied up Ricky Weevil," Judith said, sitting on the crate. "He shouldn't have laughed. The gap between his teeth gave him away."

Barney moved out into the waiting area. "I feel like I'm having a bad dream. I'm almost afraid to ask who you really are."

Judith shrugged. "Just two middle-aged women going

to meet our husbands in Boston. If we ever get there." She heard sirens. "Good. The cops are here. Let's wait until they arrest Ricky."

Renie sat down in one of the chairs. "Hey," she said to Barney, "have you got a master key to those lockers by the restrooms?"

"Yes," Barney replied. "Why?"

"Open them," she said. "There should be twenty grand in one of them."

Barney's heavy-lidded eyes widened. "Really? Oh, man, I don't—"

"There are only ten lockers," Renie interrupted. "Maybe you'll get some of the money for a reward."

"I am dreaming," Barney muttered, going back behind the counter and opening a drawer. "Whose money is it?"

"Hard to say," Judith responded. "Probably the guy who's being arrested. But it was intended for two young women who were no-shows."

"Crazy," Barney said, still muttering as he went to the lockers. Only four were locked. He got lucky on the first try. "Here's an envelope. Shall I open it?"

"Sure," Judith said.

Barney carefully used the key to tear through the envelope. "My God! You're right! There's a bunch of hunsky packets in here."

A young man wearing a police uniform entered the station. "Mrs. Flynn?" he said, looking first at Renie with unconcealed shock.

Renie pointed to Judith. "She's the one on the box. I'm just here for comic relief."

"Ah . . ." The young man blushed. "Oh. Sure." He removed his hat and introduced himself to Judith. "I'm Jason Maxwell, Williams County sheriff deputy. My partner has the suspect in custody. He's incoherent and seems to have a gash in his head. The suspect, I mean."

Judith nodded. "My cousin had to subdue him. She's Mrs. Jones. Despite appearances, she's not exactly comic relief."

"Sidekick, then," Renie said, arranging the folds of her peignoir. "Just like Chet Gundy and Wee Willie Weevil. Sometimes it's hard to tell which is which."

"Weevil?" Deputy Maxwell grew redder. "You mean the suspect is related to the daredevil guy?"

"His son," Judith said, stifling a yawn. "He's dangerous. Not only is he involved in the murder of an Amtrak attendant, but he may've caused the death of Chet Gundy. The real Willie Weevil died of an aneurysm five years ago. Oh— the Amtrak police should arrest a couple calling themselves Jack and Rosie Johnston. She glanced at Barney. "Have you seen a couple in Western gear?"

"No. The only arrivals were the Fullers, who live down the street from me." Barney stared at the cash in his hand. "What do I do with this?"

"Oh—I almost forgot," Judith said. "A couple of Ricky Weevil's accomplices were taken into custody in Wolf Point, first names, Maddie and Tiff. They were collecting this money for taking pictures at my B&B for Ricky." She smiled apologetically. "I wish you could keep some, but it is blood money."

Barney dropped the money and the envelope. "Then I don't want it."

Judith turned to Jason. "Take care of it. It's evidence. Now would you please flag down the train for us?"

The deputy awkwardly gathered up the bills and put them back in the envelope. "You have to give statements," he said. "We had to wake the sheriff up. He wants to be filled in before he charges the guy in the Porsche."

Judith shook her head. "We really can't. We have to get back on—"

"Coz," Renie broke in, "don't be a spoilsport. Your husband's a cop, you know the drill. Besides," she went on, glancing at Jason, "the locals obviously checked with the Montana and the Amtrak police. They know your name, they know your reputation. Let's not damage it by being un- cooperative."

Judith pondered Renie's words. "Well . . ."

"Thanks," Jason said. "We don't have room in the patrol car, so we'll send someone to pick you up. See you at headquarters." He hurried out the door.

"I'm beat," Renie said. "Come on, coz, let's step outside. The fresh air will perk us up. Maybe I can find my mules."

Judith shrugged. "Okay." She turned to Barney. "Thanks for helping us."

The cousins stepped into the parking lot just as the patrol car drove away. Thinking as one, they walked toward the Porsche.

"Aha!" Renie exclaimed softly. "Here are my mules. Want me to drive?"

"What?"

"Stanley is the train's next stop in about forty-five minutes. We can get there in time to catch it in this baby." She patted the car's roof. "You've got the keys. Shall I drive or will you?"

"I will," Judith said. "You drive like your father."

"Thank my father for showing me all the ropes—literally," Renie said, getting into the passenger seat as Judith slipped behind the wheel. "As a seagoing man, he taught his little girl how to tie all kinds of knots. Ever see me do monkey knots? I showed them to Oscar once, but they made him nervous."

Judith smiled as she heard the car's engine purr. "Oh, wouldn't Joe love to drive this baby?" She hit the accelerator and peeled out of the parking lot. "Watch for the signs to Stanley. I have to focus on the road."

"What finally made you realize it was Ricky all along?" Renie asked as they flew along the quiet streets of Williston.

"Rowley," Judith said. "When he and Irma boarded in Whitefish early yesterday, he saw the Cowboy Hats. We never saw them come aboard because it was so late. Ricky must've picked up the sugar beets in Missoula. The Johnstons got off to finalize their plans with him. Ricky must've inherited his father's daredevil genes. He knew how to time his move across the tracks, making it safely to the other side while letting the load of sugar beets get hit hard enough to damage the train."

"Where do you think he left the truck?"

"He'd have to lay low until he found out where the damaged engine would be replaced," Judith said, "but once he found out, he could easily arrive at the motel in Scuttle to wait for the Johnstons."

"So," Renie said, "the naked guy the Downeys saw in the motel doorway was Ricky."

Judith nodded. "Getting back to Rowley, I'll bet he saw the Zs at Whitefish. He was confused, but he may be that way, drunk or sober."

"I'm confused. The Zs got on at midnight."

"Right," Judith agreed. "The same time the Johnstons did. Jack and Rosie didn't recognize the Zs. But Dick knew all about the Weevils—including Rosie, his half sister. The Whitefish stop was around six-thirty, the same time Justin's mother got the phone call from Dick about Willie having been dead for five years."

"Why did Dick call Germaine?" Renie asked, blinking at the blur that was the countryside.

"He'd seen Maddie and Tiff's pictures of *not*-Willie," Judith said. "He'd also seen my IOU from Justin and thought we were all in cahoots. He wanted to tell Germaine he knew the truth and that the jig was up as far as the impersonation was concerned."

"Meanwhile Ricky's been hiding in plain sight as Jack Johnston."

"Always the best place," Judith said.

Renie leaned forward. "Sign ahead. Go right—merging 85 and 2."

Judith made the turn onto a straight, empty stretch of highway. "Remember you said the Johnstons looked alike in their matching Western outfits? True, but also misleading. They probably look alike because Ricky and Rosie are brother and sister."

Renie was surprised. "Really? She's got mega-teeth, but no gap."

"Neither do you, but you did when you were a kid." Judith laughed wryly. "Oddly enough, Arlene had the answer before any of this happened. She talked about the old TV cartoon, *Crusader Rabbit*, with his boon companion, Rags the Tiger. Crusader got all the glory, but Rags didn't mind. Just like Willie and Chet."

"I liked that show. Rags was pretty brave, too." Renie stared through the windshield. "How fast are we going, coz? Will we break the sound barrier?"

"I refuse to look," Judith said. "Ninety, a hundred. If we get arrested, the state patrol will take us to the train."

"Or put us in jail," Renie muttered. "We have no ID, no driver's licenses, and we're driving a stolen car. As we've mentioned earlier, what could possibly go wrong?"

"Everything else has on this trip," Judith noted. "Maybe our luck's changing. I wish I knew who killed Roy."

"I thought you did," Renie said, surprised.

"It was Jack or Rosie. If the Kloppenburgs wouldn't let Jax in, why would they act differently with Roy? They were private people. Being refused, Roy would've moved on to the Cowboy Hats next door. He was friendly and liked to chat. He'd already seen the so-called Willie and I suspect he might've mentioned having doubts about his identity. That would've scared the conspirators. They had to keep him quiet. Rowley's description of the couple by the creek struck me as odd. He called their clothes 'typical.' Mr. Peterson translated that as 'casual,' but I think Rowley was talking like a local. The couple wore Western gear, as many Montanans do."

"So when he saw them, they were already dumping poor Roy by the creek?"

"There or nearby. After the train started up again, Ricky may've moved the body. Rowley told the Amtrak cops he thought the man and woman were camping. Why? Because he thought they had a sleeping bag, not a body bag?"

Renie shuddered. "Ugh. But what about the bloodstained pillowcase?"

Judith shrugged. "Planted by the perps after the Kloppenburgs got off the train. I don't think Ricky and the others liked the Kloppenburgs much. Kloppy was responsible for the original hoax by substituting Chet Gundy for Willie Weevil. The thirty-mil policy paid off if Willie was killed during actual filming. Natural causes like an aneurysm didn't count."

"Would the Kloppenburgs have gotten that money if Willie's death had been faked to look like something else?"

"If Willie keeled over in his trailer, it's likely that only the Gundys and Kloppy knew about it. The *K*s were going to the rodeo meeting in Wolf Point, but I think they got scared when the body count started. They were still making money from the impersonation. Maybe Mrs. Kloppy was stressed and Mr. Kloppy feared for both their lives. A heart attack was a good excuse to get off the train. Besides, if Joycelynne Gundy Kloppenburg is an invalid in a Chicago institution, the Gundys and the *K*s need money to pay for her care. Pepper's relationship with Kloppy was codependent. Who'd get the royalties that were still coming in? Not knowing if Chet died of natural causes, Kloppy had a reason to be frightened. Most of the burden of maintaining the charade fell on Pepper. I'd bet real money that she saw those videos of Willie's movies at our house and got rid of them in case anybody started making comparisons—including Wayne."

"Makes sense," Renie said. "But why was Laurie Chan so upset?"

"Who knows? Maybe when she found out Mrs. Kloppy was Asian, it made her think of her birth mother. So much life and death has gone on in the past two days that anybody's emotions could go off-kilter, including Sharon Downey's. Let's face it, this hasn't been a pleasure trip for a lot of folks."

"True." Renie blinked. "I just got it. The wedding band

belonged to Rob and Joycelynne. I'll bet you figured it out when Marsha talked about nicknames."

"Oh . . . yes," Judith said diffidently. "*RK* and *JG* and the 1990 date didn't fit anybody involved—until Marsha mentioned Lynne's full first name. She'd also told us that Rob and Lynne got married a few years after Randy was born. That fit, too."

Renie nodded. "That last blur of a sign said Stanley, twenty miles."

"We'll be there in ten minutes." Judith glanced in the rear view mirror. "Uh-oh, we've got company."

"Cops?"

"Let's find out." Judith pushed down on the pedal. "Whee! I haven't driven like this since Joe and I were dating and he let me drive his MG."

Renie had her hands pressed against the dashboard. "When do we go airborne? And did I mention I was afraid of flying?"

Judith glanced again at the mirror. "We're losing them. If we were still in Montana, they'd call this the Montanabahn."

It took Renie a moment to regain her voice. "Why now?"

"Now? What do you mean?"

"After all this time, Ricky decides to act?"

"He got tired of waiting. The B&B accident set him off. Wayne told us about a PO box in Kalispell. I figure it's registered to Ricky. Wayne had to tell Ricky what happened to Chet. Then Ricky came up with his wacky plan to create enough confusion that someone could finish off the poor old coot and have photos to show that the death had stemmed from a stunt."

"But how would Ricky know that Chet would jump off the roof?"

"Chet was a daredevil, too," Judith replied. "He probably practiced doing crazy stuff all the time to stay in shape. Maddie and Tiff's photos could also be used to sue me, in case the insurance company wasn't fooled. Remember the label scrap stuck to your shoe? 'Ox,' for oxycodone, or Percocet. Willie—I mean, Chet—kept saying 'ring' before he died. I thought it meant the ring I had in my pocket. Later I realized that when my hip really hurts, I take a Percocet. Sometimes it causes ringing in my ears. If there's an autopsy, I'll bet it shows an overdose."

"By whom?"

"Rosie," Judith said. "Wasn't she with Willie, playing nurse?"

Renie looked chagrined. "I forgot."

"Ricky probably promised his half sisters a cut of the insurance money. For all we know, both of them were beneficiaries of policies we never saw. In fact, I wonder if Sister Number Two wasn't in Malta, putting together the subpoena I was handed. I quit. I'm leaving all the legal stuff to the lawyers," Judith declared. "I'll bet the Weevil and the Gundy estates are a box of bees."

"If so, the attorneys will end up with most of it," Renie remarked. "But if Ricky was so desperate for money, how could he afford a car like this and pay Maddie and Tiff twenty grand?"

"Did you look at those hunskies?"

"No. The bills had bands around them and I only got a glimpse when Barney dropped the whole bunch."

"Barney didn't look closely either," Judith said, "but from what little I could see, Ben Franklin never had slicked-back dark hair."

"They were fake? With pictures of Willie on them?"

"That's who I assumed it was. As for this car, there's only four hundred miles on it. Ricky must've bought it on his prospects."

"If he bought it at all," Renie said. "Hey, Stanley's coming . . . yikes!" She held on for dear life as Judith turned sharply at the exit.

"Now what?" Judith asked.

"Uh . . . follow this to Main Street."

"How do you know that's right?"

"I don't. I'm channeling my dad again. He always followed his nose, and my nose tells me there's a Main Street. There always is in small towns."

There was one in Stanley. "You lucked out. Next nose knowledge?"

"Try Railroad Avenue. They often have one of those."

To the relief of both cousins, there was a Railroad Avenue and an Amtrak station on the edge of the small downtown area. Judith pulled up next to the building. "The lights are on. The train must not have arrived yet."

"Trains in this country don't drive like you do," Renie said, slipping into her mules. "Shall we go inside or wait by the tracks?"

Judith didn't respond until they got out of the car. "I suppose we should go in." She looked at her watch. "Do you realize what time it is?"

"Somewhere in the wee small hours, but don't tell me. I'll get all mixed up." She stared beyond Judith. "Uh-oh. Here comes another car. I wonder if it's the one following us. It doesn't look like the cops."

"Maybe they're meeting the train," Judith said. "This is a really little town. What's close by?"

"I think Minot's next. It's got to be bigger than—" Renie stopped as a man's voice called out.

"Hold it, ladies," a husky man said, heaving himself out of the other car's driver's seat. "Where the hell you been?"

Judith peered at the newcomer, but there was no outdoor lighting except for a faint glow from inside the station. "What?"

"Just get in," the man said. "Blink's pissed off at you already."

"Blink?" Renie echoed. "Who's that?"

The husky man huffed and puffed closer. "Cut the crap. You've already given us the runaround. Your customers already left. That costs us money."

"You must be confused," Judith said. "We're—"

"Old," the man gasped. "Blink won't like this. He was

promised two hot young hookers, not a pair who've taken too many turns around the bedpost."

"Hey!" Renie cried. "You can take the bedpost and ram it up your—"

"Coz," Judith broke in, "let's not . . ."

The other man had gotten out of the car. He was tall and gaunt, a fur coat hanging loosely from his narrow shoulders. He wore dark glasses and carried a white cane. "What's this, Chunky?" he rasped. "I sense dissension."

"We got duped, Blink," Chunky replied. "Check it out for yourself."

Blink tapped his way toward the cousins and reached out to touch Renie's hand. "Feathers? What's wrong with feathers? Satin? That's good, too."

Renie yanked her hand away. "Don't paw the merchandise."

"Feisty," Blink noted. "The voice is . . . well used? Do you work carnivals?"

"What the hell does that mean?" Renie demanded. "I've never been to a carnival except for the ones at Our Lady Star of the Sea Catholic Church."

"Hmm," Blink said in a musing tone. "An interesting clientele." He moved on to Judith, touching the top of her head. "Tall. Leggy. Ample. Such qualities have their charms." He turned to Chunky. "Which is Maddie and which is Tiff?"

"Who cares?" Chunky retorted. "They're Medicare—or close to it. You want to use 'em in a nursing home?"

"That does it!" Judith said, and stomped off toward the station entrance.

"Hey!" Chunky yelled. "Get back here!"

Renie made as if to follow her cousin, but stopped. "What's our cut?"

"Coz!" Judith shouted. "Here comes the train!"

Renie slipped out of her mules, picked them up, and ran toward the tracks just as the whistle blew.

Chunky was huffing and puffing behind her. Blink waved his cane. "Come back! We can make this work!"

A bespectacled older man came out of the station as the train slowed to a stop. "Hello," he said in a squeaky voice. "Are you all getting on?"

"We are," Judith said. "We got stranded near Williston."

"Oh, that's a shame. I'm Waymore." He pointed to his name tag and squinted through thick glasses. "You girls must be tired."

"Yes," Judith said, realizing that Waymore probably didn't see much better than Blink. "Is anybody getting on or off here?"

"A family of four," he replied. "Do you see the sleepers?"

"The first one's right behind us," Judith said, keeping an eye on Blink and Chunky, who seemed to be arguing.

"Is the conductor on the platform?" Waymore asked.

"Not yet," Judith said as the door opened. Seeing Chunky approach them, she grabbed Renie's arm. "Let's go!"

Judith looked toward the door. "The stepstool's not out yet."

"Go!" Renie yelled as Chunky reached out to grab her.

Judith moved to the open door. "Help!" she cried. "Help!"

Renie was struggling with Chunky. Waymore was looking dismayed and saying, "Now, now, that's no way to treat a lady." The stepstool suddenly appeared on the ground. A small figure hurtled out of the train, hopped from the stepstool, and ran toward the scuffling Renie and Chunky.

"Hi!" Emily grabbed Chunky's leg. "Wanna play Thmack-Down?"

Renie broke free. Judith wasted no time getting onto the train. Renie was right behind her. A surprised Courtney Mueller let out a little cry. "Oh, my!"

Mr. Peterson looked equally astonished, but kept his composure. "Go ahead, Mrs. Mueller. I'll carry the twins." He picked up the two baby carriers and let Courtney go first.

Judith glanced back at the platform. Emily had grabbed Blink's cane and was running around in circles. "No ThmackDown, no thtick!" she cried in jubilation. "Ha ha!"

Jax was unloading luggage. "My God!" she exclaimed, seeing the cousins. "Where've you been?"

"To hell and back," Judith said, slumping against the luggage rack.

"Tell me about it," Jax said, "as soon as we start up again."

Renie was panting. "I . . . never . . . thought . . . I'd be . . . glad . . . to see . . . Emily."

"All aboard!" Mr. Peterson said before getting back on the train.

The Empire Builder headed east. "We're still behind schedule," the conductor said.

Judith shrugged. "Better late than never."

"Better late than dead," Renie murmured after regaining her breath. "I wonder, though—how much could we have charged at the nursing home?"

"We'd have had to charge them," Judith said. "Come on, tiger. Let's go to bed. It's been a long day."

The cousins trudged upstairs and all but fell into their bedroom. "What time is it?" Renie asked. "I took my watch off when I undressed."

"Uh . . ." Judith moved her wrist under the night-light. "I'm not sure. Did I remember to set my watch ahead?"

"How would I know?"

"Does it matter?"

Renie had climbed up into the top berth. "No."

Judith looked again at her watch. "I think mine's stopped."

"Oh. Tough."

Judith removed the watch. "To heck with it. Time's relative. 'To everything there is a season, and a time to every purpose under heaven.' Right, coz?"

"Shut the hell up," Renie muttered.

"A time to wake and a time to sleep," Judith said under her breath—and dropped into dreamland with her clothes on.

Epilogue

Judith and Joe strolled arm in arm along Boylston Street, admiring the fading autumn splendor of Boston Garden. "We're almost three weeks late for the best fall foliage," Joe said, "but you've got to admit this is pretty nice."

Judith agreed. "How lucky to have Bill's conference at the Four Seasons. The public garden, the Common, the statehouse—it's every bit as wonderful as Renie described it."

"Feel like walking over to Beacon Street?" Joe asked. "There are some wonderful old homes in the neighborhood."

"Sure," Judith said, squeezing Joe's arm. "As long as we take it slow."

"You feel rested now?"

"Oh, yes," Judith replied. "With Renie's weird sense of time, I don't think I realized we wouldn't get into Boston until midnight. I think she left out the part about a detour to D.C. But I slept in until almost eleven. Breakfast was lunch."

Joe paused at the corner of Charles Street. "We can go this way between the garden and the Common or straight ahead. Your call."

Judith shrugged. "I don't know the difference." Hearing a familiar voice, she turned around. "Here come Renie and Bill."

Joe waved. "He must've gotten sprung from his lunch meeting. Thank God I've got a couple of hours before my three-thirty interview at Bullfinch Life & Casualty. Hey," he said as Renie and Bill joined them, "want to walk the walk with us?"

Bill looked at Renie. "Are you wearing shoes?"

Renie stuck out a brown-suede-shod foot. "Yes. I told you, I wouldn't give up wearing shoes until we got home."

"Good," Bill said. "Where to?"

"Past the Common and then over to Beacon Street?" Joe suggested. "We can see the Frog Pond."

"Look at that gold dome on the statehouse!" Renie exclaimed. "But watch for cars. They don't favor pedestrians—and pedestrians don't favor cars. Lots of jaywalking and going against the lights."

"We've noticed," Joe said. "Say, we haven't had a chance to hear about your train trip. I assume you both got to relax."

"Oh," Judith said, avoiding any glance at Renie, "yes. So much interesting scenery. Good food, too. Pleasant traveling companions. It was great."

"I was kind of envious," Joe said. "Bill and I've both been on the go ever since we got here. This is really the first free time we've had. I haven't even seen the sports page since I got here."

Bill nodded. "For all I know, the TV in our suite doesn't work. The last thing I want to do at the end of the day is hear more blah-blah."

"Really," Renie murmured.

"You probably haven't missed much," Judith said.

"True," Joe agreed. "Current events pale in a city like this. Look—there's where the Freedom Trail starts." He pointed to a Visitor Information sign at edge of the Common. "I hope we have time to do that. It hits the highspots all the way across the Charles River to the USS *Constitution* Museum and Old Ironsides."

"That's a must," Bill said.

"Can we take a cab?" Renie asked.

Joe chuckled; Bill looked askance.

"Where are all those old cemeteries?" Judith asked, changing the subject.

"Two or three of them are around here," Joe said. He shot

his wife a baleful glance. "Good God, can't you stop think-ing about dead people for a couple of weeks? It's a wonder you didn't find a corpse on the train."

"Don't be silly," Judith said. "Look—people are riding on horseback across the Common. Is that the Frog Pond? What street are we on now?"

Renie grimaced. "Tremont. We're right where Madge Na-varre and I stayed when we came to Boston in 1962."

"Why the fearsome face?" Bill asked. "You've always told me the two of you had a wonderful time."

"We did." Head down, Renie walked a little faster. "It was great."

Judith's curiosity overcame her. "Come on, coz, fess up. Don't tell me you've been keeping a secret from me all these years."

Renie stopped in her tracks. "I haven't. That is, I thought I told you—or Bill—or somebody."

"What?" Judith asked.

Renie's shoulders slumped. "Madge and I were coming back to our hotel late one night. Our hotel was nice enough, but old and kind of . . . creepy. The next morning we found out that something terrible had happened a few doors away on Tremont Street."

"What was it?" Judith coaxed.

"A murder," Renie replied quietly. "The Boston Strangler had struck again."

The foursome was silent for what seemed like a long time. Then Joe and Bill burst out laughing.

"Hey," Bill said, "that was then and this is now. History won't repeat itself."

Joe grinned at Bill. "And my wife was three thousand miles away." He gave Judith a hug. "I assume you don't feel left out?"

"Oh, no," Judith asserted. "Why would I?"

Joe shrugged. "Just kidding. Let's move on. How 'bout those cemeteries?"

"Right," Bill said, taking Renie's hand. "Boppin'!"

Author's Note

The descriptions of some Empire Builder features, including the sleeper accommodations, have been altered for the sake of narrative. These details are minor, but train travel is still the best way to go.

There's no "fun" in "fund-raiser" for Judith McMonigle Flynn when she donates an overnight at Hillside Manor for the parish school's annual auction. Judith feels like she's already losing it when the winning bid goes to Norma and Wilbur Paine, who've turned the pricey item over to the younger Paines. Dinner is included, if Judith can only sort through the numerous allergies and aversions of the painfully picky Paines. The last thing she needs is another B&B guest who checks out permanently.

The odds of that happening decrease when Joe Flynn comes home early and tells his wife that his latest surveillance job has ended abruptly when the supposedly paralyzed guy suspected of insurance fraud is put out of action once and for all by a .38 Smith & Wesson. Surely one corpse in one week is enough, even for the Flynns. But if they're not careful, they'll look out the window one morning to see

ALL THE PRETTY HEARSES
Available Summer 2011 in hardcover

Wm

WILLIAM MORROW

Judith McMonigle Flynn flinched, winced, and wondered why Cousin Renie was screaming her head off while trying to batter down the back door of Hillside Manor.

"What's wrong with you?" Judith demanded, opening the door. "Are you insane or being chased by ravenous wolves?"

Renie virtually fell across the threshold. "Both," she gasped, leaning against the wall next to the pantry. "That's the last time I ever stop by the parish school office to drop off my Campbell Soup labels."

Judith gestured for Renie to follow her into the kitchen. "I didn't realize you still saved them after all these years. You haven't had a kid at Our Lady, Star of the Sea School for twenty-five years." She pulled out a kitchen chair for her cousin. "Sit. Stop hyperventilating. Coffee?"

Renie shook her head as she flopped into the chair. "Old habits die hard. Old SOTS just die," she went on, using the acronym for her fellow parishioners, "but not before they can avoid falling into the clutches of younger parents who are active school fund-raisers."

"Oh." Judith sat down across from Renie. "I managed to avoid that by going into exile out on Thurlow Street with Dan. My son's tenure at SOTS was all too brief before he had to attend public school. Since I held down two jobs, I was never an active participating parent except when I'd try to find out where he'd hidden his latest report card."

"Count your blessings," Renie murmured. She twisted around to look at the old schoolhouse clock. "Almost noon. I could've sworn it was five o'clock. The last twenty minutes seemed like hours." She reached for the sheep-shaped cookie jar on the table. "I'm hungry. They're having hamburger lunch today at school. I was tempted to wait for the delivery from Bob Burgers and steal one." She tapped the cookie jar's lid. "What's in here?"

"Stale Christmas cookies," Judith responded. "I vowed not to bake again until January tenth. Between running the B&B and all the holiday goodies, I'm tapped."

"Hmm." Renie's brown eyes twinkled. "You, too, will be dragooned into this charitable work. You're a parishioner. Contributors aren't limited to school parents. In fact, you don't even have to be a SOT."

"If you told me what it is," Judith said, "I'd know how to avoid it."

"Martha Morelli has the last of her five kids in eighth grade this year," Renie said. "You know what a demon she is for fund-raising. It's not enough to have the annual auction, the crab dinner, the St. Patrick's Day dinner, the Italian dinner, the sauerkraut dinner, The First Martyrs of the Church of Rome dinner . . ."

Judith held up a hand. "Whoa. We don't have a . . . what did you just say?"

"Oh." Renie held her head. "That's right. Bridget McDonough suggested that event a couple of years ago, but Father Hoyle pointed out that The First Martyrs in Rome were dinner. For the lions, that is. Nero's Circus Maximus was short on clowns and trained seals."

"Not all the fund-raisers are for the school, though," Judith remarked. "They had the Christmas wreath and poinsettia sale in early December, but the spring auction is the major source of school funding. It's been enormously successful."

Renie nodded. "We lucked out with some of the city's high-profile athletes moving to Heraldsgate Hill and joining the parish. But now they've either retired or been traded. That's part of the problem, so they're looking at additional revenue producers. Martha wants to put a cookbook together. Guess who she wants to design it."

Judith laughed. "That's logical. You are a graphic designer."

"Yes," Renie conceded with a longing look at the cookie jar. "But I'm trying to scale down. This year I'm only taking on the gas company's annual report, but my deadline is late January. Plus I'm doing a brochure for Key Largo Bank and re-working somebody's in-house botched newsletter for retired city light employees. Both are due in mid-February, the same as the cookbook. Martha should've asked me sooner, like in the fall."

"Why didn't she?"

"She insists she tried to get hold of me in early November, but we'd all gone on our Boston trip," Renie explained. "By the time you and I got back, it was mid-November, and Martha was caught up with Thanksgiving and Christmas. So were we, for that matter."

Judith got up from the chair. "I've got to start making Mother's lunch. If you're hungry enough to eat the sheep's head on the cookie jar, I'll make you a sandwich, too."

"No, thanks," Renie said. "I should go home. Oh—by the way, we're all supposed to contribute cookbook recipes. That includes you."

"I can do that," Judith said. "What are you going to offer?"

Renie was on her feet, rummaging in the new—and huge—handbag Bill had given her for Christmas. "Shrimp Dump."

Judith almost dropped the mustard jar she'd taken out of the fridge. "I hope you're kidding."

"No. Hey, I like it."

"Nobody else does."

"You mean like you and the rest of my family?"

"More like the rest of the world. Why not offer your Bean Glop and Clam Doodoo, too? The names alone would make most people gag."

"Hey—have you forgotten that at one of my bridal showers the guests were asked to bring their two favorite recipes and your contribution was Pottsfield Pickles and How to Can a Tuna Fish?"

"That was over forty years ago," Judith said, placing two ham slices on the cutting block in the middle of the kitchen. "Well . . . you knew I was joking. You aren't."

"That's right." Renie clutched her key ring and slung the handbag over her shoulder. "Oh—there's another new parish event on the schedule for next fall. This one you'll love."

Judith regarded her cousin warily. "What?"

"Alicia and Reggie Beard-Smythe want to sponsor a hunt club outing. Shall I sign you up now?"

"Very funny," Judith said dryly. "Will my horse have an artificial hip like mine?"

"I'm sure that could be arranged." Renie headed through the hallway to the back door. "See ya."

"Wait," Judith called. "Is this hunt club thing serious?"

Renie turned around. "Yes. There's a new hunt club over on the Eastside. Before they moved here from Virginia a couple of years ago, they were avid hunters. For a mere three hundred bucks apiece, parishioners can take part in a hunt. Horse provided, bad riding habits optional. The money goes to SOTS."

"It's a good thing all those dot.com zillionaires have moved to Heraldsgate Hill in recent years," Judith said. "The Beard-Smythes might get some of them to sign up. I assume you won't be one of them."

"Correct. As you may recall, I was the first person to ride a horse on the I-5 Interstate before it was completed. I did not want to do that, but my horse did. I never got on a horse again and don't intend to."

"Good thinking," Judith said.

"Which reminds me," Renie said, "when do the guests arrive for their free overnight?"

Judith clapped a hand to her cheek. "Oh, my God! I forgot about them. Let me check my schedule."

Renie followed her cousin back into the kitchen. "The auction was in May," Judith said, sitting down at her computer on the counter. "I completely forgot I'd offered that overnight during the slow January season." She paused, scrolling through Hillside Manor's January confirmations. "This Friday, February seventh. Norma and Wilbur Paine bought it for their children and grandchildren. I can't believe they have grandchildren old enough to stay at a B&B."

"I could never believe they had children," Renie remarked.

"Nobody as homely as the Paines should've been allowed to procreate."

Judith pointed at the names with her cursor. "Andrew and Paulina Paine, Walter and Sonya Paine, Sarah and Dennis Blair, Hannah and Wyatt Conrad, Chad and Chase Paine, Zoe Paine and Octavia Blair. Does that sound right to you?"

Renie shrugged. "The Paines did have kids in the school, but they were older than ours. I vaguely recall that Hannah was a year ahead of Tony—or was it Tom?"

"So Chad and Chase—I assume they're both boys—must belong to either Andrew or Walter Paine," Judith said. "Oh—Zoe, too. Octavia has to be Sarah's daughter. Was dinner included?"

"I'm afraid it was," Judith replied. "I must've had a weak moment."

"Does it say where these Paines live? If I've seen them at Mass, I don't think I'd recognize them."

"No," Judith said, turning away from the monitor. "The only contact information is for Norma and Wilbur. I don't recall running into any of their offspring at church. Maybe they all moved away."

"Good thinking on their part," Renie remarked, once again heading for the back door. "I'd move, too, if Norma was my mother." She stopped suddenly, a stunned expression on her round face. "My God—do you think that's why all three of our kids live so far away?"

"Probably. If I were you, I'd blame it on the Shrimp Dump."

Renie glowered at Judith. "Right. I now formally withdraw my offer to help you with the dinner Friday night."

"You didn't volunteer."

"I didn't?" Renie shrugged. "It crossed my mind. Say, maybe the Paines would like Shrimp Dump for dinner."

"I'm not that desperate."

"Let me know if you change your mind." Renie made her exit.

"Not a chance," Judith murmured under her breath, keeping an eye on Sweetums who had entered the house before Renie closed the door behind her.

Ten minutes later, Judith entered the converted tool shed that served as her mother's apartment. Gertrude Grover peered suspiciously at the sandwich her daughter set on the cluttered card-table. "You call this ham?" the old lady rasped. "It looks like linoleum to me."

"It's the ham we had for New Year's Day dinner," Judith informed her mother.

"Which New Year's?" Gertrude snapped. "How about 1995?"

"The New Year's dinner we had Saturday," Judith said patiently. "It's Tuesday. You're the one who kept ham until it turned blue."

Gertrude poked a gnarled finger at the newspaper in front of her. "You see this? Elder abuse, that's what. This is Part Two of a series on how children torture their aging parents. Spoiled pork must be one of the ways they do it. It gives old folks like me trigonomosis."

"You mean trichinosis," Judith said.

Gertrude glared at her daughter. "Isn't that what I just told you? You must be going deaf, too. You're already daffy."

"Do you want me to take a bite first?"

Gertrude snatched up the plate. "Aha! Now you want to starve me! By the time I get through to the last part of this series on Friday, I may be dead. And where's the rest of that cheesecake you bought at Begelman's Bakery for New Year's Eve?"

"We ate it," Judith replied. "Do you want some of Kristin's Fattigmann Bakkels?"

"I don't like bagels," Gertrude declared. "Especially fat ones. They're too hard to chew with my dentures."

"They're not bagels," Judith said. "They're Norwegian Christmas . . . never mind." The old lady was chomping away at the ham sandwich. Kristin's colossal output of holiday foodstuffs was probably past its pull date. Judith never ceased to be awed by her daughter-in-law's prodigious domestic enterprises. "If you want a sweet, Mother, you must've gotten ten pounds of Granny Goodness chocolates for Christmas. I assume you haven't eaten all of them in ten days."

"Ten days of what?" Gertrude asked, stabbing a fork into one of the gherkins on her plate. "I thought there were twelve days of Christmas. Or have the lunkheads in the Vatican changed that with everything else, too? And whatever happened to those two old saps, the Ringos?"

"They died," Judith said. "They were almost as old as you are. Your new Eucharistic minister is Kate Duffy, remember? She's been coming by every week for the past two years."

"I wish I could forget Kate Duffy," Gertrude muttered. "She's as bad as the Ringos. She always wants to pray with me. The last time she was here, I told her I'd been praying for her not to come. All that phony-baloney pious claptrap is as bad as your screwball cleaning lady, but in the other direction. 'Born again', huh? Once was enough with her, too."

Judith sighed. "I know Phyliss Rackley can be a trial, but she's a very good cleaning woman. As for Kate, she means well. She's had a rather hard life, at least when she was younger. I figure she's sincere, if misguided. Our family has been lucky. Somehow we managed to keep our feet planted on the ground."

"That's because us old folks went to the School of Hard Knocks," Gertrude asserted. "Common sense, that's what it is, not Satan hiding behind every bush like Phyliss says, or hearing the Holy Ghost whisper into Kate's ear. When she came by after Christmas, she told me the Holy Ghost wanted her to go to Nordquist's designer clearance."

"Ah . . . well . . . I hope the Holy Ghost gave Kate an increase in her credit limit," Judith said, edging toward the converted tool shed's door. "If I have time tomorrow, I'll bake some ginger snaps."

"Then snap to it," Gertrude said, spearing another gherkin.

Judith promised she'd try. Halfway down the walk back to the house, Arlene Rankers popped out of the massive laurel hedge that separated the two properties.

"Is Serena still here?" she asked, calling Renie by her given name.

"No," Judith replied. "She's probably home by now. Did you want to talk to her?"

Arlene didn't answer right away. In fact, her pretty face looked troubled. "I don't really know."

Judith couldn't keep from smiling. "In that case, you probably should wait to talk to her. Maybe you'll remember why you wanted to see her."

"I didn't," Arlene said. "That is, I just got a call from Mary Lou Daniels at the school." She nodded in the direction of the hill that rose up behind the Flynns' garden. The church and school were three steep blocks away and out of sight. "She called to say that Brooks was sick and she couldn't get hold of Meagan or Noah at work, so Carl just left to pick him up."

Judith knew that two of the Rankers's grandchildren attended the parish school. Brooks and his younger sister, Jade, had been enrolled in the fall after Meagan and her husband, Noah, had moved from Eugene, Oregon, to Heraldsgate Hill the previous summer. But she couldn't make any connection between Renie and the sick grandson. Unless, she mused, Renie had already donated her recipe for Shrimp Dump to the school. "What's Brooks got?" she asked.

"A bad stomachache," Arlene replied. "Three other children are sick, too. I wondered . . . oh!" She brightened. "I remember what I wanted to ask Serena. Mary Lou mentioned that your cousin had stopped by with a bag of soup labels. I thought Serena might've heard if the sick kids all had the same symptoms. It'd be a shame to have an epidemic just as school has resumed after the holidays."

Judith understood Arlene's concern. The Rankers's daughter, Meagan, was a grade school teacher at a nearby public school; her husband, Noah, had taken a new job as a salesman for a big pharmaceutical company. Finding a part-time sitter for their two children had been easy. Carl and Arlene had been eager to take on that role, not having spent much time with Brooks and Jade until the family moved north.

"Renie was there before noon," Judith said. "If anybody was waiting to be picked up in the office, she didn't tell me. I suppose the flu is going around. It usually is this time of year."

"True," Arlene said, suddenly on the alert. "I'd better go back home. Carl and Brooks will be back any minute."

Judith paused at the foot of the porch stairs. It had rained on New Year's Day, but the sun had been out ever since. The thermometer on one of the porch pillars registered forty degrees. She looked at a clump of tiny snow-drops in the flower bed next to the steps. Judith smiled. Her mother always called them "Christmas roses" because they usually bloomed the last week of December. Next to the snow-drops, she noticed that several daffodil shoots had emerged above the ground. Brave, she thought to herself. It could still snow.

"That's it!" Phyliss Rackley announced, storming out onto the porch and waving a dust-mop. "Satan's Familiar just shredded the lace curtains in Room Five. If you don't put him to sleep, I'll do it for you."

"Why," Judith asked mildly, "did you let him into Room Five?"

"Let him?" Phyliss's gray sausage curls seemed to dance in outrage. "He can go through walls, can't he? Just like the Arch Fiend himself." She lowered her voice. "The Powers of Darkness."

Judith joined the cleaning woman at the door. "How much real damage is there?"

"See for yourself," Phyliss snapped. "I've got a dust-mop to shake."

Judith carefully went up the backstairs, ever mindful of her artificial hip. Room Five was the second door on her right. Sweetums was asleep on the freshly made bed. Sure enough, almost a foot of lace fabric was ripped beyond repair. Judith pummeled the mattress. "Get you, you little stinker!" she cried. "You're not allowed upstairs."

Sweetums's plush yellow and white fur bristled as he regarded Judith with malevolent golden eyes. He yawned widely, then started to resettle himself.

"Out!" Judith yelled, scooping up the cat and carrying him into the hallway. He struggled in her grasp, but when she set him down, he merely gazed indifferently at the pitiful human's displeasure before starting to groom himself.

Judith took the ruined curtains off the rod. Fortunately—though not so fortunate in terms of income—Room Five was vacant until the weekend. She had extra curtains stored in the cupboard area down the hall. Looking out through the window with its western exposure, Judith could see the wan winter sun glinting off the bay. The mountains over on the peninsula seemed to sparkle. A barge laden with green-, blue- and rust-colored cargo containers moved smoothly southward to the city's industrial area while a super ferry pulled into the downtown slip just beyond the viaduct. Judith smiled again. Strange, she thought, how seldom I take time out to enjoy the scenery I can see from my house that others travel thousands of miles and spend thousands of dollars to see. It occurred to her that Parisians no doubt passed l'Arc de Triomphe and the Louvre without paying much attention, while Romans no doubt ignored the Colosseum and the Pantheon.

What Judith couldn't ignore was the phone. Unfortunately, it wasn't the guest phone that was on a table near the top of the main staircase. The ringing was coming from the kitchen, barely audible, but insistent. Judith wasn't going to risk a fall by dashing downstairs. After four rings, the call trunked over to her message service. After reaching the kitchen and tossing the curtains into the garbage can under the sink, she finally picked up the receiver. There was no click-click-click sound indicating an unheard message. Judith checked her caller ID screen. Norma Paine's name and number appeared. Either Norma had decided to call back later or—more likely—she was leaving one of her typical long-winded messages.

Phyliss was running the vacuum in the front parlor. Judith walked through the dining room and the entry hall to the parlor door. The cleaning woman had her back turned and was singing—or squawking—a hymn. Cringing at the third "Go down Moses," Judith waited to be acknowledged.

"What?" Phyliss demanded, silencing the vacuum. "I haven't gotten to 'bold Moses' and the 'smite' verse." She patted the vacuum bag. "That's when Moses here does his best work at deep cleaning."

Judith was used to her cleaning woman's Biblical nicknames for various appliances. The washer and dryer were Noah and Jonah. The floor polisher was Jezebel because,

Phyliss insisted, it was wayward, wanton, and woefully ignorant of God's word.

"You're right about the curtains," Judith said. "They're ruined. I've got new ones on the top shelf in the guest room storage cabinet."

Phyliss's eyes narrowed. "Did you killed Beelzebub's evil tool?"

"You know," Judith said firmly, "that Sweetums rarely goes upstairs. When we found him as a kitten shortly before I finished converting the family home into a B&B, I trained him not to go beyond the basement and the first floor."

"You can't train cats," Phyliss asserted. "They're sinister beasts."

"They're the last domestic animal to become . . . domesticated," Judith countered. "They've only been tame for five thousand years."

"Then they're slow learners," Phyliss said. "Those Egyptians thought cats were some kind of god. False idols, just like you Catholics, worshipping graven images and statues of people holding flowers or books or a bunch of house keys, which, now that I think about it, it's no wonder that statue in the backyard has got a bunch of birds hanging onto him. Whoever he is, he must not have liked cats."

Judith's shoulders slumped. She'd long ago given up trying to convince Phyliss that Catholics didn't worship statues. They were like photographs or snapshots, a reminder of someone who had lived a holy life. Phyliss remained unconvinced. Not even using the Lincoln Memorial as an inspiration to other Americans had swayed her. "I've seen pictures," she'd argued. "Abe's just sitting there, staring off into nowhere. What's inspiring about that? He could be watching TV."

Thus, Judith kept her mouth shut and went back into the kitchen. Maybe Norma Paine had finished her message. She sat down by the computer, picked up the phone, and dialed in her code.

"This," Norma said in her braying voice, "is Norma Paine. I'm calling about Friday night and your generous offer of Hillside Manor to my children and their children. Very kind

of you, as I've always wondered why you hadn't done this
before." Slight pause. "Well, better late than never, I suppose. I'm quite pleased that you included dinner instead
of just an overnight and breakfast. After all, Wilbur and I
ended up paying fourteen hundred dollars for your item, and
he insists that's going to set him back another year in his
plan to retire from his law practice at the end of this coming
year." Another pause. "Not that I wonder if he won't feel
lost without going to the office every day. In fact, I hope
he doesn't expect me to entertain him constantly. I keep re-
minding him, 'Wilbur,' I say, 'I have a life of my own, and
it keeps me very busy.' I don't think men understand what
their wives do when they're gone all day earning a living.
But I digress. What I'm calling about is that some of our
family members have food allergies. Now let me get this
right." A much longer pause. Judith had picked up a pen and
was tapping it on the counter. "Andrew is lactose intolerant.
Hannah should avoid any leafy green vegetables. Dennis insists he doesn't have diabetes, but I disagree. He's glucose
intolerant, and as you no doubt realize, that's an early stage
of diabetes. I'm very careful when I cook for him, I can tell
you that. Zoe is vegetarian. Wyatt has a severe seafood allergy. Now let me think . . ." The next pause was so long
that Judith's elbow slipped off the counter and she dropped
the pen. Retrieving it wasn't possible without bending over
and risking dislocation of her artificial hip. Instead, she took
another pen out of the drawer. And waited. "I'm not sure,"
Norma finally said, "if I have all this straight. It seems I've
left out something rather important. I'll call you later. It's so
kind of you to offer your very expensive hospitality."

"Aaargh . . ." Judith groaned, turning off the phone as Joe
Flynn entered the hallway from the back door.

"What's wrong?" he asked before taking off the new
winter jacket Judith had given him for Christmas.

"I have a Paine," Judith said. "A whole houseful of Paines.
Remember last year's school auction?"

Joe's round face looked momentarily puzzled. "Oh—you
mean that auction and dinner fund-raiser when Bill and I
tended bar?" He shook his head. "I recall very little about it,

except that I tried to auction off Oscar, and Bill told me if I did that, we could take it outside."

"Oh, God!" Judith gasped. "I forgot that part!"

"Yeah," Joe agreed, "it got kind of ugly there for a minute. And Oscar didn't even come to the auction."

Judith was on her feet, grabbing Joe by the sleeves of his jacket. "Don't you dare buy into that Oscar fantasy! He's a stuffed monkey, not a . . . a real animal." She stopped, staring into her husband's green eyes. "You and Bill weren't that drunk."

"Maybe. Maybe not." For once, the magical gold flecks weren't dancing. "Besides, he's not a monkey, he's a dwarf ape."

Judith dropped her hands. "Skip it. I'm talking about Norma and Wilbur Paine. They bought the dinner and overnight for their children and grandchildren. It's this Friday."

Joe removed his jacket and hung it on a peg in the hallway. "So?"

"So Norma just left a message with a laundry list of allergies and other prohibitions for her brood. I need to hire a dietician."

"Do a buffet," Joe suggested. "They can pick and choose."

Judith thought for a minute. "You're right. That's a good idea. The only thing I'd have to omit is shellfish. That's a bad allergy, right up there with Renie's peanut problem. The odor in the air can set off an attack." She smiled at Joe. "What would I do without you?"

"You had nineteen years to figure it out." He put an arm around his wife. "So did I. Happily, we managed to finally get it right."

Judith leaned against Joe. "Sometimes when I think of the years I spent with Dan while you were with Herself, I feel cheated. All that wasted time coping with a pair of drunks. I marvel your ex is still alive."

"She's not," Joe said. "She's pickled, preserved forever in the Florida sunshine."

"Let's hope she stays that way. I mean," Judith added quickly, "Vivian stays in Florida. I don't know why she doesn't sell the house here in the cul-de-sac instead of renting it. She's never been happy living in this part of the world."

"That's because liquor stores around here don't deliver," Joe said. "Now that she owns the house on the corner as well, she might make more money renting instead of selling. The Briscoes seem like a nice couple, and that Fairfax fellow travels a lot in his job as an auctioneer. All three newcomers seem like decent people. Quiet. Pleasant. Dull."

"Dull is good," Judith murmured. "I'd like a few months of dull." She suddenly remembered where Joe had spent the morning. "Why are you home so early? Isn't your surveillance job an eight-hour gig?"

"It was." Joe moved away from Judith, a sheepish look on his face. "Mr. Insurance Fraud is no longer able to bilk SANECO out of six million dollars for being semiparalyzed."

Judith grinned at Joe. "You caught him walking?"

Joe shook his head. "No. Somebody else caught him—with a 38. Smith & Wesson. He's dead."